Praise for Sophie Kinsella
and the Shopaholic Series

"A hilarious tale . . . hijinks worthy of classic *I Love Lucy* episodes . . . too good to pass up." —*USA Today*

"[Sophie Kinsella] gives chick-lit lovers a reason to stay home from the mall." —*Entertainment Weekly*

"Don't wait for a sale to buy this hilarious book." —*Us Weekly*

"Perfect for anyone wishing that bank statements came in more colours than just black and red." —*Mirror* (London)

"The newest Becky Bloomwood adventure is just what we've come to love and to expect from Kinsella—a bright, quick read full of self-deprecating humor." —*Raleigh (NC) News & Observer*

"If a *crème brûlée* could be transmogrified into a book, it would be *Confessions of a Shopaholic*." —*Newark Star-Ledger*

"Kinsella's heroine is blessed with the resilience of ten women, and her damage-limitation brainwaves are always good for a giggle." —*Glamour* (London)

Also by Sophie Kinsella

CONFESSIONS OF A SHOPAHOLIC

SHOPAHOLIC TAKES MANHATTAN

SHOPAHOLIC TIES THE KNOT

SHOPAHOLIC & SISTER

CAN YOU KEEP A SECRET?

THE UNDOMESTIC GODDESS

SOPHIE KINSELLA

Shopaholic
& Baby

A DELL BOOK

SHOPAHOLIC & BABY
A Dell Book

PUBLISHING HISTORY
Dial Press hardcover edition published March 2007
Dell international mass market edition / December 2007

Published by
Bantam Dell
A Division of Random House, Inc.
New York, New York

Library of Congress Catalog Card Number: 2006031793

Dell is a registered trademark of Random House, Inc., and the
colophon is a trademark of Random House, Inc.

ISBN 978-0-440-29676-8

Printed in the United States of America
Published simultaneously in Canada

www.bantamdell.com

OPM 10 9 8 7 6 5 4 3 2 1

For Oscar

Shopaholic
& Baby

Prendergast de Witt Connell
Financial Advisers

Forward House

394 High Holborn

London WC1V 7EX

Mrs R Brandon

37 Maida Vale Mansions

Maida Vale

London NW6 0YF

30 July 2003

Dear Mrs. Brandon,

It was a great pleasure to meet you and Luke the other day, and I look forward to taking on the role as your family financial adviser.

I am in the process of setting up banking arrangements and a trust fund for your unborn child. In due course we can discuss what investments you and your husband might make in the baby's name.

I look forward to getting to know you better over the coming months; please do not hesitate to contact me on any matter, no matter how small.

Yours sincerely,

Kenneth Prendergast

Family Investment Specialist

Prendergast de Witt Connell
Financial Advisers

Forward House
394 High Holborn
London WC1V 7EX

Mrs R Brandon
37 Maida Vale Mansions
Maida Vale
London NW6 0YF

1 August 2003

Dear Mrs. Brandon,

Thank you for your letter. In answer to your question, yes, there will be an overdraft facility on the baby's bank account—although, naturally, I would not expect it to be used!

Yours sincerely,

Kenneth Prendergast
Family Investment Specialist

Prendergast de Witt Connell Financial Advisers

Forward House
394 High Holborn
London WC1V 7EX

Mrs R Brandon
37 Maida Vale Mansions
Maida Vale
London NW6 0YF

7 August 2003

Dear Mrs. Brandon,

Thank you for your letter. I was intrigued to hear about the "psychic message" you recently received from your unborn child. However, I'm afraid it is impossible to access the overdraft facility at this stage. Even if, as you say, "the baby wishes it."

Yours sincerely,

Kenneth Prendergast
Family Investment Specialist

ONE

OK. DON'T PANIC. Everything's going to be fine. Of course it is.

Of *course* it is.

"If you could lift up your top, Mrs. Brandon?" The sonographer has a pleasant, professional air as she looks down at me. "I need to apply some jelly to your abdomen before we start the scan."

"Absolutely!" I say without moving a muscle. "The thing is, I'm just a teeny bit...nervous."

I'm lying on a bed at the Chelsea and Westminster hospital, tense with anticipation. Any minute now, Luke and I will see our baby on the screen for the first time since it was just a teeny blob. I still can't quite believe it. In fact, I still haven't quite got over the fact that I'm pregnant. In nineteen weeks' time I, Becky Brandon, née Bloomwood...am going to be a mother. A *mother*!

Luke's my husband, by the way. We've been married for just over a year and this is a one hundred percent genuine honeymoon baby! We traveled loads on our honeymoon, but I've pretty much worked out that we conceived it when we were staying in this gorgeous resort in Sri Lanka, called Unawatuna, all orchids and bamboo trees and beautiful views.

Unawatuna Brandon.

Miss Unawatuna Orchid Bamboo-tree Brandon.

Hmm. I'm not sure what Mum would say.

"My wife had a slight accident in the early stages of pregnancy," Luke explains from his seat beside the bed. "So she's a little anxious."

He squeezes my hand supportively, and I squeeze back. In my pregnancy book, *Nine Months of Your Life,* it says you should include your partner in all aspects of your pregnancy, otherwise he can feel hurt and alienated. So I'm including Luke as much as I possibly can. Like, last night I included him in watching my new DVD, *Toned Arms in Pregnancy.* He suddenly remembered in the middle that he had to make a business call, and missed quite a lot—but the point is, he doesn't feel shut out.

"You had an accident?" The sonographer pauses in her tapping at the computer.

"I fell off this mountain when I was looking for my long-lost sister in a storm," I explain. "I didn't know I was pregnant at the time. And I think maybe I bashed the baby."

"I see." The sonographer looks at me kindly. She has graying brown hair tied back in a knot, with a pencil stuck into it. "Well, babies are resilient little things. Let's just have a look, shall we?"

Here it is. The moment I've been obsessing over for weeks. Gingerly I lift up my top and look down at my swelling stomach.

"If you could just push all your necklaces aside?" she adds. "That's quite a collection you have there!"

"They're special pendants." I loop them together with a jangle. "This one is an Aztec maternity symbol, and this is a gestation crystal . . . and this is a chiming ball to soothe the baby . . . and this is a birthing stone."

"A birthing stone?"

"You press it on a special spot on your palm, and it takes away the pain of labor," I explain. "It's been used since ancient Maori times."

"Mm-hmm." The sonographer raises an eyebrow and squeezes some transparent gloop on my stomach. Frowning slightly, she applies the ultrasound probe thing to my skin, and instantly a fuzzy black-and-white image appears on the screen.

I can't breathe.

That's our baby. Inside me. I dart a look at Luke, and he's gazing at the screen, transfixed.

"There are the four chambers of the heart. . . ." The sonographer is moving the probe around. "Now we're looking at the shoulders. . . ." She points to the screen and I squint obediently, even though, to be honest, I can't see any shoulders, only blurry curves.

"There's an arm . . . one hand . . ." Her voice trails off and she frowns.

There's silence in the little room. I feel a sudden grip of fear. That's why she's frowning. The baby's only got one hand. I knew it.

A wave of overpowering love and protectiveness rises up inside me. Tears are welling in my eyes. I don't care if our baby's only got one hand. I'll love it just as much. I'll love it *more*. Luke and I will take it anywhere in the world for the best treatment, and we'll fund research, and if anyone even *dares* give my baby a look—

"And the other hand..." The sonographer's voice interrupts my thoughts.

"Other hand?" I look up, choked. "It's got two hands?"

"Well...yes." The sonographer seems taken aback at my reaction. "Look, you can see them here." She points at the image, and to my amazement I can just about make out the little bony fingers. Ten of them.

"I'm sorry," I gulp, wiping my eyes with a tissue she hands me. "It's just such a relief."

"Everything seems absolutely fine as far as I can tell," she says reassuringly. "And don't worry, it's normal to be emotional in pregnancy. All those hormones swilling about."

Honestly. People keep talking about hormones. Like Luke last night, when I cried over that TV ad with the puppy. I'm *not* hormonal, I'm perfectly normal. It was just a very sad ad.

"Here you go." The sonographer taps at her keyboard again. A row of black-and-white scan pictures curls out of the printer, which she hands to me. I peer at the first one—and you can see the distinct outline of a head. It's got a little nose and a mouth and everything.

"So. I've done all the checks." She swivels round on her chair. "All I need to know now is whether you want to know the gender of the baby."

"No, thank you," Luke answers with a smile. "We've talked it through at great length, haven't we, Becky? And we both feel it would spoil the magic to find out."

"Very well." The sonographer smiles back. "If that's what you've decided, I won't say anything."

She "won't say anything"? That means she's already seen what the sex is. She could just tell us right now!

"We hadn't actually *decided,* had we?" I say. "Not for definite."

"Well...yes, we had, Becky." Luke seems taken aback. "Don't you remember, we talked about it for a whole evening and agreed we wanted it to be a surprise."

"Oh right, yes." I can't take my eyes off the blurry print of the baby. "But we could have our surprise now! It would be just as magical!"

OK, maybe that's not exactly true. But isn't he desperate to know?

"Is that really what you want?" As I look up I can see a streak of disappointment in Luke's face. "To find out now?"

"Well..." I hesitate. "Not if you don't want to."

The last thing I want is to upset Luke. He's been so sweet and loving to me since I've been pregnant. Recently I've had cravings for all sorts of odd combinations—like the other day I had this sudden weird desire for pineapple and a pink cardigan. And Luke drove me to the shops especially to get them.

He's about to say something, when his mobile phone starts ringing. He whips it out of his pocket and the sonographer puts up a hand.

"I'm sorry, but you can't use that in here."

"Right." Luke frowns as he sees the caller display. "It's Iain. I'd better call him back."

I don't need to ask which Iain. It'll be Iain Wheeler, the chief marketing honcho of the Arcodas Group. Luke has his own PR company, Brandon Communications, and Arcodas is Luke's big new client. It was a real coup when he won them and it's given a fantastic boost to the company—he's already hired more staff and is planning to open loads of new European offices on the back of it.

So it's all wonderful for Brandon Communications. But as usual, Luke's working himself into the ground. I've never seen him so at anyone's beck and call before. If Iain Wheeler calls, he always, *always* calls him back within five minutes, whether he's in another meeting, or he's having supper, or even if it's the middle of the night. He says it's the service industry and Arcodas is his mega-client, and that's what they're paying for.

All I can say is, if Iain Wheeler calls while I'm in labor, then that phone is going straight out the window.

"Is there a landline I can use nearby?" Luke is asking the sonographer. "Becky, you don't mind. . . ."

"It's fine." I wave a hand.

"I'll show you," the sonographer says, getting up. "I'll be back in a moment, Mrs. Brandon."

The two of them disappear out the door, which closes with a heavy clunk.

I'm alone. The computer is still on. The ultrasound probe thing is resting next to the monitor.

I could just reach over and—

No. Don't be silly. I don't even know how to use an ultrasound. And besides, it would spoil the magical surprise. If Luke wants us to wait, then we'll wait.

I shift on the couch and examine my nails. I can wait for things. Of course I can. I can easily—

Oh *God*. No I can't. Not till December. And it's all right there in front of me . . . and nobody's about. . . .

I'll just have a teeny peek. Just really quickly. And I won't tell Luke. We'll still have the magical surprise at the birth—except it won't be *quite* so much of a surprise for me. Exactly.

Leaning right over, I manage to grab the ultrasound stick. I apply it to the gel on my stomach—and at once the blurry image reappears on the screen.

I did it! Now I just have to shift it slightly to get the crucial bit.... Frowning with concentration, I move the probe around on my abdomen, tilting it this way and that, craning my neck to see the screen. This is a lot easier than I thought! Maybe I should become a sonographer. I'm obviously a bit of a natural—

There's the head. Wow, it's huge! And that bit must be—

My hand freezes and I catch my breath. I've just spotted it. I've seen the sex of our baby!

It's a boy!

The image isn't quite as good as the sonographer's—but even so, it's unmistakable. Luke and I are going to have a son!

"Hello," I say aloud to the screen, my voice cracking slightly. "Hello, little boy!"

And now I can't stop the tears rolling down my cheeks. We're having a gorgeous baby boy! I can dress him up in cute overalls, and buy him a pedal car, and Luke can play cricket with him, and we can call him—

Oh my God. What are we going to call him?

I wonder if Luke would go for Birkin. Then I could get a Birkin to be his nappy bag.

Birkin Brandon. That's quite cool.

"Hi, little baby," I croon gently to the big round head on the screen. "Do you want to be called Birkin?"

"What are you *doing*?" The sonographer's voice makes me jump. She's standing at the door with Luke, looking appalled. "That's hospital equipment! You shouldn't be touching it!"

"I'm sorry," I say, wiping my eyes. "But I just *had* to have another quick look. Luke, I'm talking to our baby. It's just...amazing."

"Let me see!" Luke's eyes light up, and he hurries across the room, followed by the sonographer. "Where?"

I don't care if Luke sees it's a boy and the surprise is ruined. I *have* to share this precious moment with him.

"Look, there's the head!" I point. "Hello, darling!"

"Where's its face?" Luke sounds a bit perturbed.

"Dunno. Round the other side." I give a little wave. "It's Mummy and Daddy here! And we love you very—"

"Mrs. Brandon." The sonographer cuts me off. "You're talking to your bladder."

Well, how was I supposed to know it was my bladder? It looked just like a baby.

As we walk into the consultant obstetrician's room, I'm still feeling rather hot about the cheeks. The sonographer gave me this huge great lecture about how I could have done damage to myself or broken the machine, and we only managed to get away after Luke promised a big donation to the scanner appeal.

And, she said, since I hadn't been anywhere near the baby, it was very unlikely I'd seen the sex. Hmph.

But as I sit down opposite Dr. Braine, our obstetrician, I feel myself start to cheer up. He's such a reassuring man, Dr. Braine. He's in his sixties, with graying, well-groomed hair and a pinstripe suit and a faint aroma of old-fashioned aftershave. And he's delivered thousands of babies, including Luke! To be honest, I can't really imagine Luke's mother Elinor giving birth, but I guess it must have happened somehow. And as soon as we discovered I was pregnant, Luke said we had to find out if Dr. Braine was still practicing, because he was the best in the country.

"Dear boy." He shakes Luke's hand warmly. "How are you?"

"Very well indeed." Luke sits down beside me. "And how's David?"

Luke went to school with Dr. Braine's son and always asks after him when we meet.

There's silence as Dr. Braine considers the question. This is the only thing I find a tad annoying about him. He mulls over everything you say as though it's of the greatest importance, whereas you were actually just making some random remark to keep the conversation going. At our last appointment I asked where he had bought his tie, and he thought about it for five minutes, then phoned his wife to check, and it was all a total saga. And I didn't even *like* the stupid tie.

"David's very well," he says at last, nodding. "He sends his regards." There's another pause as he peruses the sheet from the sonographer. "Very good," he says eventually. "Everything's in order. How are you feeling, Rebecca?"

"Oh, I'm fine!" I say. "Happy that the baby's all right."

"You're still working full-time, I see." Dr. Braine glances at my form. "And that's not too demanding for you?"

Beside me, Luke gives a muffled snort. He's so rude.

"It's . . ." I try to think how to put it. "My job's not *that* demanding."

"Becky works for The Look," explains Luke. "You know, the new department store on Oxford Street?"

"Aah." Dr. Braine's face drops. "I *see*."

Every time I tell people what I do, they look away in embarrassment or change the subject or pretend they've never heard of The Look. Which is impossible, because all the newspapers have been talking about it for weeks. Yesterday the *Daily World* called it the "biggest retail disaster in British history."

The only plus about working for a failure of a shop is that it means I can take as much time off as I like for doctors' appointments and prenatal classes. And if I don't hurry back, no one even notices.

"I'm sure things will turn around soon," he says encouragingly. "Now, did you have any other questions?"

I take a deep breath. "Actually, I did have one question, Dr. Braine." I hesitate. "Now that the scan results are OK, would you say it's safe to . . . you know . . ."

"Absolutely." Dr. Braine nods understandingly. "A lot of couples abstain from intercourse in early pregnancy."

"I didn't mean sex!" I say in surprise. "I meant shopping."

"Shopping?" Dr. Braine seems taken aback.

"I haven't bought anything for the baby yet," I explain. "I didn't want to jinx it. But if everything looks OK, then I can start this afternoon!"

I can't help sounding excited. I've been waiting and *waiting* to start shopping for the baby. And I've just read about this fabulous new baby shop on the King's Road, called Bambino. I actually took a bona fide afternoon off, especially to go!

I feel Luke's gaze on me and turn to see him regarding me with incredulity.

"Sweetheart, what do you mean, 'start'?" he says.

"I haven't bought anything for the baby yet!" I say, defensive. "You know I haven't."

"So . . . you haven't bought a miniature Ralph Lauren dressing gown?" Luke counts off on his fingers. "Or a rocking horse? Or a pink fairy outfit with wings?"

"Those are for it to have when it's a *toddler*," I retort with dignity. "I haven't bought anything for the *baby*."

Honestly. Luke's not going to be a very good dad if he doesn't know the difference.

Dr. Braine is following our conversation, looking perplexed.

"I take it you don't wish to know the sex of the baby?" he puts in.

"No, thanks," says Luke, sounding determined. "We want to keep it a surprise, *don't* we, Becky?"

"Um . . . yes." I clear my throat. "Unless maybe you think, Dr. Braine, that we should know for very good, unavoidable medical reasons?"

I look hard at Dr. Braine, but he doesn't get the message.

"Not at all." He beams.

Drat.

It's another twenty minutes before we leave the room, about three of which are spent in Dr. Braine examining me, and the rest in him and Luke reminiscing about some school cricket match. I'm trying to be polite and listen, but I can't help fidgeting with impatience. I want to get to Bambino!

At last the appointment's over and we're walking out onto the busy London street. A woman walks past with an old-fashioned Silver Cross pram, and I discreetly eye it up. I definitely want a pram like that, with gorgeous bouncy wheels. Except I'll have it customized hot pink. It'll be *so* fab. People will call me the Girl with the Hot Pink Pram. Except if it's a boy, I'll have it sprayed baby blue. No . . . aquamarine. And everyone will say—

"I spoke to Giles from the estate agents this morning." Luke breaks into my thoughts.

"Really?" I look up in excitement. "Did he have anything . . ."

"Nothing."

"Oh." I deflate.

At the moment, we live in this amazing penthouse flat which Luke has had for years. It's stunning, but it doesn't have a garden, and there's lots of immaculate beige carpet everywhere and it's not exactly a baby type of place. So a few weeks ago we put it on the market and started looking for a nice family house.

The trouble is, the flat was snapped up immediately. Which, I don't want to boast or anything, was totally due to my brilliant styling. I put candles everywhere, and a bottle of champagne on ice in the bathroom, and loads of "lifestyle" touches like opera programs and invitations to glittering society events (which I borrowed from my posh friend Suze). And this couple called the Karlssons put in an offer on the spot! And they can pay in cash!

Which is great—except where are we going to live? We haven't seen a single house we like and now the estate agent keeps saying the market's very "dry" and "poor" and had we thought of renting?

I don't *want* to rent. I want to have a lovely new house to bring the baby home to.

"What if we don't find a place?" I look up at Luke. "What if we're cast out on the streets? It's going to be winter! I'll be heavily pregnant!"

I have a sudden image of myself trudging up Oxford Street while a choir sings "O Little Town of Bethlehem."

"Darling, we won't be cast out on the streets! But Giles said we may need to be more flexible in our requirements." Luke pauses. "I think he meant *your* requirements, Becky."

That is so unfair! When they sent over the Property Search Form, it said, "Please be as specific as possible in your wishes." So I was. And now they're complaining!

"We can forget the Shoe Room, apparently."

"But—" I stop at his expression. I once saw a Shoe Room on *Lifestyles of the Rich and Famous* and I've been hankering after one ever since. "OK, then," I say tamely.

"And we might need to be more flexible on area—"

"I don't mind that!" I say, as Luke's mobile starts ringing. "In fact, I think it's a good idea."

It's Luke who's always been so keen on Maida Vale, not me. There are *loads* of places I'd like to live.

"Luke Brandon here," Luke's saying in his businesslike way. "Oh, hi there. Yes, we've had the scan. Everything looks good. It's Jess," he adds to me. "She tried you but your phone's still switched off."

"Jess!" I say, delighted. "Let me talk to her!"

Jess is my sister. *My sister.* It still gives me such a kick to say that. All my life, I thought I was an only child—and then I discovered I had a long-lost half sister! We didn't *exactly* get on to begin with, but ever since we got trapped in a storm together, and properly talked, we've been real friends.

I haven't seen her for a couple of months because she's been away in Guatemala on some geology research project. But we've called and e-mailed each other, and she's texted me pictures of herself on top of some cliff. (Wearing a hideous blue anorak instead of the cool faux fur jacket I got her. Honestly.)

"I'm going back to the office now," Luke is saying into the phone. "And Becky's off shopping. Do you want a word?"

"Shh!" I hiss in horror. He *knows* he's not supposed to mention the word *shopping* to Jess. Making a face at him, I take the phone and put it to my ear. "Hi, Jess! How's it going?"

"It's great!" She sounds all distant and crackly. "I was just calling to hear how the scan went."

I can't help feeling touched at her remembering. She's probably hanging by a rope in some crevasse somewhere, chipping away at the rock face, but she still took the trouble to call.

"Everything looks fine!"

"Yes, Luke said. Thank goodness for that." I can hear the relief in Jess's voice. I know she feels guilty about me falling off the mountain, because I'd gone up there looking for her, because—

Anyway, it's a long story. The point is, the baby's OK.

"So, Luke says you're going shopping?"

"Just some essentials for the baby," I say casually. "Some . . . er . . . recycled nappies. From the thrift shop." I can see Luke laughing at me, and hastily turn away.

The thing about my sister Jess is, she doesn't like shopping or spending money or ruining the earth with evil consumerism. And she thinks I don't either. She thinks I've followed her lead and embraced frugality.

I did embrace it for about a week. I ordered a big sack of oats, and I bought some clothes from Oxfam and I made lentil soup. But the trouble with being frugal is, it gets so *boring*. You get sick of soup, and not buying magazines because they're a waste of money, and sticking bits of soap together to make one big revolting lump. And the oats were getting in the way of Luke's golf clubs, so in the end I chucked them out and bought some Weetabix instead.

Only I can't tell Jess, because it'll ruin our lovely sisterly bond.

"Did you see the article about making your own baby wipes?" she's saying with enthusiasm. "It should be pretty easy. I've started saving rags for you. We could do it together."

"Oh. Um...yes!"

Jess keeps sending me issues of a magazine called *Frugal Baby*. It has cover lines like "Kit Out Your Nursery for £25!" and pictures of babies dressed in old flour sacks, and it makes me feel depressed just looking at it. I don't *want* to put the baby to bed in a £3 plastic laundry basket. I want to buy a cute little cradle with white frills.

Now she's going on about something called "sustainable hemp babygros." I think I might end this conversation.

"I'd better go, Jess," I cut in. "Will you make it to Mum's party?"

My mum's having a sixtieth birthday party next

week. Loads of people are invited, and there's going to be a band, and Martin from next door is going to do conjuring tricks!

"Of course!" says Jess. "Wouldn't miss it! See you then."

"Bye!"

I switch off the phone and turn to see that Luke has managed to hail a taxi. "Shall I drop you off at the thrift shop?" he inquires, opening the door.

Oh, ha-ha.

"Bambino on the King's Road, please," I say to the driver. "Hey, do you want to come, Luke?" I add with sudden enthusiasm. "We could look at cool prams and everything and then have tea somewhere nice...."

I already know from Luke's expression that he's going to say no.

"Sweetheart, I need to get back. Meeting with Iain. I'll come another time, I promise."

There's no point being disappointed. I know Luke's working full-out on the Arcodas account. At least he made time for the scan. The taxi moves off and Luke puts his arm round me.

"You look glowing," he says.

"Really?" I beam back at him. I have to say, I do feel pretty good today. I'm wearing my fab new maternity Earl Jeans, and high wedge espadrilles, and a sexy halter-neck top from Isabella Oliver, which I've ruched up to show just a teeny hint of tanned bump.

I never realized it before—but being pregnant rocks! OK, your tummy gets big—but it's *supposed* to. And your legs look thinner in comparison. And you get this brilliant cleavage, all of a sudden. (Which I have to say, Luke is quite keen on.)

"Let's have another look at those scan pictures," he says. I delve into my handbag for the shiny roll of images and for a while we just gaze at them together: at the rounded head; at the profile of a little face.

"We're starting off a whole new person," I murmur, my eyes riveted. "Can you believe it?"

"I know." Luke's arm tightens around me. "It's the biggest adventure we'll ever go on."

"It's amazing how nature works." I bite my lip, feeling the emotions rise again. "All these maternal instincts have kicked in. I just feel like . . . I want to give our baby everything!"

"Bambino," says the taxi driver, pulling over to the pavement. I look up from the scan pictures to see the most fantastic, brand-new shop façade. The paintwork is cream, the canopy is red stripes, the doorman is dressed up as a toy soldier, and the windows are like a treasure trove for children. There are beautiful little baby clothes on mannequins, a child's bed shaped like a fifties Cadillac, a real little Ferris wheel going round and round. . . .

"Wow!" I breathe, reaching for the taxi's door handle. "I wonder if that Ferris wheel is for sale! Bye, Luke, see you later. . . ."

I'm already halfway toward the entrance, when I hear Luke calling out, "Wait!" I turn back to see a look of slight alarm on his face. "Becky." He leans out of the taxi. "The baby doesn't have to have *everything*."

TWO

HOW ON *EARTH* did I hold off baby shopping for so long?

I've reached the New Baby department on the first floor. It's softly carpeted, with nursery rhymes playing over the sound system, and huge plushy animals decorating the entrance. An assistant dressed as Peter Rabbit has given me a white wicker basket, and as I look around, clutching it, I can feel the lust rising.

They say motherhood changes you—and they're right. For once in my life I'm not thinking about myself. I'm being totally selfless! All this is for my unborn child's welfare.

In one direction are banks of gorgeous cradles and rotating tinkly mobiles. In the other I can glimpse the alluring chrome glint of prams. Ahead of me are displays of teeny-weeny outfits. I take a step forward, toward the clothes. Just look at those adorable bunny slippers. And the tiny cowhide padded jackets...and there's a massive section of Baby Dior...and, oh my God, D&G Junior...

OK. Calm down. Let's be organized. What I need is a list.

From my bag I pull *Nine Months of Your Life.* I turn to chapter eight: "Shopping for Your Baby" and eagerly start scanning the page.

> *Clothes:*
> *Do not be tempted to buy too many tiny baby clothes. White is recommended for ease of washing. Three plain babygros and six tops will suffice.*

I look at the words for a moment. The thing is, it's never a good idea to follow a book too closely. It even said in the introduction, "You will not want to take every piece of advice. Every baby is different and you must be guided by your instincts."

My instincts are telling me to get a cowhide jacket.

I hurry over to the display and look through the size labels. "Newborn baby." "Small baby." How do I know if I'm going to have a small baby or not? Experimentally I prod my bump. It feels quite small so far, but who can tell? Maybe I should buy both, to be on the safe side.

"It's the Baby in Urbe snowsuit!" A manicured hand appears on the rack in front of me and grabs a white quilted suit on a chic black hanger. "I've been *dying* to find one of these."

"Me too!" I say instinctively and grab the last remaining one.

"You know in Harrods the waiting list for these is six months?" The owner of the hand is a hugely pregnant blond girl in jeans and a stretchy turquoise-wrap top. "Oh my God, they have the whole Baby in Urbe range." She starts piling baby clothes into her white wicker basket. "And look! They've got Piglet shoes. I *must* get some for my daughters."

I've never even heard of Baby in Urbe. Or Piglet shoes.

How can I be so uncool? How can I not have heard of any of the labels? As I survey the tiny garments before me I feel a slight panic. I don't know what's in or what's out. I have no idea about baby fashion. And I've only got about four months to get up to speed.

I could always ask Suze. She's my oldest, best friend, and has three children, Ernest, Wilfrid, and Clementine. But it's a bit different with her. Most of her baby clothes are hand-embroidered smocks handed down through the generations and darned by her mother's old retainer, and the babies sleep in antique oak cots from the family stately home.

I grab a couple of pairs of Piglet shoes, several Baby in Urbe rompers, and a pair of Jelly Wellies, just to be on the safe side. Then I spot the sweetest little pink baby dress. It has rainbow buttons and matching knickers and little tiny socks. It's absolutely gorgeous. But what if we're having a boy?

This is *impossible,* not knowing the sex. There must be some way I can secretly find out.

"How many children do you have?" says the turquoise-wrap girl chattily as she squints inside shoes for sizes.

"This is my first." I gesture to my bump.

"How lovely! Just like my friend Saskia." She gestures at a dark-haired girl who's standing a few feet away. She's whippet thin with no sign of pregnancy and is talking intently into a mobile phone. "She's only just found out. *So* exciting!"

At that moment, Saskia snaps her phone shut and comes toward us, her face glowing.

"I got in!" she says. "I'm having Venetia Carter!"

"Oh, Saskia! That's fantastic!" The turquoise-wrap girl drops her basket of clothes right on my foot, and throws her arms around Saskia. "Sorry about that!" she gaily adds to me as I hand the basket back. "But isn't that great news? Venetia Carter!"

"Are you with Venetia Carter too?" Saskia asks me with sudden interest.

I am so out of the baby loop, I have no idea who or what Venetia Carter is.

"I haven't heard of her," I admit.

"*You* know." Turquoise-wrap girl opens her eyes wide. "The obstetrician! The must-have celebrity obstetrician!"

Must-have celebrity obstetrician?

My skin starts to prickle. There's a must-have celebrity obstetrician and I don't know about it?

"The one from Hollywood!" elaborates turquoise-wrap girl. "She delivers all the film stars' babies. You *must* have heard of her. And now she's moved to London. All the supermodels are going to her. She holds tea parties for her clients—isn't that fab? They all bring their babies and get these fabulous goodie bags. . . ."

My heart is thumping as I listen. Goodie bags? Parties with supermodels? I cannot *believe* I'm missing out on all this. Why haven't I heard of Venetia Carter?

It's all Luke's fault. He made us go straight for stuffy old Dr. Braine. We never even considered anyone else.

"And is she good at, you know, delivering babies?" I ask, trying to keep calm.

"Oh, Venetia's *wonderful*," says Saskia, who seems far more intense than her friend. "She's not like these old-fashioned doctors. She really *connects* with you. My boss, Amanda, had the most fabulous holistic water birth with lotus flowers and Thai massage."

Thai massage? Dr. Braine's never even *mentioned* Thai massage.

"My husband won't pay for her." Turquoise-wrap girl pouts. "He's a meanie. Saskia, you're *so* lucky—"

"How do you get a place with her?" The words come spilling out before I can stop them. "Do you have the address? Or the phone number?"

"Ooh." Turquoise-wrap girl exchanges doubtful glances with Saskia. "You're probably too late now. She'll be booked up."

"I can give you this. You could try ringing." Saskia reaches into her Mulberry bag and produces a brochure with *Venetia Carter* in elegant raised navy-blue script and a line drawing of a baby. I open it up and the first thing I see is a page of glowing testimonials, with names listed discreetly underneath. All famous! I turn to the back and there's an address in Maida Vale.

I don't believe it. Maida Vale is where we live. Oh, this is totally meant!

"Thanks," I say breathlessly. "I will."

As Saskia and her friend move away, I whip out my mobile phone and speed-dial Luke.

"Luke!" I exclaim as soon as he answers. "Thank God you answered! Guess what?"

"Becky, are you OK?" he asks in alarm. "What's happened?"

"I'm fine! But listen, we have to change doctors! I've just found out about this brilliant celebrity obstetrician called Venetia Carter. Everyone goes to her and she's amazing, apparently, and she practices near us! It couldn't be more perfect! I'm about to call her!"

"Becky, what on earth are you talking about?" Luke sounds incredulous. "We're not changing doctors! We have a doctor, remember. A very good one."

Wasn't he listening?

"I know we do," I say. "But Venetia Carter delivers all the film stars' babies! She's holistic!"

"What do you mean, 'holistic'?" Luke sounds unimpressed. God, he has such a closed mind.

"I mean everyone has a fabulous birth! She does Thai massage! I just met these two girls in Bambino, and they said—"

Luke cuts me off. "I really can't see what advantages this woman could have over Dr. Braine. We know he's experienced; we know he does a good job; he's a friend of the family...."

"But...but..." I'm hopping with frustration.

"But what?"

I'm stumped. I can't say, "But he doesn't have tea parties with supermodels."

"Maybe I want to be treated by a woman!" I exclaim with sudden inspiration. "Had you thought of that?"

"Then we'll ask Dr. Braine to recommend a colleague," Luke replies firmly. "Becky, Dr. Braine has been the family obstetrician for years. I really don't think we should run off to some unknown trendy doctor on the say-so of a couple of girls."

"But she's not unknown! That's the whole point! She treats *celebrities*!"

"Becky, just stop." Luke suddenly sounds forceful. "This is a bad idea. You're already halfway through your pregnancy. You're not changing doctors, end of story. Iain's here. I have to go. I'll see you later."

The phone goes dead and I stare at it, livid.

How dare he tell me which doctor I'm going to? And what's so great about his precious Dr. Braine? I stuff my mobile and the brochure into my bag and start furiously filling my basket with Petit Lapin baby suits.

Luke doesn't understand anything. If all the movie stars go to her, then she has to be good.

And it would be so cool. *So* cool.

I suddenly have a vision of myself lying in hospital, cradling my new baby, with Kate Winslet in the next bed. And Heidi Klum in the bed beyond that. We'd all become friends! We'd buy each other little presents, and all our babies would be bonded for life, and we'd go to the park together and be photographed by *Hello!* magazine. *Kate Winslet pushes her pram, chatting with a friend.*

Maybe *with her best friend, Becky.*

"Excuse me, do you need another basket?" A voice interrupts my thoughts, and I look up to see a salesperson gesturing at my overflowing pile of baby clothes. I've just been stuffing them into the basket without really noticing.

"Oh, thanks," I say in a daze. I take the second wicker basket from him and wander over to a display of tiny hats labeled LITTLE STAR and LITTLE TREASURE. But I can't concentrate.

I want to go to Venetia Carter. I don't care what Luke thinks.

In sudden defiance I pull out my mobile again and reach for the brochure. I move to a quiet corner of the shop and carefully punch in the number.

"Good afternoon, Venetia Carter's office," a woman's very posh voice answers.

"Oh, hello!" I say, trying to sound as charming as I can. "I'm having a baby in December, and I've heard how wonderful Venetia Carter is, and I just wondered if there was any possible chance of me arranging an appointment with her, possibly?"

"I'm sorry," the woman says in a firm but polite tone. "Dr. Carter is fully booked for the present."

"But I'm really desperate! And I really think I need a holistic water birth. And I live in Maida Vale, and I'd be willing to pay over the odds."

"Dr. Carter is absolutely—"

"I'd just like to add that I'm a personal shopper, and I'd be pleased to offer Dr. Carter my complimentary services." The words come tumbling out. "And my husband has a PR company and he could do some free PR for her! Not that she probably needs it, of course," I add hastily. "But if you could just ask her? Please?"

There's silence.

"Your name is?" says the woman at last.

"Rebecca Brandon," I say eagerly. "And my husband is Luke Brandon of Brandon Communications, and—"

"Hold on, please, Mrs. Brandon. Venetia—" Their conversation is cut off by a brisk rendition of *The Four Seasons*.

Please let her say yes. Please let her say yes....

I can hardly breathe as I wait. I'm standing next to a display of white knitted rabbits, crossing my fingers as hard as I can, clutching all my pendants for good measure, and sending silent prayers to the goddess Vishnu, who has been very helpful to me in the past. "Mrs. Brandon?"

"Hello!" I drop all my pendants. "I'm here!"

"It's likely that Dr. Carter will have an unexpected vacancy on her books. We'll be able to let you know within the next few days."

"OK," I gasp. "Thanks very much!"

REGAL AIRLINES

Mrs Rebecca Brandon
37 Maida Vale Mansions
Maida Vale
London NW6 0YF

14 August 2003

Dear Mrs. Brandon,

Thank you for your letter, and the enclosed flight itineraries, doctor's note, and scan pictures.

I agree that your unborn child has taken many flights with Regal Airlines. Unfortunately it does not qualify for air miles, since it did not buy a ticket for any of these flights.

I am sorry to disappoint and hope you choose Regal Airlines again soon.

Yours sincerely,

Margaret McNair
Customer Service Manager

THREE

I HAVEN'T MENTIONED ANYTHING more about Venetia Carter to Luke.

For a start, it's not definite yet. And for another start, if marriage has taught me one thing, it's to not bring up tricky subjects when your husband is stressed out launching offices simultaneously in Amsterdam and Munich. He's been away all week, and only arrived back last night, exhausted.

Besides which, changing doctors isn't the only tricky subject I need to broach. There's also the very slight scratch on the Mercedes (which was *not* my fault—it was that stupid bollard) and the two pairs of shoes I want him to get from Miu Miu when he goes to Milan.

It's Saturday morning, and I'm sitting in the office, checking my bank statement on my laptop. I only discovered online banking a couple of months ago—and it has *so* many advantages. You can do it any time of day! Plus, they don't send bank statements out by post, so no one (e.g., your husband) can see them lying around the house.

"Becky, I've had a letter from my mother." Luke

comes in, holding the post and a mug of coffee. "She sends her regards."

"Your mother?" I try to hide my horror. "You mean *Elinor*? What does she want?"

Luke has two mothers. His lovely, warm stepmother, Annabel, who lives in Devon with his dad and who we visited last month. And his ice-queen of a real mother, Elinor, who lives in America and abandoned him when he was little and in my opinion should be excommunicated.

"She's touring Europe with her art collection."

"Why?" I ask blankly. I have a vision of Elinor in a coach, a bundle of paintings under her arm. It doesn't seem very *her*, somehow.

"The collection is currently on loan to the Uffizi, then a gallery in Paris—" Luke breaks off. "Becky, you didn't think I meant she was taking her pictures on holiday."

"Of course not," I say with dignity. "I knew *exactly* what you meant."

"Anyway, she'll be in London later on in the year and wants to meet up."

"Luke . . . I thought you hated your mother. I thought you never wanted to see her again, remember?"

"Come on, Becky." Luke frowns slightly. "She's going to be the grandmother of our child. We can't shut her out completely."

Yes we can! I want to retort. But instead, I give an unwilling kind of half shrug. I suppose he's right. The baby will be her only grandchild. It'll have her blood in it.

Oh God, what if it *takes after* Elinor? I'm stricken by a terrible vision of a baby lying in a pram in a cream

Chanel suit, glaring up at me and saying, "Your outfit is shoddy, Mother."

"So, what are you up to?" Luke breaks into my thoughts, and too late I realize he's heading across the room toward me. Right toward my laptop.

"Nothing!" I say quickly. "It's just my bank statement...." I try to close the window I'm on, but it's frozen. Damn.

"Something wrong?" says Luke.

"No!" I say, panicking slightly. "I mean...I'll just shut the whole thing down!" I casually rip the power cord out of the back—but the screen is still powered up. The statement is there, in black and white.

And Luke's getting nearer. I'm really not sure I want him seeing this.

"Let me have a go." Luke reaches my chair. "Are you on the bank's Web site?"

"Er...kind of! Honestly, I wouldn't bother...." I position my bump in front of the screen, but Luke is peering round me. He stares at the statement for a few disbelieving moments.

"Becky," he says at last. "Does that say 'First Cooperative Bank of Namibia'?"

"Er...yes." I try to sound matter-of-fact. "I have a small online account there."

"In *Namibia*?"

"They sent me an e-mail offering me very competitive rates," I say a little defiantly. "It was a great opportunity."

"Do you respond to *every* e-mail you get, Becky?" Luke turns, incredulous. "Do you have a fine selection of Viagra substitutes too?"

I knew he wouldn't understand my brilliant new banking strategy.

"Don't get so stressy!" I say. "Why is it such a big deal where I bank? Commerce has gone global, you know, Luke. The old boundaries are gone. If you can get a good rate in Bangladesh, then—"

"*Bangladesh?*"

"Oh. Well...er...I've got a bank account there too. Just a tiny one," I add quickly, looking at his expression.

"Becky..." Luke seems to be having trouble taking all this in. "How many of these online bank accounts have you opened?"

"Three," I say after a pause. "About three."

He gives me a hard look. The trouble with husbands is, they get to know you too well.

"OK then, fifteen," I say in a rush.

"And how many overdrafts?"

"Fifteen. *What?*" I add defensively. "What's the point of having a bank account if you don't have an overdraft?"

"Fifteen overdrafts?" Luke clutches his head in disbelief. "Becky...you *are* third world debt."

"I'm playing the global economy to my advantage!" I retort. "The Bank of Chad gave me a fifty-dollar bonus just for joining!"

Luke's so blinkered. So what if I have fifteen bank accounts? Everyone knows you shouldn't put all your eggs in one basket.

"You seem to forget, Luke," I add in lofty tones, "I *am* a former financial journalist. I know all about money and investment. The bigger the risk, the bigger the profit, I think you'll find."

Luke doesn't look too impressed. "I'm aware of the principles of investment, thank you, Becky," he says politely.

"Well, then." I suddenly have a thought. "We should invest the baby's trust fund in Bangladesh too. We'd probably make a fortune!"

"Are you *crazy*?" He stares at me.

"Why not? It's an emerging market!"

"I don't think so." Luke rolls his eyes. "In fact, I've already spoken to Kenneth about the baby's fund, and we've agreed to invest it in a range of secure unit trusts—"

"Wait a minute!" I raise a hand. "What do you mean, you've spoken to Kenneth? What about *my* opinion?"

I can't believe they haven't even consulted me! Like I don't count. Like I didn't used to be a financial expert on television and get hundreds of letters a week asking for advice.

"Look, Becky." Luke sighs. "Kenneth is very happy to recommend suitable investments. You don't need to worry."

"That's not the point!" I say indignantly. "Luke, you don't understand. We're going to be *parents*. We need to make all important decisions *together*. Otherwise our child will run around hitting us and we'll end up hiding in the bedroom and never have sex again!"

"What?"

"It's true! It's on *Supernanny*!"

Luke looks totally baffled. He really should watch more TV.

"All right, fine," he says at last. "We can decide things together. But I'm not putting the baby's trust fund in some high-risk emerging market."

"Well, I'm not putting it in some stodgy old bank account where it doesn't make any profit!" I retaliate.

"Stalemate." Luke's mouth twitches. "So...what does *Supernanny* recommend when parents have fundamentally differing approaches to trust fund investment?"

"I'm not sure she's covered it," I admit. Then a sudden brain wave hits me. "I know. We'll split up the money. You invest half and I'll invest half. And we'll see who does best." I can't resist adding, "I bet it's me."

"Oh, I *see*." Luke raises his eyebrows. "So...this is a challenge, is it, Mrs. Brandon?"

"He who dares wins," I say nonchalantly, and Luke starts to laugh.

"OK. Let's do this. Half each, to be invested in anything we choose."

"You're on," I say, holding out my hand. We shake gravely, as the phone starts ringing.

"I'll get it," Luke says, and heads over to his desk. "Hello? Oh, hi there. How are you?"

I am so going to win this! I'll pick loads of brilliant investments and make the baby an absolute *mint*. Maybe I'll invest in futures. Or gold. Or...art! I just need to find the next Damien Hirst and buy a pickled cow or whatever, and then auction it for a huge profit at Sotheby's, and everyone will say how farsighted and genius I was....

"Really?" Luke is saying. "No, she never mentioned it. Well, thanks." He puts down the phone and turns to face me with a quizzical expression. "Becky, that was Giles from the real estate agents. Apparently you had a long talk earlier this week. What exactly did you say to him?"

Shit. I knew there was another tricky subject I had to broach. I should really start a list.

"Oh yes, that." I clear my throat. "I just told Giles we were willing to be more flexible in our requirements." I straighten some papers on my desk, not looking up. "Like you said. Expand our search area a bit."

"A bit?" echoes Luke incredulously. "To the *Caribbean*? He's sending us the details of eight bloody beach villas and wants to know if we'd like to arrange flights!"

"You're the one who said we had to look further afield, Luke!" I say defensively. "It was your idea!"

"I meant Kensington! Not Barbados!"

"Have you seen what we can *get* in Barbados?" I counter eagerly. "Look at this!" I push my office chair across the floor to his computer, click on a browser, and find my way onto a Caribbean realty page.

Property Web sites are the best thing *ever*. Especially the ones with virtual tours.

"See this one?" I point at the screen. "Five bedroom villa with infinity pool, sunken garden, and guest cottage!"

"Becky . . ." Luke pauses, as though thinking how to explain the situation to me. "It's in Barbados."

He is so hung up on that one detail.

"So what?" I say. "It'd be fab! The baby would learn to swim, and you could send all your e-mails from the guest cottage . . . and I could go running on the beach every day. . . ."

I have an alluring image of myself in a string bikini, pushing one of those jogger prams along a glistening white Caribbean beach. And Luke would be all tanned in a polo shirt, drinking a rum punch. He could get into surfing, and put beads in his hair again—

"I'm not putting beads in my hair again." Luke interrupts my thoughts.

That's so spooky! How on earth did he . . .

Oh, OK. I possibly may have shared my Caribbean fantasy with him before.

"Look, sweetheart," he says, sitting down. "Maybe in five, ten years' time we can think about something like this. If things go to plan, we'll have a lot of options by then. But for now it has to be central London."

"Well, what are we going to do, then?" I close the Barbados Web page crossly. "There's *nothing* on the market. It'll be Christmas and we'll be out on the streets, and we'll have to go to a homeless shelter with the baby, and eat soup. . . ."

"Becky." Luke lifts a hand to stop me. "We won't have to eat soup." He clicks one of his e-mails, opens an attachment, and presses Print. A moment later the printer springs into action.

"What?" I say. "What are you doing?"

"Here." He collects the pages and hands them to me. "This is why Giles rang. In case we were 'still considering London,' as he put it. It's just come on the market, round the corner from here. Delamain Road. But we need to be quick."

I scan the first page, taking in the words as fast as I can.

Elegant family house . . . ideal for entertaining . . . grand entrance hall . . . magnificent luxury kitchen . . .

Wow. I have to admit, this looks amazing.

Garden with architect-designed play area . . . six bedrooms . . . dressing room with walk-in shoe cupboard . . .

I catch my breath. A walk-in shoe cupboard! But surely that's just another way of saying—

"It's even got a Shoe Room." Luke is watching me with a grin. "Giles was pretty pleased about that. Shall we go and see it?"

I am so excited about this house! And not just because of the Shoe Room. I've read the details over and over, and I can just *see* Luke and me living there. Taking a shower in the frameless limestone RainJet cubicle... making coffee in the Bulthaup kitchen with its state-of-the-art appliances... and then maybe strolling out into the secluded west-facing garden with its range of mature specimen shrubs. Whatever *they* are.

It's later that day and we're walking along the leafy Maida Vale road on the way to our appointment to view it. I'm clutching the printout of the details in my hand, but I barely need to; I practically know them by heart.

"Twenty-four... twenty-six..." Luke is squinting at the numbers as we pass. "It'll be on the other side of the road...."

"There it is!" I stop dead and point across the street. "Look, there's the impressive pillared entrance and double doors with attractive fanlight! It looks fab! Let's go!"

Luke's hand holds me back as I'm about to hurry across the road. "Becky, before we go in, just a word."

"What?" I'm tugging at his hand like a dog trying to get off the leash. "What is it?"

"Try to play it cool, OK? We don't want to look too

keen. First rule of business dealing, you should always look as though you could walk away."

"Oh." I stop yanking his hand. "All right."

Cool. I can play it cool.

But as we head across the road and up to the front door, my heart's hammering. This is our house, I just know it is!

"I love the front door!" I exclaim, ringing the bell. "It's so shiny!"

"Becky . . . cool, remember," says Luke. "Try not to look so impressed."

"Oh, right, yes." I adopt the best unimpressed expression I can muster, just as the door swings open.

A very slim woman in her forties is standing on black-and-white marble tiles. She's wearing white D&G jeans, a casual top which I *know* cost her £500, and a diamond ring so huge, I'm amazed she can lift her arm.

"Hi." Her voice is a husky mockney drawl. "Are you here to see the house?"

"Yes!" At once I realize I sound too excited. "I mean . . . yeah." I affect a similar nonchalance. "We thought we'd have a look."

"Fabia Paschali." Her handshake is like wet cotton wool.

"Becky Brandon. And this is my husband, Luke."

"Well, come on through."

We follow her in, our feet echoing on the tiles, and as I look around I have to suppress a loud intake of breath. This hall is *huge*. And the sweeping staircase is like something out of Hollywood! I immediately have an image of myself trailing down it in a fantastic evening dress while Luke waits admiringly at the bottom.

"We've had fashion shoots here," says Fabia, gesturing at the staircase. "The marble is imported from Italy and the chandelier is antique Murano. It's included."

I can see she's waiting for a reaction.

"Very nice," says Luke. "Becky?"

Cool. I must be cool.

"It's all right." I give a little yawn. "Can we see the kitchen?"

The kitchen is just as amazing. It has a vast breakfast bar, a glass roof, and about every gadget known to mankind. I'm trying as hard as I can not to look overawed as Fabia runs through the appliances. "Triple oven...chef's hob...This is a rotating multisurface chopping area...."

"Not bad." I run a hand over the granite with a jaded air. "Do you have a built-in electric sushi maker?"

"Yes," she says as though I've asked something really obvious.

It has a built-in electric sushi maker!

Oh God, it's just spectacular. And so is the terrace with built-in summer kitchen and barbecue. And the drawing room fitted out with David Linley shelves. As we follow Fabia upstairs to the main bedroom I'm practically expiring, trying not to exclaim at everything.

"Here's the dressing room...." Fabia shows us into a small room lined with paneled walnut wardrobes. "This is my customized shoe cupboard...." She opens the door and we walk in.

I feel faint. Either side of us are rows and rows of shoes, lined up immaculately on suede-lined shelves. Louboutins...Blahniks...

"It's amazing!" I blurt out. "And look, we're the same size and everything. This is *so* meant to be—"

Luke casts me a warning glance. "I mean...yeah." I give an offhand shrug. "It's OK, I guess."

"Have you got kids?" Fabia glances at my stomach as we move away.

"We're expecting one in December."

"We've got two at boarding school." She rips a Nicorette patch off her arm, frowns at it, and drops it in a bin. Then she reaches in her jeans pocket and produces a packet of Marlboro Lights. "They're on the top floor now but their nurseries are still done up if you're interested." She flicks a lighter and takes a puff.

"Nurseries?" echoes Luke, glancing at me. "More than one?"

"His and hers. We had one of each. Never got round to redecorating. This is my son's...." She pushes open a white-paneled door.

I stand there, open-mouthed. It's like fairyland. The walls are painted with a mural of green hills and blue sky and woods and teddy bears having a picnic. In one corner is a painted crib in the shape of a castle; in the other is a real little red wooden train on tracks, big enough to sit on, with a toy in each carriage.

I feel an overwhelming stab of desire. I want a boy. I *so* want a little boy.

"And my daughter's is over here," Fabia continues.

I can barely tear myself away from the boy's nursery, but I follow her across the landing as she opens the door—and can't help gasping.

I have never seen anything so beautiful. It's a little girl's dream. The walls are decorated with hand-painted fairies, the white curtains are looped back with huge lilac taffeta bows, and the little cradle is festooned with broderie anglaise frills like a princess's bed.

Oh God. Now I want a girl.

I want both. Can't I have both?

"So, what do you think?" Fabia turns to me.

There's silence on the landing. I can't speak for longing. I want these nurseries more than I have ever wanted anything, ever. I want this whole house. I want to live here and have our first Christmas here as a family, and decorate a huge pine tree in the black-and-white hall, and hang a tiny stocking above the fireplace....

"Pretty nice," I manage at last, with a small shrug. "I suppose."

"Well," Fabia draws on her cigarette. "Let's show you the rest."

I feel like I'm floating as we progress through all the other rooms. We've found our house. We've found it.

"Make her an offer!" I whisper to Luke as we're peering into the hot water cupboard. "Tell her we want it!"

"Becky, slow down." He gives a little laugh. "That's not the way to negotiate. We haven't even seen it all yet."

But I can tell he loves it too. His eyes are bright, and as we come down to the hall again he's asking questions about the neighbors.

"Well...thanks," he says at last, shaking Fabia's hand. "We'll be in touch through the estate agent."

How can he restrain himself? Why isn't he getting out his checkbook?

"Thank you very much," I add, and am about to shake Fabia's hand myself when there's the sound of a key at the front door. A tanned man in his fifties comes in, wearing jeans and a leather jacket and carrying a cool art-portfolio–type thing.

"Hi, there." He looks from face to face, clearly wondering if he's supposed to know us. "How are you?"

"Darling, these are the Brandons," says Fabia. "They've been looking round the house."

"Ah. Through Hamptons?" He frowns. "I would have called if I'd known. I accepted an offer ten minutes ago. Through the other agent."

I feel a shot of horror. He's done what?

"We'll make you an offer right now!" I blurt out. "We'll offer the asking price!"

"Sorry. It's done." He shrugs and takes off his jacket. "Those Americans who looked round this morning," he adds to Fabia.

No. No. We can't be losing our dream house!

"Luke, do something." I try to speak calmly. "Make an offer! Quick!"

"You don't mind, do you?" Fabia looks surprised. "You didn't seem that keen on the place."

"We were playing cool!" I wail, all semblance of nonchalance vanishing. "Luke, I *knew* we should have said something earlier! We love the house! I adore the nurseries! We want it!"

"We'd very much like to offer above the asking price," says Luke, stepping forward. "We can act with the utmost speed and have our solicitor contact yours in the morning."

"Look, as far as I'm concerned, the house has gone," says Fabia's husband, rolling his eyes. "I need a drink. Good luck with your search." He strides away, over the tiles toward the kitchen, and I hear a fridge opening.

"I'm sorry," Fabia says with a shrug, and leads us toward the front door.

"But . . ." I trail off helplessly.

"That's OK. If the deal falls through, please let us know." Luke gives her a polite smile and slowly we walk out into the mild autumn afternoon. Leaves are drifting off the trees onto the paved path and I can smell a bonfire in the air.

I could just see myself living on this street. Pushing the baby along in a pram, waving to all the neighbors...

"I can't believe it." My voice is a little choked.

"It was just a house." Luke puts his arm round my slumped shoulders. "We'll find another one."

"We won't. We won't ever find a place like that. It was the perfect house!" I stop, my hand on the wrought-iron gate. I can't just give up. I'm not some lame giver-upper.

"Wait here," I say to Luke, swiveling on my heel. I rush back along the path, up the steps, and plant a foot in the door before Fabia can close it.

"Listen," I say urgently. "Please. Fabia, we really, really love your house. We'll pay anything you want."

"My husband's already done the deal." She shrinks back. "There's nothing I can do."

"You can talk him round! What can I do to persuade you?"

"Look." She sighs. "It's not up to me. Could you please move your feet?"

"I'll do anything!" I cry in desperation. "I'll buy you something! I work at a fashion store, I can get really cool stuff—"

I break off. Fabia is peering at my foot, jammed in the door. Then she looks at the other one.

It's not my feet she's interested in, it's my Archie Swann cowboy boots in beaten-up calfskin with the leather drawstring. Archie Swann is the new kid on the shoe block, and these exact boots were in *Vogue* last week, under "Most Coveted." I saw Fabia checking them out the moment we arrived.

Fabia raises her eyes to mine. "I like your boots," she says.

I'm momentarily speechless.

Play it cool, Becky, play it cool.

"I waited a whole year for these boots," I say at last, feeling as though I'm treading on eggshells. "You can't get them anywhere."

"I'm on the waiting list at Harvey Nichols," she bats back.

"Maybe." I force a casual tone. "But you won't get them. They only made fifty pairs and they've run out. I'm a personal shopper, so I know these things."

I am totally bluffing here. But I think it's working. She's practically salivating over them.

"Becky?" Luke is coming back up the path toward me. "What's going on?"

"Luke!" I lift a hand. "Stay there!" I feel like Obi–Wan Kenobi telling Luke Skywalker not to interfere because he doesn't understand the strength of the Force.

I wriggle out of my left boot, leaving it standing on the doormat like a totem.

"It's yours," I say. "If you accept our offer. And the other one when we exchange contracts."

"Call the agent tomorrow," says Fabia, sounding almost breathless. "I'll talk my husband round. The house is yours."

I did it! I don't believe it!

As fast as I can, in one boot and one stockinged foot, I hurry down the steps toward Luke.

"We've got the house!" I throw my arms round his neck. "I got us the house!"

"What the *fuck*—" He stares at me. "What did you say? Why are you only wearing one boot?"

"Oh...just a bit of negotiation," I say airily, and glance back at the front door. Fabia has already kicked off her gold ballet pump and thrust her jean-clad leg into the boot. Now she's turning it from side to side, fixated. "If you call the agent in the morning, I think you'll find it's a deal."

We don't even need to wait until the next morning. Less than two hours later, we're sitting in the car on the way to Mum's, when Luke's phone rings.

"Yes?" he says into his headset. "Yes. Really?"

I'm making faces at him, trying to get him to tell me what's going on, but he's keeping his eyes firmly on the road, which is really annoying. At last he switches the phone off and turns to me with the tiniest of smiles. "It's ours."

"Yes!" I squeal in delight. "I told you!"

"They're relocating to New York and want to move as soon as possible. I said we could complete by December."

"We'll have our new baby in our gorgeous new house in time for Christmas." I hug myself. "It's going to be perfect!"

"It's pretty good news." His face is glowing. "And all down to you."

"It was nothing," I say modestly. "Just good negotiating." I get out my mobile phone and am about to text Suze the good news, when all of a sudden it rings.

"Hello?" I say joyfully into it.

"Mrs. Brandon? It's Diane from Venetia Carter's office here."

"Oh!" I stiffen, and glance at Luke. "Er... hello."

"We just wanted to let you know that the vacancy *has* arisen on Dr. Carter's books. She would be very pleased to see you—and your husband if you wish—on Thursday at three P.M."

"Right," I say, a little breathless. "Um... yes, please. I'll be there! Thank you very much!"

"Not at all. Good-bye, Mrs. Brandon."

The line goes dead and I switch the phone off with trembling hands. I've got a place with Venetia Carter! I'm going to meet celebrities and have holistic Thai massage!

Now I just have to break the news to Luke.

"Who was that?" says Luke, turning on the radio. He frowns at the digital display and presses a couple of buttons.

"It was... um..." I drop my phone accidentally-on-purpose on the floor and bend down to retrieve it.

It'll be fine. He's in a good mood about the house and everything. I'll just tell him and that will be that. And if he starts objecting, I shall point out that I'm a grown-up mature woman who can choose her own medical care. Exactly.

"Er... Luke." I sit up again, a bit red in the face. "About Dr. Braine."

"Oh, yes?" Luke pulls into another lane. "By the way, I told my mother we'd organize a dinner with him and David."

A *dinner*? Oh God, this gets worse. I have to tell him, quick.

"Luke, listen." I wait until he slows down behind a truck. "I've been thinking very hard and doing some research."

Research sounds good. Even if it was just reading a piece about Hollywood baby trends on fashionmommies.com.

"And the thing is . . ." I swallow. "I want to go to Venetia Carter."

Luke makes an impatient noise. "Becky, not this again. I thought we'd agreed—"

"I've got a place with her," I say in a rush. "I've made an appointment. It's all fixed up."

"You've *what*?" He brakes at a traffic light and turns to face me.

"It's my body!" I say defensively. "I can see whoever I like!"

"Becky, we are lucky enough to have one of the most respected, renowned obstetricians in the country looking after you, and you're messing around with some unknown woman."

"For the millionth time, she's not unknown!" I exclaim in frustration. "She's huge in Hollywood! She's modern and she's in touch, and she does these amazing water births with lotus flowers. . . ."

"*Lotus* flowers? She sounds a total bloody charlatan." Luke angrily jabs his foot down on the accelerator. "I won't have you risking the health of yourself and the baby."

"She won't be a charlatan!"

I should never have mentioned the lotus flowers. I might have known Luke wouldn't understand.

"Look, darling . . ." I try a different tack. "You always say, 'Give people a chance.'"

"No, I don't." Luke doesn't even miss a beat.

"Well, then, you should!" I say crossly.

We stop at a zebra crossing and a woman walks across with a really cool green space-age-looking pram on high wheels. Wow. Maybe we should get one of those. I squint, trying to see what the logo is.

It's amazing, I never used to even *notice* prams before. Now I can't stop checking them out, even when I'm in the middle of a row with my husband.

Discussion. Not row.

"Luke, listen," I say as we move off again. "In my book it says the pregnant woman should always follow her instincts. Well, my instincts are saying really strongly, 'Go to Venetia Carter.' It's nature telling me!"

Luke is silent. I can't tell if he's frowning at the road or at what I'm saying.

"We could just go once to check her out," I say appeasingly. "One little appointment. If we hate her we don't have to go back."

We've reached Mum and Dad's drive. There's a big silver banner over the door, and a stray helium balloon reading *Happy 60th Birthday, Jane!* lands lightly on the bonnet as we pull in.

"*And* I got us the house," I can't help adding. Even though I know it isn't strictly relevant.

Luke parks the car behind a van with OXSHOTT SPECIAL EVENTS printed on the side and finally turns to face me.

"OK, Becky." He sighs. "You win. We'll go and see her."

FOUR

TO SAY THAT MUM IS EXCITED about the baby is a bit of an understatement. As we get out of the car she flies across the drive, her hair blow-dried for the party, her face all pink with excitement.

"Becky! How's my little grandchild!"

She doesn't even bother looking at my face anymore. Her attention is straight on the bump. "It's getting bigger! Can you hear Grandma?" She bends closer. "Can you hear Grandma?"

"Hello, Jane," says Luke politely. "Maybe we could come in?"

"Of course!" She snaps up again and ushers us inside the house. "Come in! Put your feet up, Becky! Have a cup of tea. *Graham!*"

"I'm here!" Dad appears down the stairs. "Becky!" He gives me a tight hug. "Come and sit down. Suze is here with the children—"

"Already!" I exclaim in delight. I haven't seen Suze for *ages*. I follow my parents into the sitting room to find Suze on the sofa next to Janice, Mum and Dad's next-door neighbor. Her blond hair is up in a knot and she's breast-feeding one of her twins. Meanwhile Janice is wriggling uncomfortably, clearly trying very hard not to look.

"Bex!" Suze's face lights up. "Oh my God! You look fantastic!"

"Suze!" I give her a great big hug, trying not to squash the baby. "How are you? And how's darling little Clemmie?" I kiss the blond little head.

"This is Wilfrid," says Suze, going a bit pink.

Damn. I always get it wrong. And to make things worse, Suze is totally paranoid that Wilfrid looks like a girl. (Which he does. Especially in that lacy romper thing.)

I quickly change the subject. "Where are the others?"

"Oh, Tarkie's got them," says Suze, looking vaguely out the window. I follow her gaze and see her husband, Tarquin, pushing my godson, Ernie, around the marquee in a wheelbarrow, with Clementine strapped to his chest.

"More!" Ernie's shrieking voice comes faintly through the window. "More, Dada!"

"That'll be you in a few months, Luke," I say with a grin.

"Mmm-hmm." He raises his eyebrows and gets out his BlackBerry. "I need to send some e-mails. I'll do it upstairs, if that's OK?"

He heads out of the room and I sit on a squashy chair near Suze. "So, guess what? We've had an offer accepted on the most *perfect* house! Look!" I get the property details out of my handbag and pass them to Mum for admiration.

"How lovely, darling!" exclaims Mum. "Is it detached?"

"Well . . . no. But it's really—"

"Is there off-street parking?" Dad squints over Mum's shoulder.

"No, there's no actual parking, but—"

"They don't need parking, Graham," Mum interrupts. "They're Londoners! They take taxis everywhere."

"Are you telling me no Londoners drive?" says Dad scoffingly. "Are you telling me that in our entire capital city, not a single resident ever gets in a car?"

"I would never drive in London." Janice gives a little shudder. "You know, they wait until you stop at the traffic lights . . . and then they *knife* you."

" 'They'?" exclaims Dad in exasperation. "Who's 'they'?"

"Marble floor. Ooh, dear." Mum looks up from the details and pulls a face. "What about the little one when it's learning to walk? You could carpet it over, perhaps. A nice Berber with flecks in so it doesn't show the dirt."

I give up.

"And my second piece of news is . . ." I say loudly, trying to haul the conversation back on track, "I'm changing doctors." I pause for effect. "I'm having Venetia Carter."

"Venetia Carter?" Suze looks up from Wilfrid in amazement. "Are you serious?"

Ha. I *knew* Suze would have heard of her.

"Absolutely." I glow with pride. "We've just heard we've got a place with her. Isn't it fantastic?"

"Is she good, then, this Dr. Carter?" Mum looks from me to Suze.

"They call her the A-list obstetrician." Suze expertly

starts to burp Wilfrid. "I read an article about her in *Harper's*. She's supposed to be wonderful!"

A-list obstetrician! That makes *me* A-list!

"She does all the supermodels and film stars," I can't help boasting. "They have tea parties and designer goodie bags and everything. I'll probably meet them all!"

"But, Becky, I thought you had a well-respected doctor." Dad looks perturbed. "Is it a good idea to be changing?"

"Dad, Venetia Carter's in a different league!" I can't help sounding impatient. "She's the absolute best. I had to beg to get a place with her."

"Well, don't forget us, love, when you're famous!" says Mum.

"I won't! Hey, do you want to see the scan?" I fish in my bag, produce the roll of pictures, and hand it to Mum.

"Look at that!" she breathes, gazing at the blurry image. "Look, Graham! Our first little grandchild. It looks *just* like my mother!"

"Your mother?" retorts Dad incredulously, grabbing the prints from her. "Are you blind?"

"Becky, I've knitted a few bits and pieces for the baby," Janice puts in timidly. "Some little matinee jackets...a shawl...a Noah's Ark set...I made *three* of each animal, just in case of mishap...."

"Janice, that's so kind of you," I say, touched.

"It's no trouble, love! I enjoy knitting. Of course, I always hoped that Tom and Lucy might..." Janice trails off with a brave, bright smile. "But that wasn't to be."

"How is Tom?" I ask cautiously.

Tom is Janice's son. He's about the same age as me,

and got married three years ago, in this big, fancy wedding. But then it all went a bit wrong. His wife, Lucy, got a tattoo and ran off with a guy who lived in a caravan, and Tom turned very weird and started building a summerhouse in his parents' back garden.

"Oh, Tom's very well! He lives mainly in the summerhouse now. We leave him food on trays." Janice looks a little beleaguered. "He says he's writing a book."

"Oh, right!" I say encouragingly. "About what?"

"The state of society." She swallows. "Apparently."

There's silence as we all digest this.

"What sort of state does he think society's in?" asks Suze.

"Not very good," whispers Janice.

"Have another cup of tea, Janice, love." Mum pats her hand comfortingly. "Or a sherry?"

"Just a small sherry," says Janice after a pause. "I'll help myself."

As she heads across the room to the drinks cabinet, Mum puts down her cup. "*Now,* Becky," she says. "Did you bring all your catalogs?"

"Here!" I reach for the bag I brought in with me. "I've got Blooming Marvellous, Great Little Trading Company, The Little White Company. . . ."

"I brought JoJo Maman Bébé," chimes in Suze. "And Italian Baby Cashmere."

"I've got all of those." Mum nods, reaching for a stack of catalogs in the magazine rack. "Have you got Funky Baba?" She waves a catalog bearing a picture of a baby in a clown costume.

"Ooh!" says Suze. "I haven't seen that one!"

"You take that," I say. "I'll take Petit Enfant. Mum, you do Luxury Baby."

With a happy sigh we all settle down to flicking through images of infants on playmats and wearing cute T-shirts and being toted in stylish baby carriers. Honestly, it's worth having a baby just for all the gorgeous *stuff*.

"I'll turn down the corner of the page if I see something you should get," says Mum in a businesslike way.

"OK, me too," I say, fixated on a spread of babies dressed up as animals. We *have* to get the baby a polar bear snowsuit. I turn down the corner and flip to the next page, which is full of adorable miniature ski-wear. And look at the tiny pom-pom hats!

"Luke, I think we should take the baby skiing from really early on," I say as he enters the room. "It'll help its development."

"*Skiing?*" He looks taken aback. "Becky, I thought you hated skiing."

I do hate skiing.

Maybe we could go to Val d'Isère or somewhere and wear the cool clothes and just not ski.

"Becky!" Mum interrupts my thoughts. "Look at this crib. It has a built-in temperature control, lullaby light show, and soothing vibrating action."

"Wow," I breathe, looking at the picture. "That's *amazing*! How much is it?"

"The deluxe version is ... twelve hundred pounds," says Mum, consulting the text.

"Twelve hundred pounds?" Luke nearly chokes on his cup of tea. "For a *crib*? Are you serious?"

"It's state of the art," points out Suze. "It uses NASA technology."

"NASA technology?" He gives an incredulous snort. "Are we planning to send the baby into space?"

"Don't you want the best for your child, Luke?" I retort. "What do you think, Janice?"

I look across the room, but Janice hasn't heard me. She's looking at the scan pictures and dabbing at her eyes with a hanky.

"Janice . . . are you OK?"

"I'm sorry, dear." She blows her nose, then takes a swig of sherry, draining the glass. "Might I top this up, Jane?"

"Go ahead, dear!" says Mum encouragingly. "Poor Janice," she adds to me and Suze in a whisper. "She's *desperate* for a grandchild. But Tom never even comes out of his summerhouse. And when he does . . ." She lowers her voice further. "He can't have had a haircut in months! And talk about shaving! I said to her, 'He'll never find a nice girl if he doesn't spruce up his appearance!' But—" She breaks off as the doorbell rings. "That'll be the caterers. I've *told* them to use the kitchen door!"

"I'll go." Dad gets up, and we all turn back to the catalogs.

"D'you think we should get a bath seat *and* a bath support?" I peer at the page. "And an inflatable travel bath?"

"Get this." Suze shows me a picture of a padded baby nest. "They're fab. Wilfie *lives* in his."

"Definitely!" I nod. "Fold the corner down!"

"These corners are getting a bit bulky." Mum looks consideringly at the catalog. "Maybe we should fold down if we're *not* interested in the page."

"Why don't you just order the entire catalog and then send back the very few things you don't want?" suggests Luke.

Now *that*'s a good—

Oh. He's being funny. Ha-di-ha. I'm about to come up with a crushing retort, when Dad's voice rings out from the hall. "Come on through, Jess. Everyone's having tea."

Jess is here!

Oh God. Jess is here.

"Quick, hide the catalogs!" I hiss, and start shoving them behind cushions in a nervous scrabble. "You know what Jess is like."

"But she might want to have a look, love!" Mum objects.

Mum doesn't really get Jess and her whole thriftiness thing. She thinks Jess is just going through a "phase," like when Suze was a committed vegan for about three weeks before totally caving in and stuffing her face with a bacon sandwich.

"She won't," says Suze, who has stayed in Jess's house and knows what she's like. She grabs Mum's copy of Funky Baba and pushes it under Wilfrid's bouncy chair just as Dad and Jess appear at the door.

"Hi, Jess!" I begin brightly, then stop in amazement. I haven't seen Jess for a couple of months and she looks absolutely spectacular!

She's all tanned and skinny and wearing cargo shorts that show off her long, toned legs. Her cropped hair has been bleached by the sun and her green sleeveless T-shirt brings out her hazel eyes.

"Hi!" she says, putting down her backpack. "Hi, Auntie Jane. Becky, how are you?"

"I'm fine!" I can't stop goggling at her. "You look great! You're so tanned!"

"Oh." Jess glances down at herself with zero interest,

then reaches in her backpack. "I brought some maize biscuits. They're made by a local cooperative in northern Guatemala." She hands Mum a box made out of rough cardboard, and Mum turns it in her fingers, perplexed.

"Lovely, dear," she says at last, and puts it down next to the teapot. "Have a fondant fancy!"

"Wow." Jess sits down on the ottoman. "Look at Clem—" She stops as I mouth "Wilfie!" behind Suze's back.

"Sorry?" says Suze.

"I was just going to ask...where's Clementine?" Jess amends. "And I can't believe Wilfie! He's huge!"

I give her a tiny grin over my cup of tea as Suze replies. God, who would have thought it? My sister and my best friend, chatting away together.

There was a time when I thought I'd lost both of them for good. Jess, because we had a great big row, and called each other names which make me wince even now to remember them. And Suze because she made a new friend called Lulu, who rides horses and has four children and thinks she's superior to everyone. I *still* can't understand why Suze likes her; in fact, it's the one subject we don't see eye-to-eye on.

"I've got something for you too, Becky." Jess delves into her backpack and produces a bunch of grubby rags. Janice recoils with a little cry of dismay.

"What's that, dear?"

"Becky and I are going to make baby wipes," says Jess.

"*Make* baby wipes?" Mum looks uncomprehending. "But love, Boots do them. You can get them in the three-for-two."

"They look a little . . . used," ventures Janice.

"We just need to boil them and soak them in a solution of oil and soap," Jess informs her. "It's far kinder to the environment. And to the baby's skin. And they're reusable. You'll save pounds in the long run."

"Er . . . fab." I gulp, and finger the rags, one of which has HM WANDSWORTH PRISON printed faintly down the side. There is no way on earth I'm having a bucket of grotty old rags in my baby's nursery. But Jess seems so enthusiastic. I don't want to hurt her feelings.

"I'll help you make a baby carrier too," she says. "Out of a pair of Luke's old jeans. It's really simple."

"Good idea!" I manage. I daren't look at Luke.

"And I've had another idea." Jess swivels on the ottoman to face me. "You don't have to say yes, but maybe you could think about it?"

"Right," I say nervously. "What is it?"

"Would you give a talk?"

"A talk?" I'm taken aback. "On what?"

"On how you kicked your spending addiction." Jess leans forward, her face all warm and sisterly. "I have a friend who's a counselor and I was telling her about you and how much you've changed. She said she thought you'd be an inspiration to a lot of the addicts in her group."

There's silence in the room. I can feel my face going puce.

"Go on, Bex." Suze nudges my foot. "You'd be great!"

"I'll come," says Luke. "When is it?"

"It wouldn't need to be formal," says Jess. "Just a friendly chat about resisting consumer pressure. Especially now that you're pregnant." She shakes her head.

"It's *ridiculous,* the amount of rubbish people feel compelled to buy for their children."

"I blame the catalogs," says Luke gravely.

"So, what do you think, Becky?" persists Jess.

"I don't really . . ." I clear my throat feebly. "I'm not sure . . ."

"Don't be embarrassed!" Jess gets up from the ottoman and comes to sit beside me on the sofa. "I'm really proud of you, Becky. And you should be proud of yourself—" Her expression changes and she shifts on the sofa. "What am I sitting on? What's this?" She reaches behind her and pulls out two glossy catalogs, with all the corners folded down.

Shit. And she *would* have picked out Luxury Baby, which has a cover picture of a baby dressed in Ralph Lauren, holding a Dior bottle and sitting in a miniature Rolls-Royce.

"Becky wasn't looking at those," says Suze in a rush. "They're not even hers. They're mine. I brought them."

I really love Suze.

Jess is leafing through Luxury Baby and flinching. "It's shocking. I mean, what baby needs an inflatable bath? Or a designer crib?"

"Oh, I know." I try to match her tones of disdain. "It's terrible. Although I probably will buy, you know, a *few* things. . . ."

"Have a look, Jess, love!" says Mum helpfully. "Becky's already found a super crib for the baby!" She rummages among the catalogs. "Where is it, now? It's got a light show . . . and vibrating action. . . ."

I stiffen in horror.

Do not show Jess the £1,200 crib.

"Here it is!" Mum holds out Funky Baba.

"Jess doesn't want to see that!" I try to grab the catalog, but Jess gets there first.

"Which page?" she says.

"Mum?" A voice interrupts us and we all look round. Standing in the doorway is a frowning guy with disheveled dark hair and stubble. He's tall and rangy and he's holding a beaten-up old paperback and I have no idea who he—

Hang on. Is that Tom?

Blimey. I barely *recognize* him. Mum's right about the shaving: he doesn't seem to have seen a razor for days.

"Dad needs help with one of his magic tricks," he says abruptly to Janice. "The rabbit's got stuck or something."

"Oh dear!" says Janice, putting down her cup. "I'd better go. Tom, say hello nicely, love."

"Hi, everyone." Tom shoots a cursory glower round the room.

"You know Suze, Becky's friend, don't you?" twitters Janice. "And have you ever met Becky's sister, Jess?"

"Hi, Tom!" says Suze cheerfully.

"Hi," says Jess.

I glance nervously over at her, all ready for some lecture about how spending a thousand pounds on a crib is a mark of the evil, decadent times we live in. But to my surprise she's not even looking at the catalog. She's let it drop onto her lap and is gazing at Tom, transfixed.

And Tom is staring back at her.

Her eyes drop to the book he's holding. "Is that *The Consumer Society: Myths and Structures*?"

"Yeah. Have you read it?"

"No, but I've read some of Baudrillard's other work. *The System of Objects.*"

"I have it!" Tom takes a step toward her. "What did you think?"

Hang on a minute.

"His concept of simulacra and simulation is pretty interesting, I thought."

Jess fiddles with the Tiffany bean I gave her. She never fiddles with that Tiffany bean. Oh my God. She fancies him!

"I'm trying to apply the collapsing of hyperrealities to my thesis of postmodern capitalistic entropy." Tom nods intently.

This is fantastic! They're good-looking and there's chemistry and they're talking English, only with weird in-words that no one else understands. It's like an episode of *The OC*, right here in Mum's living room!

I shoot a glance at Luke, who raises his eyebrows. Mum nudges Suze, who grins back. We're all totally agog. As for Janice, she looks beside herself.

"Anyway." Tom shrugs. "I should go. . . ."

Like a whirlwind, Janice springs into action.

"Jess! Dear!" she exclaims, leaping up from the sofa. "We've never really got to know each other, have we? Why don't you come back for tea, and you and Tom can carry on with your little talk?"

"Oh." Jess looks taken aback. "Well . . . I've come to see everyone here. . . ."

"You can see them later at the party!" Janice takes a firm grip on Jess's tanned arm and starts chivvying her toward the door. "Jane, Graham, you don't mind, do you?"

"Not at all," says Dad easily.

"Well, OK." Jess glances at Tom and a faint rosy color appears on her cheeks. "I'll see you later."

"Bye!" we all chorus.

The door closes behind them and we all look at each other in suppressed glee.

"Well!" says Mum, picking up the teapot. "Now, wouldn't *that* be nice! We could take down the fence and have a marquee across both lawns!"

"Mum! Honestly!" I roll my eyes. That is just like her, getting ahead of herself and imagining all sorts of ridiculous—

Ooh. The baby could be the ring bearer!

While Jess is next door, Luke is reading the paper, and Tarquin is bathing the children, Suze and I take over my old bedroom. We turn on the radio loudly and run deep, sudsy baths, and take turns perching on the edge of the tub to chat, just like in the old days in Fulham. Then Suze sits on the bed, feeding the babies in turn while I paint my toenails.

"You won't be able to do that for much longer," says Suze, watching me.

"Why?" I look up in alarm. "Is it bad for the baby?"

"No, you dope!" She laughs. "You won't be able to reach!"

That's a weird thought. I can't even *imagine* being that big. I run a hand over my tummy and the baby bounces back at me.

"Ooh!" I say. "It kicked really hard!"

"You wait till it starts poking knees out and stuff," says Suze. "It's so freaky, like having an alien inside you."

You see, this is why you need a best friend when you're pregnant. Not a single one of my baby books has said "It's so freaky, like having an alien inside you."

"Hi, darling." Tarquin is at the door again. "Shall I put Wilfie down?"

"Yes, he's finished." Suze hands over the sleepy baby, who nestles into Tarquin's shoulder as if he knows he belongs there.

"Do you like my nails, Tarkie?" I say, wriggling my toes at him. Tarquin is so sweet. When I first knew him he was totally weird and geeky and I couldn't even hold a conversation with him—but somehow he's got more and more normal as the years have gone by.

He looks blankly at my nails. "Marvelous. Come on, old chap." He pats Wilfie gently on the back. "Up to Bedfordshire."

"Tarkie's such a good dad," I say in admiration as he disappears out of the room.

"Oh, he's great," says Suze fondly as she starts feeding Clementine. "Except he keeps playing Wagner at them all the time. Ernie can sing Brunnehilde's aria from start to finish in German, but he can't speak much English." Her brow crumples. "I'm getting a bit worried, actually."

I take it back. Tarquin is still weird.

I get out my new mascara and start applying it to my lashes, watching Suze make funny faces at Clementine and kissing her fat little cheeks. She's so lovely with her children.

"D'you think I'll be a good mother, Suze?" The words pop out of my mouth before I even realize I'm thinking them.

"Of course!" Suze stares at me in the mirror. "You'll

be a brilliant mother! You'll be kind, and you'll be funny, and you'll be the best-dressed one in the playground...."

"But I don't know anything about babies. I mean, honestly, *nothing.*"

"Nor did I, remember." Suze shrugs. "You'll soon pick it up!"

Everyone keeps saying I'll pick it up. But what if I don't? I did algebra for three years, and I never picked *that* up.

"Can't you give me some parenting tips?" I put away my mascara wand. "Like...things I should know."

Suze wrinkles her brow in thought. "The only tips I can think of are the real basics," she says at last. "You know, the ones that go without saying."

I feel a twinge of alarm.

"Like what, exactly?" I try to sound casual. "I mean, I probably know about them already...."

"Well, you know." She counts off on her fingers. "Things like having a bit of first aid knowledge...making sure you've got all your equipment...You might want to book a baby massage class...." She hoists Clementine onto her shoulder. "Are you doing Baby Einstein?"

OK, now I'm freaked out. I've never *heard* of Baby Einstein.

"Don't worry, Bex!" says Suze hastily, seeing my face. "None of that really matters. As long as you can change a nappy and sing a nursery rhyme, you'll be fine!"

I can't change a nappy. And I don't know any nursery rhymes.

God, I'm in trouble.

It's another twenty minutes before Suze finishes feeding Clementine and hands her over to Tarquin.

"Right!" She closes the door behind him and turns with sparkling eyes. "No one's about. Give me your wedding ring. I just need some string or something. . . ."

"Here." I rummage in my dressing table for an old Christian Dior gift-wrap ribbon. "Will this do?"

"Should do." Suze is stringing the ribbon through the ring. "Now, Becky. Are you *sure* you want to know?"

I feel a flicker of doubt. Maybe Luke's right. Maybe we should wait for the magical surprise. But then— how will I know what color pram to get?

"I want to know," I say with resolution. "Let's do it."

"Sit back, then." Suze knots the ribbon, meets my eye, and grins. "This is exciting!"

Suze is the best. I *knew* she'd have some way to find out. She dangles the ring above my stomach and we both stare at it, transfixed.

"It's not moving," I say in a whisper.

"It will in a minute," Suze murmurs back.

This is so spooky. I feel like we're at a séance and all of a sudden the ring will spell out the name of a dead person while a window bangs shut and a vase crashes to the floor.

"It's going!" hisses Suze as the ring begins to sway on its ribbon. "Look!"

"Oh my God!" My voice is a muffled squeak. "What does it say?"

"It's going round in circles! It's a girl!"

I gasp. "Are you sure?"

"Yes! You're having a daughter! Congratulations!" Suze flings her arms round me.

It's a girl. I feel quite shaky. I'm having a daughter! I knew it. I've been having girl vibes all along.

"Becky?" The door opens and Mum is standing there, resplendent in purple sequins and matching lurid lipstick. "People will be here soon." Her eyes shoot from Suze to me. "Is everything all right, love?"

"Mum, I'm having a girl!" I blurt it out before I can stop myself. "Suze did the ring test! It went in a circle!"

"A girl!" Mum's whole face lights up. "I *thought* it looked like a girl! Oh, Becky, love!"

"Isn't it great?" says Suze. "You're going to have a granddaughter!"

"I can get out your old doll's house, Becky!" Mum is suffused with delight. "And I'll have the spare room painted pink...." She comes close and examines my bump. "Yes, look at the way you're carrying it, love. It's definitely a girl."

"And watch the ring!" says Suze. She lifts the ribbon above my stomach again and steadies it. There's utter stillness—then the ring starts moving back and forth. For a moment no one speaks.

"I thought you said a circle," says Mum at last, puzzled.

"I did! Suze, what's happening? Why's it going back and forth?"

"I dunno!" She peers at the ring, her brow wrinkled. "Maybe it's a boy after all."

We're all staring at my stomach as though we're expecting it to start talking to us.

"You are carrying high," says Mum eventually. "It could be a boy."

A minute ago she said it looked like a girl. Oh, for God's sake. The thing about old wives' tales is, they're actually total crap.

"Let's go down anyway, loves," Mum says, as music suddenly blasts from downstairs. "Keith from the Fox and Grapes has arrived. He's making all sorts of fancy cocktails."

"Excellent!" says Suze, reaching for her sponge bag. "We'll be down in a sec."

Mum leaves the room, and Suze starts applying makeup at speed while I watch in astonishment.

"Bloody hell, Suze! Are you training for the makeup Olympics?"

"You wait," says Suze, brushing sparkly shadow onto her eyelids. "You'll be able to do your makeup in three seconds flat too." She unscrews her lipstick and slashes it on. "Done!" She grabs her elegant green satin dress and steps into it, then takes a jeweled hair clasp from her bag and twists her blond hair into a knot.

"That's nice!" I say, admiring the clasp.

"Thanks." She hesitates. "Lulu gave it to me."

"Oh, right." Now that I look at it again, it isn't that nice. "So . . . how is Lulu?" I force myself to say politely.

"She's fine!" Suze's face is lowered as she wrenches her hair into place. "She's written a book, actually."

"A *book*?" Lulu never struck me as the book type.

"On cooking for your children."

"Really?" I say in surprise. "Well, maybe I should read that. Is it good?"

"I haven't read it yet," says Suze after a pause. "But obviously she's the expert, with four of them. . . ."

There's a kind of tension in her voice that I can't

place. But then Suze looks up—and her hair is such a terrible mess, we both burst out laughing.

"Let me do it." I grab the clasp, take it out of the knotted hair, brush it all out, and twist it up again, pulling little tendrils out at the front.

"Fab." Suze gives me a hug. "Thanks, Bex. And now I'm *dying* for a cosmo. Come on!"

She practically gallops out of the room, and I follow her down the stairs with slightly less enthusiasm. I guess mine will be a Virgin Fruity Bland Something.

I mean, obviously I don't mind. I'm creating a beautiful new human being and all that. But still. If I were God, I'd make it OK for pregnant women to have cocktails. In fact, I'd make it *healthy* to have cocktails. And your arms wouldn't swell up. And there wouldn't be any morning sickness. And labor wouldn't exist. . . .

Thinking about it, I'd pretty much have a whole different system altogether.

Even on virgin cocktails, it's a fabulous party. By midnight the marquee is full, and we've all had a delicious dinner. Dad has made a speech about how wonderful Mum is, as a wife and as a mother and now as a prospective grandmother. And Martin, our next-door neighbor, has performed his magic show, which was really excellent! Apart from the bit when he tried to cut Janice in half and she freaked out when he turned on the chain saw and started crying "Don't kill me, Martin!" while he kept revving it up like some horror film maniac.

It was all right in the end. Martin took off his mask and Janice was fine after she had some brandy.

And now the band is playing and we're all on the dance floor. Mum and Dad are grooving away, all rosy-cheeked and beaming at each other, the lights sparkling on Mum's sequins. Suze is dancing with one arm round Tarquin's neck and the other round Clementine, who woke up and wouldn't go back to sleep. Tom and Jess are standing at the edge of the dance floor, talking and occasionally doing a kind of awkward shuffle together. Tom looks pretty good in black tie, I noticed—and Jess's black embroidered skirt is fantastic! (I was totally sure it was Dries van Noten. But apparently it was made by a women's collective in Guatemala and cost about 30p. Typical.)

And I'm wearing my new pink dress with the hand-kerchief hem, and dancing (as best I can, given the bump) with Luke. Mum and Dad dance by and wave at us, and I smile back, trying not to cringe in horror. I know this is their party and everything. But my parents *really* don't know how to dance. Mum's wiggling her hips, completely out of time, and Dad's kind of punching the air like he's fighting three invisible men at once.

Why can't parents dance? Is it some universal law of physics or something?

Suddenly a terrifying thought hits me. We're going to be parents! In twenty years' time, *our* child will be cringing at *us*.

No. I can't let it happen.

"Luke!" I say urgently over the music. "We have to be able to do cool dancing so we don't embarrass our child!"

"I'm a very cool dancer," replies Luke. "Very cool indeed."

"No, you're not!"

"I had dance lessons in my teens, you know," he retorts. "I can waltz like Fred Astaire."

"Waltz?" I echo derisively. "That's not cool! We need to know all the street moves. Watch me."

I do a couple of funky head-wriggle body-pop maneuvers, like they do on rap videos. When I look up, Luke is gaping at me.

"Sweetheart," he says. "What are you doing?"

"It's hip-hop!" I say. "It's street!"

"Becky! Love!" Mum has pushed her way through her dancing guests to reach me. "What's wrong? Has labor started?"

Honestly. My family has *no* idea about contemporary urban street dance trends.

"I'm fine!" I say. "Just dancing."

Ow. Actually, I may have pulled a muscle or three.

"Come here, J-Lo." Luke puts his arms round me. Mum dances off to talk to Janice and I look up at Luke's glowing face. He's been in a good mood ever since that business call he took during coffee.

"What was your call about?" I ask. "Good news?"

"We've just had the go-ahead in Barcelona." His nose twitches, like it always does when he's delighted with life but wants to look deadpan. "That takes us up to eight offices, Europe-wide. All down to the Arcodas contract."

He never told me Barcelona was on the cards! That's so Luke, keeping it quiet until the deal's done. If it hadn't come off, he probably never would have said a word about it.

Eight offices. *And* London and New York. That's pretty stupendous.

The music changes to a slow track and Luke pulls me

closer. Out of the corner of my eye I notice Jess and Tom have sidled farther onto the dance floor together. *Go on,* I will Tom silently. *Kiss her.*

"So, things are going pretty well?" I say.

"Things, my darling, could not be going more fantastically." Luke meets my eyes, the teasing gone. "Seriously. We're going to treble our size."

"Wow." I digest this for a few moments. "Are we going to be squillionaires?

"Could be." He nods.

This is so cool. I have *always* wanted to be a squillionaire. We can have a building called Brandon Tower! And Luke can have his own *Apprentice*-type reality show!

"Can we buy an island?" Suze has got her own Scottish island and I've always felt a bit left out.

"Maybe." Luke laughs.

I'm about to say we need a private jet too, when the baby starts squirming around inside me. I take hold of Luke's hands and put them on my abdomen.

"It's saying hello."

"Hello, baby," he murmurs back in his deep voice. He pulls me even tighter and I close my eyes, breathing in the scent of his aftershave, feeling the music thud through me like a heartbeat.

I can't remember ever being so happy. We're dancing cheek-to-cheek, our baby is kicking between us, we've got a fabulous new house, and we're going to be squillionaires! Everything's just perfect.

BECKY BRANDON
NURSERY RHYMES SELF-TEST

MARY, MARY QUITE CONTRARY...
Had a little lamb.
And

TOM, TOM, THE PIPER'S SON...
~~Went to London to look at the~~
Fell off the wall.
And he called for his pipe.
And all the king's horses and his fiddlers three.
~~Couldn't put~~
And the dish ran away with the spoon.

LITTLE JACK HORNER...
~~He had ten thousand men~~
~~Met a pieman~~

LITTLE BOY BLUE...
~~Lost his sheep~~
Oh, fuck knows.

FIVE

OK. THIS IS MY OUTFIT for my first-ever appointment with a celebrity must-have obstetrician:

Embroidered kaftan top like Jemima Khan
Maternity jeans (with the elastic hidden in the
  pockets, *not* with a great revolting panel of
  stretchy fabric)
My new Elle Macpherson maternity underwear
  (lilac)
Prada sandals

I look pretty good, I think. I hope. I tweak my kaftan and toss my hair back at my reflection.

"Hi," I murmur. "Hi, Kate. Hi, Elle. God, fancy bumping into you. I'm wearing your underpants!"

No. Don't mention the underpants.

I scrutinize myself one final time, add a dusting of powder, then pick up my bag.

"Luke, are you ready?" I call.

"Uh-huh." Luke puts his head round the study door, his phone wedged under his chin. "Uh-huh. Hold on,

Iain." He puts his hand over the receiver. "Becky, do I really need to come?"

"*What?*" I stare at him in horror. "Of course you need to come!"

Luke runs his eyes over my face, as though assessing the full extent of my mood. "Iain," he says at last, turning back to the phone. "This is complicated." He disappears back into the office and his voice descends to a murmur.

Complicated? What does he mean, complicated? We're going to the obstetrician, end of story. I start pacing furiously around the hall, rehearsing retorts in my mind. *Can't Iain wait for once? Does our whole life have to revolve around Arcodas? Isn't our baby's birth important to you? Have you ever cared about me at all?*

Well, OK. Maybe not that last one.

At last Luke reappears at the study door. The phone's gone and he's putting on his suit jacket.

"Listen, Becky . . ." he begins.

I knew it. He's not coming.

"You've never wanted to see Venetia Carter, have you?" My words tumble out. "You're prejudiced against her! Well, fine! You go and do your business things and I'll go on my own!"

"Becky . . ." He lifts a hand. "I'm coming to the appointment."

"Oh," I say, mollified. "Well, we'd better go. It's twenty minutes' walk."

"We're going by car." He heads back into the office and I follow him in. "Iain's on his way down from the hotel group meeting. He can pick us up, we'll have a very quick meeting in the car, then I'll join you."

"Right," I say after a pause. "That sounds OK."

Actually, it sounds awful. I can't stand Iain Wheeler; the last thing I want to do is sit in a car with him. But I can't say that to Luke. There's already a slight situation over me and Arcodas.

Which was *not* my fault. It was Jess's. A few months ago, she got me into leading this big environmental protest against them, when I had no idea they were Luke's new, important client. Luke turned the whole thing round into a positive PR exercise and the Arcodas people pretended they had a sense of humor about it—but I'm not sure I've ever really been forgiven.

"And I'm not prejudiced," Luke adds, straightening his tie. "But I'll just tell you now, Becky. This obstetrician woman will have to be pretty damn good for us to cancel Dr. Braine."

"Luke, you're going to love her," I say patiently. "I know you are."

I reach into my bag to check that my phone's charged, then halt as I spot something on Luke's desk. It's a clipping from the financial pages about some new unit trust, with "Baby fund?" scribbled in the margin.

Ooh!

"So, you're thinking of putting the baby's money in a tracker fund, are you, Luke?" I say carelessly. "Interesting decision."

Luke looks taken aback for a moment, then follows my gaze.

"Maybe I am," he says in equally nonchalant tones. "Or maybe it's a double-bluff to fool the spying opposition."

"The opposition doesn't need to *spy*." I give him a kind smile. "She has her own brilliant ideas. In fact, if you need any tips, I'd be happy to help. For a small fee."

"That's quite all right," he says politely. "Going well, is it, then? Your own investment."

"Brilliantly, thanks. Couldn't be better."

"Excellent. Glad to hear it."

"Yes...that recent Japanese farming investment I made was fantastic...." I clap a hand over my mouth. "Oops! Said too much!"

"Yup, Becky. You really fool me." Luke grins. "Shall we go?"

We emerge from the building and Luke ushers me into Iain's black Mercedes limo.

"Luke." Iain nods from his seat by the window. "Rebecca."

Iain is a thickset guy in his early forties, with close-cropped salt-and-pepper hair. He's quite good-looking, actually, but has terrible skin which he covers up by having a Permatan. And he wears too much aftershave. *Why* do men do that?

"Thanks for the lift, Iain," I say in my best charming-corporate-wife manner.

"No problem." Iain's gaze drops to my swelling stomach. "Been eating too many pies, Rebecca?"

Ha-ha.

"Something like that," I say, as pleasantly as I can.

As the car pulls away, Iain takes a slurp of his take-out coffee. "How long to go before the big day?"

"Seventeen weeks."

"So, how do you fill the time until then? Don't tell me—yoga classes. My girlfriend's become a yoga nut," he adds to Luke, without giving me a chance to answer. "Load of bollocks if you ask me."

Honestly. Number one, yoga is *not* bollocks, it's a way to channel your spirit through the chakras of life, or whatever it is.

And number two, I don't need ways to fill my time, thank you.

"Actually, Iain, I'm head personal shopper at a top London department store," I inform him. "So I don't have too much time for yoga."

"A department store?" He swivels in his seat to regard me. "I didn't know that. Which one?"

I really fell into this one.

"It's . . . new," I say, examining my nails.

"Called?"

"It's called . . . The Look."

"The Look?" Iain guffaws in disbelief and nearly drops his coffee. "Luke, you didn't tell me your wife worked for The Look! Business slow enough for you, is it, Rebecca?"

"It's not that bad," I say politely.

"Not that bad? There's never been a bigger retail flop in history! I hope you've got rid of your stock options!" He guffaws again. "Not counting on a Christmas bonus, are you?"

This guy is really starting to annoy me. It's one thing for me to be rude about The Look; they're my employer. But it's quite another matter for other people to be rude.

"Actually, I think The Look is poised for a turn-around," I say coolly. "We've had a shaky start, I'll grant you, but all the basics are there."

"Well, good luck." Iain's face is creased with amusement. "Word of advice? I'd be looking for another job."

I force a smile, then turn to look out the window,

seething. God, he's patronizing. I'll show him. The Look *could* be a success. It just needs...well. It needs customers, for a start.

The car draws up to the sidewalk and the uniformed driver gets out to open the door.

"Thanks again for the lift, Iain," I say politely. "Luke, I'll see you in there."

"Uh-huh." Luke nods, frowning as he clicks open his briefcase. "I shouldn't be too long. So, Iain, what exactly was the problem with this outline?"

As the driver hands me out to the sidewalk, both men are already engrossed in paperwork.

"Will you be all right from here?" The driver gestures at the corner. "Fencastle Street's just round there, only I can't get right to it because of the bollards."

"Don't worry, I'll be fine walking from here. Oh, except I've forgotten my bag...." I reach back into the car, where Iain is talking.

"When I want that kind of decision taken, Luke, *I'll* fucking take it." His harsh tone takes me by surprise and I see Luke flinch.

It's just unbelievable. Just who does this guy think he *is*? Just because he's some business bigwig he thinks he can be rude to anyone he likes? I want to get straight back into the car and tell him exactly what I think of him.

But I'm not sure Luke would appreciate it.

"See you soon, darling." I squeeze his hand and pick up my bag. "Don't be long."

I'm a bit early for the appointment, so I take the opportunity to reapply my lipstick and give my hair a quick comb. Then I head to the corner and turn into Fencastle Street. There's a big impressive stucco building about twenty yards ahead, with *Holistic Birth Center, Venetia Carter* engraved on the glass. And on the opposite side of the street is a cluster of photographers, their lenses trained on the door.

I stop dead, my heart beating faster. It's paparazzi. They're all clicking away! Who are they— What are they—

Oh my God. It's the new Bond girl! She's walking toward the building in a pink Juicy strapless top over jeans, with a definite bump showing. I can hear the cries from the photographers: "This way, love!" and "When's the baby due?"

This is so cool!

Trying to look nonchalant, I hurry along the pavement and arrive at the door at the same time as her. The cameras are all still clicking away behind us. I'll be in all the gossip magazines with a Bond girl!

"Hi," I murmur casually as she presses the buzzer. "Hi, I'm Becky. I'm pregnant, too. I like your top!"

She looks at me as if I'm a moron, then without replying pushes the door open.

Well. She wasn't very friendly. But never mind, I'm sure the others will be. I follow her through an elegant tiled hallway and then into a large room with lilac velvet seats and a reception desk, and a huge Jo Malone candle burning on the central table.

As I head to the desk behind the Bond girl, I do a quick sweep of the room. Two girls in jeans who might *easily* be supermodels are reading *OK!* and pointing out pictures to each other. There's a heavily pregnant girl in Missoni sitting opposite in floods of tears, with a husband who's holding her hand and saying anxiously, "Sweetheart, we can call the baby Aspen if you like, I just didn't realize you were serious!"

Aspen.

Aspen Brandon.

Lord Aspen Brandon, Earl of London.

Hmm. Not sure.

The Bond girl finishes talking to the receptionist, then moves away and sits down in a corner.

"Can I help?" The receptionist is looking at me.

"Yes, please." I beam. "I'm here to see Venetia Carter. Mrs. Rebecca Brandon."

"Take a seat, Mrs. Brandon. Dr. Carter will see you presently." The receptionist smiles and hands me a brochure. "Some introductory literature. Help yourself to herbal tea."

"Thanks!" I take the brochure and sit down opposite the supermodels. Gentle panpipe music is playing over the speakers, and there are photographs of mothers and new babies pinned up on the satin-covered pinboards. The whole atmosphere is serene and beautiful. It's a million miles away from Dr. Braine's boring old waiting room, with its plastic chairs and horrible carpet and posters about folic acid.

Luke will be so impressed when he arrives. I *knew* this was the right decision! Happily I start flicking through the brochure, taking in headings here and there. *Water Birth . . . Reflexology Birth . . . Hypno Birth . . .*

Maybe I'll have a hypno birth. Whatever that is.

I'm just lingering over a picture of a girl holding a baby in what looks like a giant Jacuzzi when the receptionist summons me.

"Mrs. Brandon? Dr. Carter will see you now."

"Oh!" I put down the brochure and glance at my watch anxiously. "I'm afraid my husband isn't here yet. He should only be a few minutes. . . ."

"Don't worry." She smiles. "I'll send him in when he arrives. Please, come this way."

I follow the receptionist down the carpeted passage. The walls are covered with signed pictures of glamorous celebrity mothers sitting up in bed with newborn babies, and my head swivels as I walk. I really need to think about what I'm going to wear for the birth. Maybe I'll ask Venetia Carter for some tips.

We reach a cream-painted door and the receptionist knocks twice before opening it and ushering me in. "Venetia, this is Mrs. Brandon."

"Mrs. Brandon!" A stunningly beautiful woman with long, vivid red hair comes forward, her hand outstretched. "Welcome to the Holistic Birth Center."

"Hi!" I beam at her. "Call me Becky."

Wow. Venetia Carter looks like a movie star! She's far younger than I expected, and slighter. She's wearing a fitted Armani trouser suit and a crisp white shirt and her hair is drawn off her face with a chic tortoiseshell band.

"I'm so glad to meet you, Becky." Her voice is all silvery and melodious, like the Good Witch of the North. "Sit down, and we can have a nice talk."

She's wearing vintage Chanel pumps, I notice as I sit down. And look at that gorgeous yellow topaz strung round her neck on a silver wire.

"I want to thank you for fitting me in at such a late stage," I say in a rush as I hand over my medical file. "I really appreciate it. And I love your shoes!"

"Thank you!" She smiles. "So, let's have a look.

You're twenty-three weeks pregnant...first baby..."
Her manicured finger is running down Dr. Braine's
notes. "Any problems with your pregnancy? Is there a
reason you've left your previous medical care?"

"I just wanted a more holistic approach," I say, leaning forward earnestly. "I've been reading your brochure
and I think all your treatments sound amazing."

"Treatments?" Her pale brow wrinkles.

"Births, I mean," I amend quickly.

"Well, now." Venetia Carter takes a cream file from
a drawer, picks up a silver fountain pen, and writes
Rebecca Brandon on the front in a flowing italic script.
"There's plenty of time to decide which approach to
the birth you want. But first, let me find out more
about you. You're married, I understand?"

"Yes." I nod.

"And is your husband coming today? Mr. Brandon,
would it be?"

"He should be here." I click my tongue apologeti-
cally. "He's just having a quick business meeting outside
in the car. But he'll be here soon."

"That's fine." She lifts her head and smiles, her teeth
all perfect and shiny white. "I'm sure your husband's
very excited about having a baby."

"Oh, he is!" I'm just about to tell her all about having our first scan, when the door opens.

"Mr. Brandon is here," says the receptionist, and
Luke strides in, saying, "Sorry, sorry, I know I'm
late—"

"*There* you are, Luke!" I say. "Come and meet Dr.
Carter."

"Please!" She laughs again. "Call me Venetia—everyone does."

"Venetia?" Luke has stopped dead and is staring at Venetia Carter as though he can't believe his eyes. "*Venetia?* Is that you?"

Venetia Carter's mouth drops open.

"Luke?" she says. "Luke Brandon?"

"Do you two *know* each other?" I say in astonishment.

For an instant, neither speaks.

"We were at Cambridge," Luke says at last. "Years ago. But . . ." He rubs his forehead. "Venetia *Carter.* Did you get married or something?"

"I changed my surname by deed poll," Venetia says with a rueful smile. "Wouldn't you?"

"What was your name before you changed it?" I ask politely, but neither of them seems to hear me.

"How many years is it?" Luke still looks thunderstruck.

"Too long. *Far* too long." She runs a hand through her hair and it falls back into place in a perfect red waterfall. "Do you still see any of the old Browns gang? Like Jonathan? Or Matthew?"

"Lost touch." Luke shrugs. "You?"

"I kept up with very few of them while I was in the States. But now that I'm back in London, some of us meet up whenever we can." She's interrupted by a bleeping sound from her pocket. She reaches for a pager and switches it off. "Excuse me, I just need to make a call. I'll pop next door."

As she disappears I look at Luke. His face is all lit up as though it's Christmas Day.

"You know Venetia?" I say. "That's amazing!"

"Isn't it?" He shakes his head incredulously. "She was

part of a crowd I used to know at Cambridge. Of course, she was Venetia Grime back then."

"Grime?" I can't help a giggle.

"Hardly the best name for a doctor." He grins back. "I'm not surprised she changed it."

"And did you know her well?"

"We were at the same college." Luke nods. "She was always incredibly bright, Venetia. Incredibly talented. I always knew she'd do well in life." He breaks off as the door opens and Venetia returns.

"I'm so sorry about that!" She comes round and sits on the front of her desk, one long Armani-clad leg crossed casually over the other. "Where were we?"

"I was just saying to Luke what a coincidence it was!" I say. "You and he already knowing each other."

"Isn't it extraordinary?" She gives her silvery laugh. "Out of all the hundreds of patients I've had, I've never before had one married to an ex-boyfriend!"

My smile freezes slightly on my face.

Ex-boyfriend?

"I was just trying to remember how long we dated for, Luke," she adds. "Was it a year?"

They dated for a *year*?

"I don't remember," says Luke easily. "Long time ago."

Hang on. Just hang on a minute. Rewind. I seem to have missed a step here.

Venetia Carter used to be Luke's girlfriend at Cambridge? But...he's never referred to her. I've never even heard of a Venetia before.

I mean...not that it *matters* or anything. Why would it matter? I'm not the kind of person who gets hung up on old girlfriends from the past. I'm naturally a very nonjealous person. In fact, I probably won't even mention it.

Or maybe I will, just casually.

"So, darling, I don't remember you ever talking about Venetia," I say to Luke with a relaxed little laugh. "Isn't that funny?"

"Don't worry, Becky." Venetia leans forward with a confidential air. "I know quite well, I was never the love of Luke's life."

I feel a warm glow of delight inside me. "Oh, right," I say, trying to look modest. "Well—"

"That was Sacha de Bonneville," she adds.

What? *What?*

Luke's love of his life wasn't bloody Sacha de Bonneville! It was me! His *wife!*

"Apart from you, of course, Becky!" she exclaims, with an apologetic peal of laughter. "I was just talking about back then. In the Browns crowd. Anyway." Venetia throws back her radiant hair and picks up her file and pen again. "Back to the birth!"

"Yes," I say, regaining my composure. "Well, I was thinking about maybe having one of the water births with lotus flowers—"

"You should come along one evening, by the way, Luke," Venetia says, cutting me off. "See some of the old gang."

"I'd love to!" says Luke. "We'd love to, wouldn't we, Becky?"

"Yes," I say after a pause. "Fab idea."

"Sorry to interrupt, Becky." Venetia smiles at me. "Do carry on. A water birth, you were saying?"

We're in there for another twenty-five minutes, talking about vitamins and blood tests and a load of other stuff. But to be truthful, my mind's not really on the job.

I'm trying to concentrate, but all these distracting images keep coming into my head. Like Luke and Venetia all dressed up in Cambridge student gear, kissing passionately on a punt. (Do I mean a punt? Or a gondola? The boat thing with a pole, anyway.)

And then I keep picturing him running his hands through her long red hair. And murmuring, "Venetia, I love you."

Which is just stupid. I *bet* he never told her he loved her.

I bet . . . a thousand quid.

"Becky?"

"Oh!" I come to and suddenly realize the appointment is over. Both Luke and Venetia are standing up, waiting for me.

"So, you'll do a birth plan for me, Becky?" Venetia says as she opens the door.

"Absolutely!"

"Nothing too complicated!" She smiles. "I'd just like to get a general picture of how you envisage the birth. And Luke, I'll give you a call. I know some of the old crowd would love to see you."

"Great!" His face is animated as he kisses her on each cheek. Then the door closes and we're walking back down the corridor.

I'm not sure what Luke's thinking.

I'm not entirely sure what *I'm* thinking, to be honest.

"Well," Luke says at last. "Very impressive. Very, very impressive."

"Um . . . yes!"

"Becky." Luke suddenly stops dead. "I want to apologize. You were right and I was wrong." He shakes his head. "I'm sorry I was so negative about coming here. You're right: I was prejudiced and stupid. But you've completely made the right decision."

"Right." I nod several times. "So . . . so you think we should go with Venetia?"

"Absolutely!" He laughs, puzzled. "Don't you? Isn't this your dream come true, coming here?"

"Er . . . yes," I say, folding my Alternative Pain Relief Options leaflet into smaller and smaller quarters. "Of course it is."

"Sweetheart. Darling." Luke suddenly has a concerned frown. "If you're feeling at all threatened by my old relationship with Venetia, let me assure you—"

"Threatened?" I cut him off brightly. "Don't be ridiculous! I don't feel *threatened*."

Maybe I do feel a tad threatened. But how can I say that to Luke?

"Good, you're still here!" Venetia's silvery voice travels down the corridor and I look round to see her approaching, a clipboard in hand. "You must collect your welcome pack before you go, Becky! We have all sorts of goodies for you. And there was another thing I wanted to mention—"

"Venetia." Luke cuts her off midstream. "Let me be frank. We were just discussing the fact of . . . our previous relationship. And I'm not sure Becky feels comfortable with it." He takes my hand and I clasp his gratefully.

Venetia exhales and nods.

"Of course," she says. "Becky, I *completely* understand. If you feel at all uncomfortable, then you should certainly consider going elsewhere. I won't be offended!" She gives me a friendly smile. "All I can say is . . . I'm a professional. If you do decide to remain under my care, I'll help you achieve the very best birth experience I can. And, just in case you were *really* anxious"—her eyes twinkle at me—"I do have a boyfriend!"

"Don't worry! I'm not quite *that* insecure!" I say, joining in with her merry laughter.

She has a boyfriend! It's all OK!

I don't know how I could have thought it was anything else. God, pregnancy is making me paranoid.

"So," Venetia Carter is saying, "you two go away, have a think about it. You have my number—"

"I don't need to think about it." I beam at her. "Just show me where the welcome packs are!"

Prendergast de Witt Connell
Financial Advisers

Forward House
394 High Holborn
London WC1V 7EX

Mrs R Brandon
37 Maida Vale Mansions
Maida Vale
London NW6 0YF

20 August 2003

Dear Mrs. Brandon,

Thank you for your letter. I am aware of the investment "bet" between yourself and your husband. Please be assured I will not reveal any of your asset allocation strategies to him, nor "sell them like a Russian spy."

In answer to your query, I think an investment in gold would be a most wise choice for your child. Gold has done well over the last few years and in my opinion will continue to do so.

Yours sincerely,

Kenneth Prendergast
Family Investment Specialist

SIX

GOD, WORK'S DEPRESSING.

It's the next day, and I'm sitting at my desk in the reception area of personal shopping. Jasmine, who works with me, is slumped on the sofa. Our appointment book is empty, the phone is silent, and as I look around, the place is as dead as ever. Not a single customer. The only sign of movement out on the shop floor is Len the security guard doing his usual rounds, and he looks as fed up as the rest of us feel.

When I *think* what it used to be like at Barneys in New York, all bright and full of chatter and people buying thousand-dollar dresses . . . And all I've sold this week is a pair of fishnets and an out-of-season raincoat. This place is a disaster. And we opened only ten weeks ago.

The Look is backed by this big tycoon, Giorgio Laszlo. It was supposed to be a buzzy, high-concept department store which would take over from Selfridges and Harvey Nichols. But things started going wrong from day one; in fact, the place is a national joke.

First of all, a whole warehouse of stock got burned down and the launch had to be delayed. Then a light fixture fell from the ceiling and concussed one of the beauty assistants, right in the middle of a makeup demonstration. Then there was a suspected outbreak of Legionnaires' disease and we were all sent home for five days. It turned out to be false—but the damage was done. All the papers ran stories on how The Look was cursed, and printed cartoons showing the customers keeling over and having bits of the building fall on them. (Which were actually quite funny, but we're not allowed to say that.)

And no one's come back since we reopened. Everyone seems to think the place is still closed, or infectious, or something. The *Daily World,* who are total enemies of Giorgio Laszlo, keep sending undercover photographers to take pictures of the shop floors and run them under headings like "Still Empty!" and "How Much Longer Can This Folly Last?" The rumor is that if things don't pick up soon, the place will fold.

With a gloomy sigh, Jasmine turns a page and starts reading the horoscopes. That's the other problem: it's hard to keep your staff motivated when business is down. (Jasmine is my staff.) Before I started this job I read one of Luke's management books to get some tips on how to be a boss, and it said it was "crucial to keep giving your team compliments in bad times."

I've already complimented Jasmine's hair, shoes, and bag. To be honest, there's not a lot left.

"I like your...eyebrows, Jasmine!" I say brightly. "Where do you get them done?"

Jasmine looks at me as though I've asked her to eat baby whale. "I'm not telling you!"

"Why not?"

"It's my secret. If I tell you, you'll go there too and then you'll have my look."

Jasmine is skinny, with trails of bleached-blond hair, a nose stud, and one blue eye and one green eye. She could not look less like me if she tried.

"I won't have your look!" I retort lightly. "I'll just have good eyebrows! Go on, tell me."

"Uh-uh." She shakes her head. "No way."

I feel a surge of frustration.

"When you asked me where I have my hair done, I told you," I remind her. "I gave you a card and recommended the best stylist and got you ten percent off your first haircut. Remember?"

Jasmine shrugs. "That's hair."

"And this is eyebrows! It's *less* important!"

"That's what you think."

Oh, for God's sake. I'm about to tell her that I don't care where she gets her stupid eyebrows done (which is a lie, as I've now become obsessed with them), when I hear footsteps. Striding, heavy, senior-management kind of footsteps.

Quickly Jasmine shoves her *Heat* magazine under a pile of sweaters and I pretend to be adjusting a scarf on a mannequin. A moment later, Eric Wilmot, the marketing director, appears round the corner with a couple of smartly suited guys I've never seen before.

"And this is the personal shopping department," he says to the men with a fake-jovial air. "Rebecca here used to work at Barneys in New York! Rebecca, meet Clive and Andrew from First Results Consulting. Here to throw a few ideas around." He gives a strained smile.

Eric was only promoted to marketing director last week, when the previous one resigned. He really doesn't look like a man who's relishing his new job.

"We haven't had any customers for days," says Jasmine flatly. "It's like a morgue in here."

"Uh-huh." Eric's smile tightens.

"An empty morgue without any dead people," she clarifies. "It's *deader* than a morgue. 'Cause at least in a morgue—"

"We're all aware of the situation, thank you, Jasmine." Eric cuts her off briskly. "What we need is solutions."

"How do we get people in through the doors?" One of the consultants is addressing a mannequin. "That's the question."

"How do we maintain their loyalty?" chimes in the other one thoughtfully.

For goodness' sake. I reckon *I* could be a consultant if all you do is wear a suit and ask totally obvious questions.

"What's the unique selling point?" the first chimes in again.

"There isn't one," I say, unable to keep my mouth shut any longer. "We've got the same old stock as everyone else. Oh, and by the way, you might get ill or injured if you shop here. We need an edge!"

The three men all stare at me in surprise.

"The public perception of danger is obviously our greatest challenge," says the first consultant, frowning. "We need to counter the negative coverage, create a positive, healthy image—"

He's totally missing my point.

"It wouldn't matter!" I cut him off. "If we had something unique, that people really *wanted,* they'd come in anyway. Like, when I lived in New York I once went to a sample sale in a condemned building.

There were all these warnings outside saying Do Not Enter, Unsafe, but I'd heard they had Jimmy Choos at eighty percent off. So I went in!"

"Did they?" says Jasmine, perking up.

"No," I say regretfully. "They'd all gone. But I found a fab Gucci trench coat, only seventy dollars!"

"You went into a condemned building?" Eric is goggling at me. "For a pair of shoes?"

Something tells me he isn't going to last in this job.

"Of course! And there were about a hundred other girls there too. And if we had something fab and exclusive at The Look, they'd come here like a shot! Even if the roof was falling in! Like some really hot designer diffusion range."

This idea has been brewing in my mind for a while now. I even tried talking to Brianna, the chief buyer, about it last week. But she just nodded and asked if I could bring her the Dolce diamante dress in a size 2 because she was going to a premiere that night and the red Versace was too tight around the butt, and what did I think?

God knows how Brianna got her job. Well, actually, everybody knows. It's because she's Giorgio Laszlo's wife and used to be a model. In the press release when The Look opened it said this would qualify her perfectly to be chief buyer, as she has the "knowledge and savvy of a fashion insider."

It didn't add "unfortunately she has not one brain cell."

"Diffusion...designer..." The first consultant is scribbling in his little book. "We should speak to Brianna about that. She'll have the right connections."

"I believe she's on holiday at the moment," says Eric. "With Mr. Laszlo."

"Well, when she gets back. We'll progress that idea." The consultant snaps the book shut. "Let's move on."

They all stride off again, and I wait till they've rounded the corner before giving a harrumph of frustration.

"What's up?" says Jasmine, who has slumped back down on the sofa and is texting something on her phone.

"They'll never get anything off the ground! Brianna won't be back for weeks, and anyway, she's hopeless. They'll just have meetings and talk . . . and meanwhile the shop will go bust."

"What do you care?" Jasmine gives an indifferent shrug.

How can she just watch a business collapse and not try to do *something*?

"I care because . . . because this is where I work! It could be a success!"

"Get real, Becky. No designer's ever going to want to do an exclusive range here."

"Brianna could call in some favors," I protest. "I mean, she's modeled for Calvin Klein, Versace . . . Tom Ford. . . . She could persuade one of them, surely? God, if I had a famous designer friend—" I stop, midflow.

Hang on. Why didn't I think of this before?

"What?" Jasmine looks up.

"I *do* know a designer," I say. "I know Danny Kovitz! We could get him to do something."

"You *know* Danny Kovitz?" Jasmine looks skeptical. "Or, like, you've bumped into him once?"

"I really know him! He used to live above me in

New York. He designed my wedding dress," I can't help adding smugly.

It's so cool, having a famous friend. I knew Danny when he was a nobody. In fact I helped get him his first break. And now he's this international fashion darling! He's been in *Vogue* and had his dresses worn to the Oscars and everything. He was interviewed in *Women's Wear Daily* last month about his last collection, which he said was based on his interpretation of the decay of civilization.

I don't believe a word of it. It'll have been something he threw together at the last minute with lots of safety pins and black coffee and someone else sewed up for him.

But still. An exclusive Danny Kovitz line would be fabulous publicity. I should have thought of this before.

"If you really know Danny Kovitz, ring him up," says Jasmine challengingly. "Right now."

She doesn't *believe* me?

"Fine, I will!" I whip out my phone, find the number for Danny's mobile, and dial it.

The truth is, I haven't spoken to Danny for quite a long while. But still, we went through a lot together while I was living in New York, and we'll always have that bond. I wait for a while, but there's no reply, just a bleeping sound. He probably lost his phone and canceled it or something.

"Problem?" Jasmine raises one immaculate eyebrow.

"His cell phone isn't working," I say coolly. "I'll call his office." I dial international directories, get a New York number for Danny Kovitz Enterprises, and dial. It's nine thirty A.M. in New York, which means there's not much chance of Danny being up, unless he's had an all-nighter. But I can leave a message.

A male voice answers. "Danny Kovitz Enterprises. May I help?"

"Oh, hi there!" I say. "It's Becky Brandon here, née Bloomwood. I'd like to speak to Danny Kovitz."

"Please hold the line," the voice says politely. Some kind of rap blasts my eardrum for a few moments, then a bright female voice comes on the line.

"Welcome to the Danny Kovitz fan club! For full membership information, please press one—"

Oh, for God's sake. I switch off and dial the main number again, avoiding Jasmine's gaze.

"Danny Kovitz Enterprises. May I help?"

"Hi, I'm an old, very close friend of Danny's," I say briskly. "Please put me through to his personal assistant."

The rap booms in my ear again, then a woman is saying, "Danny Kovitz's private office, Carol speaking. How may I help?"

"Hi, Carol!" I say in my most friendly manner. "I'm an old friend of Danny's and I've been trying to contact him through his cell number but it doesn't work. Could you possibly put me through to him? Or leave a message?"

"Your name?" says Carol, sounding skeptical.

"Becky Brandon. Née Bloomwood."

"And will he know what this is in regard to?"

"Yes! We're friends!"

"Well, I'll pass your message to Mr. Kovitz. . . ."

Suddenly I hear a familiar voice, faintly in the background, saying, "I *need* a Diet Coke, OK?"

That's Danny!

"He's there, isn't he?" I exclaim. "I just heard him! Could you quickly put me through? Honestly, I just want a very quick—"

"Mr. Kovitz is . . . in a meeting," says Carol. "I'll be sure to pass your message on, Ms. Broom. Thanks for your call." The line goes dead.

I switch off the phone, seething. She's not going to pass anything on, is she? She didn't even take my number!

"So," says Jasmine, who's been watching all along. "Close friends, are you?"

"We *are*," I say furiously.

OK. Think. There has to be a way to get through to him. There *has* to be. . . .

Wait a minute.

I scrabble for the phone again and dial international directories. "Hi," I say to the operator. "The name is Kovitz, the address is Apple Bay House, on Fairview Road, if you could put me straight through. . . ."

A few moments later a voice answers. "Hello?"

"Hi, Mrs. Kovitz," I say in my most charming manner, "it's Becky here. Becky Bloomwood? Do you remember me?"

I always liked Danny's mum. We have a good old chat, and she asks all about the baby and I ask all about her award-winning gardens in Connecticut, and the conversation ends with her expressing sympathetic indignation at the way I was treated by Danny's staff, especially after I was the one who first introduced his work to Barneys (I reminded her about that, just casually), and promising to get Danny to call me.

And literally about two minutes after we've finished talking, my cell phone rings.

"Hi, Becky! Mom says you called?"

"Danny!" I can't help shooting a triumphant glance at Jasmine. "Oh my God, it's been ages. How are you?"

"I'm great! Except my mom just gave me a total *rocket*. Jesus!" Danny sounds a bit shaken. "She was like, 'Don't you stop appreciating your friends, young man.' And I'm like, 'What are you talking about?' And she's like—"

"Your assistants wouldn't put me through," I explain. "They thought I was a fan. Or a stalker or something."

"I do get stalkers." Danny sounds quite proud of himself. "I have two at the moment, both named Joshua. Isn't that wild?"

"Wow!" I can't help feeling impressed, even though I know I shouldn't be. "So . . . what are you up to at the moment?"

"I'm taking some time to work on my new collection," he says with a practiced smoothness. "I'm reinterpreting the whole Far Eastern vibe. Right now I'm at the concept stage. Gathering influences, that kind of thing."

He doesn't fool me. "Gathering influences" means "Going on holiday and getting stoned on the beach."

"Well, I was just wondering," I say quickly. "Could you do me a massive favor? Could you do a little diffusion line for this shop I work for in London? Or even just one exclusive piece."

"Oh," he says, and I can hear him opening a can. "Sure. When?"

Ha! I *knew* he'd say yes.

"Well . . . soon?" I cross my fingers. "In the next few weeks? You could come to London for a visit. We'd have a blast!"

"Becky, I don't know...." He pauses to slurp at his drink, and I imagine him in some trendy SoHo office, lounging on an office chair, in those ancient jeans he always used to wear. "I have this Far East trip lined up...."

"I saw Jude Law in the street the other day," I add casually. "He lives quite close to us."

There's silence.

"Or I guess I could swing by," Danny says at last. "London's on the way to Thailand, right?"

Yes! I have total R.E.S.P.E.C.T.

For the rest of the day Jasmine barely says a word, just keeps shooting me awed looks. And Eric was totally impressed to hear that I'd made some "proactive advancement on the project," as he put it.

If only we had some customers, this job wouldn't be too bad after all. And on the plus side, the fact that we don't have anything to do has given me time to read my new issue of *Pregnancy* magazine.

"Hey, your phone's ringing in your bag," says Jasmine as she comes from the reception area. "It's been ringing all day, actually."

"Thanks for telling me!" I say sarcastically. I hurry to my desk, grab the phone, and click it on.

"Becky!" comes Mum's excited voice. "At last! So, darling. How was the famous celebrity obstetrician? We're all longing to know! Janice has been in and out all day!"

"Oh right. Let me just..." I close the door and sit down on my desk chair, marshaling my thoughts.

"Well . . . it was amazing! Guess what, I met a Bond girl in the waiting room!"

"A Bond girl!" Mum draws in breath. "Janice, did you hear that? Becky met a Bond girl in the waiting room!"

"And the place is lovely, and I'm going to have a holistic water birth, and they gave me this lovely welcome pack all full of spa vouchers. . . ."

"How wonderful!" says Mum. "And she's a nice lady, is she? The doctor?"

"Very nice." I pause for a moment, then add casually, "She's Luke's ex-girlfriend. Isn't that a coincidence?"

"Ex-girlfriend?" Mum's voice sharpens a little. "What do you mean, ex-girlfriend?"

"You know! Just someone he went out with ages ago. At Cambridge."

There's silence down the phone.

"Is she attractive?" says Mum.

Honestly.

"She's quite attractive. But I don't see what that has to do with anything."

"Of course not, darling." There's a scuffly sort of pause, and I'm positive I can hear Mum whispering something to Janice. "Do you know why she and Luke split up?" she suddenly asks.

"No. I don't."

"Haven't you asked him about it?"

"Mum," I say, trying to keep my patience. "Luke and I have a very secure, trusting marriage. I'm not going to *quiz* him, OK?"

What does she think I should do, issue Luke a questionnaire? I mean, I know Dad turned out to have had a slightly more colorful past than anyone might have suspected (affair with train stewardess; secret love child; handlebar mustache). But Luke's not like that—I know he's not.

"And anyway, it was all ages ago," I add, sounding more defiant than I mean to. "And she's got a boyfriend."

"I don't know, Becky love." Mum exhales sharply. "Are you sure this is a good idea? Pregnancy can be a . . . *tricky* time for a man. What about going back to that nice gentleman doctor?"

I'm starting to feel a bit insulted here. What does Mum think, that I can't hold on to my husband?

"We're with Venetia Carter now," I say obstinately. "It's all signed and sealed."

"Oh well, darling. If you're sure. What's that, Janice?" There's another scuffling at the other end. "Janice says, was it Halle Berry you met?"

"No, it was the new one. The blond Rollerblade champion. Mum, I'd better go. I've got a call waiting. Give my love to everyone. Bye!" I switch off the phone, and a second later it rings again.

"Bex! I've been trying you all day! How was it?" Suze's excited voice peals down the line. "Tell me everything. Are you having the Thai water birth?"

"Maybe!" I can't help beaming. "Oh, Suze, it was fab! You get massage, and reflexology, and I met a Bond girl, and there were paparazzi waiting outside and we got photographed together! We'll be in *Hello!*"

"That's so cool!" Suze's voice rises to a squeak. "God, I'm so jealous. I want another baby now, and have it there."

"You don't actually have it at the center," I explain.

"You have all the appointments there, but she's linked to the Cavendish Hospital."

"The Cavendish? The one with all the double beds and wine lists?"

"Yes." I can't help a smirk.

"You're so *lucky*, Bex! And what's Venetia Carter like?"

"She's fab! She's really young, and cool, and she has all these really interesting ideas about childbirth, and"—I hesitate—"and she's Luke's ex-girlfriend. Isn't that amazing?"

"She's . . . what?" Suze sounds like she can't believe her ears.

"She's Luke's ex. They went out at Cambridge together."

"You're having your baby delivered by Luke's ex-*girlfriend*?"

First Mum, then Suze. What's wrong with everyone?

"Yes!" I say defensively. "Why not? It was years ago and it only lasted about five minutes. And she's attached to someone else now. What's the problem?"

"It just seems a bit . . . *weird*, don't you think?"

"It's not weird! Suze, we're all grown-ups. We're all mature, professional people. I think we can get past some old, meaningless fling, don't you?"

"But I mean, she'll be . . . you know! Poking about."

This thought had crossed my mind. But then, is it any worse than Dr. Braine poking about? To be honest, I'm in denial about this whole birth business happening at all. I'm half hoping they'll invent some new labor-substitute device by the time I reach my due date.

"I'd be paranoid!" Suze is saying. "I once met this ex of Tarkie's—"

"Tarquin has an *ex*?" I say in astonishment, before I realize how this sounds.

"Flissy Menkin. Of the Somerset Menkins?"

"Of course," I say, as though I have a clue what the Somerset Menkins might be. They sound like china pots. Or some kind of galloping disease.

"I knew she was going to be at this wedding last year, and I practically spent the whole *week* getting ready. And that was with clothes on!"

"Well, I'll get a really good bikini wax," I say airily. "And maybe I'll have a cesarean. And the point is, she's the top baby-deliverer in the country! She should be used to it by now, don't you think?"

"I s'pose." Suze still sounds doubtful. "But still. Bex, if I were you, I'd steer clear. Go back to your other doctor."

"I don't *want* to steer clear." I feel like stamping my foot. "And I totally trust Luke," I add as an afterthought.

"Of course!" says Suze hastily. "Of course you do. So...did he chuck her, or the other way around?"

"I don't know," I admit.

"Hasn't he *told* you?"

"I haven't asked him! It's irrelevant!" Suze is starting to rattle me with all her questions. "Guess what? I got Crème de la Mer in the welcome pack," I say to distract her. "And a voucher for Champneys!"

"Ooh!" Suze perks up. "Can you take a guest?"

I'm not going to let Suze and Mum freak me out. They don't know anything about it! Luke and I have a totally stable, trusting relationship. We're having a *baby* together. I feel totally secure.

On the way home that night I pop into Hollis Franklin quickly, just to look at baby linen. Hollis Franklin is such a gorgeous shop, it's got a Royal Warrant and apparently the Queen herself shops there! I spend a happy hour looking at different thread counts, and by the time I arrive back home, it's seven. Luke is in the kitchen, drinking a beer and watching the news.

"Hi!" I say, putting down my bags. "I got the baby some sheets from Hollis Franklin!" I pull out a tiny crib sheet embroidered with a tiny crest in each corner. "Isn't that adorable?"

"Very nice," says Luke, examining it. Then he catches sight of the price tag and blanches. "Jesus. You paid that for a baby sheet?"

"They're the best," I explain. "They're four hundred thread count!"

"Does the baby *need* four hundred thread count? You realize it'll throw up on these sheets?"

"The baby would *never* throw up on a Hollis Franklin sheet!" I say, indignant. "It knows better than that." I pat my bump. "Don't you, darling?"

Luke rolls his eyes. "If you say so." He puts the sheet down. "And what's in the bigger bag?"

"Matching sheets for us. The duvet cover's coming separately, and the pillow shams as soon as they're in stock—" I break off at his appalled expression. "Luke, we'll have the crib in our bedroom! We have to coordinate!"

"*Coordinate?*"

"Of course!"

"Becky, really—" Luke's attention is drawn to the

TV screen. "Hold on, it's Malcolm." He turns up the volume and I take the opportunity to shove the Hollis Franklin sheets behind the door, where Luke might forget about them.

Malcolm Lloyd is the chief executive of Arcodas, and he's being interviewed in the business slot about why he's planning to make a bid for some airline company. Luke watches intently, beer in hand.

"He should stop doing that jerky thing with his hand," I say, watching the interview too. "He looks really awkward. He should go on media training."

"He's already been on media training," says Luke.

"Well, it was rubbish. You should get someone new." I take off my jacket, dump it on a chair, and massage my aching shoulders.

"Come here, sweetheart," says Luke, noticing me. "I'll do it."

I pull a chair over and sit down in front of him, and he starts kneading my tight muscles.

"Luke, that reminds me," I say, still watching Malcolm. "Does Iain always talk to you like that?"

Luke's fingers stop moving briefly. "Like what?"

"The way he did in the car yesterday. He's so unpleasant!"

"That's just his business style. Arcodas has a different working culture."

"But it's awful!"

"Well, we're just going to have to get used to it." Luke sounds a bit defensive and snappy. "We're playing with the big boys now. Everyone's just got to—" He stops himself.

"What?" I twist my head, trying to see his expression.

"Nothing," says Luke after a moment. "Just... thinking aloud. Let's turn this off." He kisses me on the top of my head. "Shoulders feel better now?"

"A million times. Thanks."

I get up, pour myself a glass of orange-cranberry mix, and flip the TV over to *The Simpsons*. Meanwhile, Luke picks up the *Evening Standard* and starts leafing through the pages. A bowl of olives is on the counter, and we pass it back and forth between us.

There now, isn't this nice? Just a nice quiet evening at home. Just the two of us, relaxing together in our stable relationship. Not thinking about old girlfriends or anything like that.

In fact, I'm so relaxed, maybe I *will* bring the subject up. Just in a casual way. To show I don't care one way or the other.

"So... that must have been weird for you," I say lightly. "Coming across Venetia again after all those years."

"Uh-huh." Luke nods absently.

"Why did you and she break up?" I say, still lightly. "Just out of interest."

"God knows." Luke shrugs. "It was a long time ago."

You see? It was so long ago, he can't even remember. It's ancient history. I really don't care what the gory details were. In fact, let's talk about something else. Current affairs or something.

"Did you love her?" I hear myself saying.

"*Love?*" Luke gives a short laugh. "We were students."

I wait for him to expand on the subject, but he turns a page of the paper and frowns at a headline.

That is not an answer. "We were students" is not an answer.

I open my mouth to demand "What's that supposed to mean?" Then, after a moment's thought, I close it again. This is ridiculous. I'd never even met Venetia Carter till yesterday—and already Mum and Suze have made me all paranoid. Of *course* he never loved her.

I'm not going to ask him anything else about their relationship. I'm not even going to think about it. Subject officially closed.

SHORT QUIZ FOR LUKE BRANDON

1. How would you describe the relationship you had with your old girlfriend Venetia?
   a) Passionate Romeo/Juliet-style romance.
   b) V. boring relationship.
   c) I never really liked her.
   d) She stalked me.

2. In general, do you prefer girls' names that begin with
   a) R
   b) B
   c) V
   d) Don't know.

3. Have you ever been in love? If so, with how many people?
   a) Your wife and only your wife, because she taught you what love really is.
   b) Your snooty girlfriend Sacha, the bitch who stole the luggage.
   c) Your student girlfriend Venetia, with whom you had a brief fling but never mentioned her, so how could you have been in love with her?
   d) Other.

4. What do you think of long red hair?
   a) It's a bit obvious and show-offy.
   b) It swishes too much.

(Please turn over and complete remaining three sections.)

Prendergast de Witt Connell
Financial Advisers

Forward House
394 High Holborn
London WC1V 7EX

Mrs R Brandon
37 Maida Vale Mansions
Maida Vale
London NW6 0YF

28 August 2003

Dear Mrs. Brandon,

Thank you for your letter.

I fear you have misconstrued the meaning of an "investment in gold." I would strongly recommend you purchase gold bullion through a recommended broker, rather than, as you suggest, "get the starfish pendant out of the Tiffany catalog, and maybe a ring."

Please do not hesitate to contact me again should you need further guidance.

Yours sincerely,

Kenneth Prendergast
Family Investment Specialist

SEVEN

I'M NOT REALLY GOING to give Luke a questionnaire. In fact I've thrown it in the bin for various reasons, namely:

1) We have a mature, trusting marriage where you don't quiz each other on what color hair you prefer.

2) He would never have time to fill it in (especially the section "describe the qualities of your wife you most admire in 500 words").

3. I have *far* more important things to think about. Suze and I are going to a big baby fair at Earl's Court today, and there's going to be about five hundred stands, plus freebies, and a mother-and-baby fashion show, and the biggest collection of prams under one roof in Europe!

As I come out of the tube station, there are already crowds streaming toward the entrances. I have never seen so many pushchairs in my life, and we haven't even got in yet!

"Bex!"

I turn to see Suze, in a fantastic lime sundress, holding the handles of her double buggy. Wilfrid and

Clementine are sitting up, side by side, wearing the cutest stripy hats.

"Hi!" I hurry over and give her a big hug. "Isn't this fab?"

"I've got our tickets in here. . . ." Suze rifles in her bag. "Plus vouchers for a smoothie each . . ."

"Has Tarquin got Ernie today?"

"No, my mother's looking after him. They'll have a lovely day together," Suze adds fondly. "She's going to teach him how to pluck a pheasant."

It's not just Tarquin. Suze's entire family really is the weirdest.

As we enter the fair, I can't help a tiny gasp. This place is *huge*. All around are gigantic photographs of babies, and colorful stalls, and promo girls handing out carrier bags. The music from *The Lion King* is playing out of loudspeakers, and a clown on stilts is juggling foam bananas.

"So," says Suze in a businesslike manner as we join the queue. "Have you got a list?"

"List?" I echo vaguely. I can't stop looking around at everyone's prams and changing bags and babies' outfits. A few people are smiling at the sight of Wilfrid and Clementine, sitting up side by side with their bright blue eyes, and I beam back proudly.

"Your list of baby gear," says Suze patiently. "What do you still need?" She rifles in the envelope containing the tickets. "Here we are. The New Baby Checklist. Do you have a sterilizer yet?"

"Er . . . no." My eyes are fixated on a bright red stroller with a cool polka-dot hood. That would look fab going down the King's Road.

"Or a nursing pillow?"

"No."

"Are you planning to use an electric breast pump?"

"Urgh." I recoil slightly. "Do I have to? Ooh, look, they've got mini cowboy boots!"

"Bex..." Suze waits till I turn. "You do know having a baby is about more than buying them clothes, don't you? You do have . . . realistic expectations?"

"I have totally realistic expectations!" I say with slight indignation. "And I'm going to get everything on that list. I'm going to be the best-prepared mother *ever*. Come on, let's get started."

As we head down between the stands, my head is swiveling from side to side. I've never seen so many gadgets . . . and baby outfits . . . and adorable-looking toys. . . .

"You'll need a car seat," Suze is saying. "Some fix into the car, and some also clip onto wheels. . . ."

"OK." I nod vaguely. I can't get that excited by car seats, to be honest.

"And look, here's a sterilizer and bottle system," says Suze. She pauses by the Avent stand and picks up a leaflet. "They have microwave ones . . . electric ones. . . . Even if you're breast-feeding, you'll need to express. . . ."

My attention has been caught by a stand named Disco Baby. "Hey, Suze!" I interrupt her. "Baby leg warmers!"

"Right." She nods. "Do you want a four-bottle sterilizer or a six-bottle sterilizer, or—"

"And rattles in the shape of little glitter balls! Suze, *look*!"

"Oh my God." Suze's face lights up. "I *have* to buy those for the twins." She abandons the Avent leaflets, grabs her double buggy, and pushes it over. There are little "disco girl" and "disco boy" sweatshirts, and the cutest little baseball caps.

"I just wish I knew what I was *having*," I say, picking up a tiny pink skirt and stroking it longingly.

"Did you try the ancient Chinese chart?" says Suze.

"Yes. It said I was having a boy."

"A boy!" Suze's face lights up.

"But then I found this Web site called Analyze Your Cravings, and according to that, I'm having a girl." I sigh in frustration. "I just want to *know.*"

Suze looks perplexed, then reaches for a hat. "Buy this. It's unisex."

I buy the hat and a pair of the most fabulous kitsch platform bootees, and a Groove Baby miniature dressing gown. At the next stall I buy a baby beach towel and mini-sunshade, and a remote-controlled Winnie the Pooh mobile. I'm getting quite laden, to be honest, but Suze just keeps stashing all her stuff in the double buggy. Prams are so handy for shopping. I'd never quite appreciated it before.

And we've got all day here.

"Suze, I need a pram," I say, making a snap decision.

"I know." She nods vigorously. "The Pram City stand is just here, behind Zone C. You'll probably need a whole travel system, and you might want to get a lightweight buggy for traveling. . . ."

I'm barely listening as I head for the Pram City sign. The entrance is decorated with bunting and balloons, and as I step through, I can see prams stretching into the distance like an endless chrome shrubbery.

"Hi!" I say to a man in a green jacket and PRAM CITY badge. "I need a pram straightaway."

"Of course!" He beams at me. "We normally deliver within four weeks—"

"No, I need one *now*," I interrupt. "To take away. I don't mind what kind."

"Ah." His face falls. "These are all for display only, I'm afraid. . . ."

"Please?" I give him my most winsome smile. "You must have one you can sell me. Just one little pram? Some old one you don't need anymore?"

"Um . . . right." He glances nervously at my stomach. "I'll . . . see what I can do."

He bustles away, and I look around at the trendy prams. Suze is swooning over some state-of-the-art double buggy on a special podium of its own, and to my right, a pregnant woman and her husband are pushing an amazing contraption upholstered in black leather, with built-in drink holders.

"I *knew* you'd like it." The woman is glowing with pleasure.

"Of course I do." The man kisses the back of her neck, cradling her bump. "Let's order it."

I feel a sudden pang, deep inside. I want to try out prams with Luke. I want to go as a couple, and push prams around and for Luke to kiss me like that.

I mean, I know it's a hectic time for him and he's really busy at work. I know he's never going to be some New Man who knows every brand of diaper and wears a fake pregnancy stomach. But still, I don't want to have to do *everything* on my own.

And I bet he'd love that black leather one too. It's probably even got a BlackBerry holder.

"Hey, Bex." Suze comes over, pushing the twins

with one hand and the state-of-the-art buggy with the other. "Do you think I need a new pram?"

"Er..." I look at the twins. "Isn't that double buggy quite new?"

"Yes, but, I mean, this one's really maneuverable. It would be really practical! I think I should get it. I mean, you can't have too many prams, can you?"

There's a kind of lust in her eyes. Since when did Suze become such a pramaholic?

"Definitely," I say. "Maybe I should get it too!"

"Yes!" says Suze in delight. "Then we'd be matching! Have a go!" She hands it to me and I push it about for a bit. It is pretty cool, I have to say.

"I love the squidgy handles," I say, squeezing them.

"Me too! And the cool wheel design."

This is just how we used to be in clothes shops together. God, I *never* thought I'd get as excited by a pushchair as I do about a dress.

"Madam?" The assistant is back. "Here we are. I can let you buy this model today. Seventy pounds."

He's pushing an old-fashioned coach pram in an uninspiring shade of gray, with a pink lacy pillow and quilt. Suze stares at it, aghast.

"Bex, you can't put the baby in that!"

"It's not for the *baby*," I say. "It's for my shopping!" I plonk all my carrier bags inside and grasp the handles. "That's better!"

I pay for it, and prize Suze away from the hi-tech buggy, and we head off to the Refreshment Zone, passing lots of stalls on the way. I buy a paddling pool, and a box of building blocks and a huge teddy and just sling them all on top of the pram. And there's still room for loads more! Honestly, I should have bought a pram *years* ago.

"I'll get the coffees," says Suze as we near the café area.

"I'll be there in a sec," I say absently. I've spotted a stand with vintage-style hobbyhorses, which are absolutely gorgeous. I'll buy one for the baby and one each for Suze's children.

The only trouble is, there's a massive queue. I maneuver the pram into line as best I can and lean on the handles with a sigh. I'm quite tired actually, after all this walking. In front of me is an old woman in a dark red raincoat. She turns, then pulls an expression of horror as she sees me leaning on the pram.

"Let this young lady through!" she exclaims, tapping the woman in front of her. "She has a baby *and* she's expecting! The poor thing's exhausted—look at her!"

"Oh!" I say, taken aback. Everyone is moving aside like I'm royalty, and the raincoat woman is urging me to push the pram forward. "Um . . . I don't actually have a . . ."

"Come through, come through! How old's your wee one?" The old woman peers into the pram. "I can't see the poor little thing for all your gubbins!"

"Er . . . well . . ."

The stand owner is beckoning me forward encouragingly. Everyone's waiting for me to go first.

OK. I know I should be honest. I do know that.

But the queue's gigantic, and Suze is waiting . . . and what does it *really* matter if there's a baby in here or not?

"Is it a boy or a girl?" the old woman persists.

"It's . . . a girl!" I hear myself saying. "She's asleep," I add hurriedly. "I'd like four hobbyhorses, please."

"Ah, the dear little thing," says the old woman fondly. "And her name?"

Ooh! Names!

"Tallulah," I say impulsively. "I mean...Phoebe. Tallulah-Phoebe." I hand the stall owner the money, take the hobbyhorses, and somehow balance them on the pram. "Thanks very much!"

"You be a good girl, Tallulah-Phoebe," the old woman is clucking into the pram. "You be good for your mum and the new arrival."

"Oh, she will!" I say brightly. "Nice to meet you! Thanks very much!" And I hastily wheel the pram away, feeling a giggle rise inside. I turn the corner and immediately spot Suze at the coffee counter, chatting to a girl with highlights and an off-road pushchair and three children in matching stripy tops tied to it with reins.

"Hi, Bex!" she calls. "What do you want?"

"Can I have a decaf cappuccino and a choc chip muffin?" I call back. "And I *have* to tell you what just happened—" I break off as the girl with highlights turns.

I don't believe it.

It's Lulu.

Lulu, Suze's horrible friend from the country. My heart sinks like a stone as I wave cheerfully. What's she doing here? Just as we were having such a good time.

They're coming over toward me now, all the toddlers trailing in their wake like kites being dragged along a beach. Lulu is looking as sensible-mummy as ever, in her pink cords and white shirt and pearl earrings, which probably all came out of the same sensible-mummy catalog.

Oh God, I know that's really bitchy. But I can't help

it. Lulu has rubbed me the wrong way ever since the first time we met and she totally looked down on me because I didn't have any kids. (And also maybe because I took my bra off in front of all the children to entertain them. But I was really desperate, OK? And it's not like they *saw* anything.)

"Lulu!" I force a smile. "How are you? I didn't know you were coming today!"

"I didn't know myself!" Lulu's voice is so sharp and posh, it makes me wince. "I was offered a sudden promotion opportunity. For my new children's cookbook."

"Yes, Suze told me about that. Congratulations!"

"And congratulations to you!" Lulu eyes my bump. "We'll have to get together sometime! Talk baby things!"

Lulu has never been anything other than mean and patronizing to me, all the times I've met her. But now suddenly because I'm having a baby we're supposed to be friends?

"That would be super!" I say pleasantly, and Suze shoots me a look.

"There's a section on pregnancy in my cookbook, actually...." Lulu rifles in her bag for a shiny book, illustrated with a photo of herself holding an armful of vegetables in her kitchen. "I must send you a copy."

"Like, on cravings and stuff?" I take a sip of decaf. "I could do with some good nonalcoholic cocktail recipes."

"I've called it 'Think of the Baby.'" She frowns slightly. "It's shocking, what some people put in their bodies while they're pregnant. Additives...sugar..."

"Right." I hesitate, chocolate muffin halfway toward my mouth, then defiantly stuff it in. "Mmm, yum."

I can see Suze hide a giggle.

"Would your children like some?" I add, breaking it into crumbly pieces.

"They don't eat chocolate!" Lulu snaps, looking horrified, as though I've tried to peddle them cocaine. "I've·brought some dried banana snacks."

"Lulu, sweetie?" A girl in a headset ducks down to our table. "Are you ready to come and do the radio interview? And then we'd like a photo of you and all the kids."

"Absolutely." Lulu bares her teeth in her horsey smile. "Come along Cosmo, Ivo, Ludo...."

"Go Dasher, go Dancer," I mutter.

"See you later!" says Suze with a strained smile as they walk off. And all of a sudden I feel a bit ashamed. Lulu is Suze's friend and I should make the effort. I'm going to be nice about her, I suddenly resolve. If it kills me.

"So...that was great, seeing Lulu!" I try to inject some warmth into my voice. "She's right, we should all get together and have a good chat. Maybe we should meet up later on and have tea or something—"

"I don't want to." Suze's low voice takes me by surprise. I look over, and she's staring down into her cappuccino. Suddenly I recall Suze's reaction at Mum's house when I mentioned Lulu. That kind of tension in her face.

"Suze, have you and Lulu fallen out?" I say cautiously.

"Not exactly." Suze won't look up. "I mean...she's done a lot for me. She's been so helpful, especially with the children...."

The trouble with Suze is, she never wants to be

nasty. So she always starts off bitching about people with a little speech about how lovely they are really.

"But..." I prompt her.

"But she's so bloody perfect!" As Suze raises her head, her cheeks are all pink. "She makes me feel like a total failure. Especially when we go out together. She always has homemade risotto or something and her children *eat* it. And they're never naughty, and they're all really bright...."

"Your children are bright!" I retort indignantly.

"Lulu's kids are all reading Harry Potter!" Suze sounds despairing. "And Ernie can't even really *speak* much, let alone read. Apart from German phrases from Wagner. And Lulu keeps asking me if I played Mozart to him in the womb, and have I thought about extra tuition, and I just feel so inadequate...."

I feel a hot surge of outrage. How *dare* anyone make Suze feel inadequate!

"Suze, you're a brilliant mother!" I say. "And Lulu's just a cow. I knew it, the moment I met her. Don't listen to her anymore. And don't read her stupid cookbook!" I put an arm round Suze's shoulders and squeeze tight. "If you feel inadequate, how do you think *I* feel? I don't even know any nursery rhymes!"

"Good afternoon!" Lulu's amplified voice suddenly booms out from behind us, and we both turn round. She's sitting on a raised platform, opposite a woman in a pink suit, with a small audience watching. Two of her children are on her lap, and behind her are huge posters for her book, with a notice saying "Signed Copies Available."

"A lot of parents are simply *lazy* when it comes to feeding their children," she's saying with a pitying smile.

"In my experience, all children like the taste of such things as avocado, monkfish, or a good homemade polenta."

Suze and I exchange glances.

"I've got to feed the twins," mutters Suze. "I'll go and do it in the 'Mother and Baby' area."

"Do it here!" I protest. "They've got highchairs—"

"Uh-uh." She shakes her head. "No way, not with Lulu around. I've only brought a couple of jars. I'm *not* letting her see those."

"D'you want some help?" I volunteer.

"No, don't worry." She eyes my pram, piled high with the hobbyhorses, the paddling pool, and the teddy. "Bex, why don't you go round again and this time maybe look for basics? You know, things the baby will actually *need*?"

"Right, yes." I nod. "Good idea."

I head down the aisles as fast as I can, trying to get away from Lulu's grating voice.

"Television is the most *dreadful* influence," she's saying. "Again, I would say it's just sheer laziness on the part of the parents. My children have a program of stimulating educational activities—"

Stupid woman. Trying to ignore her, I pull out my fair guide and am looking around to get my bearings, when a large sign attracts my attention. FIRST AID KITS £40. Now, *that's* what we need.

Feeling rather grown-up and responsible, I park the pram and start to peruse the kits. They all come in cool cases, with different things in sections. Plasters . . . rolls of bandages . . . and the cutest little pink scissors. I can't believe I've never bought a first aid kit before. They're fab!

I take the kit up to the checkout, where a lugubrious-looking man in a white coat is sitting on a stool. He starts tapping at his till and I pick up a MediSupply Professional catalog, which is pretty dull. It's mostly rolls of elastic tape, and industrial-size bottles of aspirin, and—

Ooh. A stethoscope. I've *always* wanted a stethoscope.

"How much is the stethoscope?" I say casually.

"Stethoscope?" The man gives me a suspicious look. "Are you a doctor?"

Honestly. Are only doctors allowed to buy stethoscopes, or something?

"Not exactly," I admit at last. "Can I still have one?"

"Everything in the catalog is available to order online." He gives a grudging shrug. "If you want to pay £150. They're not toys."

"I know they're not!" I say with dignity. "I actually think every parent should have a stethoscope in the house for emergency purposes. And a home heart defibrillator," I add, turning the page. "And—"

I stop midflow. I'm staring at a picture of a smiling pregnant woman clasping her stomach.

Baby's Gender Predictor Kit.
   Conduct a simple test in the privacy of your own home. Results accurate and anonymous.

My heart is doing a kind of jig. I could find out. Without having another scan. Without telling Luke.

"Um . . . is this available online too?" I ask, my voice a bit husky.

"I've got those here." He rootles in his drawer and produces a large white box.

"Right." I swallow. "I'll take it. Thanks." I hand over my credit card and the man swipes it.

A voice comes from behind me. "How's little Tallulah-Phoebe?" It's the woman in the dark red raincoat again. She's clutching a hobbyhorse wrapped up in plastic, and peering into the ever-more-laden pram, which I parked by the display of first aid boxes. "She is a good girl, isn't she? Not a peep!"

I feel a prickle of alarm.

"She's, um . . . sleeping," I say quickly. "I'd leave her alone, actually. . . ."

"Let me just have a little look! I don't know *how* she can sleep with all these packages on her pram. *Can* you, Tallulah-Phoebe?" the woman croons, pushing aside all my plastic bags.

"Please leave her alone!" I start toward the pram. "She's very sensitive . . . she doesn't like strangers—"

"She's gone!" the old woman cries, and stands bolt upright, pale with fear. "The baby's gone! Only her little blanket's left!"

Shit.

"Um . . ." My face floods with color. "Actually . . ."

"Miss, your credit card doesn't work," says the man at the till.

"It must work!" I turn back, momentarily distracted. "I only got it last week—"

"A baby's been abducted!"

To my horror, the raincoat woman has bustled out of the stand and accosted a security guard, still clutching the lacy blanket. "Little Tallulah-Phoebe's gone! A baby's disappeared!"

"Did you hear that?" a blond woman cries out in horror. "A child's been abducted! Call the police, someone!"

"No, she hasn't!" I call. "There's been a . . . a misunderstanding. . . ." But no one hears.

"She was asleep in her pram!" The raincoat woman's gabbling to anyone who will listen. "And then it was just her blanket! These people are evil!"

"A baby's gone!"

"They just grabbed her!"

I can hear the news spreading like wildfire among passersby. Parents are summoning their children to their sides with sharp cries. To my horror I see a pair of security guards heading toward me, their walkie-talkies crackling.

"They'll have dyed her hair and changed her clothes by now," the blond woman is saying hysterically. "She'll be halfway to Thailand!"

"Madam, the fair entrances were secured as soon as we got the alert," says a security guard in a terse voice. "No one's coming in or out until we've found this baby."

OK, I have to take control. I have to tell them it's a false alarm. Yes. Just admit I invented Tallulah-Phoebe in order to queue-jump, and I'm sure everyone will understand—

No, they won't. They'll lynch me.

"It's gone through. Do you have a PIN number?" says the man at the till, who looks totally unmoved by all the fuss. I jab it in on autopilot and he hands me the bag.

"Her child's missing . . . and she's *shopping*?" says the blond woman in tones of horror.

"Can you give a full description of the child, ma'am?" one of the guards says, approaching me. "National police have been informed, and we've got a call out to the airports...."

I am never going to tell a lie again. Never.

"I...um..." My voice isn't working properly. "I should probably...explain something."

"Yes?" Both men are looking at me expectantly.

"Bex?" Suddenly I hear Suze's voice. "What's going on?" I look up, and there's Suze, pushing the double buggy with one arm and holding Clementine in the other.

Thank God, thank God, thank God—

"*There* you are!" I say, grabbing Clementine from Suze, my voice high with relief. "Come here, Tallulah-Phoebe!"

I hug Clementine tight, trying to hide the fact that she's leaning out of my arms in a desperate attempt to get back to Suze.

"Is this the missing child?" A security guard is looking Clementine up and down.

"Missing child?" Suze looks incredulous. She turns and takes in the crowd around us. "Bex, what on earth—"

"I completely forgot that you'd taken little Tallulah-Phoebe off for lunch!" I say in shrill tones. "Silly me! And everyone thought she'd been kidnapped!" I'm desperately imploring her with my eyes to play along.

I can see her brain working it all out. The great thing about Suze is that she knows me pretty well.

"*Tallulah-Phoebe?*" she says at last, in tones of incredulity, and I give a slight, shamefaced shrug.

"Baby Tallulah-Phoebe's back!" The raincoat woman

is spreading the news joyfully among the passersby. "We've found her!"

"You know this woman?" The security guard regards Suze with narrowed eyes.

"She's my friend," I say quickly, before they arrest Suze for abducting her own baby. "Actually, I think we should probably go...." I squish Clementine into my pram as best I can amid all the packages, and maneuver it into a getaway position.

"Mama!" Clementine is still stretching out her hands toward Suze. "Mama!"

"Oh my God!" Suze's face lights up like a beacon. "Did you hear that? She said Mama! Clever *girl*!"

"We're off now," I say hurriedly to the guards. "Thank you *so* much for all your help. You've got a great security system...."

"Wait a minute." One of the guards is frowning in suspicion. "Why did the baby say 'Mama' to this lady?"

"Because...she's called Mamie," I say desperately. "Clever Tallulah-Phoebe, that's your aunty Mamie! Aunty Mama! Let's go home now...."

I can't quite look at Suze as we head toward the exits. On the loudspeakers, the DJ is saying, "And baby Tallulah-Phoebe has been *found,* safe and well...."

"So, do you want to tell me what that was all about, Bex?" Suze says at last, without turning her head.

"Er..." I clear my throat. "Not really. Shall we go and have a cup of tea instead?"

EIGHT

SUZE AND I spend the rest of the day together, and it's just fab. We dump all our parcels in Suze's enormous Range Rover, then she drives to the King's Road and we have tea at a great children-friendly place with ice-cream sundaes and everything. (I am *always* having crayons on the table from now on.) Then we go to Steinberg & Tolkien, and I buy a vintage cardigan and Suze buys an evening bag, and then it's time for supper, so we go to Pizza on the Park, where a jazz group is warming up and they let the twins bang their fists on the drums.

And then at last, we lift the sleeping babies into the Range Rover and Suze gives me a lift home. It's about ten by the time we drive in past the porter's lodge and pull up in front of the entrance to the building. I call Luke on my mobile to help us upstairs with all my stuff.

"Wow," he says as he takes in the pile of bags on the ground. "So, is this it? Is the nursery complete now?"

"Um . . ." It's just occurred to me that I never did buy a sterilizer. Or a nursing pillow or any diaper rash cream. But never mind. I've still got fifteen weeks to go. Plenty of time.

As Luke struggles into the flat with the paddling pool and hobbyhorse and about six carriers, I quickly take the bag with the Gender Predictor Kit and hide it in my underwear drawer. I'll have to choose a moment when he's out.

Suze has popped into the bathroom to change one of the twins and as I emerge from the bedroom she's lugging both car seats down the corridor.

"Come and have a glass of wine," Luke says.

"I'd better get going," she says regretfully. "But I'll have a glass of water if you've got one."

We head into the kitchen, where a CD is softly playing Nina Simone songs. A half-empty bottle of wine is open on the counter, with two glasses next to it.

"I'm not having wine," I begin.

"That wasn't for you," says Luke, filling a glass of water from the fridge. "Venetia popped round earlier."

I feel a shot of surprise. Venetia was here?

"There's some extra paperwork we need to fill out," Luke continues. "She passes this way anyway, so she dropped it off on her way home."

"Right," I say after a pause. "That was . . . helpful of her."

"She's just left, actually." Luke hands Suze the glass. "You missed her by a few minutes."

Hang on. It's gone ten o'clock. Does that mean she's been here *all evening*?

I mean, not that I mind or anything. Of course I don't. Venetia is just Luke's friend. His beautiful, ex-girlfriend, platonic old friend.

I'm aware of Suze's eyes boring into me, and quickly look away.

"Bex, can you show me the nursery before I leave?" she says, her voice strangely high-pitched. "Come on."

She practically hustles me down the corridor and into the spare room, which we're calling the nursery even though we'll have moved by the time the baby arrives.

"So." Suze shuts the door and turns to face me, agog.

"What?" I shrug, pretending I don't know what she means.

"Is that normal? To 'pop round' to your ex's house and stay all evening?"

"Of course it is. Why shouldn't they catch up?"

"Just the two of them? Drinking *wine?*" Suze utters the word like some Baptist teetotal preacher.

"They're friends, Suze!" I say defensively. "Old... very good... platonic... friends."

There's silence in the little room.

"OK, Bex," Suze says at last, lifting her hands as though in surrender. "If you're sure."

"I am! I'm totally, completely, one hundred percent..." I trail off and start fiddling with a Christian Dior bottle warmer. I'm clicking the lid on and off like some obsessive-compulsive. Suze has wandered over to the wicker toy hamper and is examining a little woolly sheep. For a while we're both silent, not even looking at each other.

"At least..."

"What?"

I swallow several times, not wanting to admit it. "Well," I say at last, trying to sound matter-of-fact. "What if... just hypothetically... what if I *weren't* sure?"

Suze raises her head and meets my gaze. "Is she pretty?" she says in equally matter-of-fact tones.

"She's not just pretty. She's stunning. She's got red shiny hair and these amazing green eyes and really toned arms...."

"Cow," says Suze automatically.

"And she's clever, and she wears great clothes, and Luke really likes her...." The more I say, the less confident I'm feeling.

"Luke *loves* you!" Suze cuts in. "Bex, remember, you're his wife. You're the one he chose. She's the reject."

That makes me feel better. "Reject" makes me feel a lot better.

"But that doesn't mean she's not after him." Suze starts pacing up and down, pensively tapping the woolly sheep on her palm. "We have several options here. One: she genuinely is just a friend and you've got nothing to worry about."

"Right." I nod earnestly.

"Two: she came by this evening to check the lay of the land. Three: she's totally going after him. Four—" She stops herself.

"What's four?" I say in dread.

"It isn't four," says Suze quickly. "I reckon it's two. She came to scope things out. See the home territory."

"So . . . what do I do?"

"You let her know you're onto her." Suze raises her eyebrows meaningfully. "Woman-to-woman."

Woman-to-woman? Since when did Suze get so worldly-wise and cynical? She sounds like she should be wearing a pencil skirt and blowing cigarette smoke in some film noir.

"When are you seeing her again?" she asks.

"Next Friday. We've got a checkup appointment."

"OK." Suze sounds firm. "Go in there, Bex, and stake your claim."

"Stake my claim?" I say uncertainly. "How do I do that?" I'm not sure I've staked my claim on anything before. Except maybe a pair of boots in a Barneys sale.

"Give off discreet little signals," Suze says in knowledgeable tones. "Show her Luke belongs to you. Put your arm round him...talk about your great life together....Just nip any little ideas she might have in the bud. And make sure you look fabulous. But not like you've made any effort."

Discreet little signals. Our great life together. Look fabulous. I can do that.

"How's Luke about the baby, by the way?" Suze asks casually. "Is he excited?"

"Yes, I think so. Why?"

"Oh, nothing." She shrugs. "I just read this piece in a magazine the other day about men who can't cope with the idea of becoming a father. Apparently they often have affairs to compensate."

"Often?" I echo in dismay. "How often?"

"Er...about half the time?"

"Half?"

"I mean...a tenth," Suze amends hastily. "I can't remember what it said, actually. And I'm sure that's not Luke. But still, it might be worth talking to him about fatherhood. The article said some men can only see the pressures and stresses of having a child, and you have to paint a positive picture."

"Right." I nod, trying to take all this information in. "OK. I'll do that. And Suze..." I pause awkwardly.

"Thanks for not saying 'I told you so.' You told me to steer clear of Venetia Carter and...maybe you were right."

"I would *never* say 'I told you so'!" exclaims Suze in horror.

"I know you wouldn't. But loads of people would."

"Well, they shouldn't! And anyway, maybe *you* were right, Bex. Maybe Venetia's not interested in Luke and it's all totally innocent." She puts the woolly sheep down and pats it on the head. "But I'd stake your claim anyway. Just to be sure."

"Oh, don't worry." I give a determined nod. "I will."

Suze is so right. I need to give Venetia the message: *Keep your hands off my husband.* In a subtle way, of course.

As we arrive at the birth center on Friday I'm dressed in my best "looking fabulous with no effort" outfit of Seven maternity jeans (frayed), a sexy red stretchy top, and my new Moschino killer heels. Which are a bit dressy maybe, but the frayed jeans compensate. When we arrive, the waiting room is pretty empty, with not a celebrity in sight, but I'm so psyched up I don't mind.

"Becky?" Luke looks down at my hand, gripping his. "Are you all right? You seem tense."

"Oh...you know," I say. "I've just got a few concerns."

"I'm sure you have." He gives an understanding nod. "Why not share them with Venetia?"

Yu-huh. That was the general plan.

We sit down on the plushy chairs, and I pick up a

magazine, and Luke opens the *FT* with a rustle. I'm about to turn to "Your Baby's Horoscope" when I remember Suze's words yesterday. I should talk to Luke about fatherhood. This is the perfect time.

"So . . . it's exciting, isn't it?" I say, putting my magazine down. "Becoming parents."

"Mmm-hmm." Luke nods and turns a page.

He doesn't sound that excited. Oh God, what if he's secretly daunted by a life of diapers and is seeking refuge in another woman's arms? I have to paint a *positive* picture of parenthood, like Suze said. Something really good . . . something exciting to look forward to . . .

"Hey, Luke," I say, suddenly inspired. "Imagine if the baby wins a gold medal at the Olympic Games."

"Sorry?" He raises his head from the *FT.*

"The Olympics! Imagine if the baby wins a gold medal at something. And we'll be its parents!" I look at him for a reaction. "Won't it be great? We'll be so proud!"

My mind is totally seized by this idea. I can totally see myself at the stadium in 2030 or whenever, being interviewed by Sue Barker, telling her how I knew my child was destined for greatness, even from the womb.

Luke appears a bit bemused.

"Becky . . . have I missed something? What makes you think our child will win an Olympic gold?"

"It might! Why shouldn't it? You have to *believe* in your children, Luke."

"Ah. Fair enough." Luke nods and puts his paper down. "So, which sport did you have in mind?"

"The long jump," I say after some thought. "Or maybe the triple jump, because it's less popular. It'll be easier to win a gold."

"Or wrestling," suggests Luke.

"Wrestling?" I look at him indignantly. "Our child's not doing wrestling! It might hurt itself!"

"What if its destiny is to become the world's greatest-ever wrestler?" Luke raises his eyebrows. For a few moments I'm flummoxed.

"It's not," I say at last. "I'm its mother and I know."

"Mr. and Mrs. Brandon?" The receptionist calls over and we both look up. "Dr. Carter will see you now, if you'd like to go through."

I feel a flurry of nerves. OK, here I go. Stake my claim.

"Come on, darling!" I put my arm firmly round Luke's shoulders and we head down the corridor, me staggering slightly because I'm thrown off-balance.

"Hello, you guys!" Venetia is coming out of her room to greet us. She's dressed in black trousers and a sleeveless pink shirt cinched with the most fabulous shiny black crocodile belt. She kisses us both on each cheek and I catch a whiff of Chanel's Allure. "Great to see you again!"

"It's great to see you too, Venetia," I say, raising my eyebrow in an ironic if-you-have-any-plans-to-steal-my-husband-you-can-forget-about-them way.

"Marvelous. Come on in. . . ." She ushers us into the room.

I'm not sure she noticed my eyebrow maneuver. I might have to be more obvious.

Luke and I sit down, and Venetia perches on the front of her desk, dangling her Yves Saint Laurent heels. God, she's got a good wardrobe for a doctor. Or even not for a doctor.

"So. Becky." She opens her notes and studies them

for a moment. "First of all, we have the blood test results back. All your levels are fine . . . although we might want to watch that hemoglobin. How are you feeling?"

"I'm feeling great, thanks," I say at once. "Very happy, very *loving* . . . Here I am, in a wonderful marriage, expecting a baby . . . and I've never felt closer to Luke in my life." I reach out and grab Luke's hand. "Wouldn't you agree, darling? Aren't we particularly close at the moment? Spiritually, mentally, emotionally, and . . . and . . . sexually!"

There. Take that.

"Well . . . yes," says Luke, looking slightly stunned. "I suppose we are."

"That's lovely to hear, Becky," Venetia says, giving me a strange look. "Although I was really meaning your own physical state. Any faintness, nausea, that kind of thing?"

Oh, right.

"Er . . . no, thanks," I say. "I'm fine."

"Well, then. Let's pop you up and we can have a look." She gestures to the examination table and I obediently get up onto it. "Lie back, make sure you're comfortable. . . . Is that a little stretch mark I see?" she adds gaily as I lift up my top.

"A stretch mark?" In horror I grab the metal sidegrip and try to struggle up. "I can't have! I use a special oil every night, and a lotion in the morning, and—"

"Oops, my mistake!" says Venetia. "Just a stray fiber from your T-shirt."

"Oh." I collapse in slight posttraumatic shock and Venetia starts feeling my abdomen.

"Although, of course, stretch marks normally appear at the last minute," she adds conversationally. "So you may still get them. Those last few weeks of pregnancy can be cruel. I see my patients waddling in, desperate for their babies to be out...."

Waddling?

"I'm not going to waddle," I say with a little laugh.

"I'm afraid you will." She smiles back. "It's nature's way of slowing you down. I always think it's only fair to give my first-time patients a heads-up on the realities to come in pregnancy. It isn't all roses and sunshine, you know!"

"Absolutely," puts in Luke. "We appreciate that, don't we, Becky?"

"Yes," I mutter as Venetia wraps a blood pressure cuff round my arm.

This is a lie. I don't appreciate it. And just to make it crystal clear: I am *never* going to waddle.

"Blood pressure's just a little high...." She frowns at the screen. "Make sure you take it easy, Becky. Try to take a rest every day, or at least get the weight off your feet. And try to stay nice and calm...."

Stay calm? How am I supposed to do that when she's telling me I've got stretch marks and am going to waddle?

"Now, let's have a listen...." She smears some gel on my stomach and gets out the Doppler, and I relax a little. This is my favorite bit of every appointment. Lying back, listening to the baby's heartbeat going *wow, wow, wow* over the fuzzy background noise. Remembering that there's a little person in there.

"That all sounds fine...." Venetia moves away to the desk and scribbles something on her notes. "Oh, Luke, that reminds me—I spoke to Matthew the other day and he'd love to meet up. And I found that article by

Jeremy we were talking about. . . ." She rifles in her desk drawer and holds out an old copy of the *New Yorker.* "He's come such a long way since Cambridge. Have you read his book on Mao?"

"Not yet," says Luke, heading toward the desk and taking it from her. "I'll read this when I have time. Thanks."

"You must be busy," Venetia says sympathetically. She pours a glass of water from the cooler and offers one to Luke. "How are all the new offices working out?"

"Good." Luke nods. "The odd hiccup, of course . . ."

"But it's fabulous that you've got Arcodas as a client." She leans on the desk, frowning intelligently. "It *must* be the way forward, to diversify out of finance. And Arcodas's rate of expansion is phenomenal—I was reading a piece about it in the *FT.* Iain Wheeler sounds very impressive."

Er . . . hello?

They've completely abandoned me on my back, like an upturned beetle. I clear my throat loudly and Luke turns round.

"Sorry, sweetheart! Are you all right?" He hurries over and offers me a hand.

"Sorry, Becky!" says Venetia. "Just getting you some water. You seem a little dehydrated. It's vital to keep your fluids up. You should really be drinking at least eight glasses of water a day. Here you are."

"Thanks!" I smile at her as I take the glass, but as I sit down, suspicions are circulating darkly round my mind. Venetia's very chatty with Luke. *Too* chatty. And trying to make out I had a stretch mark. And the way she keeps flicking her hair about like a hair model in a TV ad. It's not exactly doctorly, is it?

"So!" Venetia is behind her desk again, writing on my notes. "Did you have any questions? Issues you'd like to raise?"

I glance at Luke, but he's pulled his phone out of his pocket. I can just hear the faint *bzzz* as it vibrates.

"Excuse me," he says. "I'll pop outside. Carry on without me." He gets up and leaves the room, closing the door behind him.

So it's just the two of us. Woman-to-woman. I can feel the room prickling with tension.

At least . . . it's prickling on my side.

"Becky?" Venetia shows her perfect white teeth in a smile. "Is there anything you'd like to talk about?"

"Not really," I reply pleasantly. "As I said, everything's fine. I'm fine. . . . Luke's fine. . . . Our relationship couldn't be better. . . . You know this is a honeymoon baby?" I can't resist adding.

"Yes, I heard all about your wonderful honeymoon!" Venetia exclaims. "Luke said you went to Ferrara while you were in Italy?"

"That's right." I give a reminiscent smile. "It was so romantic. We'll always share it as a wonderful memory."

"When Luke and I visited Ferrara, we couldn't tear ourselves away from those *fabulous* frescoes. I'm sure he told you?" Her eyes are all wide and innocent.

Luke and I never went to any frescoes in Ferrara. We sat at the same outdoor restaurant all afternoon, drinking Prosecco and eating the yummiest food I've ever had. And he never mentioned he'd been there before with Venetia. But *no way* am I admitting that to her.

"Actually, we didn't go to the frescoes," I say at last, examining my nails. "Luke told me all about them, of course. But he said he thought they were overrated."

"Overrated?" Venetia seems taken aback.

"Uh-huh." I fix my gaze dead on hers. "Overrated."

"But...he took masses of pictures of them." She gives an incredulous laugh. "We talked about them for hours!"

"Yes, well, we talked about them all night!" I shoot back. "About how overrated they are."

I casually fiddle with my wedding ring, making sure my engagement diamond glints under the lights.

I'm his wife. I know what he thinks about frescoes.

Venetia opens her mouth, then closes it again, looking flummoxed.

"Sorry about that!" Luke enters the room, putting his phone away, and Venetia immediately turns to him.

"Luke, d'you remember those frescoes in—"

"Ow!" I clutch my stomach. "Ouch."

"Becky! Darling!" Luke hurries to my side in alarm. "Are you all right?"

"Just a little twinge." I give him a brave smile. "I'm sure it's nothing to worry about." I glance in triumph at Venetia, who is frowning as though she can't quite work me out.

"Have you had these pains before?" she says. "Can you describe them?"

"They've gone now," I say blithely. "I think it was just a stitch."

"Let me know if you have any other pains," she says. "And remember to take things easy. That blood pressure shouldn't be a problem, but we don't want it to edge any higher. Did your previous doctor explain to you about preeclampsia?"

"Absolutely," Luke says, glancing at me, and I nod.

"Good. Well, you take care. You can call me any-time. And before you go..." Venetia opens her desk diary. "We *must* arrange an evening for us all to meet up. The twenty-fourth...or the twenty-sixth? Assuming I'm not delivering a baby, of course!"

"The twenty-sixth?" Luke nods, consulting his BlackBerry. "OK with you, Becky?"

"Fine!" I say sweetly. "We'll be there."

"Marvelous. I'll call some of the others. It's so great to have made contact again, after so many years." Venetia sighs and puts her pen down. "To be honest, it's been pretty hard, starting again in London. My old friends have their lives; they've moved on. Besides which, I don't always keep sociable hours, and Justin travels abroad a lot, of course." Her bright smile slips a little.

"Justin is Venetia's boyfriend," Luke explains to me.

The boyfriend. I'd almost forgotten he existed.

"Oh, right," I say politely. "What does he do?"

"He's a financier." Venetia reaches for a framed pic-ture of a dull-looking man in a suit, and as she surveys it her whole face lights up. "He's incredibly driven and motivated, a bit like Luke. I sometimes feel left behind when he's pursuing a deal. But what can I do? I love him."

"*Really?*" I say in surprise. Then I realize how that sounded. "I mean...er...great!"

"He's the reason I came to London." Her eyes are still fixed on the picture. "I met him at a party in L.A. and just fell hook, line, and sinker."

"You moved all this way?" I say, incredulous. "Just for him?"

"That's what love's about, surely? You do crazy things for no rhyme or reason." Venetia looks up, her green eyes shining. "If my job has taught me one thing, Becky, it's that love is the only thing. Human love. I see it every time I deliver a baby right into its mother's arms . . . every time I see a fresh, eight-week-old heart beating on the screen and watch the faces of its parents . . . every time my patients come back, second or third time around. It's love that makes the babies. And you know what? Nothing else matters."

Wow. I am totally blown away.

She's not after Luke, after all. She's in love with the boring guy! And to be honest, that little speech has practically got me in tears.

"You're so right," I say huskily, clutching Luke's arm. "Love is all that counts in this crazy, mixed-up world we call . . . the world."

I'm not sure that came out right, but who cares? I have completely misjudged Venetia. She's not a man-eater; she's a warm, beautiful, loving human being.

"I really hope Justin will be able to make the twenty-sixth." She finally puts the picture back in its place with a fond pat. "I'd love for you to meet him."

"Me too!" I say with genuine enthusiasm. "I'm looking forward to it."

"See you soon, Ven." Luke kisses Venetia. "Thanks very much."

"Bye, Becky." Venetia gives me a warm, friendly smile. "Oh, and I nearly forgot. I don't know if you'd be at all interested, but a journalist from *Vogue* called me up yesterday. They're doing a big feature on London's yummiest mummies-to-be and wanted me to put forward some names. I thought of you."

"Vogue?" I stare at her, frozen.

"You may not be interested, of course. It would involve a photo shoot of you in the baby's nursery, an interview, hair and makeup.... They'll provide designer maternity clothes...." She gives a vague shrug. "I don't know—is that your kind of thing?"

I'm practically hyperventilating. Is it my kind of thing? Is having my makeup done and wearing designer clothes and being in *Vogue*... my kind of thing?

"I think that's a yes," says Luke, looking at me in amusement.

"Great!" Venetia touches him on the hand. "Leave it to me. I'll fix it up."

Rebecca Brandon
37 Maida Vale Mansions
Maida Vale
London NW6 0YF

18 August 2003

Dear Fabia,

I just wanted to say how much we love your gorgeous, beautiful house. It's the Kate Moss of houses!!* In fact, it's so stunning, I think it deserves to appear in *Vogue*, don't you?

That reminds me of a teeny favor I wanted to ask. Coincidentally, I am being interviewed by *Vogue*—and I wondered if I could use the house for the photo shoot?

I also wondered if I could put up some personal props and say that Luke and I live there already? After all, we will by the time the magazine comes out . . . so it makes sense, really!

In return, if there is anything I can do for you or any fashion item you would like me to track down, I will be only too glad!

With very best wishes,

Becky Brandon

* Not in size, obviously.

FABIA PASCHALI

DATE: 19/8/03

TO: Rebecca Brandon

Becky,

1. Chloe Silverado bag, tan

2. Matthew Williamson purple beaded kaftan top, size 6

3. Olly Bricknell Princess shoes, green, size 39.

Fabia

Oxshott School for Girls

Marlin Road
Oxshott
Surrey
KT22 OJG

From the School Librarian
Mrs L Hargreaves

23 August 2003

Dear Becky,

How nice to hear from you after all these years, and I do indeed remember you as a pupil here. Who could forget the girl who started the "friendship handbags" craze of 1989?

I am delighted you are to appear in *Vogue*—and it is, as you say, a surprise. Though I must assure you, the teachers did not sit in the staff room, saying "I bet Becky Bloomwood never makes it into *Vogue*."

I will be sure to buy an issue, although I think it unlikely the headmistress will sanction buying an official commemorative copy for each pupil, as you suggest.

With very best wishes,

Lorna Hargreaves
Librarian

P.S. Do you still have a copy of *In the Fifth at Malory Towers*? There is a rather large fine on it.

NINE

I'M GOING to be in *Vogue*! Last week Martha, who is the girl writing the Yummiest Mummies-to-Be feature, rang up and we had the most brilliant long chat.

Maybe I did make up a few teeny things. Like my daily exercise regime. And having freshly crushed raspberries for breakfast every morning, and how I write poetry to my unborn child. (I can always get some out of a book.) Plus I've said we already live in the house on Delamain Road, because it sounds better than living in a flat.

But the point is, we *will* be living in it very soon. It's practically ours already. And the girl was really interested to hear about the his and hers nurseries. She said she thought they'd be a highlight of the shoot. A highlight!

"Becky?"

A voice cuts into my thoughts and I look up to see Eric heading across the floor toward me. Quickly I hide my lists under a MaxMara catalog and scan the shop floor to make sure there isn't some lurking customer I've missed. But there's no one. Trade hasn't exactly picked up in the last few days.

Truth be told, we've had yet another disaster. Some-one in marketing decided to start a "word on the street" campaign, hiring students to talk about The Look and hand out leaflets in cafés. Which would have been great if they hadn't handed them to a gang of shoplifters, who proceeded to come in and pinch the entire range of Benefit cosmetics. They were caught—but even so. The *Daily World* had a total field day, about how "The Look is so desperate, it's now inviting in convicted criminals."

The place feels emptier than ever, and to cap it all, five members of the staff resigned this week. No won-der Eric looks so grumpy.

"Where's Jasmine?" He glances around the personal shopping reception area.

"She's . . . in the stock room," I lie.

Actually, Jasmine is asleep on the floor in one of the dressing rooms. Her new theory is, since there's noth-ing to do at work, she might as well use the time to sleep and go clubbing at night. So far, it's working out pretty well.

"Well, it was you I wanted to see, anyway." He frowns. "I've just had the contract through for the Danny Kovitz deal. Very demanding, this friend of yours. He's specified first-class travel, a suite at Claridge's, a limo for his personal use, unlimited San Pellegrino 'stirred, to take the bubbles out' . . ."

I stifle a giggle. That is so typical of Danny.

"He's a big, important designer," I remind Eric. "Talented people all have their little quirks."

" 'For the duration of the creative process,' " Eric reads aloud, " 'Mr. Kovitz will require a bowl of at least ten inches in diameter, filled with jelly beans. No green ones.' I mean, what *is* this nonsense?" He flicks the paper in exasperation. "What's he expecting, that someone's just going to sit for hours, removing green jelly beans and disposing of them?"

Ooh. I love green jelly beans.

"I don't mind taking care of that," I say casually.

"Fine." Eric sighs. "Well, all I can say is, I hope all this effort and money is worth it."

"It will be!" I say, surreptitiously touching the wooden desk for luck. "Danny's the hottest designer around! He'll come up with something totally brilliant and directional and now. And everyone will flock to the store. I promise!"

I really, *really* hope I'm right.

As Eric stalks off again I wonder whether to call Danny and see if he's had any ideas yet. But before I can do so, my cell phone rings.

"Hello?"

"Hi," comes Luke's voice. "It's me."

"Oh, hi!" I lean back in my chair, ready to have a chat. "Hey, I've just been hearing about Danny's contract. You'll never guess what—"

"Becky, I'm afraid I can't make this afternoon."

"What?" My smile slips away.

This afternoon is our first prenatal class. It's the one that birth partners come to, and we do breathing and make friends for life. And Luke promised to be there. He *promised*.

"I'm sorry." He seems distracted. "I know I said I'd be there, but there's a . . . crisis at work."

"A *crisis*?" I sit up, concerned.

"Not a crisis," he amends at once. "It's just . . . something's happened which isn't so good. It'll be fine. Just a hiccup."

"What's happened?"

"Just . . . a minor internal dispute. I won't go into it. But I'm really sorry about this afternoon. I wanted to be there." He does sound genuinely torn up. There's no point getting cross with him.

"It's OK." I hide a sigh. "I'll be fine on my own."

"Couldn't someone else go with you? Suze, per-haps?"

That's an idea. I was Suze's birth partner, after all. We're pretty close friends. And it would be nice to have some company.

"Maybe." I nod. "So, will you still be all right for this evening?"

Tonight we're going out with Venetia and her boyfriend and all Luke's old friends from Cambridge. I've been really looking forward to it; in fact, I'm hav-ing my hair blow-dried especially.

"Hope so. I'll keep you posted."

"OK. See you later."

I ring off and am about to dial Suze's number, when I remember she's taking Ernie to some new playgroup this afternoon. So she won't be able to make it. I lean back in my chair, thinking hard. I could just go on my own; I mean, I'm not scared of a bunch of pregnant women, am I?

Or else . . .

I pick up my phone again and speed-dial a number.

"Hey, Mum," I say as soon as I get through. "Are you doing anything this afternoon?"

The prenatal class is being held in a house in Islington and is called Choices, Empowerment, Open Minds, which I think is a really good title. I *definitely* have an open mind. As I walk along the street toward the house, I see Mum pull up in her Volvo and park—after about eight attempts, a small crash with a dustbin, and the help of a lorry driver who gets out of his cab to guide her in.

"Hi, Mum!" I call as she gets out at last, looking a bit flustered. She's wearing smart white trousers, a navy blazer, and shiny patent loafers.

"Becky!" Her face lights up. "You look wonderful, darling. Come along, Janice!" She bangs on the car window. "I brought Janice along. You don't mind, do you, love?"

"Er... no," I say in surprise. "Of course not."

"She was at a loose end, and we thought we might go to Liberty's afterward to look at fabrics for the nursery. Dad's painted it yellow, but we haven't decided on curtains...." She glances at my bump. "Any inklings on whether it's a boy or a girl?"

My mind flicks to the Gender Predictor Kit, still hidden in my underwear drawer three weeks after I bought it. I keep getting it out, then losing my nerve and putting it back. Maybe I need Suze as moral support.

"Not really," I say. "Not yet."

The passenger door opens and Janice gets out, trailing a bundle of knitting.

"Becky, love!" she says breathlessly. "Do you need to bleep the door, Jane?"

"Close it, *then* I'll bleep it," orders Mum. "Give it a good slam."

I can see a pregnant girl in a brown dress ringing the

bell of a house several doors down. That must be the place!

"I was just listening to a message from Tom," Janice says, bundling her knitting into a straw bag, together with a mobile phone. "I'm seeing him later. He'll be full of Jess! It's Jess this, Jess that—"

"Jess?" I stare at her. "And Tom?"

"Of course!" Her whole face is shining. "They do make a lovely couple. I don't want to hope, but..."

"Now, remember, Janice," says Mum firmly. "You can't chivvy these young things."

Jess and Tom are going out? And she hasn't even told me? *Honestly.* I asked her the morning after the party what was going to happen with Tom, and she just looked all embarrassed and changed the subject. So I assumed it hadn't taken.

I can't help feeling a bit miffed. The whole point of having a sister is that you phone her up and tell her about your new boyfriend. Not keep her totally out of the loop.

"So...Jess and Tom are in a relationship?" I say, to make sure.

"They're very close." Janice nods vigorously. "Very, very close. And I have to say, Jess is a super girl. We get on like a house on fire!"

"Really?" I try not to sound too surprised, but I can't see Janice and Jess having much in common.

"Oh yes! We all feel like family. In fact, Martin and I have put off our cruise next summer, just in case we have a—" She breaks off. "Wedding," she whispers.

Wedding?

OK. I need to talk to Jess. Now.

"Here we are," says Mum as we approach the door,

which has a sign on it: PLEASE ENTER AND REMOVE YOUR SHOES.

"What exactly happens at a prenatal class?" asks Janice, slipping off her Kurt Geiger sandals.

"Breathing and stuff," I say vaguely. "Preparing for the birth."

"It's all changed since our day, Janice," puts in Mum. "They have childbirth coaches these days!"

"Coaches! Like tennis players!" Janice seems tickled by this idea. Then her smile drops and she clasps my arm. "Poor little Becky. You have no idea what you're letting yourself in for."

"Right," I say, a bit spooked. "Well...er...shall we go in?"

The class is being held in what looks like a normal sitting room with beanbags arranged in a circle, on which several pregnant women are already sitting, with their husbands awkwardly perched beside them.

"Hello." A slim woman with long dark hair and yoga trousers comes over. "I'm Noura, your prenatal teacher," she says in a quiet voice. "Welcome."

"Hi, Noura!" I beam at her and shake hands. "I'm Becky Brandon. This is my mum...and this is Janice."

"Ah." Noura nods knowingly and takes Janice's hand. "It's a real pleasure to meet you, Janice. You're Becky's...partner? We have another same-sex couple coming later on, so please don't feel—"

Oh my God! She thinks—

"We're not lesbians!" I cut her off hurriedly, trying not to giggle at Janice's bemused expression. "Janice is just our neighbor. She's going to Liberty's with Mum afterward."

"Oh, I see." Noura seems a bit let down. "Well, welcome, the three of you. Take a seat."

"Janice and I will get the coffees," says Mum, heading toward a table at the side of the room. "You sit down, Becky love."

"So, Becky," says Noura as I lower myself gingerly onto a beanbag. "We're going round the room, introducing ourselves. Laetitia has just explained she's having a home birth. Where are you having your baby, Becky?"

"With Venetia Carter at the Cavendish," I say, trying to sound nonchalant.

"Wow," says a girl in a pink dress. "Doesn't she do all the celebrities?"

"Yes. Actually, she's a really close friend," I can't resist adding. "We're going out tonight."

"And have you considered what kind of birth you would like?" continues Noura.

"I'm having the water birth with lotus flowers and Thai massage," I say proudly.

"Wonderful!" Noura marks something on her list. "So you'd ideally like an active birth?"

"Er..." I picture myself lolling in a nice warm pool, with music playing and lotus flowers floating about, and maybe a cosmopolitan in my hand. "No, I think probably quite inactive, actually."

"You want an...inactive birth?" Noura appears nonplussed.

"Yes." I nod. "Ideally."

"And pain relief?"

"I've got a special Maori birthing stone," I say confidently. "And I've done yoga. So I'll probably be OK."

"I see." Noura looks as though she wants to add something else. "Right," she says at last. "Well. There are birth plan forms in front of you and I'd like everyone to fill one in. We'll take all the ideas as points of discussion."

There's a murmuring as everyone picks up their pencils and begins to chat to their partners.

"I'd also love to hear from Becky's mother and Janice," Noura adds, as Mum and Janice rejoin the group. "It's a privilege to hear from older women who have been through birth and motherhood and can share their wisdom."

"Of course, dear! We'll tell you all about it." Mum gets out a packet of mints. "Polo? Polo, anyone?"

I pick up my pencil, then put it down again. I must just quickly text Jess and find out what's going on. I take out my phone, find her cell number, and type out a text.

OMG Jess!!! R U going out w Tom????

Then I delete it. Too excited. She'll get all freaked out and never reply.

Hi Jess. How R U doing? Bex

That's better. I press Send and turn my attention back to the birth plan. It's a list of questions, with space to fill in answers.

1. What are your priorities in early labor?

I think hard for a moment, then write: "Look good."

2. How will you cope with pain in the early stages (e.g., warm bath, rock on all fours)

I'm about to write "Go shopping," when my mobile pings. It's a text back from Jess!

Fine, thanks. Jess

That is *so* Jess. Two words, giving nothing away. I immediately text back.

Are you seeing Tom??

"Sheets in, everybody." Noura's clapping her hands. "If you could all stop writing..."

Already? God, this is like a school test. I hand my paper in last, pushing it into the middle so Noura won't see it. But she's leafing through all of them, nodding as she reads. Then she stops.

"Becky, under 'priorities in early labor' you've put 'Look good.'" She raises her head. "Is that a joke?"

Why is everyone staring at me? Of course it's not a joke.

"If you look good, you feel good! It's natural pain-relief. We should all have makeovers or get our hair done...."

I'm getting frowns and titters from around the room, all except a girl in a fab pink top, who's nodding in agreement.

"See you there!" she says. "I'd rather do that than rock on all fours."

"Or go shopping," I add. "It cures morning sickness, so—"

"Shopping cures *morning sickness*?" Noura interrupts me. "What are you talking about?"

"Whenever I felt sick in the first few weeks, I used to go to Harrods and buy a little something to take my mind off it," I explain. "It really worked."

"I used to order stuff online," agrees the girl in pink.

"You could add it to your list of remedies, maybe," I suggest helpfully. "After ginger tea."

Noura opens her mouth, then closes it again. She turns to another girl, who has her hand up, just as my phone beeps with another text.

> Kind of. J

Kind of? What does kind of mean? I quickly type.

> Janice thinks U R getting married!
> Bex

I press Send. Ha. That'll wind her up.

"OK. Let's move on." Noura is in the center of the room again. "From glancing through these answers, it's clear that a lot of you are concerned by the thought of labor and how you'll cope with it." She looks around the group. "My first response is: don't worry. You *can* cope. All of you."

A nervous laugh goes around the room.

"Yes, contractions can be intense," Noura continues. "But your bodies are designed to withstand them. And what you must remember is, it's a *positive* pain. I'm sure you'll both agree?" She looks over at Mum and Janice, who has got out her knitting and is clicking away.

"*Positive*?" Janice looks up, horrified. "Ooh no, dear.

Mine was agony. Twenty-four hours in the cruel summer heat. I wouldn't wish it on any of you poor girls."

"They have better drugs these days," chimes in Mum. "My advice is take everything they've got."

"But there are natural, instinctive methods you can use," Noura puts in quickly. "I'm sure you found that rocking and changing position helped with the contractions?"

Mum and Janice exchange doubtful glances.

"I wouldn't have said so," says Mum kindly.

"Or a warm bath?" Noura suggests, her smile tightening.

"A bath?" Mum laughs merrily. "Dear, when you're gripped by agony and wanting to die, a bath doesn't really help!"

I can tell Noura's getting a bit frustrated, by the way she's breathing more deeply and balling her hands into fists.

"But it was worth it in the end? The pain seemed a small price to pay, compared to the life-affirming joy?"

"Well..." Mum gives me a doubtful glance. "Of course, I was delighted to have my little Becky. But I did keep it at the one child. We both did, didn't we, Janice?"

"Never again." Janice shudders. "Not if you paid me a million pounds."

As I glance around the room I can see that all the girls' faces have frozen. Most of the men's too.

"Right!" says Noura, making an obvious effort to stay pleasant. "Well, thank you for those...inspirational words."

"No trouble!" Janice waves her knitting cheerily.

"We're going to try a small breathing exercise now,"

Noura continues, "which, believe it or not, *will* help with the contractions of early labor. I want you all to sit up straight and do some shallow breaths. In...out... that's right...."

As I'm doing my shallow breaths, there's a ping from my mobile.

What?????

Ha! I stifle a giggle and text back.

Is it love???

A few moments later my phone pings again with a new message.

We're having a few problems.

Oh God. I hope Jess is OK. I didn't mean to tease her.

It's quite tricky, doing shallow breathing *and* texting at the same time. So I abandon the shallow breathing and type.

What problems? Why didn't u tell me?

"Who are you texting, love?" says Janice, who has also abandoned shallow breathing and is consulting her knitting pattern.

"Oh...just a friend," I say lightly as another text arrives. Jess must have abandoned whatever she's doing too.

```
I didn't want to bother you, it's
stupid.
```

Honestly. How can Jess think she's bothering me? I *want* to know about her love life. I start texting U R my sister!!! when Noura claps her hands for attention.

"Relax, everyone. Now, we're going to try a simple exercise, which should put your minds at rest. Your partner is going to take your arm and twist it, giving you an old-fashioned Chinese burn. And you are going to breathe *through* the pain. Focus your minds, stay relaxed. . . . Partners, don't be afraid to increase the pressure! And you'll see how you're a lot tougher than you thought! Becky, I'll take you, if that's OK?" she adds, coming over.

My stomach flips nervously. I don't like the sound of an old-fashioned Chinese burn. Or even a newfangled one. But I can't wimp out; everyone's looking at me.

"All right, then," I say, gingerly holding out my arm.

"Obviously the pain of labor will be more intense than this, but just to give you an idea . . ."

She grasps my forearm. "Now *breathe*. . . ."

"Ow!" I say as she suddenly twists my arm. "Ow, that *hurts*!"

"Breathe, Becky," instructs Noura. "Relax."

"I am breathing! Owwwww!"

"The pain's getting stronger now. . . ." Noura ignores me. "Imagine the contraction is peaking. . . ."

I'm panting hard as she twists my skin even harder.

"And now it's ebbing . . . it's gone." She releases my arm and gives me a smile. "You see, Becky? You see how you coped with that, despite your fears?"

"Wow." I'm almost breathless.

"Do you think you learned something valuable there?" She gives me a knowing look. "Something that puts your fears into perspective?"

"Yes." I nod earnestly. "I learned I *definitely* want an epidural."

"Have a general anesthetic, darling," interjects Mum. "Or a nice cesarean!"

"You can't *have a general anesthetic*." Noura stares at her incredulously. "They don't just hand them out, you know!"

"Becky's going to the top place in London!" Mum retorts. "She can have anything she wants! Now, darling, if I were you, I'd have the Thai massage and the water birth *before* labor begins, then the epidural and aromatherapy to follow...."

"This is *labor*!" Noura shouts, clutching her hair. "You're having a baby, not ordering from a bloody room-service menu!"

There's a shocked silence.

"I'm sorry," she says, more calmly. "I ... don't know what came over me. Let's have a short break. Help yourselves to drinks."

She heads out of the room, and a muted babble of chatter breaks out.

"Well!" says Mum, raising her eyebrows. "I think someone needs to do their shallow breathing! Janice, shall we go to Liberty now?"

"Just let me finish this row...." Janice clicks frantically with her knitting needles. "There! All done. Coming, Becky?"

"I dunno," I say, torn. "Maybe I should stay to the end of the class."

"I don't think that Noura knows what she's talking

about!" Mum says conspiratorially. "*We'll* tell you everything you need to know. And you can help me choose a new handbag!"

"OK, then." I get to my feet. "Let's go!"

By the time I've finished shopping with Mum and Janice and had my hair appointment, it's gone six. I arrive home to find Luke in the study. The lights are off, and he's just sitting there in the gloom.

"Luke?" I put my bags down. "Is everything OK?"

He starts at my voice, and raises his head. I peer at him in surprise. His face is taut, with a deep crease between his brows. "It's fine," he says at last. "Everything's fine."

It doesn't sound like it's fine to me. I come into the study, perch on the desk opposite him, and study his face.

"Luke, what was the crisis at work today?"

"It's not a *crisis.*" He musters a smile. "I used the wrong word. It was just...an incident. Nothing important. It's all been resolved."

"But—"

"How are you?" He strokes my arm. "How was the class?"

"Oh." I cast my mind back. "Er...it was fine. You didn't miss much. Then I went shopping with Mum and Janice. We went to Liberty's and Browns...."

"You haven't been overdoing it?" He surveys me with concern. "Did you take a rest? Remember what Venetia said about your blood pressure?"

"I'm fine!" I wave an arm in the air. "Never felt better!"

"Well." Luke glances at his watch. "We should be going soon. I'll take a quick shower and call a taxi." His voice is cheerful enough, but as he gets up I notice a tense set to his shoulders.

"Luke . . ." I hesitate. "Everything's all right, isn't it?"

"Becky. Don't worry." Luke takes both my hands in his. "Everything's fine. We have little crises every day. It's the nature of the job; you know it is. We deal with them and we move on. Maybe I am more preoccupied than usual. I'm just very busy right now."

"Well . . . OK," I say, mollified. "Go and have your shower."

He heads down the corridor to our bedroom and I dump my bags in the hall. I am quite tired, actually, after my afternoon with Mum and Janice. Maybe I'll have a shower too, after Luke's finished. I could use my revitalizing rosemary gel and do some invigorating yoga stretches.

Or else I could have a quick Kit Kat. I go into the kitchen and am just getting the box down, when the doorbell rings. That can't be the taxi already.

"Hello?" I say into the intercom.

"Hi, Becky?" A crackly voice comes back. "It's Jess." Jess?

I press the buzzer in astonishment. What's Jess doing here? I didn't even know she was in London.

"The taxi's booked for fifteen minutes' time." Luke puts his head round the kitchen door, wearing only a towel.

"You'd better get some clothes on," I say. "Jess is just coming up in the lift!"

"Jess?" Luke looks taken aback. "We weren't expecting her, were we?"

"No." I hear the gentle chime of the doorbell to our apartment and start giggling. "Quick, get dressed!"

I swing the door open to see Jess, dressed in jeans, sneakers, and a tight brown tank top, which actually looks quite cool in a seventies, retro way.

"Hi!" She gives me a stiff hug. "How are you, Becky? I've been seeing my tutor, and I thought I'd drop by. I tried ringing, but the line was busy. Is it OK?"

She looks slightly nervous. Honestly! As if I'm going to say no, it's not, go away.

"Of course!" I warmly clasp her back. "It's fab to see you. Come on in!"

"I brought a present for the baby." She reaches in her rucksack and pulls out a brown romper, with *I Will Not Pollute the World* printed on the front in beige.

"Er...fab!" I say, turning it over in my fingers. "Thanks!"

"It's made of natural hemp," Jess says. "Are you still planning an all-hemp wardrobe for the baby?"

All-hemp? What on earth is she—

Oh. Maybe I did say something like that at Mum's party, just to stop her lecturing me about evil bleached cotton.

"I'm going...part hemp, part other fabrics," I say at last. "For...er...biodiversity."

"Excellent." She nods. "And I meant to say, I can get you a changing table on loan. There's a women's student cooperative which lends out baby equipment and toys. I've brought the number."

"Right!" I quickly kick the door of the nursery shut before she spots my Circus Tent changing station with integrated puppet show, which arrived yesterday from

Funky Baba. "I'll . . . bear that in mind. Come and have a drink."

"Have you made the baby wipes yet?" Jess follows me into the kitchen.

Not the baby wipes again. I can't tell her I threw all the rags away at Mum's house.

"Er, not yet . . ." I hastily cast around. "But I've done some other stuff." I grab a striped tea towel from the rack and tie a knot in the end. "This is a homemade organic toy," I say casually, turning round. "It's called Knotty."

"That's great." Jess examines it. "What a simple concept. Far better than any manufactured rubbish."

"And I'm planning to . . . paint this spoon with non-toxic natural paint." Feeling emboldened, I take a wooden spoon from the drawer. "I'll give it a face and call it Spoony."

God, I'm good at this eco-recycling lark. Maybe I'll start my own newsletter!

"Anyway, let me get you a drink." I pour Jess a glass of wine and plonk down opposite her. "So. What's going on? I couldn't *believe* it when Janice said you were going out with Tom!"

"I know," says Jess. "I'm sorry, I should have told you. But it's been so . . ." She breaks off.

"What?" I say, agog. Jess is staring into her glass without drinking.

"It's not really working out," she says at last.

"Why not?"

Jess is silent again. She hasn't really cracked this whole talking-about-boyfriends thing, has she?

"Go on," I cajole. "Everything you say is totally safe with me. I mean . . . you do *like* him, don't you?"

"Of course I do. But..." She exhales. "It's just..."

"Becky?" Luke puts his head round the door. "Oh, hi, Jess. I don't want to break things up, but we should be going soon...."

"You have plans," says Jess, stiffening. "I'll go."

"No!" I put a hand on her arm. The one time Jess ever drops in on me and asks my advice, I'm *not* sending her away. This is exactly what I imagined us doing when I first met her. Two sisters, popping round to each other's places, talking about boys....

"Luke." I make a snap decision. "Why don't you go on ahead and I'll join you at the bar?"

"Well, if you're sure." Luke kisses me. "Good to see you, Jess!"

He heads out of the kitchen and as I hear the front door close I rip open a mini-packet of Pringles. "So. You like him...."

"He's great." Jess is fiddling with the rough skin on one of her fingers. "He's bright, and interesting; he has sound views...and he's good-looking. I mean, that goes without saying."

"Absolutely!" I say after a pause.

To be honest, Tom has never done it for me. (Despite Janice and Martin's conviction that I've been hopelessly in love with him my whole life.) But to each their own.

"So the problem is..." I circle my hands, prompting her.

"He's so *needy*. He calls me about ten times a day; he sends cards covered with kisses...." Jess looks up with a disparaging expression and I can't help feeling a bit sorry for poor old Tom. "Last week he tried to get my name tattooed on his arm. He phoned me to tell me he was doing it, and I got so angry, he stopped after *J*."

"He's got a *J* on his arm?" I can't help giggling.

"Up near his elbow." She rolls her eyes. "It looks ridiculous."

"Well, maybe he was trying to look cool," I suggest. "You know, Lucy wanted him to get a tattoo but he wouldn't. He probably just wanted to impress you."

"Well, I'm not impressed. And as for Janice..." Jess thrusts her fingers through her cropped hair. "She rings me up nearly every day on some pretense or other. Have I had any thoughts about Tom's Christmas present? Do I want to join them on a wine-tasting weekend to France? I've really had enough of it. So I'm thinking of ending it."

I look up in dismay. *Ending* it? But what about the baby being a ring-bearer?

"You can't give up just because of a few little details!" I protest. "I mean, apart from the tattoo, are you getting on OK? Do you ever argue?"

"We had a pretty big argument the other day." Jess nods as she says it.

"About what?"

"Social policy."

Oh, this just proves it. They're made for each other!

"Jess, talk to Tom," I say on impulse. "I bet you can work things out. Just for the sake of a tattoo..."

"It's not just that." Jess wraps her arms round her knees. "There's... something else."

"What is it?"

With an intake of breath, it hits me. She's pregnant too. It has to be. God, how cool! We'll have babies together and they'll be cousins and we'll take cute pictures of them playing in the grass together. . . .

"I've been offered a two-year research project in Chile." Jess's voice pricks my bubble.

"Chile?" My mouth drops open in dismay. "But that's . . . miles away."

"Seven thousand," she says, nodding.

"So . . . are you going to go?"

"I haven't decided. But it's a fantastic opportunity. It's a team I've wanted to join for years."

"Right," I say after a short silence. "Well, then . . . you should go."

I have to be supportive. This is Jess's career. But I can't help feeling a bit doleful. I've only just got to know my long-lost sister, and now she's disappearing off to the other side of the world?

"I've pretty much decided that I will." She raises her head and I find myself looking right into her speckly hazel eyes. I've always thought Jess had pretty eyes.

Maybe the baby will have speckly hazel eyes just like that.

"You'll have to send me lots of pictures of my niece or nephew," says Jess, as though reading my mind. "So I can see it grow up."

"Of course! Every week." I bite my lip, trying to digest all this. "So . . . what about Tom?"

"I haven't told him yet." She hunches her shoulders. "But it'll mean the end for us."

"Not necessarily! You could have a long-distance relationship. . . . There's always e-mail. . . ."

"For *two years*?"

"Well . . ." I trail off. Maybe she's right. They met

only a few weeks ago. And two years is a pretty long time.

"I can't give up a chance like this for some . . . *man*." She sounds like she's arguing with herself. Maybe she's more torn than she's letting on. Maybe, underneath it all, she really has fallen for Tom.

But even I can see it. Jess's work has been her life. She can't just abandon it now.

"You have to go to Chile," I say firmly. "It'll be amazing for you. And it'll work out with Tom. Somehow."

The Pringles seem to have disappeared, so I get up and head for the cupboard. I open the door and survey the shelves dubiously. "We're out of chips. . . . I'm not supposed to eat nuts. . . . We've got some old Ritz crackers. . . ."

"Actually, I brought some popcorn," says Jess, looking a bit pink about the face. "Toffee flavored."

"You what?" I gape at her.

"It's in my rucksack."

Jess brought toffee flavored popcorn? But . . . that's not organic. Or nutritious. Or made from farm-cooperative potatoes.

I stare in astonishment as she reaches inside her rucksack for the packet. A DVD comes out too, all shiny in its cellophane, and she stuffs it back, her cheeks reddening further.

Hang on a moment.

"What's that?" I grab it. "*Nine Months?* Jess, that's not your kind of film!"

Jess looks totally caught out.

"I thought it might be your kind of film," she says at last. "Especially now."

"You brought this for us to watch together?" I say incredulously, and after a moment she nods.

"I just thought..." She clears her throat. "If you were at a loose end..."

I cannot believe how touched I feel. The first time we ever spent an evening together I tried to get Jess to watch *Pretty Woman,* and believe me, it was not a success. But now here she is with popcorn and a Hugh Grant film. And telling me about her boyfriend. Just like I imagined having a sister would be like.

"But you have to go out." Jess is shoving the DVD back into the rucksack. "In fact, you should get going...."

I feel a rush of affection for her—and all of a sudden I don't want to go anywhere. Why would I spend the evening in some crowded bar, talking to a lot of snobby Cambridge graduates I don't even know, when I could be spending time with my sister? I can meet Venetia's Mr. Wonderful some other time. Luke won't mind.

"I'm not going anywhere," I say firmly, and tear open the popcorn. "Let's stay in and have fun."

We have the best evening. We watch *Nine Months*— Jess does Sudoku puzzles at the same time, but that's OK because I'm reading *Hello!* magazine—and we conference-call Suze to ask her advice on Tom, and then we order pizza. And Jess doesn't even tell me how we could have made our own for 30p.

She leaves around eleven, saying that I must be tired, and I go to bed, wondering how late Luke will be. He must be having a good time too, to be out this long. When at last a stripe of light from the doorway lands on my face and makes me blink, I realize I must have fallen asleep, because I could have sworn I was receiving an Oscar from the Queen.

"Hi!" I sit up sleepily. "What time is it?"

"Just gone one," whispers Luke. "I'm sorry I woke you."

"It's OK." I reach for the bedside light and switch it on. "So, how was it?"

"It was good!" There's an enthusiasm in Luke's voice that I wasn't expecting. I rub my bleary eyes and focus on him. His face is glowing and he has a kind of lightness and animation about him which I haven't seen in weeks, if not months. He strips off his tie and throws it on a chair. "I'd forgotten how much I had in common with all these old friends," he says. "We talked about things I haven't even thought about for years. Politics...the arts...My old friend Matthew runs a gallery now. He invited us to an exhibition. We should go!"

"Wow!" I can't help smiling at Luke's eagerness. "How fantastic!"

"It was great, just taking a break from business." He shakes his head wonderingly. "I should do it more. Get things in perspective. Relax a bit." He starts unbuttoning his shirt. "So, how was your evening with Jess?"

"It was fab! We watched a movie and ate pizza. And I have to tell you her news...." I suddenly yawn. "Maybe tomorrow." I snuggle back down into the pillows and watch Luke get undressed. "So, what's Venetia's famous boyfriend like? Is he as boring as he looks in the picture?"

"He wasn't there," Luke says, hanging up his suit trousers.

I stop comfortably snuggling and turn my head in surprise. Venetia's boyfriend wasn't there? But I thought the whole point of the evening was to introduce us to Justin the wonder-boy financier.

"Oh, right. How come?"

"They've split up."

"They've *split up*?" I haul myself to a sitting position in bed. "But . . . I thought she loved Justin more than anyone else. I thought she moved halfway across the world to be with him and they were the happiest couple in the whole universe."

"She did." Luke shrugs. "They were. Until three days ago. She was pretty upset about it."

"Right," I say after a pause. "I see."

Suddenly the evening has taken on a totally different slant. It wasn't Luke being introduced to Venetia's long-term boyfriend. It was a newly single Venetia crying on Luke's shoulder.

"So . . . did Venetia break it off?" I ask casually. "Or did he?"

"I'm not sure which of them ended it." Luke heads into the bathroom. "Apparently he's gone back to his wife now."

"His *wife*?" My voice shoots up like a rocket. "What do you mean, 'his wife'?"

"Venetia thought they were separated in all but name." Luke turns on the taps and I can barely hear him. "She's had a tough time, romantically, poor old Ven. She always seems to fall for married men and get into complicated situations."

I'm trying to stay calm here. Shallow breaths. Do not overreact.

"What kind of situations?" I ask lightly.

"Oh, I don't know." Luke is squeezing toothpaste onto his brush. "Divorce proceedings . . . some scandal with a senior doctor at the hospital where she worked . . . There was an injunction in LA. . . ." He frowns at the tube. "We're nearly out of this stuff."

Divorce proceedings? Injunctions? Scandals?

I can't reply. My mouth is opening and shutting like a goldfish. Every instinct in my body is on red alert.

She's after Luke.

I watch Luke cleaning his teeth as though with Venetia's eyes. He's wearing only pajama bottoms, and he's still tanned from the summer, and the muscles of his shoulders are rippling faintly as he brushes. Oh God, oh God. Of *course* she's after him. He's good-looking and he owns a multimillion-pound company and they had a romance when they were much younger. Maybe he was her first love and she's never given her heart to anyone else.

Maybe she was *his* first love.

There's a hollow kind of feeling in my stomach. Which is ridiculous, bearing in mind how much is in my stomach right now.

"So!" I try to sound confident and lighthearted. "Do I need to be worried?"

Luke's splashing water on his face. "What do you mean?"

"I . . ." I can't bring myself to say it. What am I implying, that I don't trust him? "She could maybe try going after single men!" I change tack. "Then life wouldn't be so complicated for her!" I give a small laugh, but as Luke turns, he's frowning.

"Venetia's made some . . . unwise choices. But none

of them were deliberate or out of malice. She's just a hopeless romantic."

He's defending her. I feel totally wrong-footed.

A bleep suddenly comes from Luke's jacket. He comes out of the bathroom, drying his face, and takes his phone out of his pocket.

"It's a text from Venetia." He looks at it and smiles. "Look. It's a picture of this evening."

I take the phone from him and study the display. There's Venetia, dressed for off duty in long, rangy jeans, a leather jacket, and high, spiky boots. She's gazing at the camera with a confident smile, her arm round Luke like she owns him.

Home-wrecker flashes through my brain before I can stop it.

Well, she's not wrecking this home. No way. Luke and I have been through a lot over the years, and it'll take more than some swishy-haired, spiky-heeled doctor to break us up. I'm 110 percent confident.

Mrs R Brandon
37 Maida Vale Mansions
Maida Vale
London NW6 0YF

10 September 2003

Dear Mrs. Brandon,
I regret to inform you that your application to found
an online bank, "Becky's Online Bank for Girls," has
been turned down by the committee.

There were many grounds for the decision, in
particular your statement that to run an online bank
"you just need a computer and somewhere to put all
the money."

I wish you success in any further ventures, but
suggest that banking is not one of them.

Yours sincerely,

John Franklin
Internet Business Committee

TEN

MAYBE I'M NOT *110* percent confident. Maybe just 100 percent.

Or even...95.

It's a few weeks since Luke went out for that evening with Venetia, and my confidence has wobbled ever so slightly. It's not that anything has *happened,* exactly. On the surface, Luke and I are as happy as ever and nothing's wrong. It's just that...

Well, OK. Here is my evidence so far:

1) Luke keeps getting texts and smiling and sending replies straight back. And I know they're from her. And he never shows them to me.

2) He's been out with her three more times. *Without me.* One time when I'd already arranged to meet Suze, he said he might as well use the evening to see some friends, and it turned out the "friends" was Venetia. Once with all the Cambridge gang at some big fancy dinner with their old tutor, where partners weren't invited. And once for lunch, which was apparently because she was going to be "right by his office." Yeah, right. Delivering a baby in an office block?

That was when we had our teeny row, where I said

(very lightly), that wow, he was spending a lot of time with Venetia—maybe too much? Whereupon Luke replied that she was feeling low right now and needed an old friend to talk to. So I said, "Well, I feel low too when you go off partying without me!" And Luke said that meeting up with his old university friends had been the highlight of his year, and it was his chance to switch off and if I came along too, I'd understand. So I said, "I'd come if you'd *invite* me." And he said he *had* invited me, and I said—

Anyway. We said a few things.

That's all the evidence I have. I don't even know why I'm calling it evidence—it's not like I think something's actually going on. I mean . . . it's a ludicrous idea. This is Luke I'm talking about. My *husband*.

"I can't believe anything's happening, Bex." Suze shakes her head and stirs her raspberry and apricot smoothie. She's come over for the morning so we can do the gender predictor test, but so far all we've done is talk about Luke. Luckily the children are all in the living room, eating sandwiches and watching *Teletubbies* in a total trance (which Suze let them do only after I swore an oath never, ever to tell Lulu).

"I can't believe it either!" I spread my arms wide. "But they see each other all the time, and she's always texting him, and I have no idea what they talk about. . . ."

"Did you stake your claim?" Suze takes a bite of chocolate-chip cookie. "Last time you saw her?"

"Totally! But she didn't take any notice."

"Hmm." Suze ponders for a while. "Have you thought about going to another doctor?"

"I keep thinking about it. But I don't think it would make any difference. She's already made contact with

Luke, hasn't she? In fact, she'd probably love to get me out of the picture."

"And what does Luke say?"

"Oh well." I start fiddling with my straw. "He says she's all lonely and vulnerable since she split up from her boyfriend. He behaves like she's this poor tragic victim. And he always takes her side. I called her Cruella de Venetia the other day and he got really cross."

"Cruella de Venetia." Suze splutters cookie crumbs over the counter. "That's good."

"It's not good! We ended up having an argument! She's this . . . *presence* in our life, even though I never see her."

"Don't you have appointments with her?" Suze looks surprised.

"I have, but the last two times I've been to the clinic she was with a client in labor, and I got seen by one of her assistant doctors."

"She's avoiding you." Suze gives a knowing nod and slurps on her straw, her brow furrowed. "Bex, I know this is a really dreadful thing to suggest . . . but what about looking at Luke's texts?"

"I already have," I admit.

"And?" Suze looks agog.

"They're in Latin."

"Latin?"

"They both studied Latin at university," I say resent-fully. "It's their 'thing.' I don't understand a word of it. But I wrote one down." I reach in my pocket and un-furl a small bit of paper. "This is it."

We both look at the words in silence.

Fac me laetam: mecum hodie bibe!

"I don't like the sound of that," says Suze at last.

"Nor do I."

We both regard the words for a few moments longer, then Suze sighs and pushes the paper back toward me. "Bex, I hate to say it...but you should be on your guard. In fact, you should strike back. If she can spend all this time with Luke, then so can you. When was the last time you did something romantic, just the two of you?"

"Dunno. Not for ages."

"Well, then!" Suze slaps the table triumphantly. "Go to his office and take him out for lunch as a surprise. He'd love that."

That's a good idea. I never want to bother Luke at work, because he's so busy. But if Venetia can do it, then why can't I?

"OK, I'll try it," I say, cheering up. "And I'll let you know how it goes. Thanks, Suze." I drain my smoothie and put my glass down with a flourish. "So."

"So." Suze meets my eyes. "Are you ready?"

"I think so." I feel a squirm of nerves. "Let's go!"

I pull the gender predictor box toward me along the counter and tug at the plastic wrapping, my hands trembling a little. In a matter of minutes I'll know. This is almost as exciting as the birth itself!

I secretly think it's a boy. Or maybe a girl.

"Hey, Bex, wait," says Suze suddenly. "How will you fool Luke?"

"What do you mean?"

"When they deliver the baby! How will you convince him you didn't know the sex beforehand?"

I stop ripping at the plastic. That's a good point.

"I'll just act surprised," I say at last. "I'm really good

at acting—look." I put on my most astonished expression. "It's a . . . boy!"

Suze pulls a face. "Bex, that was terrible!"

"I wasn't ready," I say hastily. "Let's try again." I concentrate for a moment, then gasp. "It's a girl!"

Suze is shaking her head and wincing. "Totally fake! Bex, you need to get *into* your character. You need to use some Method."

Oh no. Here we go. Suze went to drama school for a term before university, so she thinks she's practically Judi Dench. (It wasn't a real drama school, like RADA. It was a private one where your father pays and you do cooking in the afternoon. But we don't mention that.)

"Stand up," she instructs me. "Do some loosening-up exercises. . . ." She rolls her head around and shakes out her arms. Reluctantly, I copy her. "Now, what's your motivation?"

"Fooling Luke," I remind her.

"No! Your *interior* motivation. Your *character*." Suze closes her eyes for a moment, as if communing with the spirits. "You're a new mother. You're seeing your baby for the first time. You're delighted . . . yet surprised. . . . The sex is not what you expected. . . . You've never been so amazed in your *life*. . . . Really *feel* it. . . ."

"It's . . . a *boy*!" I clutch at my chest. Suze is whirling her arms at me.

"More, Bex! Again, with passion!"

"It's a boy! My God, it's a BOY!!!" My voice resounds around the kitchen, and a spoon falls off the counter onto the floor.

"Hey, that was pretty good!" Suze looks impressed.

"Really?" I'm panting.

"Yes! You'll definitely fool him. Let's do the test."

As I head to the sink for some water, Suze rips the box open and pulls out a syringe.

"Ooh, look," she says cheerfully. "You have to have an injection."

"An *injection*?" I look round in dismay.

"'The blood test is quick and easy to perform,'" she reads aloud from the leaflet. "'Simply ask a doctor, nurse, or other qualified person to take a vial of blood from a vein.' Here's the needle," she adds, taking out a plastic box. "I'll be the doctor."

"Right." I nod, trying to hide my qualms. "Er, Suze... have you ever actually done an injection before?"

"Oh, yes." She nods confidently. "I've injected a sheep. Come on!" She's fitting the needle to the syringe. "Roll up your sleeve!"

A sheep?

"So, what do we do with the vial of blood?" I ask, playing for time.

"We send it away to the lab," says Suze, reaching for the leaflet. "'Your results will be posted to you in anonymous, discreet packaging. Please expect them within'"—she turns the page—"'approximately ten to twelve weeks.'"

What?

"Ten to twelve weeks?" I grab the leaflet from her. "What good is that? I'll have *had* it by then." I turn the pages over, trying to find some express delivery option, but there isn't one. At last I give up and subside onto a bar stool in disappointment. "Twelve weeks. There's no point even doing it!"

Suze sighs and sits down beside me. "Bex, didn't you

read any of the instructions before you bought this test? Didn't you find out how it worked?"

"Well . . . no," I admit. "I thought it would be like a pregnancy stick test. With a blue line and a pink line."

Stupid rubbishy test. It cost me forty quid too. What a total rip-off. I mean, do they think pregnant women are *that* desperate to know what sex their baby is? It's only a few months to wait, for goodness' sake. And it's not like it matters. As long as it's a healthy baby, then really, what is the—

Suze breaks into my thoughts. "Shall we do the ring test again? See what it says?"

"Ooh!" I look up, brightening. "Yes, let's."

We do the ring test five times, and decide the odds are 3–2 on it being a boy. So we make a great big list of boys' names and Suze tries to persuade me to call it Tarquin Wilfrid Susan. Yup. I don't think so.

By the time she's bundled up all the children, fed them lots of fish oil capsules (to counteract the dumbing-down effect of TV), and left, I feel a lot better. She's right—Luke and I just need to spend a bit more time together. And I've thought of a much better plan than taking him out to lunch. I mean, he goes to boring old business lunches all the time. I want to do something different. Something *romantic.*

So the next day at work, I phone down to the Food Hall and order a picnic basket of all Luke's favorite food. I've already checked with Mel, his assistant, and he hasn't got any appointments booked for lunchtime. (I didn't tell her why I was asking, because there's no way she'd keep it secret.) My plan is to surprise him and have a picnic lunch in his office and it'll be all intimate and lovely! I've even got them to put in a bottle of

champagne, a checked cloth, and a plastic "picnic" can-
delabra from Homewares, just to set the scene.

As I set off for Luke's office at lunchtime I'm feeling
quite excited. It's been ages since we did something
spontaneous like this! Plus I haven't been to Brandon
Communications for weeks, and I'm looking forward
to seeing everyone. There's been the most amazing
buzz at the company, ever since they won the Arcodas
pitch. The Arcodas Group is so huge, and so different
from all the financial clients they normally deal with, it's
been the biggest challenge they've ever faced. (I know
this from helping Luke write his motivational speeches.)

But then, what is life without new adventures and
new dreams? Brandon Communications is the best in
the business, stronger and more dynamic every year,
thriving on new enterprises. Together they can take on
any challenge, meet it, and conquer it. As a team. As a
family. (I wrote that bit.)

I arrive at the offices just before one, and sidle across
the marble foyer to Karen, the receptionist. She's talking to her colleague Dawn in a low voice, and she looks
all pink and upset. I hope nothing's wrong.

"It's not right," I can hear her saying in a guarded
voice as I approach the desk. "It's just not right. No one
should behave like that, boss or no boss. I know I'm
old-fashioned—"

"It's not," Dawn interrupts her. "It's having respect
for your fellow human beings."

"Respect." Karen nods vigorously. "How *she's* feeling, poor thing..."

"Have you seen her? Since..." Dawn trails off
meaningfully.

Karen shakes her head. "No one has."

I'm following their conversation with slight unease. What are they talking about? Who's "she"?

"Hi!" I say, and they both jump.

"Becky! Goodness!" Karen looks quite flustered at the sight of me. "What are you...Did we know you were coming today?" She starts leafing through the papers on her desk. "Dawn, is it in the appointment book?"

In the appointment book? Since when do I have to make an appointment to see my own husband?

"I just thought I'd surprise Luke. He's free at lunchtime; I've already checked. So I thought we could have a nice picnic in his office!" I nod at the basket hanging on my arm.

I'm expecting them to say, "What a lovely idea!" But instead, Karen and Dawn both look kind of nervous.

"Right!" says Karen at last. "Well. Let's just...see if..." She presses a couple of buttons on her switchboard. "Hello, Mel? It's Karen at reception here. I have Becky here. Becky Brandon. She's here to...surprise Luke." There's quite a long silence, during which Karen listens intently. "Yes. Yes, I'll do that." She looks up and smiles at me. "Take a seat, Becky. Someone will be with you shortly."

Take a seat? Someone will be with me? What on earth has *happened* to them?

"Why don't I just go straight up?" I suggest.

"We're...not quite sure where Luke is." Karen definitely looks shifty. "It's probably better if you..." She clears her throat. "Adam will be down shortly."

I don't believe this. Adam Farr is head of corporate communications at Brandon C. He's the guy they always summon for tricky situations. Luke says Adam is the consummate expert at handling people.

I'm being handled. Why am I being handled? What's going on?

"Do take a seat, Becky!" Karen says, but I don't move.

"I couldn't help overhearing you earlier," I say casually. "Is something wrong?"

"Of course not!" Karen's reply is too swift, as though she's been waiting for me to ask. "We were talking about . . . something on TV last night. Weren't we, Dawn?"

Dawn is nodding agreement, but her eyes are edgy.

"What about you?" says Karen. "Keeping well, are you, Becky?"

"Not long to go, is it?" puts in Dawn.

I try to think of a natural, friendly reply—but how can I? This whole conversation is fake. Just then, the lift doors open and Adam Farr strides out.

"Rebecca!" He has his corporate smile on and is slipping a BlackBerry into his pocket. "What a pleasure to see you!"

This guy may be the smoothest operator in the company. But he is *not* fobbing me off.

"Hi, Adam," I say almost curtly. "Is Luke around?"

"He's just finishing up a meeting," says Adam without missing a beat. "Let's go up and get you a coffee. I know everyone will be thrilled you've dropped by—"

"What meeting?" I interrupt him, and I swear I see Adam flinch.

"On finance," he says after an infinitesimal pause. "Very dull, I'm afraid. Shall we?"

Adam ushers me into the lift and we travel up for a

while in silence. Now that I'm up close to him, I can detect signs of strain in him, beneath the confident, business-y manner. There are shadows under his eyes, and he keeps tapping his fingertips together in the same rhythmic pattern, like a nervous tic.

"So . . . how's life?" I say. "You must all be really busy, with the expansion and everything."

"Absolutely." He nods.

"And is it fun, working on all these different Arcodas projects?"

There's silence. I can see Adam's fingers tapping together faster and harder.

"Of course," he says at last, and nods again. The lift doors open, and he shows me out before I can say anything else.

A few Brandon C staff are standing there, waiting for the lift, and I smile and say "Hi!" to the faces I know— but no one smiles back. At least not a genuine smile. Everyone seems taken aback to see me, and there are a few fake little flashes of teeth, and a couple of people say, "Hi, Becky," and then look down awkwardly. But nobody stops to talk. Not even to ask about the baby.

Why is everyone being so *weird*? Over by the water cooler I can see a couple of girls talking in lowered voices and glancing at me when they think I'm not looking.

My stomach starts to churn. Oh God. Have I been totally naive? What do they know? What have they seen? A sudden vision comes to me, of Luke ushering Venetia down the corridor to his office, closing the door, and saying, "Please don't disturb us for an hour."

"Becky!" Luke's resounding voice makes me jump. "Are you OK? What are you doing here?" He's striding down the corridor toward me, flanked by his second-in-command, Gary, on one side, and some guy I don't know on the other, with a bunch of people following in their wake. They all look fairly stressed out.

"I'm fine!" I say, trying to sound cheerful. "I just thought . . . we could have a picnic in your office."

Now that I say it, in front of all his staff, it sounds really stupid. I feel like Pollyanna, holding this stupid wicker basket. There's even a pink stripy bow tied round the handle, which I should have torn off.

"Becky, I have a meeting." Luke shakes his head. "I'm sorry."

"But Mel said you didn't have anything booked!" My voice is more shrill than I intended. "She said you'd be free!"

Gary and the others glance at each other and melt away, leaving Luke and me alone. My cheeks are prickling with humiliation. Why should I be made to feel stupid and in everyone's way, just for dropping in to see my husband?

"Luke, what's going on?" The words spill out before I can stop them. "Everyone's giving me weird looks. You sent Adam down to 'handle' me. Something's wrong, I know it is!"

"Becky, no one's been *handling* you," Luke says patiently. "No one's giving you weird looks."

"They are! It's like *Invasion of the Body Snatchers*! No one's even *smiling* anymore! Everyone looks so tense, and strained. . . ."

"They're preoccupied, that's all." Despite his easy veneer, Luke seems rattled. "We're all working very hard right now. Including me. I really have to go." He kisses me. "We'll have the picnic at home, OK? Adam will call you a car."

And the next minute, he's disappeared into the lift, leaving me alone with my basket and my jumping, unsettling thoughts.

A meeting. What meeting? Why didn't Mel know about it?

Now I'm envisaging him hurrying into a restaurant where Venetia is waiting, cradling a glass of wine while all the waiters watch admiringly. She gets up, and they kiss, and he says, "Sorry I'm late, my wife turned up—"

No. Stop it. *Stop* it, Becky.

But I can't. Thoughts are piling into my head, thicker and faster, like a snowstorm. They've been seeing each other every lunch hour. All the Brandon C staff know about it. That's why Karen and Dawn looked so awkward, that's why they tried to get rid of me....

The other lift is waiting with its doors open, and on impulse I get in. I reach the ground floor and walk as swiftly as I can manage out of the foyer, ignoring the calls of Karen and Dawn, just in time to see Luke being driven away by his company driver in the Mercedes. Frantically I hail a taxi, step in, and dump the basket on the seat.

"Where to, love?" asks the taxi driver.

I slam the door and lean forward.

"You see that Mercedes up ahead?" I swallow hard. "Follow it."

I can't believe I'm actually doing this. I'm tailing Luke through the streets of London. As we drive round Trafalgar Square with the Mercedes in sight, I feel like I'm in some kind of movie. I even find myself glancing through the rear window to check that there are no baddies in pursuit.

"Your boyfriend, is it?" the taxi driver suddenly says in a strong South London accent.

"Husband."

"Thought as much. Got another woman, 'as 'e?"

I feel a horrible pang in my chest. How did he know? Do I *look* like the cheated-on partner?

"I'm not sure," I admit. "Maybe. That's what I want to find out."

I sit back and watch a bunch of tourists follow their tour leader across the road. Then it occurs to me that this taxi driver is probably a total expert on people following their partners to prove adultery. He probably drives them all the time! On impulse I lean forward and slide the dividing window across.

"D'you think I should confront him? What do most people do?"

"Depends." We've reached some snarled-up traffic and the taxi driver turns round to face me. He's got a long face like a sniffer dog, and dark, mournful eyes. "Depends if you want to 'ave an open an' honest marriage."

"I do!" I exclaim.

"Fair enough. Risk is that by 'aving it out, you drive 'im into the arms of the other bird."

"Right," I say doubtfully. "So . . . what's the other option?"

"Turn a blind eye an' live a sham for the rest of your days."

Neither option sounds that great.

We're edging along Oxford Street by now, making slow progress through all the buses and pedestrians. I'm craning my neck, scanning the road ahead, when all of a sudden I glimpse Luke's Mercedes, turning into a side street.

"There! He went that way!"

"I saw 'im."

The cabbie deftly changes lanes and a few moments later we're turning into the same side street. The Mercedes is at the end of the road, turning the corner.

My hands are starting to sweat. It almost felt like a game when I first hailed the cab. But now this is serious. At some point his car is going to stop and he's going to get out and . . . then what am I going to do?

We're winding round the narrow streets of Soho. It's a bright, sharp autumn day, and a few brave people are sitting out at pavement cafés, cradling cups of coffee. All of a sudden, the taxi driver signals sharply and pulls up behind a van. "They're stopping."

I watch, breathless, as the Mercedes comes to a halt on the other side of the road. The driver opens the passenger door and Luke gets out, without even glancing in our direction. He consults a piece of paper, then heads to an unsalubrious-looking brown-painted door. He rings a buzzer and a moment later is admitted.

My gaze travels up to a battered sign hanging from a first-floor window: ROOMS.

Rooms? Luke has taken *rooms*?

I feel as if something's clenching me tightly round the chest. Something *is* going on. Venetia's up there. She's waiting for him in a black fur-trimmed negligee.

But why some grotty room in Soho? Why not the Four Seasons, for God's sake?

Because he'd get spotted. He's come here because it's out of the way. It all makes sense. . . .

"Love?" Through a haze I realize the taxi driver is talking to me.

"Yes?" I manage.

"You want to sit here and wait?"

"No!" I grab the picnic basket and thrust the door open. "Thank you. I'll . . . take it from here. Thank you so much."

"Wait a mo'." He gets out and offers me a hand to help me step down from the cab. I scrabble in my bag and give him a wodge of cash without even counting it. The taxi driver sighs, peels off a few notes, and hands the rest back.

"Not used to this game, are you, love?"

"Not really," I admit.

"You need any more help . . ." He feels in his pocket and produces a gray business card. "My brother Lou. Does a lot of work for divorce lawyers. You might want to get yourself one of those an' all. Make sure you and the kid are taken care of."

"Yes. Thanks." I pocket the card, barely aware of what I'm doing.

"Good luck, love." The taxi driver gets back in his cab, still shaking his head, and drives away.

I'm standing outside the building with the "rooms" sign. I could buzz at the door and see what happened.

No. What if she answered?

My legs suddenly feel wobbly. I need a seat. The ground floor of the building is a business print shop, and I find myself walking inside and sinking into a chair. What am I going to do? What?

"Hello there!" A voice makes me jump and I turn to see a cheerful man in a short-sleeved striped shirt. "Are you interested in some printing? We have a special offer on all our business cards. Vellum, laminated, textured . . ."

"Um . . . thanks." I nod, just to get rid of him.

"Here you are!" The man hands me a sample book and I start to leaf through it blindly. Maybe I should just go up and . . . and burst in. But what if I really do find them together?

I'm turning the pages more and more feverishly. I can't believe this is happening. I can't believe I'm here, in the middle of Soho, wondering if my husband is upstairs with another woman.

"Here's our form. If you'll just fill it in . . ." The man has come back with a clipboard and pen, which he thrusts at me. On automatic pilot I take them from him and write "Bloomwood Inc." at the top of the page.

"What kind of business are you in?" the man asks chattily.

"Um . . . double-glazing."

"Double-glazing!" The man frowns thoughtfully. "I'd suggest a nice laminated white card with a border. With the address here and your company motto here . . . Do you have a motto?"

"For . . . for all your glazing needs," I hear myself saying. "London, Paris, Dubai."

I have no idea what I'm saying. The words are just coming out of my mouth.

"Dubai!" The man looks impressed. "I'll bet they have a few windows out there!"

"They do." I nod. "It's the window capital of the world."

"Now, I *never* knew that!" the man says with interest.

I stiffen. I just heard a rumbling-footsteps kind of noise. Someone's coming down the stairs.

Luke. It has to be.

Except...that was a bit quick, surely?

"Er...thanks very much! I'll think about it...." I shove the clipboard back at the man and rush out of the shop and into the street. In front of me the brown-painted door is slowly opening and I quickly edge behind a small tree.

My entire body is clenched with dread. Blood is rushing through my ears. *Stay calm. Whatever happens, whoever he's with—*

The door swings open—and Luke steps out, followed by a couple of men in suits.

"Let's discuss it over lunch," he's saying. "There's a couple of clients I think could really benefit from that approach."

He's not with Venetia. *He's not with Venetia!*

I feel like doing a little dance on the pavement. Relief is flooding through me. *How* could I have thought he was up to anything? I'm so paranoid. I'm so stupid! I'm going to go home and totally trust him from now on....

"Ms. Bloomwood?"

The guy from the print shop has come out and is peering at me, shading his eyes from the sun. Damn. Maybe this tree wasn't such a great hiding place. I forgot my bump would be poking out.

"*Becky?*" Luke swivels and stares at me in astonishment. "Is that you?"

I feel my cheeks turning beet red as the three men peer at me. "Er...hi!" I say brightly.

"I've got a mock-up of that business card, if you'd like it." The print shop man is advancing on me.

"Thanks!" I swipe it from him. "I'll let you know."

"Becky, what are you doing here?" Luke is coming toward the tree.

"Just . . . shopping! What a coincidence!"

"As I said, Ms. Bloomwood, I recommend a laminate finish." The man from the print shop is *still* bloody talking. "But it is more pricey, so I've put in a list of options for you. . . ."

"Thanks! Actually, my husband's here, so I'll . . . I'll get back to you."

"Aha!" The print shop guy beams at Luke. "Pleased to meet you. Are you in the double-glazing trade too?"

"No, he's not." I cut him off desperately. "Thanks so much. Bye!" At last, to my relief, the print shop guy retreats toward his door and there's a pause.

"The double-glazing trade?" says Luke at last, a little bemusedly.

"He got . . . me confused with . . . someone else." I shove the mock-up card into my bag. "So, anyway, what are *you* doing here?"

"Meeting some possible new media consultants for the company." Luke still looks puzzled. "Let me introduce Nigel and Richard. My wife, Rebecca."

"Very glad to meet you, Rebecca," says Nigel, grasping my hand. "You're the one who identified the need for media training, we hear. Luke told us you weren't impressed by his client's performance."

"Oh, right!" I feel a small glow. I didn't realize Luke had taken my advice, let alone told other people about it.

"Excuse our less than salubrious office space," puts in the other man. "We've only just moved in."

"I hadn't even noticed!" I say with a shrill laugh. "Anyway, I must be off—I was just passing. . . ."

"Have a good afternoon." Luke kisses me.

"I will." I hold on to his arm for a moment. "And maybe we can have our picnic later?"

Luke winces. "No, I'm sorry. I should have said, I'll be late back tonight. New-client dinner."

"Oh." I can't help feeling disappointed. But new business is new business. "Well, never mind. Who's the client?"

"Venetia."

My smile freezes on my face. *"Venetia?"*

"Venetia Carter," Luke explains to the others. "You know, the celebrity obstetrician? Her old PR agency weren't cutting it, apparently."

Venetia's hiring Brandon Communications. I do not believe this.

"Who's going to the dinner?"

"Just me and her." Luke shrugs. "I'll be handling her account, as we're old friends."

I can't help it. Suspicions are rising up inside me, as thick and fast as ever.

"So . . . you're going to have meetings with her and everything?" I wipe my damp upper lip.

"That's the general idea, Becky." Luke raises his eyebrows quizzically. "I'll send her your love, shall I?"

"Yes!" I manage a smile. "Do that!"

Luke walks off with the two men, and I stare after them, my heart thudding.

OK, so maybe I got things a tad wrong today. But there's no doubt. She's after Luke. I know it deep down in my heart, just like I know my new orange top from eBay was a mistake.

Venetia's moving in on my husband. And I have to stop her.

Prendergast de Witt Connell
Financial Advisers

INVESTMENT SUMMARY

CLIENT: "BABY BRANDON"
SUMMARY AS OF 24 OCTOBER 2003

FUND A: "LUKE'S PORTFOLIO"

Investment holdings to date:
    Wetherby's Gilt Fund 20%
    Somerset European Growth Fund 20%
    Start Right Accumulator Fund 30%

Remainder as yet uninvested

FUND B: "BECKY'S PORTFOLIO"

Investment holdings to date:
    Gold (Tiffany necklace, ring) 10%
    Copper (bracelet) 5%
    Shares in First Mutual Bank, Bangladesh 10%
    Shares in fabbesthandbagsonline.com 10%
    Dior vintage coat 5%
    Bottle of 1964 champagne 5%
    Share in racehorse named Baby Go for It 5%
    Sunglasses "once worn by Grace Kelly" 1%

Remainder as yet uninvested

ELEVEN

I'M GOING TO TALK TO LUKE, I've decided. I'm going to be mature and grown-up and just tackle this head-on. So with total resolve I sit up in bed until he arrives home that night. It's way after midnight as the door opens, and he smells of smoke and drink and . . . oh my God. Allure.

OK. Don't panic. Just because he smells of Allure, it doesn't prove anything.

"Hi! How was the dinner?" I make sure I sound all friendly and encouraging, and not like some whingy wife out of *EastEnders*.

"It was great." Luke takes off his jacket. "Venetia's very bright. Very switched on."

"I'll . . . bet she is." I twist my hands together under the duvet, where he can't see them. "And what did you talk about? Apart from work."

"Oh, I don't know." Luke is loosening his tie. "The arts . . . books . . ."

"You never read books!" I say before I can stop myself. It's true. He doesn't, apart from how-to-run-your-magnificent-business-empire kind of books.

"Maybe not," he says, shooting me a wry look. "But I used to."

What does that mean? Before he met me? So now it's my fault he doesn't read books, is that it?

"And what else did you talk about?" I persist.

"Becky, honestly. I can't remember."

His phone beeps with a text and he checks it. He smiles, texts something back, then resumes getting undressed. I'm watching in growing disbelief and anger. How can he do that? In *front* of me?

"Was that in Latin?" I say before I can stop myself.

"What?" Luke wheels around, his hands still tugging at his shirtsleeves.

"I just happened to see..." I falter. Then I stop. Sod it. I'm not going to pretend anymore. I take a deep breath and look at Luke straight-on. "She sends you texts in Latin, doesn't she? Is that your secret code?"

"What are you talking about?" Luke takes a step forward, his brow darkened. "Have you been reading my texts?"

"I'm your wife! What does she text you about, Luke?" My voice is rising in hurt. "Latin books? Or... other things?"

"I'm sorry?" He looks bemused.

"You know she's moving in on you, don't you?"

"What?" Luke gives a short laugh. "Becky, I know you have a vivid imagination, but really...." He pulls his shirt off and dumps it in the laundry hamper.

How can he be so dense? I thought he was supposed to be *clever*.

"She's after you!" I'm leaning forward in agitation. "Can't you see it? She's a home-wrecker! That's what she does—"

"She is not after me!" Luke says, cutting me off. "To be honest, Becky, I'm shocked. I never thought of you as being possessive. Surely I'm allowed to have a few friends, for Christ's sake. Just because she happens to be female—"

"It's not that," I cut him off scornfully.

It's that she used to be his ex-girlfriend and has long swishy red hair. But I'm not going to say *that*.

"It's that..." I flounder. "It's that...we're *married,* Luke. We should share everything. We shouldn't have anything separate. I'm an open book! Look at my phone!" I gesture widely. "Look in my drawers! I don't have a single secret! Go on, look!"

"Becky, it's getting late." Luke rubs his face. "Could we do this tomorrow?"

I stare at him indignantly. What does he mean, "do this tomorrow"? We're not playing Monopoly—we're having a crucial discussion about the state of our marriage.

"Go on! Look!"

"All right." Luke lifts his hands in surrender, and heads toward my bureau.

"I don't have a single secret I'm keeping from you! You can look anywhere, poke about all you like—" I draw up sharply.

Shit. The gender predictor test. It's in the top left drawer.

"Er...except that drawer," I exclaim hastily. "Don't touch the top left drawer."

Luke stops. "I can't touch that drawer?"

"No. It's...a surprise. Or the Harrods bag on the chair," I add hastily. I don't want him seeing the receipt for my new hi-tech moisturizer. I nearly died myself when I saw the price.

"Anything else?" Luke inquires.

"Um...a couple of things in the wardrobe. Early birthday presents for you," I add defiantly.

There's silence in the bedroom. I can't quite tell what Luke is thinking. At last he turns, his face working oddly.

"So, our marriage is a completely honest, open book except for that drawer, this Harrods bag, and the back of the wardrobe?"

I sense my position on the moral high ground is not quite as strong as I thought it was.

"The point is..." I cast around. "The point is, I wasn't out all night with someone else, doing goodness knows what!"

Oh God. I sound exactly like a whingy *EastEnders* wife.

"Becky." Luke sighs and sits down on the bed. "Venetia's not 'someone else.' She's a client. She's a friend. She'd like to be *your* friend."

I turn away, pleating the duvet cover into a little fan.

"I just can't understand what your problem is. You were the one who wanted to go to Venetia in the first place!"

"Yes, but—"

I can't exactly say, I didn't know then that she was a husband stealer.

"She's going to be delivering our baby in a few weeks' time! You should be getting to know her. Feeling relaxed with her!"

I don't want her to deliver the baby flashes through my mind.

"And on that subject..." Luke stands up. "Venetia asked if we could make an appointment tomorrow. She hasn't seen you for a while and she feels bad about it. I said we'd both be there. OK?" He heads into the bathroom.

"Fine," I say morosely, and sink back into the pillows with a great sigh. My head is swirling with confused thoughts. Maybe I *am* being unreasonable and paranoid. Maybe she's not after Luke.

And she is the best obstetrician in the world, practically. OK. I'm going to make a real, real effort and see if we can be friends.

When we arrive at the Holistic Birth Center on Friday, the paparazzi are out in force and I can see why. The Bond girl *and* the new face of Lancôme are posing together on the steps, both in cool low-slung trousers and clingy tops which accentuate their teeny bumps.

"Becky, slow down!" Luke calls after me as I hurry to join them. But by the time I arrive, they've already pushed their way in through the doors. I pause hopefully on the steps, but not a single lens points toward me. In fact, the photographers are all moving away, which is pretty insulting. You'd think they'd take a picture just to be polite.

Inside, the Bond girl is ahead of me at the desk, and I can hear the receptionist saying, "And you got your invitation to tea at the Savoy? Do you need us to send a car?"

"No, thanks," says the Bond girl, nodding at the Lancôme model. "Zara and I are going together."

My heart skips a beat. Tea at the Savoy? I didn't get

an invitation to tea at the Savoy. Maybe they're going to give it to me now! I approach the receptionist with an expectant smile, already reaching for my diary so I can check the date. But she doesn't hand over any invitation.

"Take a seat, Mrs. Brandon." She smiles back. "Venetia will be with you shortly."

"Er . . . was there anything else?" I linger at the desk. "Anything I should . . . have?"

"Did you bring a urine sample?" The receptionist smiles. "That's all you need."

That is *not* what I was talking about. I wait another few seconds just in case, then stalk over to the seating area, trying to hide my disappointment. She hasn't invited me. All the celebrities will be having tea together, exchanging pregnancy stories and asking each other where they buy their premiere dresses, and I'll be sitting at home on my own.

"Becky?" Luke is regarding me, puzzled. "What's up?"

"Nothing." I can feel my bottom lip quivering. "Only she didn't invite me to the tea party. They're all going to the Savoy. All of them! Without me."

"Becky, you don't *know* there's a tea party. I'm sure . . . I mean . . ." Luke breaks off, clearly at a loss. "Look, even if she didn't, does it matter? You don't go to a doctor because of the tea parties."

I open my mouth, then close it again.

"Becky?" A melodious voice rings out. "Luke?"

Oh my God. It's her.

I haven't seen Venetia in weeks. To be honest, she'd kind of altered in my mind. I'd pictured her taller, with longer, witchier hair and flashing green eyes and kind of . . . fangs. But here she is, slim and pretty, dressed in a chic black turtleneck and smiling as though I'm her best friend.

"Great to see you!" She kisses me. "I do apologize, I've been neglecting you *shamefully*." As she says it, she glances at Luke as though they're in on some private conversation.

Or is that me being paranoid?

"Come on through!" She ushers us into her room and we all sit down. "So, Becky." Venetia opens her file. "How are you feeling?"

"Fine," I say. "Thanks."

"Baby moving well?"

"Yes, all the time." I put a hand on my tummy, and, of course, the baby's gone to sleep.

"Well, let's have a feel." She gestures toward the examination table and I go and heave myself onto it while Venetia washes her hands.

"Did I hear something about a tea party out there, Ven?" says Luke lightly. "Great publicity idea." I stare at him in astonishment and he winks.

Sometimes I really *love* Luke.

"Oh." Venetia sounds taken aback. "That's right. It's for patients at a slightly more advanced stage than you, Becky. But of course you're on the list for the next one!"

She's *so* lying. I wasn't on that list.

As her hands move over my abdomen, I can't relax. I'm staring at her hands: slim and white, with a massive diamond eternity band on the third finger of her right hand. I wonder who gave her that.

"It's a good-size baby. Breech at the moment, which means the head is up near your ribs. . . ." Venetia's frowning in concentration as she feels the baby. "If it remains in that position we'll have to discuss your options for the birth, but it's early days yet." She glances at her notes. "You're only thirty-two weeks. Plenty of time for the baby to turn. Now, let's listen to the heartbeat. . . ." She squirts gel on my stomach, and does the ultrasound. A moment later the heartbeat is going *wow-wow-wow* through the room.

"Nice, strong heartbeat." Venetia nods at me, and I nod back as best I can while lying down. For a few moments the three of us just listen to the regular, fuzzy beat. It's so weird. Here we are, all transfixed by the sound—and the baby has no idea we're listening to it.

"That's your child." Venetia meets Luke's eyes. "Pretty amazing, huh?" She leans over and straightens his tie—and I feel a spike of resentment. How dare she do that? This is *our* moment. And everyone knows that the wife straightens the tie.

"So, Venetia," I say politely as at last she turns off the ultrasound machine. "I was sorry to hear about you splitting up with your boyfriend. What a shame."

"Ah well." Venetia spreads her hands. "Some things aren't meant to be." She smiles sweetly. "How's your general health, Becky? Any aches and pains? Heartburn? Hemorrhoids?"

I don't believe it. She's *deliberately* choosing all the least sexy ailments.

"No," I say firmly. "I feel really great."

"Then you're lucky." Venetia gestures to us to sit down again. "Toward the end of pregnancy, you'll find your body will really start feeling the strain. You may suffer from acne . . . varicose veins. . . . Sex will obviously be difficult, if not impossible. . . ."

Ooh. She is an absolute cow.

"We don't have any problems in that area." I take Luke's hand and clasp it. "*Do* we, darling?"

"It's early days yet." Venetia's pleasant smile is unmoved. "Many of my patients lose their libido for good after childbirth. And of course, unfortunately, some men find their partner's new shape somewhat . . . *unattractive.*"

Unattractive? Did she just say I was unattractive?

She's wrapped a blood pressure cuff round my arm and now frowns as it deflates. "Your blood pressure's creeping higher, Becky."

I'm not bloody surprised! I glance at Luke, but he seems totally unsuspicious.

"Darling, you should mention that pain in your leg," he says. "Remember, the other evening?"

"Pain in the leg?" Venetia looks up, alert.

"It was nothing," I say quickly. "Just a twinge."

I wore my new five-inch Manolos all day at work last week. Which was maybe a mistake, as by the time I got home I could barely walk and had to get Luke to massage my calf muscle.

"You should get it checked out, even so." Luke squeezes my hand. "There's no harm being careful."

"Absolutely!" Venetia pushes back her chair. "Let's examine it, shall we, Becky? Up on the table again."

I do *not* like that glint in her eye. Reluctantly, I take off my new Wolford Stay-Ups and get on the table.

"Hmm." She takes my leg, peers at it, then rubs a hand over it. "I think I can feel the beginnings of a varicose vein!"

I stare at my smooth skin in horror. She's lying. There's not a hint of a varicose vein.

"I can't see anything there," I say, trying to stay calm.

"To you it might seem invisible, but I can detect these things very early on." Venetia pats my shoulder. "What I recommend, Becky, is you wear these surgical support stockings from now on." She takes a packet from her desk and pulls out a pair of what look like long white-mesh socks. "Put them on."

"I'm not putting those on!" I recoil in horror. I can barely bring myself to *touch* them, let alone wear them. They are the most revolting things I've ever seen.

"Becky, darling." Luke leans forward. "If Venetia says you should wear them—"

"I'm sure I haven't got varicose veins!" My voice is growing shriller. "Luke, it was my *shoes,* remember?"

"Ah," Venetia chips in. "You may have a point. Let me see what you're wearing."

She surveys my new platform wedges and shakes her head sadly.

"Those really aren't suitable for late pregnancy. Here, try these." She roots in her bottom desk drawer and produces a pair of ugly brown rubber flip-flops. "They're an orthopedic sample. I'd be glad to know what you think of them."

I stare at them in dismay. "Instead of the support stockings?"

"Oh no!" She smiles. "I think you should wear the support stockings as well. Just to be on the safe side."

Bitch. *Bitch.*

"Put them on, darling," says Luke with an encouraging nod. "Venetia's just thinking of your health."

No, she's not! I want to yell. *Can't you see what she's doing?*

But I can't. There's no way out. They're both watching me. I'm going to have to do this.

Feeling sick, I slowly pull on first one surgical stocking, then the other.

"Tug them right up!" says Venetia. "That's it, over your thighs." I slip on the horrible flip-flops. Then I pick up my new oversize Marc Jacobs (pale yellow, totally gorgeous) bag to stuff my wedges in.

"Is that your bag?" Venetia's beady eyes alight on it and I feel a clutch of dread. Not the bag. Please, not the bag.

"This is *far* too heavy for a pregnant woman!" she says, taking it from me and hefting it with a frown. "Do you know the damage you might do to your spine?" To Luke she adds, "You know, I did a year working very closely with a physical therapist. The injuries she saw, from people lugging around ridiculous-size bags!"

"Big bags are in fashion," I say tightly.

"Fashion!" Venetia gives her silvery laugh. "Fashion is bad for your health. Try this, Becky. My physical therapist supplies them." She opens a cupboard and produces a fanny pack made of khaki webbing. "Far more ergonomic for the back. You can even hide it under your T-shirt for security. . . ."

"That's great!" says Luke, taking my Marc Jacobs from Venetia and putting it on the floor where I can't reach it. "Venetia, this is so kind of you."

Kind? He has no idea what's going on here. None.

"Go on, Becky!" Venetia is like a cat playing with a half-dead mouse, relishing its suffering. "See if it fits."

With trembling hands I pull up my T-shirt, fit the khaki belt around my belly, fasten the clasp, and allow my T-shirt to fall back down. As I turn I catch a glimpse of myself in the full-length mirror fitted to the back of the door.

I want to cry. I look like a grotesque monster. My legs are two white, bulbous tree trunks. My feet resemble a granny's. I have bumps in front *and* behind.

"You look great, Becky!" Venetia has hopped onto the desk and is doing an agile, yoga-type stretch which shows off her long, lithe arms. "So, Luke, that was a marvelous meeting we had. I was really interested in what you had to say about Web links...."

Miserably, I shuffle to my seat and wait for them to finish talking about Venetia's business profile. But now they've moved on to her brochure and whether it could be improved.

"Oh, sorry, Becky!" Venetia suddenly appears to notice me. "This must be really boring. You know, the checkup's done, so if you don't want to hang around...."

"Aren't you meeting Suze and Jess for lunch?" Luke looks at me. "Why don't you shoot off? I just want to recap a few things with Venetia."

I'm rooted to the ground. I don't want to leave him here alone with her. Every instinct is telling me not to. But if I say that, he'll think I'm just being all possessive and suspicious and we'll have another huge row.

"Well, OK," I say at last. "I'll go."

"Make sure you take what you need," says Venetia, gesturing at my Marc Jacobs. "And I don't want to hear that you've been using that bag!" She wags her finger at me.

I want to *shoot* her. But there's no point arguing; Luke will only take her side. In silence I take out my

purse, phone, keys, and a few essential items of makeup.
I put them in the khaki bag and zip it shut.

"Bye, darling." Luke kisses me. "I'll call you later."

"Bye. Bye, Venetia." I can barely look her in the eye.
I leave the room and head out to the foyer.

At the reception desk I can see an excited blond girl
with the tiniest of bumps, saying, "I'm so thrilled to
have a place with Venetia!"

Yes, you are now, I think savagely. Until she makes
you look like a *freak* in front of your husband.

I'm nearly at the door, when a sudden recollection
stops me. Luke's mobile rang this morning while he was
in the shower, and I answered it. Which was *not* because I am possessive and suspicious, but because . . .

Well, OK. I thought it might be Venetia. But it
wasn't; it was John from Brandon Communications and
I never told Luke to ring him. I'd better let him know.

I retrace my steps through the waiting room, trying
to ignore the curious stares of the blond girl and her
husband. These bloody stockings are coming off as soon
as I get outside.

A woman in a blue nurse-type uniform is ahead of
me in the corridor, and as I'm shuffling along she pauses
at Venetia's door. She knocks twice, then opens the
door.

"Oh, sorry!" I hear her say. "I didn't mean to disturb . . ."

Disturb what? *Disturb what?*

My heart suddenly hammering, I hurry forward
along the corridor, and just catch a glimpse through the
doorway as the nurse retreats.

And I see them. Sitting together on the desk, talking
in low, laughing voices. Venetia's arm is resting casually

across Luke's shoulders. The other hand is entwined in his. They look happy and relaxed and intimate.

They look like a couple.

I don't know how I get to the restaurant where I'm meeting Suze and Jess. I'm walking on autopilot, like a zombie. I want to throw up every time I think about it.

They were together. They were *together.*

"Bex?"

Somehow I've pushed my way in through the glass doors and am standing in a total daze as waiters bustle around and people chatter. "Bex, are you OK?" Suze is hurrying over to greet me. Her eyes drop in dismay to my white legs. "What are you *wearing?* What's happened? Bex...can you speak?"

"I...no. I need to sit down." I totter after her to a corner table where Jess is sitting.

"What's happened?" Jess looks aghast at my appearance. She quickly pushes out a chair for me and helps me sit down. "Are you OK? Is it the baby?"

"I saw them," I manage.

"Who?"

"Luke and Venetia. Together."

"Together?" Suze claps a hand to her mouth. "Together, doing...what?"

"They were sitting on a desk, talking." I can barely get the words out. "She had her arm on his shoulders. And he was holding her hand." I look up for a reaction. Both Suze and Jess look like they're waiting for more.

"Were they...kissing?" Suze ventures.

"No, they were *laughing.* They looked all happy. I

just...I had to get out of there." I take a deep gulp of water. Suze and Jess exchange glances.

"And...that's why you put on white tights?" hazards Suze cautiously.

"No! Of course not!" I thrust down my glass, feeling the humiliation rise up again. "It was Venetia! She took away my shoes and my bag and she made me put these things on, just so I'd look all gross in front of Luke."

Suze gasps. "What a *cow*!"

"And I can't get them off." I'm near tears by now. "I'm stuck with them!"

"Come on! I'll help you!" Suze puts down her glass and reaches for one of the stockings. Jess is watching, her brow wrinkled.

"Becky...are you sure there isn't some good health reason for wearing them?"

"No! She was just doing it to be mean! She said fashion's bad for the health!"

Jess looks unmoved. "Fashion *is* bad for the health."

"Fashion is *not* bad for the health!" I erupt. "It's *good* for the health! It makes you...it makes you stay slim and stand up straight so your jacket hangs better. And take an interest in yourself so you don't get all depressed." I'm ticking the points off on my fingers. "And high heels are brilliant exercise for calf muscles...."

"Bex, have some wine," says Suze soothingly, pushing her glass over. "Just a sip won't hurt the baby. And it might...calm you down a bit."

"OK. Thanks." I take a grateful gulp.

"My obstetrician told me I could have a glass every other night," adds Suze. "He's French."

I take another sip, feeling my heart rate subside. I should have gone to France to have the baby. Or *any-*

where but Venetia Carter. Maybe I should just forget this whole hospital thing and have the baby in a shop, like I always planned. At least I'd feel relaxed and happy. At least I'd get free clothes.

"I don't know what to do." I put the wineglass down and look miserably from Suze to Jess. "I've already tried talking to Luke. He said nothing was going on and they were just friends. But they didn't look like just friends to me."

"How exactly was he holding her hand?" Suze frowns intently. "Could it just have been friendly? Is Venetia a touchy-feely person?"

"She's..." I think back. I remember her squeezing my arm, brushing a hand down my arm. "Quite," I allow at last.

"Well, maybe that's all it is! Maybe she's just one of those people that gets too close."

"Do you have any other evidence?" asks Jess.

"Not yet." I fiddle with a bread stick wrapper, wondering whether to tell them. "I followed him the other day."

"You did *what*?" Suze looks aghast. "What if he'd *seen* you?"

"He did see me. I pretended I was shopping."

"Bex..." Suze clutches her hair. "What if nothing's going on? Just seeing them holding hands isn't proof. You don't want to ruin all the trust between you and Luke."

"So, what should I do?" I look from face to face. "What should I do?"

"Nothing," says Suze firmly. "Bex, I *know* Luke loves you. And he hasn't done anything really incriminating, has he? It would be different if he'd lied to you, or if you'd seen them kissing. . . ."

"I agree." Jess nods vigorously. "I think you've got the wrong end of the stick, Becky."

"But . . ." I trail off, winding the wrapper tightly around my fingers. I don't know how to explain it; I just have a bad feeling. It's not just the texting, or the dinners. It's not even seeing them just now. It's something about *her*. It's something in her eyes. She's a predator.

But if I say that to the others, they'll say I'm imagining it.

"All right," I say at last. "I won't do anything."

"Let's order," says Suze firmly, shoving a menu at me.

"There's a set menu," says Jess, putting a typed sheet on top of the à la carte. "It's more economical, if we only have two courses and don't choose any of these ridiculous items with truffles."

I immediately want to retort that truffles are my favorite food and who cares how much they cost? But the trouble is, I kind of agree. I've never got the whole thousand-pounds-for-a-truffle thing.

Oh God. Please don't say I'm starting to agree with Jess.

"And you can help me think of how to get my own back on Lulu," adds Suze, passing the bread basket.

"Ooh," I say, cheering up. "How come?"

"She's been asked to do a TV program," Suze says with disdain. "One of those makeover shows where she goes to the house of some crap mother and tells them how to cook healthily for their children. And she's asked me to be the first crap mother!"

"No!"

"She's already put my name forward to the production company!" Suze's voice rises in indignation. "They phoned me up and said was it true that I only fed my children canned food and that none of them could speak?"

"What a *nerve*!" I take a roll and spread some butter on it. There's nothing like having someone else to hate, to make you forget your problems.

We have a great lunch, the three of us, and by the end of it I feel so much better. We all decide Lulu is the absolute pits. (Jess has never met Lulu, but I give her a pretty good description.) And then Jess relays her own problems. She told Tom about Chile and it didn't go too well.

"First he thought I was joking," she says, crumbling a roll into little bits. "Then he thought I was testing his love. So he proposed."

"He proposed?" I say in an excited squeak.

"Obviously, I told him to stop being so ridiculous," says Jess. "And now... we're not really talking." She says it in a matter-of-fact way, but I can see the sadness in her eyes. "Just one of those things." She takes a deep gulp of wine, which is *really* unlike Jess. I glance at Suze, who gives me an anxious frown.

"Jess, are you *sure* about Chile?" I say tentatively.

"Yes." She nods. "I have to go. I have to do this. I'll never get this opportunity again."

"And Tom can always come and visit you out there," Suze points out.

"Exactly. If he would just stop listening to his mother!" Jess shakes her head in exasperation. "Janice is in total hysterics. She keeps sending me pages which she's printed out from the Internet, saying Chile's a dangerous, unstable country riddled with disease and land mines."

"Is it?" I say fearfully.

"Of course not!" says Jess. "She's talking absolute rubbish." She takes a sip of wine. "There's just a few land mines, that's all. And a small cholera problem."

A few land mines? *Cholera?*

"Jess, be really careful out there," I say on impulse, and grab her hand. "We don't want anything to happen to you."

"Yes, be careful," chimes in Suze.

"I will." Jess's neck flushes pink. "I'll be fine. Thanks, anyway." As the waiter arrives with our coffees she withdraws her hand, looking awkward. "I . . like your hair clip, Becky."

She obviously wants to change the subject.

"Oh, thanks," I touch it fondly. "Isn't it fab? It's Miu Miu. Actually, it's part of the baby's trust fund portfolio."

There's silence and I look up to see both Suze and Jess staring at me.

"Bex, how can a Miu Miu hair clip be part of a trust fund portfolio?" says Suze uncertainly.

"Because it's an Antique of the Future!" I say with a flourish.

"What's an Antique of the Future?" Suze looks puzzled.

Ha. You see. I am so ahead of the game!

"It's this fab new way to invest," I explain. "It's easy-peasy! You just buy anything and keep the packaging, and then in fifty years you auction it and make a fortune!"

"Right," says Suze, looking dubious. "So, what else have you bought?"

"Um..." I think. "Quite a few things from Miu Miu, actually. And some Harry Potter figures and Barbie princess dolls...and this fab bracelet from Topshop..."

"Becky, a Topshop bracelet isn't an *investment*," says Jess, looking incredulous.

She really hasn't got the point.

"Maybe not *now*," I explain patiently. "But it will be. It'll be on the *Antiques Road Show*—you'll see!"

"Bex, what's wrong with a bank?" says Suze anxiously.

"I'm not putting the baby's money into some crappy bank like everyone else!" I say. "I'm a financial professional, remember, Suze. This is what I do."

"What you *used* to do."

"It's like riding a bike," I assure her loftily. I'm not actually that great at riding a bike, but I needn't mention that.

"So, is that it?" asks Jess. "Have you invested all the money?"

"Oh, no. I've still got loads!" I take a sip of coffee, then notice an abstract painting on the wall next to me. It's just a big blue square of oil paint on canvas, and there's a little price tag of £195. "Hey, look at that!" I say, focusing on it with interest. "D'you think I should—"

"No!" chime Jess and Suze in unison.

Honestly. They didn't even know what I was going to say.

———

I arrive home that evening to find a dark, empty flat and no Luke. *He's with her* immediately shoots through my mind.

No. He's not. Stop it. I make myself a sandwich, kick off my shoes, and curl up on the sofa with the remote. As I'm flicking down the channels looking for *Birth Stories*, which I'm addicted to (only I have to watch the crucial bit through my fingers), the phone rings.

"Hi." It's Luke, sounding hurried. "Becky, I forgot to remind you—I'm out at the Finance Awards. I'll be back late."

"Oh, right." Now I remember—I did know about the Finance Awards. In fact, Luke invited me, but I couldn't face an evening of boring old fund managers. "OK. I'll see you then. Luke..."

I break off, my heart thumping. I don't know what I want to say, let alone how to say it.

"I have to go." Luke hasn't even *noticed* my troubled silence. "See you later."

"Luke..." I try again, but the line's already dead.

I stare into space for a while, imagining the perfect conversation in which Luke asked me what was wrong and I said, Oh nothing, and he said, Yes there is, and it ended with him saying he totally loved me and Venetia was really ugly and how about we fly to Paris tomorrow?

A blaring theme song from the TV drags me from my daze and I look up at the screen. Somehow I've gone too far down the cable list, and I'm on some obscure business and finance channel. I'm just trying to remember the number for the Living Channel, when my attention is drawn to the screen by a portly guy in a dinner jacket. I recognize him. It's Alan Proctor from Foreland Investments. And there's that girl Jill from *Portfolio Management,* sitting next to him. What on earth...

I don't believe it. The Finance Awards are actually being televised! On some cable channel which nobody ever watches—but still! I sit up and focus on the screen. Maybe I'll see Luke!

"And we're live from Grosvenor House at this year's Finance Awards...." an announcer is saying. "The venue has been changed this year due to increased numbers...."

Just for fun, I reach for the phone and speed-dial Luke. The camera pans around the ballroom and I scan the screen intently, looking at all the black-tied people sitting at tables. There's Philip, my old editor at *Successful Saving,* swigging back the wine. And that girl from Lloyds who always used to wear the same green suit to press conferences...

"Hi, Becky," Luke answers abruptly. "Is everything OK?"

"Hi!" I say. "I just wondered how it's going at the Finance Awards?"

I'm waiting for the camera to pan to Luke. Then I can say, "Guess what, I'm watching you!"

"Oh... the same old, same old," Luke says after a pause. "Packed room at the Dorchester... gruesome crowds..."

The Dorchester?

I stare at the phone for a moment. Then, feeling hot and cold, I press my ear hard to the receiver. I can't hear any background babble. He's not in a crowded ball-room, is he?

He's lying.

"Becky? Are you there?"

"I . . . um . . . yes." I feel dizzy with shock. "So, who are you sitting next to?"

"I'm next to . . . Mel. I'd better go, sweetheart."

"OK," I say numbly. "Bye."

The camera's just panned to Mel. She's sandwiched between two large men in suits. There isn't an empty chair at the whole table.

Luke lied to me. He's somewhere else. With someone else.

The glitzy light and noise of the awards ceremony is jarring my nerves, and I jab the TV off. For a moment I just stare blankly, in silence—then, in a daze, I reach for the phone and find myself dialing Mum's number. I need to talk to someone.

"Hello?" As soon as I hear her safe, familiar voice, I want to burst into tears.

"Mum, it's Becky."

"Becky! How are you, love? How's the baby? Kicking away?"

"The baby's fine." I touch my bump automatically. "But I've got . . . a . . . a problem."

"What kind of problem?" Mum sounds perturbed. "Becky, it's not those people from MasterCard again?"

"No! It's . . . personal."

"Personal?"

"I . . . it's . . ." I bite my lip, suddenly wishing I'd thought before phoning. I can't tell Mum what's wrong. I can't get her all worried. Not after she warned me about exactly this happening.

Maybe I can ask her advice without giving away the truth. Like when people write to advice columnists about their "friend" and it was really *them* who got caught wearing their wife's swimwear.

"It's a...a colleague at work," I begin, my voice faltering. "I think she's planning to...to move to a different department. She's been talking to them behind my back and having lunches with them, and I've just found out she's *lied* to me...." A tear trickles down my cheek. "Do you have any advice?"

"Of course I've got some advice!" says Mum cheerfully. "Love, she's only a colleague! They come and go. You'll have forgotten all about her in a few weeks' time and moved on to someone else!"

"Right," I say after a pause.

To be honest, that wasn't the hugest help.

"Now," Mum is saying. "Have you got a diaper holder yet? Because I saw a super one in John Lewis—"

"The thing is, Mum..." I make another attempt. "The thing is, I really *like* this colleague. And I can't tell if she's seeing these other people behind my back...."

"Darling, who *is* this friend?" Mum sounds perplexed. "Have you ever mentioned her before?"

"She's just...someone I click with. We have fun, and we're having a...a joint project...and, you know, it felt like it was really working. I thought we were so happy together...." There's a huge lump in my throat. "I can't bear to lose her."

"You won't *lose* her!" says Mum, laughing. "Even if she leaves you for another department, you can still have the odd coffee together—"

"The odd coffee together?" My voice shoots out in distress. "What good is the odd coffee together?"

Tears start running down my face at the thought of

me and Luke stiffly meeting for the odd coffee, while Venetia sits drumming her nails in the corner.

"Becky?" exclaims Mum in alarm. "Sweetheart? Are you all right?"

"I'm fine." I snuffle, rubbing my face. "It's just a bit...upsetting."

"Is this girl really *that* important to you?" Mum is clearly baffled. I can hear Dad in the background, saying "What's wrong?" and there's a rustling as Mum turns away from the phone.

"It's Becky," I can hear her saying, sotto voce. "I think she's a bit hormonal, poor love...."

Honestly, I am *not* hormonal. My husband is having an *affair*.

"Becky, now listen." Mum is back on the line. "Have you talked to your friend about this? Have you asked her straight-out whether she's planning to move departments? Are you even sure you've got your facts straight?"

There's silence as I try to imagine confronting Luke when he comes home tonight. Calling him on his lie. What if he blusters and tries to pretend he was at the awards ceremony? What if he says he loves Venetia and he's leaving me for her?

Either way, I feel totally sick at the prospect.

"It isn't easy," I say at last.

"Oh, Becky." Mum sighs. "You've never been the best at facing up to things, have you?"

"No." I scuff my foot on the carpet. "I suppose I haven't."

"You're grown-up now, love," says Mum gently. "You have to *confront* your problems. You know what you have to do."

"You're right." I give a huge sigh, feeling some of the tension leave my body. "Thanks, Mum."

"You take care, darling. Don't let yourself get upset. Dad sends his love too."

"See you soon, Mum. Bye. And thanks."

I switch off the phone with a new resolve. It just shows, mothers *do* know best. Mum's made me see this whole thing clearly for the first time. I've decided exactly what I'm going to do.

I'm going to hire a private detective.

OXFORD UNIVERSITY

OXFORD · OX1 6TH

Mrs R Brandon
37 Maida Vale Mansions
Maida Vale
London NW6 0YF

3 November 2003

Dear Mrs. Brandon,

Thank you for your telephone message, which my secretary relayed to me as best she could.

I am very sorry to hear your husband may be "having an affair in Latin," as you put it. I can understand how anxious you must feel and will be pleased to translate any text messages you send me. I do hope this will prove illuminating.

Yours sincerely,

Edmund Fortescue
Professor of Classics

P.S. Incidentally, "Latin lover" is not generally taken to mean someone who talks to their lover in Latin; I do hope this is of some reassurance to you.

Denny and George

44 FLORAL STREET ~ COVENT GARDEN ~ LONDON W1

Mrs R Brandon
37 Maida Vale Mansions
Maida Vale
London NW6 0YF

4 November 2003

Dear Rebecca,

Thank you for your letter. I am sorry to hear you
have fallen out with your obstetrician.

We are touched that you have had so many happy
times in here and feel it is "the perfect place to bring
a baby into the world." However, I'm afraid we
cannot convert our shop into a temporary birthing
suite, even for an old and valued customer.

We appreciate your offer to name the baby "Denny
George Brandon"; however, I'm afraid this does not
alter our decision.

Good luck with the birth.

Very best wishes,

Francesca Goodman
Store Manager

REGAL AIRLINES

HEAD OFFICE • PRESTON HOUSE • 354 KINGSWAY • LONDON WC2 4TH

Mrs Rebecca Brandon
37 Maida Vale Mansions
Maida Vale
London NW6 0YF

4 November 2003

Dear Mrs. Brandon,

Thank you for your letter.

You appear to be under a severe misapprehension. If you gave birth midair on a Regal flight, your child would not "get free club-class travel for life." Nor would you be entitled to join your child "as its guardian."

Our flight attendants have not "all delivered zillions of babies before," and I would point out that company policy forbids us from letting any woman more than thirty-seven weeks pregnant board a Regal flight.

I hope you choose Regal Airlines again soon.

Yours sincerely,

Margaret McNair
Customer Service Manager

KENNETH PRENDERGAST

Prendergast de Witt Connell
Financial Advisers

Forward House
394 High Holborn
London WC1V 7EX

Mrs R Brandon
37 Maida Vale Mansions
Maida Vale
London NW6 0YF

5 November 2003

Dear Mrs. Brandon,

Thank you for your letter.

I was perturbed to hear of your "new genius plan." I strongly advise that you do not invest the remainder of your child's fund in so-called "Antiques of the Future." I am returning the Polaroid of the Topshop limited edition bikini, which I cannot comment on. Such purchases are not a "sure-fire win," nor can anyone make a profit "if they just buy enough stuff."

May I guide you towards more conventional investments, such as bonds and company shares?

Yours sincerely,

Kenneth Prendergast
Family Investment Specialist

TWELVE

I DON'T KNOW WHY I didn't do this before.
It's like Mum says, I need to get my facts straight. All I
need is to find out the answer to one simple question: Is
Luke having an affair with Venetia? Yes or no.

And if he *is*—

My stomach spasms at the thought and I do a few
quick shallow breaths. In. Out. In. Out. Ignore the
pain. I'll cross that bridge when I come to it.

I'm standing in West Ruislip tube station, right at the
end of the Central Line, consulting my little A–Z. I've
never been to this bit of northwest London before and I
wouldn't really have thought of it being the kind of place
where private detectives hang out. (But then, I suppose
I was really picturing downtown Chicago in the 1940s.)

I head off down the main road, glancing at my reflection in a shop window as I pass. It took me ages to
decide what to wear this morning, but in the end I
went for a simple black print dress, vintage shoes, and
oversize opaque sunglasses. Although it turns out that
sunglasses are a crap disguise. If anyone I knew spotted
me, they wouldn't think, "There's a mysterious woman

in black," they'd think, "There's Becky, wearing sun-glasses and visiting a private detective."

Feeling nervous, I start walking faster. I can't quite believe I'm actually doing this. It was all so *easy*. Like booking a pedicure. I phoned the number on the card that the taxi driver gave me, but unfortunately that par-ticular detective was about to go off to the Costa del Sol. (For a golfing holiday, not to follow a crook.) So I looked up private detectives on the Internet—and it turns out there are zillions of them! In the end I chose one called Dave Sharpness, Private Eye (Matrimonial a Specialty), and we arranged an appointment and now here I am. In West Ruislip.

I turn into a side street and there's the building ahead of me. I survey it for a few moments. This really isn't how I'd imagined it. I'd envisioned a dingy office down some alleyway with a single lightbulb swinging in the window and maybe bullet holes in the door. But this is a well-kept low-rise block with venetian blinds and a little patch of grass outside with a notice saying *Please Do Not Drop Litter.*

Well. Private detectives don't *have* to be gritty, do they? I stuff the A–Z into my bag, head toward the en-trance, and push open the glass doors. A pale woman with badly layered aubergine-dyed hair is sitting at a desk. She looks up from her paperback and I feel a sud-den pang of humiliation. She must see people like me all the time.

"I'm here to see Dave Sharpness," I say, trying to keep my chin high.

"Of course, dear." Her eyes descend to my bump ex-pressionlessly. "Take a seat."

I sit down on a brown foam chair and pick up a copy

of *Reader's Digest* from the coffee table. A moment later, a door opens and I see a man in his late fifties or even early sixties approaching me. He's paunchy, with bright white hair sticking up from a tanned head, blue eyes, and a jowly double chin.

"Dave Sharpness," he says with a smoker's wheeze, and grips my hand. "Come through, come through."

I follow him into a small office with venetian blinds and a mahogany desk. There's a bookshelf filled with legal-looking books, and a series of box files with names on them. I spot one with "Brandon" written on it. It's resting openly on the desk, and I feel a flicker of alarm. Is this what they call discreet? What if Luke came to West Ruislip for a business meeting and he walked past this window and saw it?

"So, Mrs. Brandon." Dave Sharpness has squeezed himself behind his desk and is addressing me hoarsely. "First, let me introduce myself. I had thirty years in the motor trade before turning to private investigation. Having had various painful experiences myself, I know all too well the trauma you are undergoing right now." He leans forward, his chins wobbling. "Be assured, I am one hundred and *fifty* percent committed to providing results for you."

"Right. Fab." I swallow. "Um . . . I was wondering. Could you not have my box file out on show, please? Anyone might see it on that shelf!"

"These are dummies with false names, Mrs. Brandon," Dave Sharpness says, gesturing at the shelf. "Please don't worry. Your file will be safely concealed in our client secure storage facility."

"Oh, I see," I say, feeling a bit more reassured. "Client secure storage facility" sounds pretty good.

Like some underground system with coded locks and infrared laser beams criss-crossing each other. "So... what does that consist of, exactly?"

"It's a filing cabinet in the back office." He wipes his glowing face with a handkerchief. "Locked every night by Wendy, our office manager. Now, to business." He pulls a pad of foolscap toward him. "Let's start at the beginning. You have concerns about your husband. You think he's cheating on you."

I have a sudden urge to cry out "No! Luke would *never* cheat on me!" and get up and run away.

But that would slightly defeat the point of coming here.

"I... don't know," I force myself to say. "Maybe. We've been married for a year and everything seemed great. But there's this... woman. Venetia Carter. They had a relationship in the past, and now she's come to London. He's seeing a lot of her, and he's all distant and snappy with me, and they send texts to each other in this *code,* and last night he..." I break off, breathing hard. "Anyway, I just want to find out what's going on."

"Of course you do," says Dave Sharpness, scribbling. "Why should you have to put up with the uncertainty and pain anymore?"

"Exactly." I nod.

"You want answers. Your instincts are telling you something's wrong, but you can't put your finger on it."

"That's it!" God, he totally understands.

"All you want is photographic proof of the illicit affair."

"I... er..." I'm halted. I hadn't really thought about photographic proof. All I'd thought about was getting a yes or no answer.

"Or video." Dave Sharpness looks up. "We can put all the evidence on DVD for you."

"DVD?" I echo, shocked. Maybe I haven't thought this plan through. Am I really going to hire someone to tail Luke with a video camera? What if he found out?

"Couldn't you just *tell* me if he's having an affair or not?" I suggest. "Without taking any pictures or video?"

Dave Sharpness raises his eyebrows. "Mrs. Brandon, believe me. When we uncover the proof, you're going to want to see it with your own eyes."

"You mean . . . *if* you discover any proof. I've probably got it all wrong! It's probably all perfectly . . ." I trail off at his expression.

"First rule of matrimonial investigation," he says with a lugubrious smile. "The ladies very rarely get it wrong. Feminine intuition, you see."

This guy is an expert. He should know.

"So you think . . ." I lick my suddenly dry lips. "Do you really think . . ."

"I don't think," says Dave Sharpness with a small flourish. "I discover. Whether it's one lady he's dallying with, or two, or a whole string of them, myself and my operatives will find out and furnish you with whatever proof you need."

"He's not dallying with a whole string of ladies!" I say in horror. "I know he isn't! It's just this one specific woman, Venetia Carter—" I stop as Dave Sharpness lifts a reproving finger.

"Let's find that out, shall we? Now, I'll need as much information as you can give me. All the women he knows—both his friends and yours. All the places he frequents, all his habits. I like to do a thorough job,

Mrs. Brandon. I will produce a full dossier on your husband's life, plus background on any women or other persons deemed to be relevant. There is nothing you will not know by the end of my investigation."

"Look." I try to keep my patience. "I know everything about Luke already. Except for this one tiny thing. He's my *husband*."

"If I had a pound for every lady who's said that to me..." Dave Sharpness gives a hoarse chuckle. "You fill in the details. We'll do the rest."

He holds out a fresh pad of paper. I take it from him and flip the pages, feeling uneasy.

"Do I need to...give you a photograph?"

"We'll take care of that. You just tell us about the women. Don't leave anyone out. Friends...colleagues...Do you have a sister?"

"Well...yes," I say, taken aback. "But he'd *never*...I mean, not in a million years..."

Dave Sharpness is shaking his head in ponderous amusement. "You'd be surprised, Mrs. Brandon. In my experience, if they've got one little secret, they've got a whole host of them." He hands me a pen. "Don't you worry. We'll soon let you know."

I write "Venetia Carter" at the top of the page, then stop.

What am I *doing*?

"I can't do it." I drop the pen. "I'm sorry. This just feels so weird. So *wrong*. To spy on my own husband!" I push my chair back and stand up. "I shouldn't have come. I shouldn't even be here!"

"You don't need to make your decision today," Dave Sharpness says unperturbed, reaching for a packet of toffees. "All I will say is that of the customers who react like your good self… ninety percent are back within a week. They still go ahead with the investigation, only they've lost a week. As a lady in your advanced condition…" His gaze drops meaningfully to my stomach. "Well, I'd be cracking on."

"Oh." Slowly I sink back down into the chair. "I hadn't thought of it like that."

"And we don't use the word *spying,*" he adds, wrinkling his florid nose. "No one likes to think of themselves as spying on a loved one. We prefer the term *distance observation.*"

"Distance observation." That does sound better.

I fiddle with my birthing stone, my mind spinning. Maybe he's got a point: if I walk away now, I'll only be back in a week. Maybe I should just sign on the dotted line straightaway.

"But what if my husband saw you?" I say, looking up. "What if he's totally innocent and he discovers I hired a detective? He'll never trust me again…."

Dave Sharpness holds up a hand. "Let me reassure you. All of my operatives operate with the utmost caution and discretion. Either your husband is innocent—in which case, no harm done—or he's guilty, in which case you have the proof you need to take further action. To be perfectly honest, Mrs. Brandon, it's a win-win situation."

"So there's no way at all he could find out?" I say, just to be totally sure.

"Please." Dave Sharpness chuckles again. "Mrs. Brandon, I'm a professional."

Honestly, I never realized hiring a private investigator was such hard work. It takes me about forty minutes to write down all the information Dave Sharpness wants. Every time I try to explain that I'm only interested in whether Luke's seeing Venetia, he holds up his hand and says, "Take it from me, Mrs. Brandon, you'll be interested enough if we find anything."

"That's it," I say at last, shoving the pad of paper toward him. "I can't think of anyone else."

"Excellent." Dave Sharpness takes it and runs a fingernail down all the names. "We'll get cracking on this lot. Meanwhile, we'll place your husband under what we call low-grade surveillance."

"Right," I say nervously. "What does that involve?"

"One of my highly skilled operatives will follow your husband for an initial period of two weeks, at which time we shall meet again. Any information gained in the meantime shall be communicated to you directly by myself. I *shall* require a deposit...."

"Oh," I say, feeling for my bag. "Of course."

"And as a new customer"—he rifles in his drawer and produces a small flyer—"you qualify for our special offer."

Special offer? He honestly thinks I'm interested in some stupid special offer? My *marriage* is under threat here. In fact, I'm pretty insulted he even mentioned it.

"Valid only today," Dave Sharpness continues. "Buy one, get the second half-price. It's a unique opportunity for new customers. Shame to miss out on a bargain."

There's silence. In spite of myself I'm feeling the teeniest, weeniest ripple of interest.

"What do you mean?" I give a reluctant shrug. "You get the second detective half off?"

"She's a card!" Dave Sharpness wheezes with laughter. "No, you order a second *investigation* and you'll get it half-price. Saves you coming back, you see. Wrap up all your investigatory needs in one go."

"But I don't have any other investigatory needs."

"Are you sure about that?" He raises his eyebrows. "Have a good think, Mrs. Brandon. No other little mysteries you need to clear up? No missing persons you'd like us to trace? The offer's valid only today. You'll regret it if you lose out." He hands me the flyer. "You'll see our full list of services here...."

I open my mouth to tell him I'm not interested, then find myself closing it again.

Perhaps I should just have a little think about this. I mean, it is a pretty good deal. And maybe there *is* something else I'd like to find out about. My eyes run down the headings on the flyer. I could trace an old schoolchum...or track a vehicle by GPS satellite...or simply discover more about a friend or neighbor....

Oh my God. I have it!

I'm not sure Dave really *got* the whole eyebrow thing. But I explained as fully as I could and drew him a picture and in the end he became quite enthusiastic. He said if he didn't find out where and how Jasmine was getting her eyebrows shaped, he wasn't Regional Salesman of the Year, 1989 (Southwest). I don't know what that's got to do with private detecting, but anyway. He's on the case. Both of them.

So it's done. The only thing is, I now feel horribly guilty.

The nearer I get to home the guiltier I feel, until I can't bear it anymore. I hurry into the shop at the end of our road and buy Luke a bunch of flowers and some chocolates, and at the last moment I throw in a miniature whisky.

His car is in our parking space, which means he must be home. As I travel up in the lift I start getting my story straight. My plan is: I'll just say I was at work all afternoon.

No. He might have called there for some reason and found out I took the afternoon off.

I'll say I was shopping. Nowhere near West Ruislip.

But what if someone *saw* me in West Ruislip? What if one of Luke's employees lives in West Ruislip and she was working from home and rang Luke and said, "Guess what, I've just seen your wife!"

OK, I *was* in West Ruislip. I was there for... another reason. To see a pregnancy hypnotherapist. Yes. Brilliant.

By now I've reached our front door, and as I unlock it, my heart's thumping with nerves.

"Hi!" Luke appears in the hall, holding a huge bouquet, and I stare at him, transfixed. We *both* have flowers?

Oh God. He knows.

No. Don't be stupid. How could he know? And why would that make him buy flowers?

Luke seems a little puzzled too. "These are for you," he says after a pause.

"Right," I say in a constricted voice. "Well... these are for you."

Awkwardly we exchange bouquets, and I hand Luke his chocolates and miniature whisky.

"Let's go..." Luke nods toward the kitchen, and I follow him to the area where we have a sofa and a low table. Late afternoon sunshine is blazing in through the window, and it almost feels like summer.

Luke sinks onto the sofa beside me and takes a swig from a bottle of beer on the table. "Becky, I just wanted to say I'm sorry." He rubs his brow, as though marshaling his thoughts. "I know I've been distant these past few days. It's been a strange time. But...I think I've managed to get rid of something that was bothering me."

He finally looks up, and I feel a dart of understanding. He's talking in subtext! It couldn't be clearer. *Something that was bothering me.* That's her. Venetia came on to him—and he rejected her. That's what he's trying to tell me! He turned her down!

And here I am, hiring private detectives, like I don't trust him. Like I don't love him.

"Luke, I'm sorry too!" I say in a rush of remorse. "I really am."

"For what?" Luke looks taken aback.

"For...er..." *Do* not *blurt it all out, Becky.* "For... that time I forgot to order the groceries. I've always felt really bad about it."

"Come here." Luke laughs and pulls me close for a kiss. For a while we just sit there, the sun warm on our faces. It's ages since we just sat like this. The baby is squirming energetically inside me, and we both watch as my dress jumps with the motion. It is pretty freaky, just like Suze said. But it's exciting too.

"So," says Luke, putting a hand on my stomach. "When are we going to look at prams?"

"Soon!" I put my arms round him and hug him tight in relief. Luke loves me. It's all happy again. I *knew* it would be.

TO: Dave Sharpness
FROM: Rebecca Brandon
SUBJECT: Luke Brandon

Dear Mr. Sharpness,

Just to repeat the message I left on your
answering machine, I would like you to
CALL OFF the investigation on my husband.
Repeat: CALL IT OFF. He is not having an
affair after all.

I will contact you in due course about the
deposit I paid you.

With best wishes,

Rebecca Brandon

Mrs R Brandon
37 Maida Vale Mansions
Maida Vale
London NW6 0YF

11 November 2003

Dear Mrs. Brandon,

I am delighted to enclose translations of the Latin text messages you sent me, and hope they put your mind at rest. They are all entirely innocuous: for instance, *sum suci plena* means "I'm full of life" rather than the more graphic meaning you ascribed to it.

I also think you may have been unduly concerned by the phrases *licitum dic*, *fac me*, and *sex*, which in Latin means "six."

If I can be of any further assistance, please do not hesitate to let me know. Perhaps some Latin lessons?

With very best wishes.

Yours sincerely,

Edmund Fortescue
Professor of Classics

THIRTEEN

THE WHOLE WORLD looks different when your husband isn't having an affair.

Suddenly a phone call is just a phone call. A text is just a text. A late night out isn't a reason to have a row. It even turns out *fac me* doesn't mean . . . what I thought it did.

Thank God I canceled the private detective, is all I can say. I even burned all his paperwork and receipts, so there was no chance of Luke finding out. (And then quickly invented a story about defective hair tongs when the smoke alarm went off.)

Luke is so much more relaxed these days, and he hasn't even mentioned *her* for two weeks. Except when an invitation came to a Cambridge reunion party and he said casually, "Oh yes, Ven told me about this." It's a black-tie dance at the Guildhall in London, and I'm determined to look as fab and glam as I can, like Catherine Zeta-Jones at the Oscars. Yesterday I bought the *best* dress, all clingy and sexy in midnight-blue silk, and now I need some matching heels. (And Venetia can just choke on her chicken.)

So everything's going brilliantly. We're exchanging

contracts on the house next week, and last night we talked about throwing a massive housewarming-christening party, which would be so cool. And the really big news is that Danny arrives today! He flies in this morning and is coming straight to the store to meet everyone and announce his collaboration with The Look. Then he and I are having lunch, just the two of us. I'm *so* looking forward to it.

As I arrive at The Look at nine thirty, the place is already bustling with excitement. A reception area has been set up on the ground floor, with a table of champagne glasses and a big screen showing footage from Danny's latest catwalk show. A few journalists have arrived for the press conference, and all the PR department is milling around bright-eyed, handing out media packs.

"Rebecca." Eric advances on me before I've even taken my coat off. "A word, please. Any news on the design?"

This is the only teeny little hitch. Danny said he'd submit a provisional design to us by last week. And he still hasn't. I spoke to him a couple of days ago, and he said it was pretty much there, he just needed the final inspiration. Which could mean anything. It probably means he hasn't even started. Not that I'll let Eric know this.

"It's in the final stages," I say as convincingly as I can.

"Have you seen anything?"

"Absolutely!" I cross my fingers behind my back.

"So, what's it like?" His brows narrow. "Is it a top? A dress? What?"

"It's... groundbreaking." I wave my hands vaguely. "It's a kind of... You'll have to see it. When it's ready."

Eric doesn't look convinced.

"Your friend Mr. Kovitz has just made yet *another* request," he says. "Two tickets for Euro Disney." He gives me a baleful stare. "Why is he going to Euro Disney?"

I can't help cursing Danny inside. Why can't he buy his own bloody tickets to Euro Disney?

"Inspiration!" I say at last. "He's probably going to make some satirical comment on . . . modern culture."

Eric doesn't look impressed.

"Rebecca, this plan of yours is costing a lot more time and money than I anticipated," he says heavily. "Money which could have gone into conventional marketing. It had better work."

"It will! I promise it will!"

"And if it doesn't?"

I feel a surge of frustration. Why does he have to be so *negative*? "Then . . . I resign!" I say with a flourish. "OK? Satisfied?"

"I'll hold you to that, Rebecca," Eric says with an ominous look.

"You do that!" I say confidently, and hold his gaze till he walks away.

Shit. I just offered to resign. Why on earth did I do that? I'm just wondering whether to run after Eric and say "Ha-ha, I was only joking!" when my phone starts ringing and I flip it open. "Hello?"

"Hi, Becky? Buffy."

I stifle a sigh. Buffy is one of Danny's assistants and she's been calling every evening, just to check some tiny detail or other.

"Hi, Buffy!" I force a cheerful tone. "What can I do for you?"

"I just wanted to check Mr. Kovitz's hotel room had

been ordered as he wanted it? Eighty degrees, the TV tuned to MTV, three cans of Dr Pepper by the bed?"

"Yes. I ordered it all." Suddenly something occurs to me. "Buffy, what time is it in New York?"

"It's four A.M.," she says brightly, and I stare at the phone, gobsmacked.

"You've got up at four A.M. just to check that Danny has Dr Pepper in his hotel room?"

"That's OK!" She sounds totally breezy. "It's all part of working in the fashion industry!"

"He's here!" comes a cry from the door. "Danny Kovitz is here!"

"Buffy, I have to go," I say hastily, and thrust my phone down. As I head toward the doors I glimpse a limo on the street outside and feel a prickle of excitement. It's amazing how important Danny has got!

Then the doors swing back, and there he is! He's as skinny as ever, and dressed in old jeans and the coolest black jacket, with one sleeve made out of mattress ticking. He looks tired and his curly hair is disheveled, but his blue eyes light up as he sees me, and he comes running forward.

"Becky! Oh my God, look at you." He envelops me in an enormous hug. "You look *fabulous!*"

"Look at you!" I retort. "Mr. Famous!"

"C'mon. I'm not *famous.* . . ." Danny makes a two-second stab at being self-deprecating. "Well . . . OK. Yes, I am. Isn't it wild?"

I can't help giggling. "So, is this your entourage?" I nod at the woman in a headset who has come in along-side a huge, bald secret-service–type guy.

"That's my assistant, Carla."

"I thought Buffy was your assistant."

"My second assistant," Danny explains. "And that's Stan, my bodyguard."

"You need a bodyguard?" I say in amazement. Even I didn't realize Danny had got quite that famous.

"Well, I don't really *need* him," Danny admits. "But I thought it would be cool. Hey, did you get them to put Dr Pepper in my room?"

"Three cans." I see Eric approaching and quickly steer Danny away, toward the champagne table. "So . . . how's the design coming?" I ask casually. "Only I'm getting some pressure from my boss. . . ."

A familiar defensive look comes over Danny's face.

"I'm working on it, OK?" he says. "My team had some ideas but I'm not happy with them. I need to soak up the feel of the shop . . . the vibe of London . . . maybe take inspiration from some other European cities. . . ."

Other European *cities*?

"Right. And . . . how long do you think that will take? About?"

"Let me introduce myself," cuts in Eric, who has finally caught up with us. "Eric Wilmot. Head of marketing here at The Look. Welcome to Britain." He shakes Danny's hand with a grim smile. "We're delighted to be collaborating with such a talented young designer on such an exciting fashion project."

That sentence came word-for-word out of the press release. I know, because I wrote it.

"Danny was just telling me how he's really close to coming up with a final design!" I say to Eric, praying that Danny keeps his mouth closed. "Isn't that exciting? Although no *exact* time scale yet . . ."

"Mr. Kovitz?" A girl of about twenty, wearing green boots and a very strange coat made out of what looks like cellophane, is shyly approaching. "I'm from *Fashion Student Gazette*. I just wanted to say I'm a *huge* fan. We all are, in my year at Central Saint Martins. Could I ask you a few questions about your inspiration?"

Ha. You see? I shoot a triumphant look at Eric, who just scowls back.

It's pretty exciting, being part of a major fashion launch at a major department store! Even if it is a failing, empty department store.

Everybody gives a speech, even me. Brianna announces the initiative and thanks all the journalists for coming. Eric says again how excited we are to be working with Danny. I explain that I've known Danny ever since he was first stocked at Barneys (I don't mention that all his T-shirts fell to bits and I nearly got the sack). Danny says how thrilled he is to be designer in residence at The Look, and how he's sure within six months this will be the only place to shop in London.

By the end, everyone's in a brilliant mood. Everyone except Eric.

"Designer in residence?" he says as soon as he gets me alone. "What does that mean, 'designer in residence'? Does he think we're putting him up all bloody year?"

"No!" I say. "Of course not!"

I may have to have a little chat with Danny.

At last, after draining all the champagne, the fashion journalists melt away. Brianna and Eric disappear off to their offices and I'm left alone with Danny. Or at least, with Danny and his people.

"So, shall we go for lunch?" I suggest.

"Sure!" Danny says, and glances at Carla, who immediately speaks into her headset. "Travis? Travis, it's Carla. Could you bring the car around, please?"

Cool! We're going in the limo!

"There's quite a nice place round the corner—" I begin, but Carla cuts me off.

"Buffy has made reservations at three Zagat-recommended restaurants. Japanese, French, and I believe the third was Italian. . . ."

"How about . . . Moroccan?" Danny says as the driver opens the door.

"I'll give Buffy a call," Carla says without batting an eyelid. She speed-dials as we all get into the limo. "Buffy, Carla. Could you please hold the reservations you've made and research a Moroccan restaurant for lunch? That's *Moroccan,*" she repeats, enunciating clearly. "London West One. Thanks, hon."

"I feel like a latte," says Danny suddenly. "A mocha latte."

Without missing a beat, Carla speaks into her phone again. "Hello, Travis, this is Carla," she says. "Could we please pull over at a Starbucks. That's *Starbucks.*"

Thirty seconds later, the limo draws up beside a Starbucks. Carla opens the door.

"Just a mocha latte?" she says.

"Uh-huh," Danny says, stretching out lazily.

"Anything for you, Stan?" Carla looks at the bodyguard, who is sunk in his seat, plugged into his iPod.

"Huh?" He opens his eyes. "Oh, right, Starbucks. Get me a cappuccino. Real foamy."

The car door closes and I turn to Danny in disbelief. Does he have people running after him like this all day?

"Danny . . ."

"Uh-huh?" Danny looks up from flipping through

Cosmo Girl. "Hey, are you cold in here? I feel cold." He switches on his phone and speed-dials. "Carla, the car's a little cold. OK, thanks."

That does it.

"Danny, this is ridiculous!" I exclaim. "Can't you talk to the driver yourself? Can't you get your own latte?"

Danny looks genuinely perplexed.

"Well . . . I could," he says. "I guess." His phone rings and he switches it on. "Yes, cinnamon. Oh, that's too bad." He puts his hand over the phone. "Buffy can't find a Moroccan restaurant for us. How about Lebanese fusion?"

"Danny . . ." I feel like I'm on another planet. "There's a really nice restaurant right here." I gesture outside. "Can't we just go there? The two of us, no one else?"

"Oh." Danny seems to be getting his head round this idea. "Well . . . sure. Let's do it."

We get out of the car just as Carla approaches holding a Starbucks take-out tray.

"Is something wrong?" She surveys us in alarm.

"We're going for lunch," I say. "Just Danny and me. In there." I point at the restaurant, which is called Annie's.

"Right." Carla nods vigorously, as though taking in the situation. "Great! I'll just make you a reservation. . . ." To my utter astonishment she speed-dials her phone again. "Hi, Buffy, could you please reserve a table at a restaurant called Annie's, let me spell that for you. . . ."

Buffy is in *New York*. We are standing ten feet away from the place. How does this make any sense?

"Honestly, we're fine, thanks!" I say to Carla. "See you later!" And I drag Danny across the pavement and into the restaurant.

We do have to wait a bit for a table. But I stick out my stomach as far as it will go and sigh wistfully at the maître d'—and a few minutes later we're ensconced in a corner banquette, dipping bread into yummy olive oil. Which is a relief. I was going to have to admit defeat and call Buffy.

"This is so great, being here," Danny says, as a waiter pours him a glass of wine. "Here's to you, Becky!"

"Here's to you!" I clink his wineglass with my water glass. "And here's to your fabulous design for The Look!" I force myself to leave a natural pause. "So, you were going to tell me when you thought you might have something to show us?"

"Was I?" Danny looks surprised. "Hey, you want to come to Paris with me next week? There is the *best* gay scene there—"

"Fab!" I nod. "The thing is, Danny, we kind of... sort of... need to have something quite... quickly."

"Quickly?" Danny opens his eyes wide, looking betrayed. "What do you mean, 'quickly'?"

"Well, you know! As soon as you can manage, really. We're trying to save the store, so the sooner we can get something going, the better...." I trail off as Danny fixes a reproachful gaze on me.

"I could be 'quick,' " he says, uttering the word with disdain. "I could throw together a few crap ideas in five minutes. Or I could do something *meaningful*. Which may take *time*. That's the creative process—excuse me for being an artist." He takes a gulp of wine and puts his glass down.

I can't say that a few crap ideas in five minutes sound great to me.

Can I?

"Is there a middle road?" I venture at last. "Like... some *fairly* good ideas in about... a week?"

"A *week*?" Danny looks almost more offended than before.

"Or... whatever." I back down. "You're the creative person; you know how you work best. So! What do you want to eat?"

We order penne (me) and lobster (Danny) and the special quail's-egg salad (Danny) and a champagne cock-tail (Danny).

"So, how've you been?" Danny asks as the waiter eventually retreats. "I've been having a *total* nightmare with my boyfriend, Nathan. I thought he was seeing someone else."

"Me too," I confess.

"What?" Danny drops his roll in astonishment. "You thought *Luke* was..."

"Having an affair." I nod.

"You're kidding." He seems genuinely shocked. "But you guys are so perfect."

"It's fine now," I reassure him. "I know nothing's go-ing on. But I nearly had him followed by a private de-tective."

"Get *out*." Danny is leaning forward, his eyes alight. "So, what happened?"

"I canceled it."

"Jesus." Danny chews his roll, taking this all in. "So, why did you think he was cheating?"

"There's this *woman*. She's our obstetrician. And she's Luke's ex-girlfriend."

"Ooh." Danny winces. "The ex-girlfriend. Harsh. And what's she like?"

I have a sudden flashback to Venetia making me put on those revolting surgical stockings, her eyes gleaming with triumph.

"She's a red-haired bitch and I hate her," I say, more vehemently than I meant to. "I call her Cruella de Venetia."

"And she's delivering the baby?" Danny starts laughing. "Is this for real?"

"It's not funny!" I can't help giggling too.

"I *have* to see this birth." Danny skewers an olive on a cocktail stick. "'Push!' 'I won't, you bitch!' You should sell tickets."

"Stop it!" My stomach's hurting from laughing. On the table my phone beeps with a text and I pull it over to have a look. "Hey, it's Luke! He's stopping by to say hello!" I texted Luke while we were ordering, to let him know where we were having lunch.

"Great." Danny takes a swig of his champagne cocktail. "So, you guys are cool now?"

"We're great. In fact, things are wonderful. We're going to look at prams together tomorrow." I give Danny a beatific smile.

"He doesn't even know you thought he was cheating?"

"I brought it up a couple of times," I say slowly, buttering another roll. "But he always denied anything was going on. I'm not going to mention it again."

"Or the private detective." Danny's eyes gleam.

"Obviously not the private detective." I narrow my eyes. "And don't say a *word*, Danny."

"I wouldn't!" Danny exclaims innocently, and takes another slurp of champagne cocktail.

"Hi, guys!" I turn to see Luke making his way through the crowded restaurant. He's wearing his new Paul Smith suit and has his BlackBerry in his hand. He gives me a tiny wink, and I force myself to stay composed, even though I want to smile wickedly as I remember this morning. And no, I'm not explaining. Let's just say that if I'm so "unattractive" and "unsexy" like Venetia said, then why did Luke . . .

Anyway. Moving on.

"Danny! Long time."

"Luke!" Danny leaps up and claps him on the back. "Great to see you!"

"Congratulations on all your success!" Luke pulls out a chair from a neighboring table. "I can't stay long, but I wanted to say welcome to London."

"Cheers, mate." Danny puts on the worst cockney accent I have ever heard. He drains his champagne cocktail and gestures to a waiter to bring him another one. "And congratulations to you guys!" He runs a hand lightly over my tummy, then flinches as the baby kicks. "Jesus. Was that *it*?"

"It's exciting!" Luke nods with a smile. "Only a few weeks to go!"

"Jesus." Danny's still staring at my stomach. "What if it's a girl in there? Another little Becky Bloomwood. You better get back to the office, Luke, and earn some money. You're gonna need it."

"Shut up!" I hit him on the arm. But Luke's already getting up from his seat. "I was only passing, anyway. Iain's waiting for me in the car. See you again, Danny. Bye, sweetheart." He kisses me on the forehead, then peers out the restaurant window as though searching for something.

"What is it?" I say, following his gaze.

"It's . . ." Luke frowns. "I wasn't going to say anything, but for the last few days I've felt as though I'm being followed."

"Followed?"

"I'm seeing the same guy around the place all the time." Luke shrugs. "He was outside the office yesterday, and I saw him just now."

"But who on earth—" I come to a halt.

Shit. No. It *can't* be.

I canceled them. I know I did. I phoned and left a message on Dave Sharpness's answering machine. And I sent an e-mail.

I look up to see Danny's delighted gaze on me.

"You think someone's *following* you, Luke?" he says, raising his eyebrows. "Like . . . a private detective, maybe?"

I will kill him.

"It's probably nothing!" My voice is a bit strangled. "Just coincidence!"

"Probably." Luke nods. "Strange, though. See you later." He touches my hand, and we both watch him wend his way between the tables.

"Trust is a beautiful thing between a married couple," observes Danny. "You two are very lucky."

"Shut up!" I'm scrabbling for my phone. "I have to call them off!"

"I thought you already did."

"I did! Days ago! It's all a mistake!" I find Dave Sharpness's card and jab in the number, my fingers fumbling in agitation.

"How do you think Luke will react when he finds out you're having him trailed?" asks Danny conversationally. "I'd be quite pissed if it were me."

"You are really *not* helping." I glare at him. "And thanks for mentioning private detectives!"

"Oh, I'm sorry!" Danny claps his hand over his mouth in mock apology. "Because he would never have worked it out on his own."

I'm through to voice mail, and I take a deep breath.

"Mr. Sharpness. It's Becky Brandon here. There seems to have been some confusion. I would like you to *stop* following my husband, Luke. I do not want any investigation. Please call off your operatives at once. Thank you." I switch off the phone and take a gulp of Danny's champagne cocktail, breathing hard. "There. Done."

Prendergast de Witt Connell
Financial Advisers

Forward House
394 High Holborn
London WC1V 7EX

Mrs R Brandon
37 Maida Vale Mansions
Maida Vale
London NW6 0YF

20 November 2003

Dear Mrs. Brandon,

Thank you for your letter.

I have noted your new shareholding in the London Cappuccino Company.

I would recommend you do not make any further share purchases simply because of "fab shareholder perks" such as free coffee. You should be looking for solid, long-term growth prospects.

In answer to your other query, I am not aware of any jewelry companies which give away free diamonds to their shareholders.

Yours sincerely,

Kenneth Prendergast
Family Investment Specialist

FOURTEEN

I JUST HOPE they got my message. Or the one I left last evening. Or the one I left this morning. I must have blocked Dave Sharpness's voice mail completely, telling him to stop the investigation. But until I speak to him myself, I can't be positive the message has got through.

Which means the surveillance could still be on.

As we leave the flat together the next morning to go to the pram center, all my senses are on high alert. I feel sure someone's watching us. But where? Hiding in the trees? Sitting in a parked car with a long lens trained on us? I edge down the steps of the building, my eyes darting from side to side. There's an electronic clicking sound to my left, and I instinctively shield my face with my hand—until I realize it's not a camera, it's someone opening their car.

"Are you all right, darling?" Luke is watching me, bemused.

The postman comes by, and I shoot a suspicious glance at him. Is he *really* the postman?

Oh, yes. He is.

"OK." I hurry to Luke. "Let's get in the car. Now."

We should have bought a car with blacked-out windows. I *told* Luke all along. And a built-in fridge.

My mobile rings just as we reach the gates of our block, and I jump a mile. That timing is too coincidental. It'll be the private detective, telling me he's in the boot of the car. Or he's in the building opposite, with a sniper rifle aimed at Luke. . . .

Stop it. I didn't hire an assassin. It's fine.

Even so, as I get my phone out, my hands are trembling. "Er . . . hello?" I say nervously.

"Hi, it's me!" comes Suze's breezy voice, with the clamor of children's voices in the background. "Listen, if they have a twin Urban Baby cozy-toes in red trim, will you get it for me? I'll pay you back."

"Oh. Er . . . of course." I grab a pen and scribble it down. "Anything else?"

"No, that's it. I'd better go! Talk later!"

I put my phone away, still feeling jumpy. We're being followed—I just know we are.

"So, where is this place?" Luke consults the leaflet and starts pressing buttons on his sat nav. The map pops up and he pulls a face. "It's bloody miles away. Do we have to go here?"

"It's the best place in London! Look!" I read from the leaflet. "You get to try all the top-quality prams on a variety of terrains and a consultant will help guide you through the maze."

"The maze of pram-buying or a literal maze?" inquires Luke.

"I don't know," I admit, after searching through the leaflet. "But anyway, it's got the widest choice and Suze said we should go there."

"Fair enough." Luke raises his eyebrows and does a

U-turn. Then he frowns at the rearview mirror. "That car looks familiar."

Shit.

Trying to appear casual, I swivel my head to see. It's a brown Ford and a guy is driving it. A dark-haired, pockmarked, private detective kind of guy.

Shit shit shit.

"Let's listen to the radio!" I say. I start tuning in to different stations, turning the volume up, trying to distract him. "And anyway, so what if it's familiar? There are lots of brown Fords in the world. Who knows how many? Probably . . . five million. No, ten . . ."

"Brown Ford?" Luke gives me a strange look. "What?"

I turn my head again. The brown Ford has disappeared. Where did it go?

"I meant that convertible BMW we passed," Luke says, turning the radio down. "It looked like Mel's husband's car."

"Oh, right," I say after a pause, and subside. Maybe I'll just keep my mouth shut for a bit.

I hadn't quite realized it would take an hour to get to Pram City. It's a warehouse based right out in North London, and there's a special park-and-ride scheme where you get on a bus. I didn't realize that, either. But still. It'll be worth it when we have the most cool uber-pram in the world!

As we descend the bus steps, I have a surreptitious scope around—but I can't see anyone who looks like a private investigator. It's mostly pregnant couples like us.

Unless . . . maybe Dave Sharpness has hired *another preg-nant couple* to trail us?

No. I'm getting paranoid. I have to stop obsessing about this. Anyway, would it be the worst thing in the world if Luke found out? At least I care about our marriage. In a way, he should be *flattered* I'm having him followed.

Exactly.

We head toward the vast doors along with all the other couples, and as we enter, I can't help feeling a little glow of pleasure. Here we are, choosing prams together. Just like I always imagined!

"So!" I beam up at Luke. "What do you think? Where shall we start?"

"Jesus," Luke says, looking around. It's a big domed building, with vicious air-conditioning and nursery rhymes playing over the sound system. Colorful ten-foot banners hanging from the rafters read STROLLERS, ALL-TERRAINS, TRAVEL SYSTEMS, TWINS AND MORE.

"What do we need?" Luke rubs his brow. "A pram? A travel system? A buggy?"

"It depends." I try to sound knowledgeable, but the truth is I'm still foxed by this whole pram and pushchair business. Suze tried to explain the system to me, but it was just like going to press conferences when I was a financial journalist. I glazed over at the pros and cons of swiveling front wheels—and then when she finished I was too embarrassed to admit I hadn't taken in a word.

"I've done some research," I add, and reach in my bag for my Pram List, which I hand to Luke with pride. Over the last few weeks, every time I've seen a cool pram or buggy, I've written down its name—and it hasn't been easy. I had to chase one all the way down High Street Kensington.

Luke is leafing through the pages in disbelief. "Becky, there's about thirty prams here."

"Well, that's the long list! We just need to whittle it down a bit."

"May I help you?" We both look up to see a guy with a round head and close-cropped hair approaching us. He's wearing a short-sleeved shirt and a Pram City badge saying *My Name Is Stuart,* and he's propelling a purple buggy along with one expert hand.

"We need a pram," says Luke.

"Ah." Stuart's eyes drop to my stomach. "Congratulations! Is this your first visit here?"

"First and only," says Luke firmly. "Not wishing to be rude, but we'd like to get everything wrapped up in one visit, wouldn't we, Becky?"

"Absolutely!" I nod.

"Of course. Glenda? Take care of this, please? Back to Section D." Stuart pushes the purple buggy across the shiny floor to a girl about ten yards away, then turns back to us. "Now, what kind of a pram were you looking for?"

"We're not quite sure," I say, glancing at Luke. "I think we need some help."

"Of course!" Stuart nods. "Step this way."

He leads us into the center of the Travel Systems area, then stops, like a museum guide.

"Every couple is different," he says in a singsong voice. "Every baby is unique. So before we go any further, I'd like to ask you a few questions about your lifestyle, the better to steer your choice." He reaches for a small pad of paper which is attached to his belt by springy wire. "Let's look at terrain. What will you be requiring of your vehicle? Pavement walking and shopping? Off-road hiking? Extreme mountaineering?"

"All of them," I say, slightly mesmerized by his voice.

"*All* of them?" exclaims Luke. "Becky, when do you ever go extreme mountaineering?"

"I might!" I retort. "I might take it up as a hobby!" I have an image of myself lightly pushing a pram up the foothills of Everest while the baby goos happily up at me. "I don't think we should rule anything out at this stage."

"Uh-huh." Stuart is scribbling some notes. "Now, will you require the pram to fold down quickly and easily for car use? Will you want it to convert to a car seat? Will you be looking for something light and maneuverable or sturdy and secure?"

I glance at Luke. He looks as flummoxed as I feel.

Stuart relents. "Let's look at some models. That'll get you started."

Half an hour later, my head is spinning. We've looked at prams that turn into car seats, pushchairs that fold up with hydraulic action, buggies with bicycle wheels, prams with special-sprung German mattresses, and an amazing contraption that keeps the baby out of pollution and is "ideal for shopping and lattes." (I love that one.) We've looked at foot muffs, raincovers, changing bags, and canopies.

To be honest, I'm ready for a latte now myself, but Luke is still totally engrossed. He's poring over the framework of a pushchair with the hugest, most rugged wheels I've ever seen. It's upholstered in khaki camouflage and looks like a great big Action Man toy.

"So, it has an articulated chassis," he's saying with interest. "How does that affect the turning circle?"

For God's sake. It's not a car.

"You can't beat the turning circle on this model." Stuart's eyes are gleaming as he demonstrates. "The Warrior is the Humvee of off-roaders. You see the sprung axle?"

"The Warrior?" I echo, aghast. "We're not getting a pram called the Warrior!"

Both men ignore me.

"It's a great piece of engineering." Luke takes hold of the handles. "Feels good."

"This is a *man's* pram. It's not a fashion pram." Stuart glances with slight disdain at the Lulu Guinness printed stroller I'm holding on to. "We had an ex-SAS guy in here the other day, Mr. Brandon." He lowers his voice. "This is the pram he chose."

"I like it a lot." Luke's pushing it back and forth. "Becky, I think we should get this."

"OK." I roll my eyes. "That can be your one."

"What do you mean, my one?" Luke stares at me.

"I want to get *this* one!" I say defiantly. "It's got a limited edition Lulu Guinness print and built-in iPod holder. And look at the sun canopy. It's fab!"

"You cannot be serious." Luke runs his eyes dismissively over it. "It looks like a toy."

"Well, your one looks like a tank! I'm not pushing that down the street!"

"I would *just* point out," interjects Stuart delicately, "while applauding both your choices, that neither of these models has the car seat and lie-flat facilities that you were originally seeking."

"Oh." I look at the Lulu Guinness stroller. "Oh, right."

"Might I suggest you regroup, have coffee, and work out your needs? It may be that you need more than one vehicle. One for off-roading, one for nipping around the shops."

That's a thought.

Stuart hurries off toward another couple, and Luke and I head toward the café.

"OK," I say as we reach the tables. "You go and get the coffees. I'll sit here and work out exactly what we need."

I pull out a chair, sit down, and get out a pen and my Pram List. On the back I write *Pram Priorities* and draw a grid. The only way to do this is to be totally rigorous and scientific.

A few minutes later, Luke approaches with a tray of drinks. "Get any further?" he asks, sitting down opposite me.

"Yes!" I look up, my face flushed from the effort. "OK. I've been working it out logically . . . and we need five prams."

"Five?" Luke nearly drops his coffee. "Becky, one small baby cannot possibly need five prams."

"It does! Look." I show him my grid. "We need a travel system with a carry-cot and a car seat for when it's tiny." I count off on my fingers. "We need an off-road jogger for going on walks. We need that shopping-and-lattes one for the city. We need the whizzy folding-up one for the car. And we need the Lulu Guinness one."

"Why?"

"Because . . . it's cool," I say defensively. "And all the other yummy mummies will have one."

"The other yummy mummies?" Luke gives me a blank look. Honestly. Doesn't he remember anything?

"In *Vogue*! I have to be the yummiest!"

Stuart is passing the café area, and Luke beckons him over.

"Excuse me. My wife is now talking about buying *five* prams. Please, can you explain to her that this is totally unreasonable?"

"You'd be surprised, sir," says Stuart, giving me a confidential wink. "We do see a lot of repeat custom. And if you wanted to get all the pram-buying wrapped up in the one trip, it *might* make sense. . . ." He trails off at Luke's stony expression and clears his throat. "Why not try out a few models on our all-terrain stroller course? That'll give you a real idea."

The all-terrain stroller course is at the back of the store, and Stuart helps us take all our "possibles" over to it.

"We at Pram City are very proud of our stroller course," he says, effortlessly pushing five buggies along in a straight line. "As you go around it, you'll find every surface that the pram may encounter in its lifetime, from the shiny marble of a shopping mall to the pebbly beach of a summer holiday to the stone steps of a cathedral. . . . Here we are!"

Wow. I am quite impressed. The stroller course is about thirty meters long, like some kind of racetrack, and all the way round, people are pushing prams and calling out to each other. In the gravel section, one girl has got totally stuck with her pink umbrella buggy, and in the beach section, two toddlers are chucking sand at each other.

"Cool!" I grab the shopping-and-lattes stroller and head for the start. "Race you, Mr. Warrior."

"You're on." Luke takes hold of the enormous khaki handles, then frowns. "How do I release the brake?"

"Ha! Loser!" I start dashing over the pavement section with my nippy stroller. A moment later I see Luke starting to push his monster along, and soon he's gaining on me.

"Don't you *dare*!" I say over my shoulder, and pick up the pace.

"The Warrior is invincible," Luke says in a film-trailer voice. "The Warrior admits no defeat."

"Can the Warrior do a *twirl*?" I retort. We're on the marble surface by now, and my stroller is amazing! I push it with one finger and it practically does a figure eight. "You see? It's absolutely—" I look up to see Luke already on the gravel. "You missed your compulsory figures!" I call in outrage. "Twenty-second penalty!"

The Warrior is pretty cool on gravel, it has to be said. It just kind of crunches the stones into submission. Whereas my stroller is a bit . . . crap.

"Need any help there?" Luke inquires as he watches me pick my way across. "Having trouble with your inferior pram?"

"I don't plan to take the baby to any gravel pits," I retort kindly. I reach the grass and accidentally-on-purpose bump my pram into Luke's.

"Trouble with your steering?" He raises his eyebrows.

"Just testing your airbags," I say airily. "They don't seem to be working."

"Very kind of you. Shall I test yours?" He bumps his pram into mine, and with a giggle I shove him back again. At the side fence I can see Stuart watching us in slight alarm.

"Any decisions yet?" he calls out.

"Oh yes," Luke calls back, nodding. "We want three Warriors."

"Shut up!" I hit Luke with the back of my hand and he starts to laugh.

"Make that four—" He breaks off as his mobile rings. "Hang on a sec." He takes it out and lifts it to his ear. "Luke Brandon. Oh, hi."

He lets go of the pram and turns away. Maybe I'll have a go with the Warrior now. I take hold of the massive handles and give it an experimental push.

"You're kidding," I hear Luke saying sharply. I wheel the Warrior round till I'm facing him. His face is tight and pale, and he's listening with an intent frown to whoever's on the phone. *Is everything OK?* I mouth at him, but he immediately swivels away and takes several paces away from me.

"Right," I can just hear him saying. "We have to . . . think about this." He's rumpling his hair as he walks along the stroller course, not even noticing the couple with the three-wheeler who have to dodge him.

Feeling slightly anxious, I start following him with the Warrior. What's happened? Who's that on the phone? I bump the wheels down some steps, and at last I catch up with him at the sandy beach section. As I draw near I feel a nervous flip. He's standing still, clutching his phone, his face etched with tension.

"That's not an option," he keeps saying in the same

low voice. "It's not an option." All of a sudden he notices me and his whole face jolts.

"Luke..."

"I'm talking, Becky." He sounds rattled. "Could I have some privacy, please?" He strides off down the sand, and I gaze after him, feeling as though I've been punched in the face.

Privacy? From me?

My legs are trembling as I watch him striding away. What went wrong? One minute we were pushing prams and laughing and teasing each other and now...

Suddenly I'm aware of my own mobile ringing inside my bag. I have a sudden mad conviction it's Luke, apologizing—but I can see him on the other side of the stroller course, still talking.

I pull out my phone and switch it on. "Hello?"

"Mrs. Brandon?" comes a crackly voice. "Dave Sharpness here."

Oh, for God's sake. Of all the times.

"At last!" I snap, taking out my worry on him. "Listen, I canceled you! What are you doing, still following my husband?"

"Mrs. Brandon." Dave Sharpness chuckles. "If I had a penny for every woman who phones up to cancel the next day and then regrets it—"

"But I *did* want you to cancel!" I feel like hitting the phone in frustration. "My husband knows someone's been following him! He saw one of your men!"

"Ah." Dave Sharpness sounds taken aback. "Now, that should *not* have happened. I'll speak to the operative concerned—"

"Call them all off! Call everybody off right this

minute before my marriage gets ruined! And don't phone me again!"

The phone is getting more and more crackly.

"I'm losing you, Mrs. Brandon," I hear Dave Sharpness's voice faintly. "My apologies. I'm on the road to Liverpool."

"I said, stop the investigation!" I say, as loudly and clearly as I dare.

"What about our findings? That's why I was ringing. Mrs. Brandon, I have a full report available for you...." His voice disappears into a sea of static.

"Findings?" I stare at the phone, my heart suddenly thumping. "What do you...Mr. Sharpness? Are you there?"

"...really think you should see the photographs..."

The crackle suddenly switches to a continuous tone. He's gone.

I'm paralyzed, standing on the sand, one hand still clutching the Warrior. Photographs? He surely doesn't mean—

"Becky." Luke's voice startles me so much that I jump, flipping my phone into the air. He bends down to pick it up from the sand, and hands it back. I can't quite look at him as I take it with shaky hands and shove it in my pocket.

Photographs of what?

"Becky, I have to go." Luke sounds as strained as I feel. "That was...Mel. Slight office emergency."

"Fine." I nod and start pushing the Warrior back to the beginning of the course. My eyes are fixed straight ahead. I feel numb. Photographs of what?

"Let's get the Lulu Guinness pram," says Luke as we reach the start. "I really don't mind."

"No. Get the Warrior." I swallow, trying to press back the sudden lump springing up in my throat. "It doesn't matter."

All the fun and easyness has disappeared. I feel cold with apprehension. Dave Sharpness has got evidence of Luke doing...something. And I have no idea what.

FIFTEEN

I DON'T BOTHER with the sunglasses this time. Nor do I bother smiling at the receptionist. I sit bolt upright on the same brown foam chair, shredding a tissue to bits, thinking, *I can't believe it.*

I couldn't do anything over the weekend. I had to wait until Luke went off to work this morning. I made sure he'd really gone (by looking out the window and then calling him twice in the car to make sure he hadn't turned round) and then plucked up the courage to ring Dave Sharpness's office. Even then, I practically did it in a whisper. I spoke to the receptionist, who refused to give me any details of the findings over the phone. So here I am, at eleven o'clock in the morning, in West Ruislip again.

The whole thing feels surreal. It was supposed to be *canceled.* They weren't supposed to *find* anything.

"Mrs. Brandon." I look up, feeling like a patient at a doctor's office. There's Dave Sharpness, sounding more sepulchral than ever. "Would you like to come through?"

As he ushers me into the office, he looks so pitying, I can't bear it. Instantly I decide to put on a brave face. I'll pretend I'm not bothered if Luke's having an affair. I was only wanting to know out of idle curiosity. In fact, I'm *glad* he's having an affair, because I wanted a divorce all along. Yes.

"So you found something," I say nonchalantly as I take a seat. "Interesting." I attempt a careless little smile.

"This is a difficult time for you, Mrs. Brandon." Dave Sharpness leans heavily forward on his elbows.

"No it's not!" I say overbrightly. "I really don't care. Actually, I've got a boyfriend and we're going to run away together to Monaco, so I'm absolutely fine about all of this."

Dave Sharpness doesn't look taken in.

"I think you do care." His voice descends yet lower. "I think you care very much." His bloodshot eyes are so mournful, I can't hold out anymore.

"OK, I do care!" I sniff. "Just tell me, OK? Has he been seeing her?"

Dave Sharpness opens a manila folder and surveys the contents, shaking his head.

"This part of the job is never easy." He sighs, shuffles the papers, then looks up. "Mrs. Brandon, your husband has been leading quite the double life."

"Double life?" I gape at him.

"I'm afraid to say, he's not the man you thought he was."

How can Luke not be the man I thought he was? What's he talking about?

"What do you mean?" I say, almost aggressively.

"Last Wednesday, one of my operatives trailed your husband from his place of work. He checked into a hotel under a false name. He ordered cocktails for several...women. Of...a certain type. If you know what I mean, Mrs. Brandon."

I'm so gobsmacked, I can't speak. Luke? Women of a certain type?

"My highly skilled operative followed up his alias." Dave Sharpness gives me an impressive look. "He discovered that there has been trouble at that particular hotel in the past. There have been...regrettable incidents with women." Dave Sharpness looks at his notes with a distasteful expression. "All of which have been hushed up and paid off. He's clearly a powerful man, your husband. My operative further discovered several sexual harassment charges which were never pursued...a joint allegation of bullying against himself and a colleague, again hushed up...."

"Stop it!" I cry, unable to listen anymore. "You must have got your information wrong! You or your operative. My husband doesn't drink cocktails with women of a certain type! He would never *bully* anyone! I know him!"

Dave Sharpness sighs. He leans back in his chair and rests his hands on his huge stomach.

"I feel for you, Mrs. Brandon, I really do. No wife wants to hear that her husband is less than perfect."

"I'm not saying he's *perfect,* but..."

"If you knew the number of deceivers out there." He eyes me lugubriously. "And the wife is always the last to know."

"You don't understand!" I feel like slapping him. "This can't be Luke. It just *can't* be!"

"It's hard to come to terms with the truth." Dave Sharpness is inexorable. "It takes great courage."

"Stop patronizing me!" I say furiously. "I do have courage. But I also *know* my husband isn't a bully. Give me those notes!" I grab the folder from him, and a pile of shiny black-and-white photographs falls out onto the desk.

I stare at them in confusion. They're all pictures of Iain Wheeler. Iain outside Brandon Communications. Iain Wheeler walking up the steps of a hotel.

"This isn't my husband." I look up. "This is *not* my husband."

"Now we're getting somewhere." Dave Sharpness nods in satisfaction. "Your husband has two sides to his personality, as it were—"

"Shut up, you stupid man!" I shout, exasperated. "It's Iain! You've followed the wrong person!"

"What?" Dave Sharpness sits up. "Literally the wrong person?"

"This is one of his clients. Iain Wheeler."

Dave Sharpness grabs one of the prints and stares at it for a few seconds.

"This isn't your husband?"

"No!" I suddenly spot a photo of Iain getting into his limo. I grab it and point at Luke, who is in the background on the other side of the car, barely in focus. "*That's* Luke! *That's* my husband."

Dave Sharpness's breathing is getting heavier as he looks from Luke's blurry head to the photos of Iain, to his notes, and back to Luke.

"Lee! Get in here!" he shouts, suddenly sounding far less smooth-caring-professional and more pissed-off-South-London-geezer.

A few moments later, the door opens and a skinny guy of about seventeen pokes his head round the door, holding a Game Boy.

"Er . . . yeah?" he says.

This is the highly skilled operative?

"Lee, I've had it with you." Dave Sharpness bangs his hand furiously on the table. "This is the second time you've buggered up. You've only followed the wrong bloody man. This isn't Luke Brandon." He jabs at the pictures. "*This* is Luke Brandon!"

"Oh." Lee rubs his nose, looking unconcerned. "Shit."

"Yes, shit! Yes, I've a good mind to fire your bloody arse." Dave Sharpness's neck has turned bright pink. "How d'you get the wrong man?"

"Dunno!" says Lee defensively. "I got his picture out of the paper." He reaches in the folder and pulls out a clipping from the *Times*.

I know this picture. It's a candid shot of Luke and Iain chatting at an Arcodas press conference. "There, see?" says Lee. "It says, 'Luke Brandon, right, confers with Iain Wheeler, left.' "

"They got the caption the wrong way round!" I practically spit at him. "There was an apology the next day! Didn't you *check* it!"

Lee's eyes have already drifted back to his Game Boy.

"Answer the lady!" bellows Dave Sharpness. "Lee, you're a waste of bloody space!"

"Look, Dad, it was a mistake, all right?" whines Lee. *Dad?*

This is the last time I ever get a private detective off the Internet.

"Mrs. Brandon . . ." Dave Sharpness is obviously trying to calm himself. "I can only apologize. We will of course restart the investigation at no extra charge to yourself, this time focusing on the correct personage—"

"No!" I cut him off. "Just stop, OK? I've had enough."

I'm suddenly feeling shaky. *How* could I ever have hired someone to spy on Luke? What am I doing in this crappy place? Abruptly I stand up. "I'm going. Please don't contact me ever again."

"Of course." Dave Sharpness hastily pushes his own chair back. "Lee, get out of the way! If I can just give you the other findings, Mrs. Brandon..."

"*Other* findings?" I turn on him, incredulous. "You really think I want to hear anything else you've got to say?"

"There was the matter of the eyebrows?" Dave Sharpness coughs delicately.

"Oh. Oh, right." I come to a halt. I'd forgotten about that.

"It's all in here." Dave Sharpness takes the opportunity to press the manila folder into my arms. "Details of the therapist and the treatment, photographs, surveillance notes..."

I want to throw the folder right back in his face and stalk out.

Only... Jasmine *does* have really good eyebrows.

"I might have a look just at that bit," I say at last, as stonily as I can.

"You'll also find a few other pieces of information in there," Dave Sharpness says, hurrying after me to the door, "that had been collated in regard to your husband's case. Your friend Susan Cleath-Stuart, for example. Now, she's a *very* rich young lady."

I feel sick. He's been checking out *Suze*?

"Apparently, her fortune has been estimated at—"

"Shut *up*!" I wheel round savagely. "I never want to see or hear from you again! And if any of your firm follows Luke or any of my friends, I'm calling the police."

"Absolutely," says Dave Sharpness, nodding as though this is a brilliant idea which he came up with. "Understood."

I totter to the end of the street and hail a taxi. It chugs off and I sit clinging to the handstrap, unable to relax until we're well out of West Ruislip. I can hardly bear to look at the manila folder sitting on my lap like a horrible guilty secret. Although now that I think about it, it's probably *better* that I brought it away. I'm taking all this information and I'm putting it straight in the shredder. And then I'll shred the shreds. I never want Luke to know what I did.

I can't believe I even went down this road. Luke and I are married. We shouldn't spy on each other. It's practically in the marriage vows, "To love, to cherish, and never hire a private detective in West Ruislip."

We should trust each other. We should *believe* each other. On impulse I take out my mobile and dial Luke's number. "Hi, darling!" I say as soon as I get through. "It's me."

"Hi! Is everything—"

"Everything's fine. I was just wondering." I take a deep breath. "That phone call you took the other day, at the pram shop. You seemed a bit upset. Is everything all right?"

"Becky, I'm sorry about that." He sounds truly remorseful. "I really am. I . . . lost it for a moment. There's been a small problem here. But it'll work itself out, I'm sure. Don't worry."

"Right." I exhale. I hadn't even realized I was holding my breath.

It's work. That's all it is. Luke always has little problems and blips that need sorting out, and sometimes he gets stressed. That's what happens when you run an enormous company.

"I'll see you later, sweetheart. All set for the big night out?"

It's the college reunion tonight. I'd almost forgotten. "Can't wait! Bye, Luke."

I put my phone away and take a few deep breaths. The main thing is, Luke has no idea I even went near a private detective. And he'll never find out.

As we reach the familiar terrain of West London I open up the folder and start leafing through the photos and surveillance notes. I might as well find out about Jasmine's eyebrows before I get to shredding. I come across a blurry shot of Suze walking down High Street Kensington, and I close my eyes, feeling another wave of shame. I've made some terrible mistakes in my life, but this is the worst by a million zillion miles. How could I have exposed my best friend to some seedy private detective?

The next ten or so pictures are all of Venetia, and I pass over those quickly. I don't want to see her. Then there's a couple of Mel, Luke's assistant, coming out of the office . . . and then . . . Oh my God, is that *Lulu*?

I stare at the print, bewildered. Then I remember mentioning her when I was making the list of women that Luke knows. I said that Luke didn't get on with her, and Dave Sharpness nodded knowingly and said, "That's often the smokescreen." Stupid man. He obviously got the idea that Luke and Lulu were secretly having a torrid affair or something—

Hang on. I blink, and peer more carefully at the photograph. That can't be . . .

She can't be . . .

I clap a hand over my mouth, half shocked, half trying not to laugh. OK, I know hiring a private detective was a stupid thing to do. But this is *so* going to cheer Suze up.

I'm just stuffing all the prints and papers back into the folder when my mobile rings. "Yes?" I say cautiously.

"Becky, it's Jasmine!" comes an animated voice. "Are you coming in, or what?"

I sit up in surprise. First of all, I didn't think anyone would even notice I was late. And second, since when did Jasmine ever raise her voice above a bored, monosyllabic drawl?

"I'm on my way," I say. "What's up?"

"It's your mate Danny Kovitz."

I feel a grip of alarm. Please don't say he's lost interest. Please don't say he's pulled out.

"Is there . . . a problem?" I can hardly bear to say it.

"No way! He's finished his design! He's here with it now. And it's amazing!"

Finally, *finally,* something is going well! I arrive at The Look and head straight up to the boardroom on the sixth floor, which is where everybody has assembled to see the design.

Jasmine meets me at the lift, her eyes sparkling.

"It's so cool!" she says. "Apparently he was working all night to get it right. He says coming to Britain gave him exactly the final inspiration he needed. Everyone's really excited. It's going to be a sell-out! I've been texting my friends and they all want one."

"Great!" I say in astonishment.

I don't know what I'm more surprised by, Danny

finishing his design so quickly or Jasmine coming to life.

"In here..." She opens the heavy pale-wood door, and I can hear Danny's voice as we enter the board-room. He's sitting on the long table, holding forth to Eric, Brianna, and all the marketing and PR personnel.

"It was just that final concept I needed to crack," he's saying. "But once I got it..."

"It's so different!" Brianna is saying. "It's so *original*."

"Becky!" Danny suddenly notices me. "Come and see the design! Carla, come over here."

He beckons her over—and I gasp.

"You *what*?" My voice shoots out in horror before I can stop it.

Carla's wearing a T-shirt with gathered seams and Danny's trademark ragged, pleated sleeves. The back-ground is pale blue, and on the front there's a little stylized sixties-type drawing of a red-headed doll. Un-derneath is the single printed phrase:

SHE'S a RED-HAiRED BiTCH and I HATE HER

I look at Danny and back at the T-shirt and back at Danny.

"You can't...." My mouth isn't working properly. "Danny, you can't...."

"Isn't it great?" says Jasmine.

"The magazines will *love* it." A girl from PR is nod-ding enthusiastically. "We've already given *InStyle* a teeny sneak preview and it's going in their must-have column. And with the signature carrier bag too... *Everyone* is going to want one."

"It's such a brilliant slogan!" says someone else. "'She's a red-haired bitch and I hate her'!"

The whole room laughs. Except me. I'm still in shock. What's Venetia going to say? What's Luke going to say?

"We're going to have it on bus stops, on posters, in magazines...." the PR girl is saying. "Danny had a fab idea, which is to run it as a maternity T-shirt too."

My head jerks up in horror. He what?

"Great idea, Danny!" I say, shooting daggers at him.

"I thought so." He beams back innocently. "Hey, you could wear one for the birth!"

"So, where did you get your inspiration, Mr. Kovitz?" asks an eager young marketing assistant.

"Who's the red-haired bitch?" The PR girl chimes in with an easy laugh. "I hope she won't mind having a thousand T-shirts printed about her!"

"What do you think, Becky?" Danny wickedly raises his eyebrows at me.

"Does Becky *know* her?" says Brianna in surprise. "Is this a real person?"

Everyone suddenly looks interested.

"No!" I gabble in alarm. "No! Not at all! She isn't... I mean...I was just...thinking. Why don't we broaden the design? We could have blond and brunette versions too."

"Nice idea," says Brianna. "What do you think, Danny?"

For a heart–stopping moment I think he's going to say "No, it has to be red–haired because Venetia is red–haired." But thank God, he nods.

"I like it. Pick your own bitch." He suddenly gives a huge, catlike yawn. "Is there any more coffee?"

Thank God. Disaster averted. I'll take a blond version home and Luke will never know about the original.

"We need this!" says Carla, pouring out the coffee. "We were up all night. Danny finalized the design at around two A.M. Then we found an all-night silk screener in Hoxton, and they made up the prototypes for us."

"Well, we appreciate your efforts," says Eric ponderously. "On behalf of The Look, I would like to thank you, Danny, and your team."

"Gratitude accepted," says Danny charmingly. "And I would like to thank Becky Bloomwood, whose brainchild this collaboration was." He starts applauding, and reluctantly I smile back. You can never stay cross with Danny for long. "To Becky, my muse," Danny adds, lifting the fresh cup of coffee that Carla has poured for him. "And the little musette."

"Thanks." I lift my cup back toward him. "To you, Danny."

"You're his *muse*?" Jasmine breathes beside me. "That's so cool!"

"Well . . ." I shrug nonchalantly. But inside I'm pretty chuffed. I have always wanted to be a fashion designer's muse!

It just shows. Whenever life seems total rubbish, it always turns around. Today has been approximately a million times better than I expected. Luke isn't leading a double life after all. Danny's design is going to be a sell-out. And I'm a muse!

By the end of the day I've changed my clothes a few

times, because fashion muses do like to experiment with their looks. I finally decide on a pink chiffon empire-line dress which I can just squeeze over my bump, with one of Danny's prototype T-shirts layered on top, together with a green velvet coat and a black feather hat.

I must start wearing more hats if I'm going to be a muse. And brooches.

At five thirty Danny appears at the entrance to personal shopping and I look up in surprise. "Are you still here? Where've you been?"

"Oh . . . just hanging out in menswear," he says casually. "That guy Tristan who works there . . . he's pretty cute, huh?"

"Tristan's not gay." I give Danny a look.

"Yet," Danny says, and picks up a pink evening dress from our Cruisewear department. "This is *gross.* Becky, you should not be stocking this dress."

He's totally hyper at the moment, the way he always gets when he's finished a design. I remember this from New York.

"Where are all your 'people'?" I ask, rolling my eyes. But Danny doesn't even get the irony.

"Drawing up contracts," he says vaguely. "And Stan took the car to go sightseeing. He's never been to London before. Hey, shall we have a drink?"

"I've got to go home." I glance reluctantly at my watch. "I have this reunion thing tonight."

"Just a quick drink?" Danny wheedles. "I've barely *seen* you. Hey, what's with the hat?"

"Do you like it?" I touch it, a little self-conscious. "I just felt like feathers."

"Feathers." Danny's surveying me with an interested frown. "Great idea."

"Really?" I glow with pride. Maybe he'll base his whole new collection on feathers, and it'll be my idea! "Hey, if you want to draw a little sketch of me or any-thing..." I say casually, but Danny isn't listening. He's walking around me, an interested frown on his face.

"You should wear a feather boa," he says suddenly. "Like, an oversize one. Like... *huge*."

An oversize feather boa. That's so brilliant. It could be the next big thing! It could be the new Fendi baguette!

"There are feather boas in accessories!" I say. "Come on!" I grab my bag and zip it up, first making sure the manila folder is safely in there. I'm going to shred it as soon as I get home. When Luke isn't looking.

We head down the escalators to the ground floor, where the accessories department is located.

"We're closing...." begins Jane, the accessories man-ager, but then she sees it's us.

"Sorry," I say breathlessly as Danny heads to a stand displaying feather boas and scarves. "We won't be long. It's just we're having a key fashion moment here...."

"*There*," says Danny, garlanding me with colorful feather boas. "Like, the biggest feather boa you ever saw." He's tying eight boas together into a massive sausage-shaped one. "This is a great look."

I feel a frisson as he drapes the boa round me. We're making fashion history, right here! We're setting a whole new trend! Next year everyone will be wearing huge Danny Kovitz boas. Celebrities will wear them to the Oscars, high street shops will rip them off....

"The Giant Boa," Danny says as he ties back a stray

feathery strand. "The Giant. It's fabulous. Take a look!" He swivels me round to face the mirror, and I gasp.

"Er...wow!"

"Great, isn't it?" He beams at me.

To be absolutely truthful, I gasped because I look so stupid. You can hardly see my head for feathers. I look like an enormous, pregnant feather duster.

But I mustn't be narrow-minded. This is fashion. People probably thought skinny jeans looked ridiculous when they first saw them.

"Amazing," I breathe, trying to get the feathers out of my mouth. "You're a *genius,* Danny."

"Let's go and have that drink." Danny is flushed with animation. "I'm in the mood for martinis."

"Can you put these boas on my account?" I say to Jane. "There's eight of them. Thanks!"

We head out of the shop on a total high, and I lead Danny round the corner into Portman Square. The street lamps are on, and some people in black tie are coming out of the Templeton Hotel. They eye me weirdly as we pass and I hear a couple of giggles, but I just hold my head higher. If you're going to be at the cutting edge of fashion, you're going to get a few strange looks.

"Shall we go to the bar here?" I suggest, coming to a halt. "It's a bit dull, but it's right here."

"As long as they can mix a drink..." Danny pushes open the heavy glass doors and ushers me in. The Templeton Bar is a very *beige* bar: beige carpet, plushy chairs, and waiters in beige uniforms. It's crowded with business types, but I can see some space by the piano.

"Let's nab that table over there," I say to Danny— and then I stop dead.

It's Venetia. Sitting in the corner a few yards away, her hair glowing under the lights, with a suited guy and another smart woman. I don't recognize either of them.

"What?" Danny peers at me. "Is something wrong?"

"It's..." I swallow and jerk my head discreetly toward her. Danny follows my gaze and gasps theatrically in delight.

"Is that Cruella de Venetia?"

"Shut up!" I squeak.

But it's too late: Venetia's turned. She's seen us. She's getting up and coming across, an impossibly elegant figure in a black trouser suit and heels, her hair as immaculate as ever, a wineglass in her hand.

It's fine, I tell myself. Calm down. I don't know why my heart is pounding and my fingers are sweaty.

Oh. Well...maybe because in my bag is a folder containing ten long-lens pictures of Venetia. But she doesn't *know* that, does she?

"Becky!" She smiles and kisses me on both cheeks. "My favorite client. How are you? Only four weeks to go now, isn't it?"

"That's right. So...um...how are you, Venetia?" My voice is jerky and my face has turned red—but other than that I think I'm acting quite naturally. "This is my friend, Danny Kovitz."

"Danny Kovitz." Her eyes light up in recognition. "It's an honor. I bought one of your pieces in Milan recently. In Corso Como. A beaded jacket?"

"I know the one!" says Danny eagerly. "I'll bet you look fabulous in it."

Why's he being nice to her? He's supposed to be on *my* side.

"Did you buy the pants?" he's saying now. "Because

we did them in two styles, a capri and a boot cut. You'd look great in the capri pants."

"No, I just bought the jacket." She smiles at him, then glances at me. "Becky, you seem hot in all those . . . feathers. Are you OK?"

"I'm . . . fine!" I blow a couple of feathers off my lipstick. "This is Danny's new fashion concept."

"Right." Venetia gives my giant feather boa a dubious look. "Only, you know, it's not healthy for you to overheat during pregnancy."

Typical. Bossing me about again. Telling me fashion's unhealthy. But the truth is, I am starting to sweat in all these layers, so reluctantly I unpeel the boa and take off my coat.

There's a weird silence. For a moment I'm not quite sure why Venetia is staring at my chest. Then my stomach plunges as I realize I'm wearing Danny's T-shirt. I glance down, and there it is, clear as day.

SHE'S a RED-HAiRED BiTCH and I HATE HER

Shit.

"Actually, I'm quite cold!" I clamp the boa round my neck again, trying desperately to cover up the words. "Brrrrr! It's freezing in here. Isn't it freezing, for the time of year?"

"What does that say?" Venetia says in a peculiar voice. "On your T-shirt."

"It's nothing," I say, flustered. "Nothing! It's just a . . . joke! I mean, obviously it's not *you*. It's another red-haired bitch. Er . . . woman. Person."

This is not going well.

"Good work, Becky," says Danny in my ear. "Tactful."

Venetia is inhaling deeply, as though trying to control herself. She looks pretty annoyed, now I come to notice it.

"Becky," she says at last. "Might we have a little talk?"

"Talk?" I echo nervously.

"Yes, talk. The two of us. Speaking to each other alone. If you wouldn't mind?" She glances at Danny.

"Sure. I'll get us some drinks." He disappears off to the bar and I feel a quailing inside as I turn to face Venetia. There's a frown line between her eyes and she's tapping her fingers against the stem of her glass. She looks like a young, glamorous headmistress who's about to tell me I've let down the whole school.

"So!" I muster a bright tone. "How are you?"

She can't read your mind, I'm telling myself feverishly. *She doesn't know you had her trailed. She can't prove the T-shirt is about her. Just act innocent.*

"Look, Becky." Venetia drains her glass in one gulp. "Let's cut the crap."

I stare at her in shock. Did she just say "crap"?

"We were trying to spare you any unpleasantness." Venetia's frown deepens. "We wanted to be as...I don't know...as amicable as possible. But if *this* is the attitude you're going to take..." She gestures at the T-shirt.

I'm missing something here. In fact, I'm missing everything.

"What do you mean, 'we'?" I say.

Venetia gazes at me as though suspecting a trick. Then, very slowly, her expression changes. She exhales and rubs her brow. "Oh God," she says, almost as though to herself.

I feel a thud of foreboding deep inside. A kind of hot nausea is slowly rising through me. She can't mean what I—

She can't.

The noise and chatter of the bar has dwindled to a rushing in my ears. I swallow several times, trying to keep a grip on myself. I know I thought something might be going on. I know I talked about it with Suze and Jess and Danny.

But all of a sudden, standing here now, I realize I didn't ever really think it was true. Not really. Not *really*.

"What are you saying?" I can't quite control my voice. "Exactly."

A waiter is passing with a tray of drinks, and Venetia puts out a hand to stop him.

"Vodka tonic on the rocks, please," she says. "Straightaway. Anything for you, Becky?"

"Just . . . tell me." My eyes burn into hers. "Tell me what you're talking about."

The waiter moves away and Venetia thrusts a hand through her hair. She looks a little ruffled by my reaction. "Becky . . . this was always going to be difficult. You should know, Luke feels terrible about what's been going on. He really cares about you. He'll be livid that I've spoken to you, even."

For a few moments I can't reply. I'm just staring at her, my whole body tensed up. I feel like I've swung into some parallel universe.

"What are you saying?" I repeat huskily.

"He really doesn't want to hurt you." Venetia leans

closer, and I get a sickening waft of Allure. "As he keeps saying . . . he made a mistake. Pure and simple. He married the wrong person. But that's not your fault."

Something starts stabbing at my chest. For a moment I'm not sure I can speak, for shock.

"Luke didn't marry the wrong person," I manage at last. "He married the *right* person. He loves me, OK? He *loves* me."

"You met right after he split up from Sacha, didn't you?" Venetia nods, even though I haven't replied. "He told me all about it. You were a refreshing change, Becky. You make him laugh. But you're hardly on the same level. You don't *really* understand what he's about."

"I do." My throat isn't working properly. "I totally understand Luke! We went round the world on our honeymoon—"

"Becky, I've known Luke since he was nineteen." She cuts across me, invincible, inexorable. "I *know* him. What we had at Cambridge was powerful. It was intoxicating. He was my first real love. I was his. We were like Odysseus and Penelope. When we saw each other again in my consulting room . . ." She breaks off. "I'm sorry. But we both knew, instantly. It was just a matter of when and where."

My legs seem to have turned to dust. My face is numb. I'm clutching my stupid feathers, trying to find a pithy, witty . . . something. But my head feels like a heavy lump of flannel. I have a horrible feeling there are tears on my cheeks.

"It's been appalling timing." Venetia takes her drink from the waiter. "Luke didn't want to say anything until after the baby came. But I think you deserve to know the truth."

"We went looking at prams together yesterday." My voice comes out thick and rushed. "How come he went to look at prams, then?"

"Oh, he's excited about the baby!" says Venetia in surprise. "He wants to see his child as much as possible after..." She pauses delicately. "He wants the whole thing to be amicable. But obviously that depends on you."

I can't listen to her sweet, poisonous voice anymore. I have to get away.

"You're wrong, Venetia," I say, struggling clumsily into my coat. "You're deluded. Luke and I have a strong, loving marriage! We laugh, and we talk, and we have sex...."

Venetia just looks at me with infinite pity. "Becky, Luke's just playing along to keep you happy. You don't have a marriage. Not anymore."

I don't wait to say good-bye to Danny. I head straight out of the bar on stumbling legs and hail a taxi. All the way home, Venetia's words are going round and round in my brain, until I want to throw up.

It can't be true, I keep telling myself. It can't be.

Of course it can, a small voice replies. *It's what you suspected all along.*

I let myself into the flat and immediately hear Luke moving around in the kitchen.

"Hi!" he calls out.

My throat's too tight to answer. I feel paralyzed. At last Luke pops his head round the door. He's already in dress trousers and a crisp Armani dress shirt. His bow tie is loose around his neck, ready for me to tie it like I always do.

I stare at him wordlessly. *Are you leaving me for Venetia? Is our whole marriage a sham?*

"Hi, darling." He takes a sip of wine.

I feel like I'm standing on a cliff edge. The moment I speak, it will all be over.

"Becky? Sweetheart?" Luke takes a few steps toward me, looking puzzled. "Are you OK?" He peers curiously at the feathers.

I can't do it. I can't ask him. I'm too frightened of what I'll hear.

"I'll go and get ready," I whisper, unable to meet his eye. "We need to leave soon."

I head to the bedroom and strip off, bundling Danny's T-shirt into the bottom of the wardrobe where Luke will never look. Then I take a quick shower, hoping it'll make me feel better. But it doesn't. As I catch sight of myself in the mirror, wrapped in a towel, I look scared and pale.

Come on, Becky. Chin up. Think glam. Think Catherine Zeta-Jones. I get out my slinky new midnight-blue dress and slip it on, thinking this at least will cheer me up. But somehow the dress doesn't look as good as it did before. It's not clingy, it's puckering. I haul at the zipper but it won't go up.

It's too small.

My perfect dress is too small. I must have grown some more. My bump, or my thighs, or somewhere. My whole body's suddenly got huge.

I can feel my chin wobbling, but desperately clamp my lips shut. I am *not* going to cry. I wrench off the dress as best I can and head to the wardrobe to find something else. And then I glimpse myself in the mirror, and freeze. I'm waddling.

I'm a white, fat, waddling...monstrosity.

I sit down on the bed, feeling dizzy. My head is pounding and there are spots before my eyes. No wonder he chose Venetia.

"Becky, are you OK?" Luke is at the door, surveying me in alarm. I hadn't even noticed him.

"I..." Tears are blocking my throat. "I'm..."

"You don't look well. Why don't you lie down? I'll bring you some water."

As I watch him go, Venetia's voice is in my head like a coiled snake. *He's playing along to keep you happy.*

"Here we are." Luke's voice makes me jump. He hands me a glass of water and two chocolate biscuits. "I think you should rest for a while."

I take the glass without drinking. Suddenly everything feels like acting. He's acting. I'm acting.

"What about the reunion?" I say at last. "We need to go soon."

"We can be late. Or we can miss it. Darling, have some water, lie down...."

Reluctantly I take a sip of water, then put my head on the pillow. Luke tucks the duvet over me and quietly leaves the room.

I don't know how long I lie there for. It feels like about thirty seconds. Or six hours. Afterward I work out it was about twenty minutes.

And then I hear the voices. His voice. And her voice. Approaching down the corridor.

"...hope you don't mind..."

"No, absolutely. Luke, you did the right thing to call. So, how's the patient?"

I open my eyes, and it's a nightmare come true. There, looming in front of me, is Venetia.

She's changed into a full-length strapless black taffeta ball gown with a swirly skirt. Her hair is pinned up in a chignon, and diamonds are flashing at her ears. She looks like a princess.

"Luke says you're not feeling well, Becky?" Her smile is syrupy sweet. "Let's have a look."

"What are *you* doing here?" I spit out.

"Luke called me. He was worried!" Venetia puts a hand on my head and I flinch. "Let me see if you've got a temperature." She sits on the bed with a rustle of taffeta and opens a little medical case.

"Luke, I don't want her here!" With no warning, tears are spilling from my eyes. "I'm not ill!"

"Open." Venetia is advancing a thermometer toward my mouth.

"No!" I turn my head away like a baby refusing its porridge.

"Come on, Becky," Venetia says in cajoling tones. "I just want to take your temperature...."

"Becky." Luke takes my hand. "Come on. We can't take any risks."

"I'm *not* ill—" My words are stifled as Venetia jams the thermometer in my mouth and stands up.

"I really don't think she should come tonight," she says in a low voice, drawing Luke aside. "Can you persuade her to stay here and rest?"

"Of course." Luke nods. "Please send our apologies."

"You're staying behind too?" Venetia frowns. "Luke, I really think..." She beckons Luke out of the room and I can hear low murmurings coming from the corridor.

A few moments later Luke appears around the door again, holding a jug of water.

Someone's tied his bow tie up, I suddenly notice. I want to burst into tears.

"Becky. Sweetheart, Venetia thinks you should take it easy."

I stare at him silently, the thermometer still in my mouth.

"I'll stay with you, of course. If you want me to." He hesitates awkwardly. "But . . . if you didn't mind me popping out just for half an hour, there are a lot of people coming to this reunion I'd like to see."

My throat is thickening. Fresh tears are springing to my eyes. I can see it all plainly now. He wants to go to the party with Venetia. They've probably engineered this whole thing.

What am I going to do, beg him not to? I've got more pride than that.

"Fine," I mumble, turning my head away so he can't see my tears. "Go."

"What?"

"Fine." I take the thermometer out of my mouth. "Go."

There's a rustle as Venetia comes into the room again. "Let's have a look." She studies the thermometer with a small frown. "Yes, you're slightly feverish. Let's give you some paracetamol. . . ."

She hands me two tablets and I gulp them down with the water which Luke brought in.

"You're sure you'll be OK?" he says, watching me anxiously.

"Yes. Enjoy yourself." I pull the duvet over my head and feel my tears drenching the pillow.

"Bye, sweetheart." I can feel Luke patting the duvet. "Get some rest."

There's some muffled talking, and then in the distance I hear the door slam. That's it. They've gone.

It's about half an hour before I even move. I push back the duvet and wipe my wet eyes. I get out of bed, stagger into the bathroom, and look at myself. I'm a fright. My eyes are red and puffy. My cheeks are tear-stained. My hair is all over the place.

I splash my face with water and sit down on the edge of the bathtub. What am I going to do? I can't just stay here all night, wondering and worrying and imagining the worst. I'd rather just catch them. I'd rather just see it for my own eyes.

I'll go there. The thought hits me like a bullet.

I'll go to the reunion right now, this minute. What's to stop me? I'm not ill. I'm fine.

I head back into the bedroom with a fresh determination. I fling open my wardrobe doors and pull out a black chiffon maternity kaftan that I bought in the summer and never wore because it felt too tentlike. OK. Accessories. A few long, glittery necklaces...a pair of sparkly heels...diamond earrings...I wrench open my makeup case and apply as much as I can, as quickly as I can.

I take a step back and look at myself head to foot in the mirror. I look...fine. Not exactly my most polished outfit ever, but fine.

Adrenaline is beating through me as I grab an evening bag and stuff my keys, mobile, and purse into it. I wrap a shawl around myself and head out the front door, my chin jutting with resolve. I'll show them. Or I'll catch them. Or . . . *something.* I'm not some helpless victim who's tamely going to lie in bed while her husband's with another woman.

I manage to catch a cab straight outside our building, and as it zooms off I sit back and practice my confrontation lines. I need to hold my head high and be sarcastic yet noble. And not burst into tears or hit Venetia.

Well, maybe I could hit Venetia. A ringing slap on her cheek, after I've laid into Luke.

"You're still *married,* by the way," I rehearse under my breath. "Forget something, Luke? Like your *wife?*"

We're getting near now, and I feel light-headed with nerves . . . but I don't care. I'm still going to do it. I'm going to be strong. As the taxi draws up, I hand a wodge of crumpled money to the driver and get out. It's started to rain, and a cold breeze is cutting right through my chiffon kaftan. I need to get inside.

I totter over the open square toward the grand stone entrance of the Guildhall and through the heavy oak doors. Inside, the reception area is full of pale blue helium balloons in bunches, and banners reading CAMBRIDGE REUNION, and a huge pin board covered in old photographs of students. In front of me a group of four men are slapping each other on the back and exclaiming things like "I can't believe you're still alive, you bastard!" As I hesitate, wondering where to go, a girl in a red ball gown sitting behind a cloth-draped table smiles up at me.

"Hello! Do you have your invitation?"

"My husband has it." I try to sound calm, like any normal guest. "He arrived earlier than me. Luke

Brandon?" The girl runs a finger down her list, then stops.

"Of course!" She smiles at me. "Do go in, Mrs. Brandon."

I follow the group of bantering guys into the great hall and accept a glass of champagne on autopilot. I've never been here before and I didn't realize how huge it was. There are massive stained-glass windows and ancient stone statues, and an orchestra is playing in the gallery, amplified over the roar of chatter. People in evening dress are milling and chatting and collecting food from a buffet, and some are even dancing old-fashioned waltzes, like something out of a film. I look around, trying to spot Luke or Venetia, but the room is so busy with women in beautiful dresses, and men in black tie, and even a few particularly dashing men in tails. . . .

And then I see them. Dancing together.

Luke was right, he does waltz as well as Fred Astaire. He's skimming Venetia around the floor like an expert. Her skirt is twirling, and her head is thrown back as she smiles up at Luke. They're perfectly in time with each other. The most glamorous couple in the room.

I'm rooted to the spot as I watch them, my kaftan clinging damply to my shins. All the sarcastic, feisty phrases I prepared have shriveled on my lips. I'm not sure I can breathe, let alone speak.

"Are you all right?" A waiter is addressing me, but his voice seems to be coming from miles away and his face is out of focus.

I never once waltzed with Luke. And now it's too late.

"She's falling!" I can feel hands grabbing at me as my

legs give way beneath me. My arm bashes against something and there's a ringing in my ears and the sound of a woman shouting "Get some water! There's a pregnant woman here!"

And then everything goes dark.

SIXTEEN

I THOUGHT MARRIAGE was forever. I really did. I thought Luke and I would grow old and gray together. Or at least old. (I'm not intending to go gray, ever. Or wear those gross dresses with elastic waistbands.)

But we're not going to grow old together. We're not going to sit on benches together, or watch our grandchildren play. I'm not even going to make it past thirty with him. Our marriage has failed.

Every time I try to speak I think I'll cry, so I'm not really speaking. Luckily there's no one here to speak to. I'm in a private room at the Cavendish Hospital, which is where they brought me last night. If you want attention at a hospital, just arrive with a celebrity doctor in black tie. I've never *seen* so many nurses running around. First they thought I might be in labor, and then they thought I might have preeclampsia, but in the end they decided I was just a bit overtired and dehydrated. So they put me in this bed, with a saline drip. I should be going home today, after I've been checked out.

Luke stayed with me all night too. But I couldn't bring myself to talk to him. So I pretended I was asleep, even this morning when he quietly said, "Becky? Are you awake?"

Now he's gone off to take a shower and I've opened my eyes. It's a really nice room, with soft green walls and even a little sofa. But who cares, when my life is over? What does anything matter anymore?

I know two out of three marriages fail, or whatever it is. But I honestly thought...

I thought we were...

Roughly, I brush a tear away. I'm *not* going to cry.

"Hello?" The door opens and a nurse pushes in a trolley. "Breakfast?"

"Thanks," I say, my voice croaky, and I sit up as she plumps my pillows around me. I take a sip of tea and eat a piece of toast, just so the baby has something to keep it going. Then I check my reflection in my compact mirror. God, I look like crap. I've still got on the remnants of last night's makeup, and my hair has frizzed from the rain. And the so-called "hydrating" drip has done nothing for my skin.

I *look* like a reject.

I gaze at myself, feeling bitter. It's what happens to everyone. You get married and you think everything's great, but all the time your husband was having an affair and then he leaves you for another woman with red swishy hair. I should have seen it coming. I never should have relaxed.

I gave that man the best years of my life, and now I'm tossed aside for a newer model.

Well, OK, I gave him a year and a half of my life. And she's older than me. But still.

There's another movement at the door and I stiffen. A moment later it opens and Luke cautiously makes his way in. There are faint shadows beneath his eyes, I notice, and he's cut himself shaving.

Good. I'm *glad* he did.

"You're awake!" he says. "How are you feeling?"

I nod, clamping my lips together. I'm not going to give him the satisfaction of seeing me upset. I'm going to keep my dignity, even if it means I can only talk in monosyllables.

"You look better." He sits down on the bed. "I was worried about you."

Again I hear Venetia's cool, assured voice: *Luke's just playing along to keep you happy.* I look up and meet his gaze, willing him to give himself away, searching for some chink in his façade. But he's putting on the best act I've ever seen. A concerned, loving husband at his wife's bedside.

I've always known Luke was good at PR. It's his job. It's made him a millionaire. But I never realized he could be this good. I never knew he could be this... double-faced.

"Becky?" Now he's searching my face. "Is everything OK?"

"No. It's not." There's silence as I summon up all my strength. "Luke... I know."

"You know?" Luke's tone is easy but at once there's a guarded look in his eyes. "Know what?"

"Don't pretend, OK?" I swallow hard. "Venetia told me. She told me what's been going on."

"She *told* you?" Luke gets to his feet, his face aghast. "She had no right—" He breaks off and turns away. And I feel a sickening thud deep inside me. Everything is suddenly hurting. My head, my eyes, my limbs.

I hadn't realized how hard I was clinging to a last

shred of hope. That somehow Luke would sweep me up in his arms, explain everything away, and tell me he loved me. But the shred's melted away. It's all over.

"Maybe she thought I ought to know." Somehow I muster tones of cutting sarcasm. "Maybe she thought I'd be interested!"

"Becky...I was trying to protect you." Luke turns, and he looks genuinely miserable. "The baby. Your blood pressure."

"So, when were you planning to tell me?"

"I don't know." Luke exhales, pacing to the window and back again. "After the baby. I was going to see how things...played out."

"I see."

Suddenly I can't do this anymore. I can't be dignified and grown-up. I want to yell and scream at him. I want to burst into sobs and throw things.

"Luke, please...just go." My voice is barely above a whisper. "I don't want to talk about this. I'm tired."

"Right." He doesn't move an inch. "Becky..."

"What?"

Luke rubs his face hard, as though trying to scrub away his problems. "I'm supposed to be going to Geneva. The De Savatier Investment Fund launch. It could not have come at a worse time. I can cancel...."

"Go. I'll be fine."

"Becky..."

"Go to Geneva." I turn away and stare at the green hospital wall.

"We have to talk about this," he perseveres. "I have to explain."

No. No no no. I'm not listening to him tell me all about how he fell for Venetia, and he never meant to hurt me but he just couldn't help himself, and he still sees me as a good friend.

I'd rather not know anything about it, ever.

"Luke, just leave me *alone*!" I spit it out without turning my head. "I told you, I don't want to talk about it. And anyway, I'm supposed to stay calm for the baby. You're not supposed to upset me."

"Right. Fine. Well, I'll go then."

Luke sounds pretty upset himself now. Well, tough luck.

I'm aware of him walking across the room, his tread slow and reluctant.

"My mother's in town," he says. "But don't worry, I've told her to leave you alone."

"Fine," I mumble into the pillow.

"I'll see you when I get back. Should be around Friday lunchtime. OK?"

I don't respond. What does he mean, he'll *see* me? When he comes round to move all his stuff into Venetia's flat? When he summons a meeting with his divorce lawyers?

There's a long silence and I know Luke's still there, waiting. But then, at last, I hear the door open and close, and the faint sound of his footsteps disappearing down the corridor.

I wait ten minutes before I lift my head. I feel surreal and kind of blurry, as though I'm in the middle of a dream. I can't quite believe this is all really happening. I'm eight months pregnant and Luke's having an affair with our obstetrician and our marriage is over.

Our marriage is over. I repeat the words to myself, but

they don't ring true. I can't make them register. It seems only five minutes ago that we were on honeymoon, blissfully lazing on the beach. That we were dancing at our wedding in Mum's back garden, me in Mum's old frilly wedding dress and a lopsided flower garland. That a whole press conference was stopping still for him to pass me a twenty-quid note so I could buy a Denny and George scarf. Back in the days when I barely knew him, when he was the sexy mysterious Luke Brandon and I wasn't even sure he knew my name.

I feel a wrenching pain deep inside, and all of a sudden tears are spilling onto my cheeks, and I'm burying my sobbing head in the sheets. How can he leave me? Hasn't he *enjoyed* being married to me? Haven't we had fun together?

Before I can stop it, Venetia's voice slides into my head. *You were a refreshing change, Becky. You make him laugh. But you're hardly on the same level.*

Stupid . . . stupid . . . *cow*. Bitch. Skinny . . . horrible . . . pretentious . . .

I wipe my eyes and sit up and take three long breaths. I'm not going to think about her. Or any of it.

There's a knocking at the door. "Mrs. Brandon?" It sounds like one of the nurses.

"Er . . . hang on. . . ." I hastily splash some water onto my face from my drinking jug, and wipe it with the sheet. "Yes?"

The door opens and the pretty nurse who brought me my breakfast smiles at me. "You have a visitor."

My mind leaps in one joyous bound to Luke. He's come back, he's sorry, it was all a mistake. . . .

"Who is it?" I grab my compact from the cabinet, grimace at my reflection, and tug at my frizzy hair.

"A Mrs. Sherman?"

I nearly drop the compact in dismay. Elinor? Elinor's *here*? I thought Luke told her to leave me alone.

I haven't seen Elinor since our wedding in New York. Or at least...our "wedding" in New York. (It was all a bit complicated in the end.) We've never really got on, mainly on account of her being a snobby, ice-cold bitch, who abandoned Luke when he was tiny and totally screwed him up. And the way she was rude to Mum. And the way she didn't let me in to my own bloody engagement party! And—

"Are you OK, Rebecca?" The nurse looks at me in slight alarm, and I realize I'm breathing harder and harder. "I can tell her you're asleep if you like."

"Yes, please. Tell her to go away."

I'm in no state to see anyone right now. Not with my face all pink and my eyes still teary. And why should I make any effort to see Elinor? Surely the only advantage of splitting up with your husband is that you don't need to see your mother-in-law anymore. I won't miss her, and she won't miss me.

"Fine." The nurse comes over and squints at my drip. "A doctor will be along soon to check you over, then I should think you'll be going home. Should I tell Mrs. Sherman that you'll be leaving?"

"Actually..."

A new thought has just struck me. There's an even bigger advantage to splitting up with your husband. *You don't have to be polite to your mother-in-law anymore.*

I can say what I like to Elinor. I can be as rude as I like. For the first time in days, I feel a streak of cheer.

"I've changed my mind. I'll see her after all. Just let me get ready...." I reach for my makeup bag and clumsily knock it to the floor. The nurse picks it up and gives me an anxious look.

"Are you OK? You seem very on edge."

"I'm fine. I was just a bit . . . upset earlier. I'll be fine."

The nurse disappears, and I open my makeup bag. I dab on some eye gel and brush myself with bronzer. I am not going to look like a victim here. I'm not going to look like some poor pathetic wronged wife. I have no idea what Elinor knows, but if she even *mentions* Luke and me splitting up, or dares to look pleased about it, I'll . . . I'll tell her the baby isn't Luke's, that it was fathered by my prison penpal Wayne and the whole scandal's going to hit the papers tomorrow. That'll freak her out.

I spray myself with perfume and quickly slick on some lip gloss as I hear footsteps approaching. There's a knock at the door and I call, "Come in." A moment later it swings open—and there she is.

She's wearing a mint-green suit and the same Ferragamo pumps she buys every season, and she's carrying a crocodile Kelly bag. She's thinner than ever, her hair a lacquered helmet, her face pale and stretched-looking. Which figures. When I worked in Barneys in New York, I saw women like Elinor every single day. But over here she looks . . . Well, there's no other word for it: *weird*.

Her mouth moves a millimeter, and I realize this is her greeting.

"Hi, Elinor." I don't bother trying to smile. She'll just assume I've had Botox too. "Welcome to London."

"London is so tawdry these days," she says with disapproval. "So tasteless."

She's just unbelievable. The whole of London is tasteless?

"Yeah, especially the Queen," I say. "She has *no* idea."

Ignoring me, Elinor stalks to a chair and sits down on the edge of it. She surveys me stonily for a few moments. "I gather you left the doctor I recommended, Rebecca. Who are you seeing now?"

"Her name's . . . Venetia Carter." I feel a knife of pain as I say the name. But Elinor doesn't react a smidgen. She can't know.

"Have you seen Luke?" I venture.

"Not yet." She pulls off a pair of calfskin gloves and runs her eyes over my hospital-gowned frame. "You've put on a lot of weight, Rebecca. Does this new doctor approve?"

You see? This is what she's like. Not "How are you?" or "Don't you look blooming?"

"I'm pregnant," I snap. "And I'm having a big baby."

Elinor's expression doesn't soften. "Not too large, I hope. Oversize babies are vulgar."

Vulgar? How dare she call my lovely baby vulgar?

"Yes, well, I'm glad it's going to be big," I say in defiance. "That way there'll be more room for . . . the tattoos."

I can just about see a jolt of shock pass across her practically immobile face. That'll bust her stitches. Or staples. Whatever's holding her together.

"Didn't Luke tell you about our tattoo plans?" I adopt a surprised tone. "We've found a special newborn-baby tattooist who comes right into the delivery room. We thought we'd have an eagle on its back, with our names in Sanskrit. . . ."

"You are not tattooing my grandchild." Her voice is like gunfire.

"Oh yes, we are. Luke *really* got the tattoo bug while we were on honeymoon. He has fifteen of them!" I smile blandly at her. "And as soon as the baby's born he's going to get its name tattooed on his arm. Isn't that sweet?"

Elinor's gripping her Kelly bag so hard, the veins are standing up. I can tell she doesn't know whether to believe me or not.

"Have you decided on a name?" she says at last.

"Uh-huh." I nod. "Armageddon for a boy, Pomegranate for a girl."

For a moment she seems unable to reply. I can tell she's desperate to raise her eyebrows, or frown, or *something*. I almost feel sorry for her real face, trapped under the Botox like a caged animal.

"Armageddon?" she manages at last.

"Isn't it great?" I nod again. "Macho, but kind of elegant. And unusual!"

Elinor looks like she's going to explode. Or implode.

"I will not have this!" she suddenly erupts, rising to her feet. "Tattooing! These names! You're . . . irresponsible beyond—"

"'Irresponsible'?" I interrupt in disbelief. "Are you serious? Well, at least we're not planning to *abandon*—" I stop abruptly, feeling like the words are too hot for my mouth. I can't do it. I can't bring myself to launch a full-blown attack on Elinor. I haven't got the energy, for a start. And anyway . . . I feel distracted. All of a sudden my head is buzzing with thoughts.

"Rebecca." Elinor approaches the bed, her eyes

snapping. "I have no idea if you're being frank with me——"

"Shut up!" I lift a hand, not caring if I'm rude. I have to concentrate. I have to think this through. I'm suddenly starting to see things clearly, like a tune falling into place.

Elinor walked out on Luke. Now Luke's walking out on our baby. It's history repeating itself. Does Luke *realize* this? If he just saw it . . . if he just understood what he was doing . . .

"Rebecca!"

I look up, as though out of a daze. Elinor looks like she wants to pop with exasperation.

"Oh, Elinor . . . I'm sorry," I say, all rancor gone. "It was lovely of you to come by, but I'm a bit tired now. Please drop round for tea sometime."

Elinor looks like the wind has been taken out of her sails. I think she was probably squaring up for a fight too.

"Very well," she says frostily. "I'm staying at Claridge's. Here are the details of my exhibition."

She hands me an invitation for a private viewing, along with a glossy brochure entitled "The Elinor Sherman Collection." It's illustrated with a photograph of an elegant white plinth, on top of which is resting another, smaller white plinth.

God, I don't understand modern art.

"Thanks," I say, eyeing it dubiously. "We'll be sure to make it. Thanks for coming. Have a nice day!"

Elinor gives me one last, narrowed look, then picks up her gloves and Kelly bag and strides out of the room. As soon as she's gone, I bury my head in my hands, trying to think. Somehow I have to get through to Luke.

He doesn't want to do this. Deep in his heart, I know he doesn't. I feel like he's been lured away by the evil fairies and I just need to break the spell.

But how? What do I do? If I call him, he'll brush me off and promise to call back later and never will. His e-mails are read by his secretaries.... It's not exactly a subject for a text....

I have to write a letter.

It hits me like a thunderbolt. I have to write a letter, like in the old days before phone calls and e-mail. God, yes. I'll compose the best letter I've ever written in my life. I'll explain all my feelings, and his. (He sometimes needs them explained to him.) I'll put the case before him plainly.

I'm going to save our marriage. He doesn't want a broken family—I know he doesn't. I *know* he doesn't.

A nurse is passing by the door, and I call out, "Excuse me?"

"Yes?" She looks in with a smile.

"Would it be possible to get some writing paper?"

"There's some in the hospital shop, or..." She frowns in thought. "One of my colleagues has some, I think. Just hang on a moment...."

A moment later she's back, with a pad of Basildon Bond. "One sheet enough?"

"I may need more than that," I say momentously. "Could I have ... three?"

I cannot believe how much I've written to Luke. Once I started, I just couldn't stop. I had no idea there was so much pent up inside me.

I started off talking about our wedding and how

happy we were then. Then I talked about all the things we love to do together, and how much fun we've had and how excited we were when we discovered we were having a baby. Then I moved on to Venetia. I didn't call her by name. I called her the Threat to Our Marriage. He'll know what I'm talking about.

And now I'm on page seventeen (one of the nurses ran down and bought me my own pad of Basildon Bond) and I'm getting to the main bit. The plea to him to give our marriage another shot. Tears are running down my face, and I keep having to break off to snuffle into a tissue.

In our vows, you promised to love me forever. I know you think you don't anymore. I know there are other women in this world, who are maybe cleverer and maybe can speak Latin. I know you've had an . . .

I can't bring myself to write the word *affair*—I just can't.

I'll just put a dash, like they used to in old-fashioned books.

I know you've had an————. But it doesn't have to ruin everything. I'm prepared to put the past behind us, Luke, because I believe above anything else that we belong together. You, me, and the baby.

We can be a happy family. I know we can. Please don't give up on us. Maybe you're secretly scared of parenthood, but we can do it together! Like you said, it's the biggest adventure we'll ever have.

I break off from writing to wipe my eyes. I need to finish this now. I need some way for him to show me . . . to answer . . . to let me know . . .

Suddenly it comes to me. We need a great big tall

tower, just like in romantic movies. And we'll meet at
the top at midnight. . . .

No. I get too tired by midnight. We'll meet at the
top at . . . six o'clock. The wind will be blowing and
Gershwin will be playing and I'll see from his eyes that
he's put Venetia behind him forever. And I'll say simply,
"Are you coming home?" And he'll say—

"Are you OK, Becky?" The nurse pops her head
round the door. "How's it going?"

"Nearly finished." I blow my nose. "Where's a tall
tower in London? If I wanted to meet someone."

"Dunno." The nurse wrinkles her nose. "The Oxo
Tower's pretty tall. I went there the other day. They've
got a viewing platform and a restaurant. . . ."

"Thanks!"

*Luke, if you love me and want to save our marriage, meet
me at the top of the Oxo Tower at six o'clock on Friday. I will
be waiting at the viewing platform.*

Your loving wife,

Becky.

I put my pen down, feeling totally drained, as though
I've just composed a Beethoven symphony. All I have
to do now is FedEx the letter to his Geneva office . . .
and then just wait till Friday night.

I fold the seventeen pages in half, and am trying un-
successfully to cram them into the matching Basildon
Bond envelope, when my mobile rings on the cabinet.

Luke! Oh my God. But he hasn't read the letter yet!

With trembling hands I grab the phone, but it's not
Luke after all. It's a number I don't recognize. It isn't
Elinor calling to lecture me, is it?

"Hello?" I say cautiously.

"Hello, Becky? It's Martha here."

"Oh." I push my hair back off my face, trying to place the name. "Er . . . hi."

"Just checking you're still all set for the shoot on Friday?" she says chattily. "I can't wait to see your house!"

Vogue. Shit. I'd totally forgotten about it.

How could I forget about a *Vogue* photo shoot? God, my life must really be in pieces.

"So, is everything OK?" Martha's voice is trilling gaily down the phone. "You haven't had the baby yet, or anything?"

"Well, no . . ." I hesitate. "But I am in hospital." As I say the words I realize I shouldn't really have my mobile on in a hospital. But this is *Vogue* on the phone. There must be an exemption for *Vogue,* surely.

"Oh no!" Her voice falls in dismay. "You know, we're having such bad luck with this piece! One of the yummy mummies had her twins early, which was *really* annoying, and the other has had pre-eclampy-something and is on bed rest! We can't do the interview or anything! Are you on bed rest?"

"I . . . hang on a minute. . . ."

I put the phone down on the bed, trying to galvanize my spirits. I have never felt less like having my picture taken in my life. I'm fat, I'm tear-stained, my hair is ter- rible, my marriage is crumbling away. . . . I give a deep, shuddery sigh, and then catch sight of my blurry reflec- tion in a nearby glass-fronted cupboard. Hunched over, head drooping. I look defeated. I look *awful.*

In an immediate reflex action I sit up straighter. What am I saying? Is my *life* over too? Just because my husband had an affair?

No way. I'm not going to feel sorry for myself.

I'm not going to give up. Maybe my life *is* in pieces. But I can still be yummy. I'll be the yummiest bloody mummy-to-be they've ever seen.

I lift the phone to my ear again. "Hi, Martha?" I say, trying to sound breezy. "Sorry about that. It's all fine for the shoot on Friday. I'm coming out of hospital today, so I'll be there!"

"Great!" I can hear the relief in Martha's voice. "Can't wait! It'll only take two or three hours, and I promise we won't exhaust you! I'm sure you have lots of lovely clothes, but our stylist will bring along some pieces too. . . . Now let me just check your address. You live at thirty-three Delamain Road?"

I never got that stuff for Fabia, it suddenly occurs to me. But I've still got time. It'll be fine.

"Yes, that's right."

"Lucky thing, those houses are amazing! We'll see you there then, eleven o'clock."

"See you then!"

I switch off the phone and breathe out hard. I'm going to be in *Vogue*. I'm going to be yummy. And I'm going to save my marriage.

FROM: Becky Brandon
TO: Fabia Paschali
SUBJECT: Tomorrow

_____

Hello, Fabia!

Just to confirm, I will be coming tomorrow
with a *Vogue* crew and the shoot will last
from around 11am till 3pm.

I have got the purple top and the Chloe
bag, but unfortunately, although I've
tried everywhere, I can't locate the Olly
Bricknell shoes you want. Is there
anything else that you'd like?

Again, thanks so much and look forward to
seeing you tomorrow!

Becky

FROM: Fabia Paschali
TO: Becky Brandon
SUBJECT: Re: Tomorrow

_____

Becky,

No shoes, no house.

Fabia

Prendergast de Witt Connell
Financial Advisers

Forward House
394 High Holborn
London WC1V 7EX

Mrs R Brandon
37 Maida Vale Mansions
Maida Vale
London NW6 0YF

26 November 2003

Dear Mrs. Brandon,

Thank you for your letter.

I have noted your new shareholdings in Sweet Confectionery, Inc., Estelle Rodin Cosmetics, and The Urban Spa plc. I cannot, however, agree that these are the "best investments in the world."

Please let me reiterate. Free chocolates, samples of perfume, and discount spa treatments—while pleasant—are no sound basis for investment. I urge you to reconsider your current investment strategy and would be pleased to advise you further.

Yours sincerely,

Kenneth Prendergast
Family Investment Specialist

SEVENTEEN

THESE BLOODY, BLOODY SHOES. There is not a single pair of them left in London. Especially not in green. No wonder Fabia wants them, they're like the Holy Grail or something, except there aren't even any clues in paintings. I spent yesterday trying all my contacts, every supplier I know, every shop, *everywhere*. I even called my old colleague Erin at Barneys in New York and she just laughed pityingly.

In the end, Danny stepped in to help. He made some calls around and finally tracked down a pair to a model he knows who is on a shoot in Paris. In return for a sample jacket, she gave them to a friend who was coming over to London last night. He met up with Danny and now he's going to deliver them to me.

That's the plan. But he isn't here yet. And it's already five past ten and I'm starting to panic. I'm standing on the corner of Delamain Road, dressed in my yummiest outfit of red print wrap dress, Prada heels, and a vintage-style fake fur stole, and all the cars keep slowing down to look. In hindsight, this wasn't the best place to meet. I must look like some eight months' pregnant hooker for pervy people.

I take out my phone and, yet again, redial Danny's number. *"Danny?"*

"We're here! We're coming. We're just driving over a bridge . . . whoa!"

Danny was supposed to be dropping the shoes round last night—only he went off clubbing instead, with some photographer he met on holiday. (Don't ask. He started to tell me about the night they spent together in Marrakech, and honestly, I had to put my hands over the baby's ears.) He's shrieking with laughter, and I can hear the roar of his friend's Harley-Davidson. How can he be having fun? Doesn't he know how stressed out I am?

I've barely slept since Luke has been gone. And when I *did* get to sleep last night, I had the most awful dream. I dreamed I went to the top of the Oxo Tower, but Luke didn't show up. I stood for hours in the wind and gale and rain pouring down on me and then at last Luke appeared, but he'd somehow turned into Elinor and she started yelling at me. And then all my hair fell off. . . .

"Excuse me!"

A woman holding two small children by the hand is approaching, and giving me an odd look.

"Oh. Sorry." I come to, and move out of the way.

In real life, I haven't spoken to Luke since he left. He's tried to call several times, but I just sent short texts back saying sorry I missed him and everything's OK. I didn't want to talk to him until he'd read my letter—which only happened last night, according to the tracking system. Somebody at the Geneva office signed for it at 6:11 p.m., so he must have read it by now.

The die is cast. By six o'clock tonight I'll know, one way or another. Either he'll be there, waiting for me, or...

Nausea rises through me and I shake my head briskly. I'm not going to think about it. I'm going to get through this shoot first. I take a bite of a Kit Kat for energy, and glance down again at the printed page that Martha e-mailed me. It's an interview with one of the other yummy mummies-to-be from the article, which Martha said would "give me an idea." The other yummy is called Amelia Gordon-Barraclough. She's posing in a vast Kensington nursery wearing a beaded kaftan and about fifty-nine bracelets, and all her quotes sound totally smug.

"We commissioned all our nursery furniture from artisans in Provence."

Well. Huh. I'll say we got all ours from artisans in ... outer Mongolia. No, we *sourced* it. People in glossy magazines never just buy something from a shop, they source it, or discover it in a junkyard, or get left it by their famous designer godmother.

"My husband and I do couples' yoga together twice a day in our 'retreat room.' We feel it creates harmony in our relationship."

With a pang, I have a sudden memory of Luke and me doing couples' yoga on our honeymoon.

At least, we were doing yoga, and we were a couple.

A lump is rising in my throat. No. Stop it. Think confident. Think yummy. I'll say that Luke and I do something much *cooler* than yoga. Like that thing I read about the other day. Qi-something.

My thoughts are broken by the roar of a motorbike,

and I look up to see a Harley speeding along the quiet residential street.

"Hi!" I wave my arms. "Here!"

"Hey, Becky!" The motorbike comes to a throbbing halt beside me. Danny pulls off a motorbike helmet and leaps off the back, a shoe box in his hand. "There you go!"

"Oh, Danny, thanks." I give him an enormous hug. "You saved my life."

"No problem!" Danny says, getting back on the bike. "Let me know how it goes! This is Zane, by the way."

"Hi!" I wave at Zane, who is in leathers from head to foot and raises a hand in greeting. "Thanks for the delivery!"

The motorbike zooms off again. I take hold of the handle of my suitcase, which is filled with spare outfits and props, and pick up the armful of flowers I bought this morning to make the house look nice. I head toward number thirty-three, somehow manhandle the case up the steps, and ring the doorbell. There's no answer.

After a pause I ring again and call "Fabia!" But there's still no reply.

She can't have forgotten it's this morning.

"Fabia! Can you hear me?" I beat on the door. *"Fabi-a!"*

There's dead silence. No one's there. I feel a beat of panic. What am I going to do? *Vogue* will be here any—

"Cooee! Hello there!" A voice from the street heralds me and I turn to see a girl leaning out of the window of a Mini Cooper. She's skinny, has glossy hair, a

Kabbala bracelet, and a huge engagement rock. She has to be from *Vogue*.

"Are you Becky?" she calls.

"Yes!" I force a bright smile. "Hi! Are you Martha?"

"That's right!" Her eyes are running up and down the stories. "You've got a *gorgeous* house! I can't wait to see inside!"

"Oh. Er... thanks!"

There's an expectant pause and I lean casually against one of the pillars. Like I'm just hanging out on my front steps. Like people do.

"Everything all right?" asks Martha, looking puzzled.

"Fine!" I attempt an easy gesture. "Just, you know... enjoying the air..."

I'm thinking frantically. Maybe we could do the whole shoot out here on the steps. Yes. I could say the front door is the best feature of the house and the rest of it isn't worth bothering with....

"Becky, have you lost your key?" says Martha, still looking puzzled.

Genius. Of course. Why didn't I think of that?

"Yes! Silly me!" I hit myself on the head. "And none of the neighbors have got one, and there's no one in...."

"Oh no!" Martha's face falls.

"I know." I give a regretful shrug. "I'm really sorry. But if we can't get in..."

As I say the words, the front door opens and I nearly fall into the house. Fabia has appeared, rubbing her eyes and wearing an orange Marni dress.

"Hi, Becky." She sounds so *drifty*. Like she's on tranquilizers or something.

"Wow!" Martha's face lights up. "Someone *was* in! How lucky! Who's this?"

"This is Fabia. Our . . . lodger."

"Lodger?" Fabia wrinkles her nose.

"Lodger and good friend," I amend hastily, putting an arm round her. "We're very close. . . ."

Thank God, down on the street a car has pulled up behind the Mini and is starting to hoot.

"Oh, shut up!" says Martha. "Becky, we're just going to get some coffees. Can I get you anything?"

"No, I'm fine, thanks! I'll just wait here at home. At my home." I put a proprietorial hand on the doorknob. "See you soon!"

I watch the car disappear, then wheel round to Fabia. "I thought you weren't in! OK, we need to get going. I've got the stuff for you. Here's the bag, and the top. . . ." I hand her the carriers.

"Great." Her eyes focus on them greedily. "Did you get the shoes?"

"Of course!" I say. "My friend Danny got a model to bring them over from Paris. Danny Kovitz, the designer?"

As I produce the box, I feel a dart of triumph. No one else in the world can get hold of these. I am *so* connected. I wait for Fabia to gasp or say, "You're incredible!" Instead she opens the shoe box, peers at them for a few moments, then wrinkles her brow.

"These are the wrong color." She puts the lid back on and pushes them toward me. "I wanted green."

Is she color-blind? They're the most gorgeous shade of pale sage green, plus they have *Green* printed in big letters on the box.

"Fabia, these *are* green."

"I wanted more of a . . ." She waves an arm. "Bluey-green."

I'm trying really hard to keep my patience. "Do you mean . . . turquoise?"

"Yeah!" Her face brightens. "Turquoise. That's what I meant. These ones are too pale."

I do not believe it. These shoes have traveled all the way from Paris via a fashion model and a world-famous designer and she doesn't want them?

Well, I'll have them.

"Fine," I say, and take the box back. "I'll get you the turquoise pair. But I really need to get into the house. . . ."

"I don't know." Fabia leans against the door frame and examines a drawn thread on her sleeve. "It's not that convenient, to be honest."

Not convenient? It has to be convenient!

"But we agreed on today, remember? The people from *Vogue* are already here!"

"Couldn't you put them off?"

"You don't put *Vogue* off!" My voice rises in agitation. "They're *Vogue*!"

She gives one of her careless shrugs, and all of a sudden I'm livid. She knew I was coming. It was all planned. She can't do this to me!

"Fabia." I lean close, breathing hard. "You are not wrecking my only chance to be in *Vogue*. I got you the top. I got you the bag. I got you the shoes! You have to let me into this house, or . . . or . . ."

"Or *what*?" says Fabia.

"Or . . . I'll phone up Barneys and get you black-listed!" I hiss in sudden inspiration. "That won't be much fun if you're living in New York, will it?"

Fabia turns pale. Ha. Gotcha.

"Well, where am I supposed to go?" she says sulkily, taking her arm off the door frame.

"I don't know! Go and have a hot-stone massage or something! Just get out!" I shove my suitcase into the house and push past her into the hall.

Right. I have to be quick. I snap open my case, take out a silver-framed picture of me and Luke at our wedding and put it prominently on the hall table. There. It looks like my house already!

"Where is your husband, anyway?" says Fabia, watching me with folded arms. "Shouldn't he be doing this too? You look like some kind of single mother."

Her words hit me unawares. For a few seconds I don't trust myself to answer.

"Luke's...abroad," I say at last. "But I'm meeting him later on. At six o'clock. At the viewing platform at the Oxo Tower. He'll be there." I take a deep breath. "I know he will."

There's a hotness in my eyes and I blink fiercely. I'm not going to disintegrate.

"Are you all right?" Fabia stares at me.

"It's just...quite an important day for me." I get out a tissue and dab my eyes. "Could I have a glass of water?"

"Jesus." I can hear Fabia muttering as she heads toward the kitchen. "It's only bloody *Vogue*."

OK. I'm getting there. Twenty minutes have passed, Fabia has finally gone, and the house is really feeling as though it's mine. I've taken down all Fabia's photographs and replaced them with ones of me and my family. I've put *B* and *L* initial cushions on the sofa in the living room. I've arranged flowers in vases everywhere. I've memorized the contents of the kitchen cupboards and even planted some Post-it notes on the fridge, saying things like "We need more organic quinoa, darling" and "Luke—remember Couples' Qi-gong on Saturday!"

Now I'm hastily decanting some of my own shoes into Fabia's shoe cupboard, because they're bound to ask me about my accessories. I'm just counting how many pairs of Jimmy Choos there are, when the doorbell suddenly rings, and I jump in a flurry of panic. I shove the rest of the shoes into the cupboard, check my reflection, and head down the stairs with trembling legs.

This is it! All my *life* I've wanted to itemize my clothes in a magazine!

As I reach the hall I do a quick recap in my head. Dress: Diane von Furstenberg. Shoes: Prada. Tights: Topshop. Earrings: present from Mum.

No, that's not cool enough. I'll call them . . . model's own. No, *vintage*. I'll say I found them sewn into a 1930s corset which I bought from an old atelier in a backstreet in Paris. Perfect.

I swing open the front door, plastering a bright smile on my face—and freeze.

It's not *Vogue*. It's Luke.

He's wearing an overcoat and holding an overnight case and it looks like he didn't shave this morning.

"What the hell is this?" he says with no preamble, lifting up my letter.

I stare back at him, dumbstruck. This isn't right. He's supposed to be at the Oxo Tower looking all romantic and loving. Not here on the doorstep, disheveled and moody.

"I . . ." I swallow. "What are you doing here?"

"What am I *doing* here?" he echoes incredulously. "I'm reacting to this! You didn't answer any of my calls, I had no bloody idea what was going on. . . . 'Meet me at the top of the Oxo Tower.'" He shakes the letter at me. "What *is* all this crap?"

Crap?

"It's not crap!" I cry, stung. "I was trying to save our marriage, in case you hadn't realized—"

"Save our marriage?" He stares at me. "At the Oxo Tower?"

"It works in films! You were supposed to turn up, and it was all supposed to be lovely, like in *Sleepless in Seattle.* . . ."

My voice is thickening with disappointment. I *so* thought it was going to work. I *so* thought he was going to be there, and we'd run into each other's arms, and be a happy family again.

"OK, I'm obviously missing something." Luke is frowning down at the letter again. "This letter doesn't even make *sense*. 'I know you had an————' Blank. What did I have? An embolism?"

He's mocking me. I can't bear it.

"An affair!" I yell. "An affair! Your affair with Venetia! I know about it, remember? And I just thought maybe you wanted to give our marriage another shot, but obviously not, so please just go. I have a *Vogue* shoot to do." I brush angrily at my tear-filled eyes.

"My *what*?" He seems genuinely shell-shocked. "Becky, you're joking."

"Yeah, right." I make to close the door, but he grabs my wrist hard.

"Stop." Luke's voice is like thunder. "I don't know what the fuck's going on. I get this letter out of the blue . . . you're accusing me of having an affair. . . . You can't run away without explaining."

Has he moved in to a parallel universe? Did someone hit him over the head or something?

"You admitted it yourself, Luke!" I practically shriek in frustration. "You said you'd been trying to 'protect' me, because of my blood pressure or whatever. Remember that?"

Luke's eyes are scanning my face, back and forth, as though searching for answers.

"The conversation we had in the hospital," he says suddenly. "Before I left."

"*Yes!* Does it all come flooding back now?" I can't help sounding sarcastic. "You were planning to tell me after the baby. You were going to see how things 'played out.' You basically admitted it—"

"I wasn't talking about having a fucking *affair*!" Luke explodes. "I was talking about the crisis situation with Arcodas!"

"I . . ." The wind is instantly taken out of my sails. "Wh-what?"

I suddenly notice two children standing on the pavement, staring at us. I guess we do look quite conspicuous, what with my huge bump and everything.

"Let's adjourn inside," I say in dignified tones. Luke follows my gaze.

"Right. Yes. Let's . . . do that."

He steps into the house and I close the door. For a

moment there's silence in the hall. I don't know what to say. I feel totally thrown.

"Becky... I don't know what wrong end of what stick you've got hold of." Luke exhales long and hard. "There's been some trouble at work and I've been trying to shield you from it. But I'm not having an affair. With *Venetia*?"

"But she told me you were."

Luke looks astounded. "She can't have done."

"She did! She said you were leaving me for her. She said—" I bite my lip. It's too painful to remember everything Venetia said.

"This is just... bloody... *madness.*" Luke shakes his head in exasperation. "I don't know what kind of conversation you had with Venetia, what kind of... crossed wires or misinformation...."

"So you're saying nothing's been going on between you? Nothing at all?"

Luke clutches his hair, closing his eyes briefly. "Why would you think anything was going on?"

"*Why?*" I stare up at him. "Luke, are you *serious*? Where do I start? All those times you've gone out with her, just you and her. All those texts in Latin, which you wouldn't tell me about. And everyone was so weird toward me at the office... and I saw you sitting together on her desk... and you lied, the night of the Finance Awards...." My voice is starting to wobble. "I knew you weren't really there...."

"I lied because I didn't want to *worry* you!" Luke sounds more fraught and angry than I've ever heard him. "My staff were weird to you at the office because I'd sent round an e-mail saying that nobody, but *nobody*, was to mention the company problems to you. On pain of being fired. Becky...I've been trying to protect you."

I have a sudden flashback to him, sitting at his desk in the gloom, his brow creased. That was weeks ago. He's been moody and absent ever since.

But then why would Venetia have said...

Why would she have...

"She told me you were leaving me for her." My voice is really jumping around now. "She said you'd still want to visit the baby." I give a sudden sob.

"*Leaving* you? Becky, come here." Luke wraps his arms tightly around me, and all of a sudden I'm burying my head in his chest, tears streaming into his shirt. "I love you," he says firmly. "I'm never leaving you. Or little Birkin."

How did he...

Oh. He must have found my list of names.

"It's Armageddon now," I correct him, through my snuffles. "Or Pomegranate. That's what I told your mother."

"Excellent. I hope she passed out."

"Nearly." I try to smile, but I can't. It's all still too raw. I've had weeks and weeks of worrying and imagining and fearing the worst. I can't just snap my fingers and act normal again.

"I thought I was going to be a single mother." I gulp. "I thought you loved her. I didn't know why you were being so weird. It's been awful. If you had problems at work you should have *told* me."

"I know I should." He's silent for a bit, resting his chin on my head. "To be honest, Becky...it's been nice to have somewhere to escape from it all."

I lift my head up and study Luke. He looks grim.

And tired. It suddenly hits me. He looks really, really tired.

"What's been going on?" I wipe my face. "What's the trouble? You have to tell me now."

"Arcodas," he says shortly.

"But I thought it was all going so well," I say, confused. "I thought that's why you were opening the new offices."

"I wish I'd never fucking pitched for them." He sounds so bleak, I feel a thud of dread.

"Luke...what's happened?" I say nervously. "Let's sit down." I make my way into Fabia's sitting room and sink into a squashy suede sofa.

"A load of things," says Luke, following me. He raises his eyebrows briefly at the *B* and *L* cushions, then sits down, resting his head in his hands. "You don't want to know."

"I do. I want to know everything. From the start."

"It's been a nightmare." He turns his face toward me. "The main nightmare being a harassment claim."

"Harassment?" I gape at him.

"Sally-Ann Davies. Remember her?"

"Of course." I nod. "What happened?"

Sally-Ann has worked for the company ever since I've known Luke. She's quite reserved, but really sweet and reliable.

"There were...incidents between her and Iain. She says he came on to her in an aggressive, unpleasant manner. She made a complaint. Which he laughed off."

"God, how awful," I breathe. "So...what did you..."

"I believe Sally-Ann one hundred percent." Luke sounds totally resolute.

I'm silent. My mind has flashed back to the manila file from Dave Sharpness's office. The dossier he collected on Iain. All those hushed-up cases.

Should I tell Luke?

No. Not unless I have to. It would raise so many awkward questions, and he might get angry when he hears what I did. Anyway, I shredded everything in the file, so I haven't even got the evidence anymore.

"Yes," I say slowly. "I'd believe her too. So... what did Iain say?"

"Nothing that I'd care to repeat." Luke's face is tight. "He accused her of inventing the story to get a promotion. His opinion of women is pretty unspeakable."

I frown, trying to think back over the past weeks. "Was that when you couldn't come to my prenatal class?"

"That was the start of it, yes." He massages his brow. "Becky, I couldn't tell you. Believe me, I wanted to, but I knew how upset you'd get. And Venetia had just told me you needed to stay calm."

Stay calm. Yup, that plan really worked.

"So what happened?"

"Sally-Ann was incredibly generous-spirited about it. She said she wouldn't take it any further if she could be moved to another account. Which obviously we did. But the whole company was upset by it." He sighs. "To be honest, Arcodas have been difficult to work with, right from the start."

"Iain's awful, isn't he?" I say bluntly.

"It's not just him." Luke shakes his head. "The whole

ethos. They're bullies, all of them." A shadow passes over his face. "And now . . . it's happened again."

"With Sally-Ann?"

Luke shakes his head. "Amy Hill, one of our assistants, was reduced to tears by another of the Arcodas team. He got violently angry and she said she felt physically threatened."

"You're kidding."

"They walk round my company like they bloody *own* it." He exhales sharply, as though trying to keep a grip on himself. "I called a meeting and requested that the member of Arcodas staff in question apologize to Amy."

"And did he?"

"No." Luke's face twists. "He wants her fired."

"Fired?" I'm aghast.

"His story is, she's incompetent, and if she could get the job done he wouldn't need to get tough. Meanwhile, all my staff are up in arms. They're writing me e-mails of protest, refusing to touch the Arcodas account, threatening to resign. . . ." Luke thrusts his hands through his hair, looking totally beleaguered. "Like I said, it's a nightmare."

I subside back onto Fabia's sofa, trying to take all this in. I can't believe Luke has been walking around with all of this to worry about for so long. Saying nothing. Trying to protect me.

Not having an affair after all.

I run my eyes over his averted face. He could still be lying, it occurs to me. Even if the stuff about Arcodas is true. He could still be seeing Venetia. *He's just playing along to keep you happy* runs through my mind for the thousandth time.

"Luke, please," I say in a rush. "Please. Tell me the truth once and for all. Are you seeing her?"

"What?" Luke turns to me, astounded. "Becky, I thought we'd dealt with this—"

"She said you were acting." I twist my fingers miserably. "All this could just be put on. To . . . to keep me happy."

Luke turns to face me square-on and takes both my hands in his, tight.

"Becky, we're not seeing each other. Nothing is going on. I don't know how I can put it any more plainly."

"So why did she say you were seeing each other?"

"I don't *know.*" Luke sounds at the end of his rope. "I honestly have no idea what she was talking about. Look, Becky, you're just going to have to trust me. Can you do that?"

There's silence. The truth is, I don't know. I don't know if I can trust him anymore.

"I want a cup of tea," I mumble at last, and get up.

I thought everything would be better when we'd talked, when we'd got it all out in the open. But here it is, out in the open like an exhibit on a podium. And I still don't know what to believe. Without meeting Luke's eye, I head into the kitchen and start opening all Fabia's hand-built cupboards, looking for the tea. God, this is supposed to be my house. I'm supposed to *know* where the tea is.

"Try that one," says Luke, as I open a cupboard filled with saucepans and bang it shut again, except it won't bang because it's so expensive and well-made. "The corner cupboard?"

"Oh, right." I open it and locate a box of tea bags. I put them on the counter and lean against it, all energy gone. Meanwhile Luke has headed over to the huge glass doors at the back and is staring out at the garden, his shoulders rigid.

This isn't how I planned our reunion. Not one bit.

"What are you going to do about Arcodas?" I say at last, twisting the string of a tea bag. "You can't fire Amy."

"Of course I'm not going to fire Amy."

"So, what are your options?"

"Option one: I patch things over," says Luke without moving his head. "Take the flak, smooth down some feathers, and carry on."

"Until it happens again," I say.

"Exactly." Luke turns with a grim little nod. "Option two: I call a meeting with Arcodas. Tell them straight, I'm not having my staff bullied. Get an apology for Amy. Make them see reason."

"And option three?" I can tell there's an option three from his expression.

"Option three: if they won't cooperate"—he pauses for a long time—"we refuse to work for them. Withdraw from the contract."

"Would that be possible?"

"It would be possible." He presses the heels of his hands into his eyes and rubs them. "It would be fucking expensive. There's a penalty if we quit within the first year. Plus we've opened Europe-wide offices on the strength of this contract. It was supposed to be our brave new world. Our gateway to bigger and better things."

I can hear the heavy disappointment in his voice. And suddenly I want to throw my arms around him tight. It was so exciting when Brandon Communications won the Arcodas pitch. They worked so hard to get it. It seemed like such a prize.

"So, what are you going to do?" I ask tentatively.

Luke has picked up an antique nutcracker from a side table. He starts rotating the handle, his face set.

"Or else I could tell my staff they just have to get on with it. A few might leave, but the others would knuckle down. People need jobs. They'll put up with shit."

"And have a miserable company."

"A miserable, profitable company." His voice has an edge which I don't like. "We're in this to make money, remember?"

The baby suddenly kicks me hard inside and I wince. Everything's so...achy-painy. Me. Luke. The whole horrible situation.

"You don't want that," I say.

Luke doesn't move a muscle. His face is flint-hard. Anyone watching would think he didn't agree or hadn't heard or didn't care. But I know what's inside his head. He loves his company. He loves it when it's thriving and successful and happy.

"Luke, the staff at Brandon C..." I take a step toward him. "They're your *family*. They've been loyal to you all these years. Think how you'd feel if Amy was your daughter. You'd want her employer to take a stand. I mean...you're your own boss! The whole point is, you don't *have* to work with anyone."

"I'll talk to them." Luke's eyes are still focused downward. "I'll have it out. Maybe we can make it all work."

"Maybe." I nod, trying to sound more hopeful than I feel.

Suddenly Luke puts the nutcracker back on the table and looks up. "Becky, if I end up pulling out of the Arcodas deal . . . we won't be squillionaires. You understand that."

I feel a pang. It was pretty exciting when it was all going so well and we were going to conquer the world and fly around in private jets. And I was planning to buy these amazing £1,000 stiletto boots from Vivienne Westwood.

Anyway. There's a £50 version in Topshop. I'll get those instead.

"Maybe not right now." I lift my chin defiantly. "But we will be when you pull off your next big deal. And in the meantime"—I look around the fabulous designer kitchen—"we're doing pretty well. We can buy an island some other year." I think for a moment. "Actually, islands are totally over. We didn't want one."

Luke stares at me for a moment, then gives a sudden snort of laughter.

"You know something, Becky Bloomwood? You are going to be one hell of a mother."

"Oh!" I color, totally taken by surprise. "Really? In a good way?"

Luke comes across the kitchen and rests his hands gently on my bump. "This little person is very lucky," he murmurs.

"Except I don't know any nursery rhymes," I say, a bit gloomy. "I won't be able to get it off to sleep."

"Nursery rhymes are overrated," says Luke confidently. "I'll read it pieces from the *FT*. That'll send it off."

We both gaze down at my swollen tummy for a while. I still can't quite get my head round the fact that there's a baby inside my body. Which has got to come out...somehow.

OK, let's not go there. There's still time for them to invent something.

After a while Luke raises his head. He has a strange, unreadable expression on his face.

"So...tell me, Becky," he says lightly. "Is it Armageddon or Pomegranate?"

"What?" I look at him, confused.

"This morning, when I got home, I was trying to work out where you'd gone. I rooted around in your drawers for clues...." He hesitates. "And I came across that gender predictor test. You've found out, haven't you?"

My heart gives an almighty thud. Shit. I should have thrown the test away. I'm so *stupid*.

Luke's smiling, but I can see a trace of hurt in his eyes. And suddenly I feel really terrible. I don't know how I could have been planning to leave Luke out of such an important moment. I don't even quite know anymore why I was so desperate to find out the sex. Who cares?

I put one of my hands on his and squeeze it. "Actually, Luke...I didn't do the test. I don't know."

Luke's rueful expression doesn't change.

"Come on, Becky. Just tell me. If only one of us is going to be surprised, there doesn't seem much point in waiting anymore."

"I didn't do the test!" I insist. "Honestly! It was going to take too long and you had to have an injection...."

He doesn't believe me. I can see it from his face. We'll be in the delivery room and they'll say "It's a boy!" or whatever, and all he'll think is "Becky already knew."

A lump suddenly rises in my throat. I don't want it to be like that. I want us to find out together.

"Luke, I *didn't* find out," I say desperately, tears stinging my eyes. "I really, honestly didn't! I wouldn't lie to you. You have to believe me. It's going to be an amazing . . . wonderful . . . surprise. For *both* of us."

I'm gazing up at him, my whole body tense, my hands clutching my skirt. Luke's eyes are scanning my face.

"OK." His brow finally relaxes. "OK. I believe you."

"And I believe you too." The words fall out of my mouth with no warning.

But now I've said them, I realize they're true. I could demand more proof that Luke's not seeing Venetia. I could get him followed again. I could be totally paranoid and miserable forever.

In the end, you have to choose whether or not to trust someone. And I do choose to trust him. I do.

"Come here." Luke draws me in for a hug. "It's OK, sweetheart. It's all going to be fine."

After a while I pull away from Luke. I take a deep breath, trying to compose myself, and get down a couple of mugs. Then I turn to him.

"Luke, why did Venetia say you were having an affair if you weren't?"

"I have no idea." Luke looks mystified. "Are you absolutely *sure* that's what she meant? You couldn't have misinterpreted what she was saying?"

"No!" I retort crossly. "I'm not that stupid! It was totally obvious what she meant." I rip off a piece of Fabia's paper towels and blow my nose on it. "And just so you know, I'm *not* having our baby delivered by her. Or going to any of her stupid tea parties."

"Fine." Luke nods. "I'm sure we can go back to Dr. Braine. You know, he's e-mailed me a couple of times, just to see how you are."

"Really? That's so sweet of him. . . ."

The doorbell rings and I start. It's them. I'd almost half kind-of forgotten.

"Who's that?" says Luke.

"It's *Vogue*!" I say in agitation. "The whole reason I'm here! For the photo shoot!"

I hurry into the hall, and as I see my reflection in the mirror I feel a jerk of dismay. My face is blotchy; my eyes are all bloodshot and puffy; my smile is strained. I can't remember my way round the house. I've totally forgotten all my yummy quotes. I can't even remember who my *underpants* are by. I can't do it.

The doorbell rings again, twice.

"Aren't you going to answer?" Luke has followed me into the hall.

"I'll have to cancel!" Woefully, I turn to face him. "Look at me. I'm a mess! I can't be in *Vogue* like this!"

"You'll be wonderful," he replies firmly, and strides to the front door.

"They think it's our house!" I hiss after him in panic. "I told them we live here."

Luke shoots me a what-do-you-take-me-for? glance over his shoulder, and swings open the door.

"Hello!" he says, in his most confident, head-of-a-huge-important-company voice. "Welcome to our home."

Makeup artists should hereby get the Nobel Prize for adding to human happiness. And so should hairdressers.

And so should Luke.

It's three hours later and the shoot is going brilliantly. Luke totally charmed all the *Vogue* people as soon as they arrived, and was completely convincing as we showed them around the house. They totally think we live here!

I feel like a different person. I certainly *look* like a different person. My blotchiness has been totally covered up, and the makeup artist was really sweet about it. She said she'd seen far worse and at least I wasn't off my head on coke. Or six hours late. And at least I hadn't brought some stupid yappy dog. (I get the feeling she's not that keen on models.)

My hair looks totally fab and shiny, and they brought the most amazing clothes for me to wear, all in a trailer which they've parked outside. And now I'm standing on the sweeping staircase in a Missoni dress, beaming as the camera clicks, feeling just like Claudia Schiffer or someone.

And Luke is standing at the bottom of the staircase, smiling encouragingly up at me. He's been here all along. He canceled all the rest of his morning meetings, and took part in the interview and everything. He said having a baby put other things into perspective and he thought fatherhood would change him as a person. He said he thought I was more beautiful right now than he'd ever seen me (which is a total lie, but still). He said...

Anyway. He said loads of nice things. *And* he knew who painted the picture above the fireplace in the sitting room when they asked. He's brilliant!

"Shall we move outside now?" The photographer looks questioningly at Martha.

"That's a nice idea." She nods, and I walk down the stairs, carefully holding up my dress.

"Maybe I could wear the Oscar de la Renta dress?"

The stylist brought the most amazing purple evening dress and cloak, which was apparently made for some pregnant movie star to wear to a premiere but she never did. I just *have* to try it on.

"Yes, that'll look spectacular against the grass." Martha heads to the back of the hall and squints through the glass doors. "What an amazing garden! Did you landscape it yourselves?"

"Absolutely!" I glance at Luke.

"We hired a gardening company, obviously," he says, "but the concept was all ours."

"That's right." I nod. "Our inspiration was a kind of Zen...meets...urban structure...."

"The positioning of the trees was crucial to the project," Luke adds. "We had them moved at least three times."

"Wow." Martha nods intelligently and scribbles in her notebook. "You're real perfectionists!"

"We just care about design," Luke says seriously. He shoots me a quick wink and I try not to giggle.

"So, you must be looking forward to seeing your little child out there on the lawn." She looks up with a smile. "Learning to crawl...and walk..."

"Yes." Luke takes my hand. "We certainly are."

I'm about to add something, but my stomach suddenly tightens, like someone squeezed it with both hands. It's been doing it for a while, now that I think about it—but that time was kind of stronger. "Ooh," I say, before I can stop myself.

"What?" Luke looks alert.

"Nothing," I say quickly. "So, shall I put on the cloak?"

"Let's get your makeup touched up," says Martha. "And shall we do a sandwich run?"

I head across the hall, reach the front door, and stop. My stomach just tightened up again. It's unmistakable.

"What is it?" Luke is watching me. "Becky, what's going on?"

OK. Don't panic.

"Luke," I say as calmly as I can, "I think I'm in labor. It's been going on for a while now."

My stomach tightens again, and I start shallow panting, just like Noura said in that lesson. God, it's amazing how I'm coping instinctively.

"A *while*?" Luke strides over to me, looking alarmed. "How long, exactly?"

I think back to when I first became aware of the sensations. "About five hours? Which means I'm probably . . . five centimeters dilated, maybe?"

"Five centimeters dilated?" Luke stares at me. "What does that mean?"

"It means I'm halfway there." My voice suddenly trembles with excitement. "It means we're going to have a baby!"

"Jesus Christ." Luke whips out his mobile phone and jabs at it. "Hello? Ambulance service, please. Quick!"

As he gives the address I feel suddenly shaky around the knees. This wasn't supposed to happen until the nineteenth. I thought I had three more weeks to go.

And maybe I should have gone to more than one prenatal class.

"What's going on?" Martha says, looking up from her notes. "Shall we do the garden shots now?"

"Becky's in labor," Luke says, putting his phone away. "I'm afraid we'll have to go."

"In *labor*?" Martha drops her notebook and pen and scrabbles to pick them up. "Oh my God! But it's not due yet, is it?"

"Not for three weeks," says Luke. "It must be early."

"Are you all right, Becky?" Martha peers at me. "Do you need drugs?"

"I'm using natural methods," I gasp, gripping my necklace. "This is an ancient Maori birthing stone."

"Wow!" says Martha, scribbling. "Can you spell *Maori*?"

My stomach tightens again and I clutch the stone harder. Even with the pain, I can't help feeling exhilarated. They're right, birth *is* an amazing experience. I feel as if my whole body is working in harmony, as if this is what it was designed to do all along.

"Have you got a bag packed?" says Martha, watching me in alarm. "Aren't you supposed to have a bag?"

"I've got a suitcase," I say breathlessly.

"Right," says Luke, snapping his phone shut. "Let's get it. Quick. Where is it? And your hospital notes."

"It's . . ." I break off. It's all at home. Our real home.

"Um . . . it's in the bedroom. By the dressing table." I look at him in slight desperation. Luke's eyes snap with sudden understanding.

"Of course," he says. "Well . . . I'm sure we can make a stop-off if we need to."

"I'll nip up and get it for you," says Martha helpfully. "Which side of the dressing table is it?"

"No! I mean . . . um . . . actually, there it is!" I point at a Mulberry hold-all that I've suddenly spotted in the hall cupboard. "I forgot, I put it there so as to be ready."

"Right." Luke drags it out of the cupboard, with some effort, and a tennis ball falls out of it.

"Why are you taking tennis balls to hospital?" asks Martha, looking puzzled.

"For . . . er . . . massage. Oh God . . ." I grip the Maori stone tightly and breathe deeply.

"Are you OK, Becky?" says Luke, looking anxious. "It seems to be getting worse." He looks at his watch. "Where's this bloody ambulance?"

"They're getting stronger." I manage to nod through the pain. "I should think I'm probably about six or seven centimeters dilated by now."

"Hey, the ambulance is here." The photographer pokes his head through the front door. "It's just pulling up."

"We should get going." Luke holds out his arm to me. "Are you able to walk?"

"I think so. Just about."

We head out the front door and pause on the top step. The ambulance is blocking the whole road, its blue light flashing round and round. I can see a few people watching, on the other side of the street.

This is it. When I come out of hospital . . . I'll have a baby!

"Good luck!" calls Martha. "Hope it all goes well!"

"Becky . . . I love you." Luke squeezes my arm tight. "I'm so proud of you. You're doing amazingly! You're so calm, so composed. . . ."

"It just feels totally natural," I say with a kind of humble awe, like Patrick Swayze telling Demi Moore what heaven is like at the end of *Ghost*. "It's painful... but it's beautiful too."

Two paramedics have got out of the back of the ambulance and are coming toward me.

"Ready?" Luke glances down at me.

"Uh-huh." I take a deep breath and start walking down the steps. "Let's do it."

EIGHTEEN

HUH. I DON'T BELIEVE IT, I wasn't in labor after all. I don't have a baby or *anything*.

It doesn't make any sense, in fact I still think they might have been wrong. I had all the symptoms! The regular contractions, and the back pain (well, a slight achy feeling), just like in the book. But they sent me home and said I wasn't in labor or prelabor or even approaching labor. They said they weren't real labor pains.

It was all a bit embarrassing. Especially when I asked for the epidural and they laughed. They didn't have to laugh. Or phone up their friends and tell them. I *heard* that midwife, even though she was whispering.

It's also made me rethink this whole giving-birth thing. I mean, if that wasn't the real thing... what on earth is the real thing like? So after we got back from the hospital I had a long, frank talk with Luke. I said I'd given it some careful thought and come to the conclusion that I couldn't do labor, and we were going to have to find some other solution.

He was really sweet about it, and *didn't* just say "Love, you'll be fine" (like that stupid midwife phone advisory service). He said I should line up every form of pain relief I could, never mind about the cost. So I've hired a reflexologist, a hot-stone-massage person, an aromatherapist, an acupuncturist, a homeopath, and a doula. Plus I've taken to phoning the hospital every day, just to make sure their anesthetists haven't all gone ill or been trapped in a cupboard or anything.

And I chucked out that stupid birthing stone. I always thought it was rubbish.

It's now a week later, and nothing's happened since, except I'm bigger and more lumbery than ever. We went to see Dr. Braine yesterday, and he said everything seemed just fine and the baby had turned into the right position, which was good news. Hmph. Good news for the baby, maybe. Not for me. I can hardly walk anymore, let alone sleep. Last night I woke up at three A.M. and felt so uncomfortable I couldn't even lie in bed, so I went and watched this program on cable called *True-Life Births—When Trauma Goes Bad*.

Which was maybe a mistake, in hindsight. But luckily Luke was awake too, and he made me a cup of hot chocolate to calm me down and said it was really unlikely we'd ever be stuck in a snowdrift with twins about to be born and no doctors for two hundred miles. And at least now we knew what to do if we were.

Luke isn't sleeping well either at the moment, and it's all because of the Arcodas situation. He's been talking to his lawyers every day, and having consultations with his staff, and has endlessly tried to set up a meeting with the Arcodas senior team to have it all out. But Iain has canceled twice with no notice—and then he disappeared off on some trip. So nothing's resolved yet, and the longer it all goes on, the tenser Luke gets. It's like we're both on some ticking fuse, just . . . *waiting*.

I've never been good at waiting. For babies, or phone calls, or sample sales...or anything.

The only positive thing right now is that Luke and I are about a million times closer than we have been for months. We've talked about everything over the past week. His company, plans for the future...one night we even got out all the honeymoon photos and looked through them again.

We've talked about everything...except Venetia.

I tried. I tried to tell him what she was really like, over supper, after we got back from the hospital that day. But Luke was just incredulous. He said he still couldn't believe that Venetia said she and he were having an affair. He said they were genuinely just old friends—and maybe I'd made a mistake or misinterpreted what she meant.

Which made me want to hurl my plate at the wall and shout, "How stupid do you think I *am*?" But I didn't. It would have turned into a big row, and I really didn't want to ruin the evening.

And I haven't pushed the subject since then. Luke's so hassled, I can't bring myself to. As he says, we never have to see Venetia again if we don't want to. He's given her notice as a PR client, Dr. Braine will deliver the baby, and Luke's promised he won't make any plans to meet up with her. As far as he's concerned, it's a brief chapter of our life which has closed.

Only...I can't close it. Deep down, I'm still obsessed. I *didn't* make a mistake. She *did* say that she and Luke were having an affair. She nearly ruined our marriage—and now she's just getting away with it.

If I could just *see* her...if I could tell her what I think of her....

"Bex, you're grinding your teeth again," says Suze patiently. "Stop it." She arrived half an hour ago, laden with homemade Christmas presents from Ernie's school fair. Now she brings over a cup of raspberry leaf tea and an iced Santa Claus cookie and puts them down on the counter. "You have to stop stressing about Venetia. It's not good for the baby."

"It's all right for you! You don't know what it's like. No one made you wear hideous stockings and said you don't have a marriage anymore and your husband was leaving you...."

"Look, Bex." Suze sighs. "Whatever Venetia said... Whether she did say that or not..."

"She did!" I look up, indignant. "That's what she said, word for word! Don't you believe me either?"

"Of course I do!" says Suze, backtracking. "Of course. But you know, when you're pregnant, things can seem worse than they really are.... You can overreact...."

"I am not overreacting! She tried to steal my husband! What, you think I'm deluded? You think I made it all up?"

"No!" says Suze hastily. "Look, I'm sorry. Maybe she did go after him. But... she didn't get him, did she?"

"Well... no."

"So. Just let it go. You're having a baby, Bex. *That's* the important thing, isn't it?"

She looks so anxious, I can't tell her my secret fantasy of bursting into the Holistic Birth Center unannounced and telling everyone exactly what a deceitful home-wrecker Venetia Carter really is.

Then how holistic would she look?

"All right," I say at last. "I'm letting it go."

"Good." Suze pats my arm. "So, what time do we have to leave?"

I'm going back to The Look today, even though I'm officially now on maternity leave, because they're opening the waiting list for the new Danny Kovitz line. Danny is going to be there from twelve noon, signing T-shirts for people who register, and the store has already had hundreds of inquiries!

The whole thing has suddenly become huge news—helped by Danny being photographed the other night in a clinch with the new guy in *Coronation Street*. All the papers have suddenly taken up the story and we've had loads of publicity. Danny was even on *Morning Coffee* this morning, assessing spring fashions on the sofa (he said all the outfits were hideous, which they loved) and telling everyone to come to The Look.

Ha! And it was all my idea to get him involved.

"Let's go in a few minutes," I say, glancing at my watch. "There's no rush. They can't exactly fire me for being late, can they?"

"I guess not. . . ." Suze edges back to the sink, past our brand-new Warrior pushchair, which is in the corner, still in its packaging. There wasn't room for it in the nursery, and the hall is cluttered with a Bugaboo (they were on special offer) and this cool three-wheeler which has an integrated car seat. "Bex, how many prams did you order?"

"A few," I say vaguely.

"But where are you going to *keep* them all?"

"It's OK," I assure her. "I'm having a special room for them in the new house. I'll call it the Pram Room."

"A Pram Room?" Suze stares at me. "You're having a Shoe Room and a Pram Room?"

"Why not? People don't have enough different rooms. I might have a Handbag Room too. Just a small one..." I take a sip of raspberry leaf tea, which according to Suze helps speed up labor, and wince at the revolting taste.

"Ooh, what was that?" says Suze, alert. "Did you feel a twinge?"

Honestly. This is the third time she's asked about twinges since she arrived this morning.

"Suze, it's not due for another two weeks," I remind her.

"That doesn't mean anything!" says Suze. "Those dates are all a conspiracy by doctors." She studies me closely. "Do you feel like sweeping the floor or cleaning out the fridge?"

"The fridge is clean!" I say, a bit offended.

"No, you dope!" says Suze. "It's the nesting instinct. When the twins were due I suddenly got this mania for ironing Tarkie's shirts. And Lulu always starts vacuuming the whole house."

"Vacuuming?" I look at her dubiously. I can't imagine having an urge to vacuum.

"Totally! Loads of women scrub the floor—" She breaks off as the buzzer sounds, and picks up the entry phone. "Hello, the Brandon residence!" She listens for a moment, then presses the entry button. "It's a delivery. Are you expecting something?"

"Ooh, yes!" I put my cup down. "It'll be my Christmas things!"

"Presents?" Suze brightens. "Is there one for me?"

"Not presents," I explain. "Gorgeous decorations. It was so weird—I had this sudden urge yesterday, like I *had* to get Christmas all sorted before I had the baby. So

I've ordered new angels for the tree, and an Advent candle, and this gorgeous nativity scene...." I take a bite of cookie and munch it. "I've got it all planned for the new house. We'll have a huge Christmas tree in the hall, and garlands everywhere, and gingerbread men which we can put on red ribbons...."

The doorbell sounds and I head to the door. I open it to see two men holding massive cardboard boxes, plus a huge bulky parcel which must be the life-size models of Mary and Joseph.

"Blimey!" says Suze, staring at them. "You'll need a Christmas Decoration Room too."

Hey. That's not a bad idea!

"Hi!" I beam at the men. "Just put them anywhere, thank you so much...." I scribble a signature and turn to Suze as the guys head out again. "I must show you the baby's Christmas stocking—" I stop. Suze is looking from me to the boxes and back again with a strange, animated expression. "What?"

"Bex, this is it," she says. "You're nesting."

I stare at her. "But...I haven't cleaned anything."

"Every woman's different! Maybe you don't clean— you order things from catalogs! Was it like...this sudden really strong desire which you couldn't fight?"

"Yes!" I can't help a gasp of recognition. "Exactly! The catalog came through the door...and I just *had* to order from it. I couldn't stop myself!"

"There you go!" Suze says, satisfied. "It's all part of nature's grand plan."

"Wow," I breathe, totally awestruck by my own body. I wasn't shopping, I was nesting! I *must* tell Luke.

"And you really don't feel like cleaning anything?" Suze adds curiously. "Or tidying up?"

I prod my feelings experimentally. "I don't *think* so. . . ."

"You don't feel like washing up those plates?" Suze gestures to the breakfast things in the sink.

"No," I say definitely. "No urge at all."

"It just shows." Suze shakes her head in wonderment. "Every pregnancy is different."

A new thought has suddenly struck me. "Hey, Suze, if I'm nesting, maybe I'll have the baby soon! Like this afternoon!"

"You can't!" says Suze in dismay. "Not before your shower!" Immediately she claps her hand over her mouth.

Shower? Does she mean . . . baby shower?

"Are you throwing me a baby shower!" I can't help beaming with excitement.

"No!" says Suze at once. "I . . . that's not . . . it wasn't . . . I'm not . . ."

Her face has turned bright pink and she's twisting one leg around the other. Suze is such a hopeless liar.

"Yes, you are!"

"Well, OK," she says in a rush. "But it's a *surprise*. I'm not going to tell you when it is."

"Is it today?" I say at once. "I bet it's today!"

"I'm not telling you!" she says, all flustered. "Stop talking about it. Pretend I never said anything. Come on, let's go."

We take a taxi to The Look, and as we draw near I cannot believe my eyes. This is better than I could have hoped for, in a million years.

There are queues of people snaking round the block

as far as I can see. There must be hundreds of them, mostly girls in cool-looking outfits, chattering in groups or on mobile phones. Everyone's holding a helium balloon with THE LOOK—DANNY KOVITZ printed on it, and music is playing from speakers, and one of the girls from PR is giving out bottles of Diet Coke and "Danny Kovitz" lollies.

The whole atmosphere is like a party. A TV crew from *London Tonight* is filming the scene and a radio presenter is interviewing the girl at the head of the queue, and as we get out I can see a woman introducing herself to a young, rangy girl as a scout from Models One.

"This is *amazing*," Suze breathes beside me.

"I know!" I'm trying to look cool, but a huge grin is spreading across my face. "Come on, let's go inside!"

We fight our way to the head of the queue, and I show my pass to the security guard. As he opens the door to let us in, I can feel the swell of girls pushing forward behind me.

"Did you see that girl?" I can hear furious voices behind me demanding. "She just shoved her way in! Why does she get to queue-barge just because she's pregnant?"

Oops. Maybe we should have gone in a side door.

Inside, there's another queue of excited, chattering girls. It winds through accessories, past huge screens showing Danny's latest catwalk collection, up to a mirrored, art deco table behind which Danny is sitting on a huge throne-like chair. Above him a banner reads *EXCLUSIVE—MEET DANNY KOVITZ!* and in front of him three teenage girls in identikit military jackets and ponytails are gawking at him in total awe as he signs plain white T-shirts for them. He meets my eye and winks.

"Thanks," I mouth back, and blow him a kiss. He is a total, one hundred percent star.

Plus, I know he will be *loving* all this.

A small distance from the table, Eric is being interviewed by another TV crew, and as I approach I can hear him speaking.

"I did always feel strongly that The Look should be considering joint design initiatives..." he's saying importantly. Then suddenly he notices me watching. He breaks off, flushing slightly. "Ahem. Let me introduce Rebecca Brandon, our head of Personal Shopping, who originated the idea...."

"Hi there!" I head over to the camera with a big, confident smile. "Eric and I worked as a team on this project and I think it heralds a new day for The Look. And all those people who laughed at us can *eat their words*."

I give a few more sound bites to the interviewer, then make an excuse and leave Eric to it. To my astonishment, I've just spotted Jess standing uncomfortably by the sunglasses, all on her own in jeans and a parka. I told her about the launch today, but I really wasn't sure she'd come along.

"Jess!" I call out as I near her. "You made it!"

"This is incredible, Becky." Jess is looking around at the milling crowds. "Congratulations."

"Thanks!" I beam at her. "Isn't it great? Have you seen all the TV crews?"

"There was a guy from the *Times* outside," says Jess, nodding. "And the *Standard*. The media coverage is going to be huge." She gives a little smile. "Becky Brandon does it again."

"Well..." I shrug, flushing. "So, how are things? How are preparations going for Chile?"

"Oh, fine." Jess heaves a sigh.

The thing with Jess is, it can be a bit hard to tell what mood she's in. She has a slightly gloomy air about her even when she's happy. (Which is just the way she is—I'm not being mean or anything.) But as I look at her now, I think she's genuinely miserable.

"Jess... what's up?" I put a hand on her arm. "Things aren't fine."

"No," says Jess. "They're not." She looks up, and to my horror I see her eyes are shimmering. "Tom's disappeared."

"Disappeared?" I say, aghast.

"I wasn't going to say anything. I didn't want to get you worried. But no one's seen him for three days. I think he's sulking."

"About you leaving?"

She nods and I feel a pang of anger at Tom. Why does he have to be such a self-obsessed flake?

"He sent one text to his parents to say he's safe. That's it. He could be anywhere. And Janice blames me, of course...."

"This isn't your fault! He's just a—" I stop myself.

"Do *you* have any ideas where he might be, Becky?" Her brow is all crinkled up. "You've known him all your life."

I shrug, at a loss. Knowing Tom, he could have done anything. He could have gone to the tattoo parlor and asked them to tattoo *Jess, Don't Go* on his genitals.

"Look... he'll turn up," I say at last. "He's not completely stupid. He's probably just gone off on a bender somewhere."

"Hi, Becky." I look up to see Jasmine coming toward us, holding an armful of scarves and hats, her cheeks pink with exertion.

"Hey, Jasmine! Isn't this amazing? What's it like upstairs?"

"Mayhem." She rolls her eyes. "Customers everywhere. Thank God we've got the extra staff."

"Isn't it cool?" I beam, but Jasmine gives an unenthusiastic scowl.

"I preferred it the way it was. We're all going to have to stay late tonight, you know. I haven't had a moment to myself."

"This way, the shop may not go bust," I point out, but Jasmine doesn't look impressed.

"Whatever..." Her face suddenly snaps in shock. For a moment she's speechless. "Becky...have you had your eyebrows done?"

I wondered when she was going to notice!

"Oh," I say casually. "Yes, I have. Nice, aren't they?" I smooth one down with my finger.

"Where did you go?" she demands.

"I'm afraid I couldn't say," I tell her in tones of regret. "It's a bit of a secret. Sorry about that."

Jasmine's chin is set in fury. "Tell me where you went!"

"No!"

"Jasmine!" a girl is calling from the escalators. "Have you got those scarves for the customer?"

"You found out where I go, didn't you?" she spits. "You must have spied on me."

"How could I have done that?" I say innocently,

glancing at my reflection in a nearby mirror. My eyebrows *do* look pretty spectacular, though I say it myself. It's this Indian woman in Crouch End who does them. You go to her house and she threads and plucks and it takes forever. But it's worth it.

"Jasmine!" the girl calls louder.

"I've got to go." Jasmine shoots me a last, evil look.

"Bye then!" I say cheerily. "I'll bring the baby in to see you."

Jess has been following the whole conversation, looking utterly bemused. "What's the big deal about eyebrows?" she says as Jasmine stalks off.

I survey Jess's eyebrows. They're brown and tufty and it's obvious that no pair of tweezers, brush, or eyebrow pencil has ever been near them.

"I'll show you one day," I say as my phone starts to ring. I take it out and flip it open. "Hello?"

"Hi," says Luke's voice in my ear. "It's me. I gather the launch is a huge success. It's just been on the news. Well done, darling!"

"Thanks! It is pretty amazing...." I take a few steps away from Jess and turn in behind a rack of chiffon beaded shrugs. "So...what's the latest?" I add in a lower voice.

"We've had the meeting. I've just come out of it."

"Oh my God." I clutch the phone tighter. "And how did it go?"

"Couldn't have been worse."

"That good, huh?" I try to joke, but my heart sinks. I was so hoping Luke might be able to salvage the situation.

"I don't think anyone's ever stood up to Iain before. He doesn't like it. Jesus, they're a bunch of unpleasant thugs." I can hear the anger in Luke's voice. "They think they own the world."

"They practically do own the world," I point out.

"They don't own me." Luke sounds resolute. "Or my company."

"So, what are you going to do?"

"I'm talking to the whole staff this afternoon." He pauses and I picture him at his desk in his shirtsleeves, tugging at his tie to loosen it. "But it looks like we're going to pull out of the deal. There's no way we can work with these people."

So that's it. The whole Arcodas-deal-conquering-the-world dream is ended. All Luke's hopes and plans dashed. I feel a growing, overwhelming fury at Iain Wheeler. How *dare* he treat people so badly and just get away with it? He needs someone to expose him.

"Luke, I have to go," I say with sudden resolve. "I'll see you later. We'll talk about it tonight."

I switch off, quickly search through my phone numbers, and speed-dial. After four rings there's a reply.

"Dave Sharpness."

"Oh, hi, Mr. Sharpness," I say. "It's Becky Brandon here."

"Mrs. Brandon!" His hoarse voice lifts. "What a delight to hear from you again! I hope you're keeping well?"

"Er... fine, thanks." Two girls walk past, and I edge away to an empty spot behind a display of wigs.

"Is there another matter we might be able to help you with?" Dave Sharpness is saying. "Our surveillance operatives have undergone full retraining, you'll be pleased to hear. And I can offer you a twenty percent discount on all investigations—"

"No!" I cut him off. "Thanks. What I need is that dossier you did for me. I shredded it. But now . . . I need it. Do you have a copy you could get to me?"

Dave Sharpness gives his throaty chuckle.

"Mrs. Brandon, if I could count the number of ladies I've known who destroy some vital piece of evidence in a fit of pique. Then, when the divorce court looms, they're on the phone wondering if we keep copies. . . ."

"I'm not getting divorced!" I say, trying to keep my patience. "I need it . . . for a different reason. Do you have a copy?"

"Well, now. Ordinarily, Mrs. Brandon, I would have a copy to you within the hour. However. . ." He pauses.

"What's wrong?" I say anxiously.

"Unfortunately, there's been a slight mishap with the client secure storage facility." Dave Sharpness exhales. "Our office manager, Wendy, and a pot of coffee. I won't go into details, but some of our archives are . . . well, to put it bluntly, a bit of a mess. We've had to throw a lot of it out."

"But I need it! I need everything you've got on Iain Wheeler. You know, that guy you thought was my husband? Any photos, or evidence of those hushed-up cases . . ."

"Mrs. Brandon, I'll do my best. I'll have a search through, see what I've got. . . ."

"And can you courier it round as soon as you find anything?"

"Will do."

"Thanks," I say. "I really do appreciate it."

I switch off the phone, my heart beating fast. I'll get

that evidence. And if it's all ruined, I'll just commission another investigation. We'll bring Iain Wheeler down.

Jess appears again through the crush, holding a Danny Kovitz balloon. She looks a bit surprised to see me lurking behind the wigs.

"Hi, Becky," she says, as I come out into the main throng. "I just saw Suze and she's trying on about a hundred things. D'you feel like a cup of tea?"

"Actually . . . I feel a bit tired," I say, as a customer nearly elbows me in the stomach. "I might head home soon and have a rest. I'll just say good-bye to everyone. . . ."

"Good idea." Jess nods vigorously. "Save your energy for tomor—" She stops.

"Tomorrow?" I say, puzzled. "What's happening tomorrow?"

"I mean . . . for the baby." Jess's eyes slide away evasively. "For the birth. Whenever it is."

What on earth is she . . .

And then it hits me. She's in on the secret too. That's what she let slip!

My surprise baby shower is tomorrow!

SURPRISE BABY SHOWER— POSSIBLE OUTFITS

1. Pink PARTY glittery T-shirt, maternity jeans, silver shoes
   PROS: Will look fab.
   CONS: Won't look like I was surprised.

2. Nightie and dressing gown, no makeup, hair ratty
   PROS: Will look surprised.
   CONS: Will look crap.

3. Juicy Couture jogging tracksuit
   PROS: Will look informal yet sleek. Like Hollywood celebrity relaxing at home.
   CONS: Do not fit into Juicy Couture jogging tracksuit.

4. Maternity "Ginger Spice" Union Jack dress and matching wig, bought in summer sale, 90% off
   PROS: Have not had a chance to wear it yet.
   CONS: No one else may be in fancy dress.

Prendergast de Witt Connell
Financial Advisers

Forward House
394 High Holborn
London WC1V 7EX

Mrs R Brandon
37 Maida Vale Mansions
Maida Vale
London NW6 0YF

3 December 2003

Dear Mrs. Brandon,

Thank you for your letter.

I cannot agree with any of your points and will answer only by saying that investment is not supposed to be "fun." I assure you that I would not change my mind if I could see your collection of 1930s lipstick cases. And I doubt very much they—or any part of your portfolio—will "make you a million."

Yours sincerely,

Kenneth Prendergast
Family Investment Specialist

NINETEEN

IF ONLY I KNEW what *time* I was being surprised.

It's eight o'clock the following morning, and I'm dressed and made up and all ready. In the end I went for a pink wrap dress and suede boots. Plus I had my nails done last night, and bought some flowers and tidied the flat up a bit.

Best of all, I rooted through all my old boxes of stuff till I found this gorgeous card I once bought in New York. It has a little crib on it, with tiny presents dotted around—and glittery writing saying: Thanks for Throwing Me a Surprise Baby Shower, Friends! I *knew* I'd have a need for it one day.

I also found a somber gray one saying, Sorry to Hear of Your Business Troubles, but I ripped that one up. Stupid card.

I haven't heard anything from Dave Sharpness yet. And I haven't mentioned it to Luke, even though I'm bursting to. I don't want to raise his hopes until I know I have the evidence.

Luke's in the kitchen, drinking a strong black coffee before he leaves for work. I wander in and watch him for a moment. His jawline is tense and he's stirring sugar into his espresso cup. He does that only when he needs a five-thousand-volt boost of energy.

He notices me and gestures to the bar seat opposite. I heave myself up and rest my elbows on the granite.

"Becky ... we need to talk."

"You're doing the right thing," I say at once. "You know you are."

Luke nods. "You know, I already feel free. They were oppressing me. They were oppressing the whole company."

"Exactly! You don't *need* them, Luke! You don't need to run around after some arrogant, think-they-own-the-world company...."

Luke lifts a hand. "It's not as simple as that. There's something I need to tell you." He pauses, stirring his coffee round and round, his face intent. "Arcodas haven't paid us."

"What?" I stare at him, uncomprehending. "You mean ... at *all*?"

"Once, right at the beginning. But nothing since. They owe us ... well, a lot."

"But they can't not pay you! People have to pay their bills! I mean, it's against the—"

I break off, reddening. I've just remembered a few store card bills stuffed into my dressing table drawer, which I might not *totally* have paid yet.

But that's different. I'm not a huge multinational company, am I?

"They're notorious for this. We've been chasing them, threatening them...." Luke rubs his brow. "While we were still doing business, we were confident we'd get the money. Now, we may have to sue."

"Well then, sue!" I say defiantly. "They won't get away with it!"

"But in the meantime..." Luke lifts his cup, then puts it down again. "Becky, to be honest, things aren't great. We expanded fast. Too fast, in hindsight. I have leases to pay, salaries to pay...we're hemorrhaging money. Until we manage to get back on our feet again, cash flow is going to be an issue."

"Right." I gulp. *Hemorrhaging money.* That's about the worst expression I've ever heard. I have a sudden horrible vision of money pouring out of a great hole, day after day.

"We'll need to borrow more than I thought to buy the house." Luke winces and takes a gulp of coffee. "It may delay things by a few weeks. I'll call the agent today. I should be able to square it with everyone."

He drains his cup and I notice a deep stress groove running between his brows which wasn't there before. Bastards. They gave that to him.

"You still did the right thing, Luke." I grab his hand and hold it tight. "And if it means losing a bit of money, well...so what?"

Just wait. Just you wait, Iain bloody Wheeler.

On impulse I get down off my stool, go round to Luke's side of the counter, and put my arms around him as best as I can. The baby's so huge it doesn't really have room to jump around anymore, but it's still squirming every now and then.

Hey, baby, I telegraph it silently. *Don't come out till I've had my baby shower, will you?*

I read the other day that a lot of mothers experience a genuine communication with their unborn babies, so

I'm trying to send it the odd little message of encouragement.

Tomorrow would be fine. Maybe lunchtime?

If you make it out in less than six hours, I'll give you a prize!

"I should have listened to you, Becky." Luke's wry voice takes me by surprise. "You were the one protesting against Arcodas in the first place. And you never liked Iain."

"Loathed him." I nod.

No, I'm not telling you what the prize is. Wait and see.

There's a ring at the buzzer and he lifts the receiver. "Hi, bring it up." To me he says, "It's a package."

I stiffen. "A courier package?"

"Uh-huh." He shrugs his coat on. "Are you expecting something?"

"Kind of." I swallow. "Luke...you might want to see this package. It could be important."

"It's not more bed linen, is it?" Luke doesn't look enthusiastic.

"No! It's not bed linen! It's—" I break off as the doorbell rings. "You'll see." I hurry into the hall.

"Package for you. Please sign here," mumbles the courier as I open the door. I scribble on his electronic pad, grab the Jiffy bag, and turn to see Luke coming into the hall.

"Luke, I have something pretty major here." I clear my throat. "Something which could...change things. And you need to be open-minded about where I got it...."

"Shouldn't you give that to Jess?" Luke is squinting at the Jiffy bag.

"Jess?" I follow his gaze and for the first time see *Miss Jessica Bertram* typed on the label.

I feel a plunge of disappointment. It isn't from Dave Sharpness after all, it's some stupid thing for Jess.

"How come Jess is getting parcels delivered here?" I say, unable to hide my frustration. "She doesn't live here!"

"Who knows?" Luke shrugs. "Sweetheart, I need to get going." He runs his eyes over my swollen stomach. "But I'll have my mobile on, and my pager. . . . If there are *any* signs at all . . ."

"I'll call." I nod, turning the Jiffy bag over in my fingers. "So, what am I supposed to do with this?"

"You can give it to Jess—" Luke stops himself. "Sometime. Whenever you see her next."

Hang on a minute. The overcasual way he said that . . .

"Luke, you know, don't you?" I exclaim.

"Know what?" His mouth twitches suspiciously as he picks up his briefcase.

"You *know*! About the . . . you know!"

"I have no idea what you're talking about." Luke looks as though he wants to laugh. "By the way, Becky, on a completely unrelated matter . . . could you possibly be in at around eleven this morning? We're expecting the gas man."

"No, we're not!" I point at him, half-accusing, half-giggling. "You're setting me up!"

"Have a wonderful time." Luke kisses me, and then he's out the door and I'm left alone.

I linger in the hall for a bit, just looking at the door. I almost wish I'd gone in with Luke today, to show moral support. He looks so stressed. And now he's got to face all his staff. And his finance people.

Hemorrhaging money. My stomach gives a nasty flip. No. Stop it. Don't think about it.

There's still two hours to go before eleven, so I put on a Harry Potter DVD to distract myself, and open a box of chocolate snowmen, just because it's the festive season. It's got to the bit where Harry sees his dead parents in the mirror, and I'm reaching for a tissue, when I happen to glance out the window—and see Suze. She's standing in front of our building, in the little car park next to the landscaped garden, and she's looking straight up at the window.

Immediately I duck down out of view. I hope she didn't spot me.

After a few moments I cautiously raise my head again and she's still standing there. Only she's been joined by Jess! In slight excitement I glance at my watch. Ten forty. Not long now!

The only thing is, they both seem quite perturbed. Suze is gesturing with a frown, and Jess is nodding. They must have a problem. I wonder what it is. And I can't even help.

As I'm watching, Suze gets out her phone. She dials, and as the phone in the flat rings, I jump guiltily and move away from the window.

OK. Act casual. I take a deep breath, then lift the receiver.

"Oh, hi, Suze!" I say, in my most natural manner. "How are you doing? You're probably in Hampshire on your horse or somewhere."

"How did you know it was me?" says Suze suspiciously.

Shit.

"We've got . . . Caller ID," I fib. "So, how are you?"

"I'm great!" says Suze, sounding totally stilted. "Actually, Bex, I was just reading this article about pregnant women, and it said you should go for a twenty-minute walk every day for health. So I was thinking maybe you should go on one. Like . . . now. Just round the block."

She wants to get me out of the way! Right. What I'll do is play along but not make it look too obvious.

"A twenty-minute walk," I say in thoughtful tones. "That sounds like a good idea. Maybe I will."

"Not any *more* than twenty minutes," Suze adds hurriedly. "Just twenty minutes exactly."

"OK!" I say. "I'll go right now."

"Cool!" Suze sounds relieved. "Er . . . see you . . . sometime!"

"See you!"

I hurry to the hall, put on my coat, and head downstairs in the lift. When I step outside, Suze and Jess have disappeared. They must be hiding!

Trying to look just like any normal pregnant woman having a twenty-minute walk, I head toward the gates, my eyes swiveling from left to right.

Oh my God, I just saw Suze behind that car! And there's Jess crouching behind the low wall!

I can't let them know I can see them. I can't giggle. Keeping my composure, I reach the gates—and spot a familiar spring of curly brown hair behind a rhododendron bush.

No. I don't believe it. Is that *Mum*?

I get past the gates and burst into laughter, muffling the sound with my hands. I hurry along the pavement, find a bench in the next street, and flick through *Heat* magazine, which I hid inside my coat so Suze wouldn't see. Then, on the dot of twenty minutes, I get up and turn my steps back toward home.

As I walk through the gates again there's no sign of anyone. I let myself in and take the lift to the top floor, feeling bubbles of anticipation. I head to our apartment, put my key in the lock, and turn.

"Surprise!" A chorus of voices greets me as I swing the door back wide. And the weird thing is, even though I was expecting it, I feel a genuine shock to see so many friendly faces clustered together. Suze, Jess, Mum, Janice, Danny . . . and is that *Kelly*?

"Wow!" I drop *Heat* without even meaning to. "What on earth—"

"It's your shower!" Suze is glowing pink with pleasure. "Surprise! We fooled you! Come in, have a glass of Buck's Fizz. . . ."

She ushers me into the sitting room, and I can't believe the transformation. There are pink and blue helium balloons everywhere, and a huge cake sitting on a silver stand, and a pile of presents, and bottles of champagne on ice. . . .

"This is just . . ." My voice suddenly wobbles. "It's just . . ."

"Don't cry, Bex!" says Suze.

"Have a drink, love!" Mum thrusts a glass into my hand.

"I knew we shouldn't surprise her!" Janice looks alarmed. "I said it would be too much of a shock for her system!"

"Surprised to see me?" Kelly has bounded up to me, her face shining with excitement and Stila shimmer makeup.

"Kelly!" I fling my drink-free arm around her. I met Kelly in Cumbria, when I was looking for Jess. I was only just pregnant then, and didn't even know it yet. It seems *years* ago now.

"Were you really surprised, Bex?" Suze looks at me, her face full of suppressed glee.

"Totally!"

And it's true. OK, I knew it was happening. But I had no idea anyone would make so much effort! Every time I look around, I notice something else, like the silver "baby" confetti sprinkled over the table, or the little booties hanging from all the pictures. . . .

"You ain't seen nothing yet," says Danny, taking a swig of champagne. "OK, everyone, line up, unbutton your jackets, on the count of three . . ."

I watch, bemused, as they scramble into place, like some kind of motley chorus line.

"One . . . two . . . three!"

Everyone, from Mum to Jess to Kelly, flings open their jackets. And underneath they're all wearing matching Danny Kovitz T-shirts, just like the one he designed for The Look. Except the picture is of a little doll-like pregnant girl. And underneath is the slogan:

SHE'S a YuMMY MuMMY and WE LOVE HER

I can't speak.

"She's overwhelmed!" Mum comes bustling up. "Take a seat, love. Have a snack." She thrusts a platter of tiny Chinese duck pancakes at me. "Waitrose's own brand. They're very good!"

"Open your presents," instructs Suze, clapping her

hands. "Then we've got party games. Hey, everyone sit down, Bex is going to open her presents...." She heaves all the gift-wrapped parcels into a pile in front of me, then tinkles a fork in her glass. "Now, I have a little speech to make about the presents. Attention!"

Everyone turns expectantly toward Suze and she makes a little bow.

"Thank you! Now, when I was planning this baby shower, I asked Jess what she thought we should buy Becky. And Jess said, 'There's nothing left, she's bought all of London already.'"

There's the hugest roar of laughter around the room, and I feel my cheeks turn beet-red. OK, maybe I did go a tad overboard. But the point is I had to. I mean, I'll be far too busy to go shopping after the baby's born. I probably won't go near a shop for a *year.*

"So!" resumes Suze, her eyes sparkling. "Jess suggested we should *make* things. And that's what we've done."

They've *made* things?

Oh God, they haven't all made baby wipes, have they?

"We'll start with mine." Suze hands me a rectangular package and I start ripping off the silver paper in slight apprehension.

"Oh, wow," I breathe as I see what it is. *"Wow."*

It's not baby wipes. It's an exquisite photo frame, made out of creamy painted wood, with tiny little mirrors and mother-of-pearl set into it. Inside, instead of a photograph, is a cartoon of a stick girl holding a baby in front of a house.

"You can put a picture of the baby in it," Suze is

explaining. "But for now, I've drawn a picture of you in front of your new house."

I look at the picture more closely and can't help bursting into laughter. The cartoon house has been divided up into rooms and each one given a label. "Pram Room." "Nappy Room." "Lipstick Room." "Visa Bill Room" (in the cellar). "Antiques of the Future Room."

An Antiques of the Future Room! That's actually a *brilliant* idea.

As I open my other presents I'm totally overwhelmed. Kelly's is a tiny patchwork quilt, with patches contributed by all the lovely friends I made in Scully. Janice's is a tiny red hand-knitted jumper with *Baby's First Christmas* embroidered on the front. Mum's is the matching Father Christmas hat and booties. Danny's is the *coolest* designer distressed romper suit ever.

"Now mine," says Jess, placing the largest present of the lot in front of me. It's wrapped in a patchwork of old, crumpled wrapping papers, one of which is printed with the words *Happy 2000!*

"Be careful taking the paper off!" says Jess as I start to unwrap it. "I can use it again."

"Er . . . OK!" Gently I peel the paper away and fold it up. There's a layer of tissue paper underneath, and I pull it away to see a box about two feet high, made of pale, polished wood. Puzzled, I turn it around to face me—and it's not a box after all. It's a little cupboard with double doors and tiny porcelain handles. And *Baby's Shoes* carved into the front.

"What—" I look up.

"Open it up." Jess's face is shining. "Go on!"

I tug it open, and there are little shelves, sloped and

lined with white suede. On one of them is resting the smallest pair of red baseball boots I've ever seen.

It's a little tiny Shoe Room.

"Jess..." I can feel tears welling up. "You *made* this?"

"Tom helped." She gives a self-deprecating shrug. "We did it together."

"But it was Jess's idea," chips in Suze. "Isn't it brilliant? I *wish* I'd thought of it...."

"It's perfect." I'm totally bowled over. "Look at the way the doors fit...and the way the shelves are carved...."

"Tom always was good with his hands." Janice clamps a hanky to her eyes. "This can be his memorial. We'll probably never have a tombstone."

I exchange looks with Mum, who pulls a familiar Janice-has-lost-it expression.

"Janice, I'm *sure* he's not dead—" Jess begins.

"We can engrave his dates on the back," Janice continues. "If you don't mind, Becky, love."

"Er...well no," I say uncertainly. "Of course not."

"He's not dead, Janice!" Jess almost yells. "I know he's not!"

"Well, where is he?" Janice pulls her hanky from her eyes, which are smudgy with mauve eye shadow. "You broke that boy's heart!"

"Wait!" I suddenly remember. "Jess, I got a package for you this morning. Maybe it's from him."

I hurry to the hall and bring back the parcel. Jess rips it open and a CD falls out. On it is written simply "From Tom."

We all stare at it for a moment.

"It's a DVD," says Danny, picking it up. "Put it on."

"It's his last will and testament!" cries Janice hysterically. "It's a message from beyond the grave!"

"It's not from beyond the grave," Jess snaps, but as she heads to the DVD player I can see that she's gone pale.

She presses Play and crouches down on the floor. We all wait in silence as the screen flickers. Then suddenly there's Tom, facing the camera, against a blue sky. He's wearing an old green polo shirt and looks pretty disheveled.

"Hi, Jess," he says momentously. "By the time you see this, I'll be in Chile. Because . . . that's where I am now."

Jess stiffens. *"Chile?"*

"Chile?" Janice shrieks. "What's he doing in Chile?"

"I love you," Tom's saying. "And I'll move to the other side of the world if that's what it takes. Or farther."

"Oh, that's so romantic," sighs Kelly.

"He's such a stupid *prat*," Jess says, knocking a fist against her forehead. "I'm not going out there for three months!"

But her eyes are glistening, I notice.

"Look what I've found you." Tom is holding a chunk of some black shiny rock up to the camera. "You'll love this country, Jess."

"He'll get cholera!" Janice is saying in agitation. "Or malaria! Tom's always had a weak system—"

"I can get work as a carpenter," Tom is saying. "I can write my book. We'll be happy here. And if Mum gives you any grief, just remember what I told you about her."

"Told you?" Janice looks up sharply. "What did he tell you?"

"Er...nothing." Jess hastily presses Stop and whips the DVD out of the machine. "I'll watch the rest later."

"So!" says Mum cheerily. "He's alive, Janice love. That's good news!"

"Alive?" Janice is still in a state of hysteria. "What's the use of being alive in Chile?"

"At least he's out in the world!" says Jess with sudden passion. "At least he's doing something with his life! You know, he's been really depressed, Janice. This is just what he needs."

"I know what my son needs!" Janice retorts indignantly as the doorbell rings. I heave myself to my feet, glad of an excuse to get out of the line of fire.

"I'll just get this...." I head into the hall and pick up the entry phone. "Hello?"

"I have a delivery for you," comes a crackly voice.

My heart skips a beat. A delivery. This has to be it. It *has* to be. As I press the buzzer I can hardly breathe. I'm telling myself firmly not to hope, it'll be another package for Jess, or a catalog, or a computer part for Luke....

But when I open the door, there's a motorbike courier standing in his leathers, holding a big padded envelope, and I already recognize Dave Sharpness's writing in bold black marker pen.

I lock myself in the cloakroom and feverishly rip the envelope open. There's a manila folder inside, marked "Brandon." On the front is stuck a Post-it note, with a scribbled message: *Hope this helps. Any further assistance required, do not hesitate. Yours, Dave S.*

I open it up, and it's all there. Copies of all the notes, transcripts of conversations, photos...I leaf through, my heart thumping. I'd forgotten quite how much stuff they had collected on Iain Wheeler. For a crappy private detective agency in West Ruislip, they actually did a great job.

I quickly bundle it all up again and head into the cool, empty kitchen. I'm about to pick up the phone to call Luke, when it rings, making me jump.

"Hello?"

"Hello, Mrs. Brandon," comes an unfamiliar male voice. "Mike Enwright from the Press Association here."

"Oh, right." I stare at the phone, puzzled.

"I just wondered if you could comment on rumors that your husband's company is going down?"

I feel a shiver of shock.

"It's not going down," I say robustly. "I have no idea what you're talking about."

"News is, he's lost the Arcodas account. And the latest rumor is Foreland Investment is going the same way."

"He has not *lost* Arcodas!" I exclaim, furious. "They have parted ways for reasons which I cannot discuss. And for your information, my husband's company is as strong as ever. Stronger! Luke Brandon has been courted by high-caliber clients all his career, and he always will be. He is a man of immense integrity, talent, intelligence, good looks, and . . . and dress sense."

I break off, breathing hard.

"OK then!" Mike Enwright is chuckling. "I get the picture."

"Are you going to quote all that?"

"I doubt it." He chuckles again. "But I like your attitude. Thanks for your time, Mrs. Brandon."

He rings off and, flustered, I run water into a glass. I

have to talk to Luke. I dial his direct line and get through on the third ring.

"Becky!" Luke sounds alert. "Has anything—"

"No, it's not that." I check outside the kitchen door and lower my voice. "Luke, the Press Association just rang. They wanted a quote about you"—I swallow—"going down. They said Foreland were leaving you."

"That is bullshit!" Luke's voice erupts in anger. "Those Arcodas fuckers are feeding stories to the press."

"They couldn't really damage you, could they?" I say fearfully.

"Not if I have anything to do with it." Luke sounds resolute. "The gloves are off. If they want to fight, we'll fight. We'll take them to court if it comes to it. Charge them with harassment. Expose the whole bloody lot of them."

I feel a huge surge of pride as I hear him speak. He sounds like the Luke Brandon I first met. Assured and in charge of the situation. Not running around after Iain Wheeler like some lackey.

"Luke, I've got something for you." My words spill out. "I have . . . material on Iain Wheeler."

"What did you say?" says Luke after a pause.

"There were some old cases of harassment and office bullying that were hushed up. I've got a whole dossier on him, right here in my hands."

"You've got *what*?" Luke sounds flabbergasted. "Becky . . . what are you talking about?"

Maybe I won't get into the whole private-detective-in-West-Ruislip story just now.

"Don't ask me how," I say hurriedly. "I just do."

"But how—"

"I said don't ask! But it's true. I'll have it all biked round to the office. You should probably have your lawyers ready to take a look. There are photos, notes, all kinds of evidence.... Honestly, Luke. If this all comes out...he's finished."

"*Photos*? You've been taking photos of Iain?"

"Er...not me, exactly..."

"Becky, what *is* this?" he demands. "What the hell have you been up to?"

"I'll explain later. Just trust me, Luke, please. This is going to help you, I promise."

"Becky..." Luke's voice is incredulous. "You constantly amaze me."

"I love you," I say impulsively. "Cream them." I put the phone down and push my hair back with sweaty hands. I take a few gulps of water, then speed-dial Luke's regular courier firm and order a bike.

In half an hour or so, the folder will be with Luke. I just *wish* I could see his face when he opens it.

"Hi, Bex!" I jump as Suze comes sauntering into the kitchen. Her expression changes as she sees me. "Bex...are you OK?"

"I'm...fine!" I put on a hasty smile. "Just taking some time out."

"We're going to play games next!" Suze opens the fridge and gets out a carton of orange juice. "Guess the baby food...hunt the nappy pin...celebrities' babies' names..."

I can't believe the trouble she's gone to, organizing all this.

"Suze...thanks so much," I say. "It's all *amazing*. And my photo frame!"

"It came out well, didn't it?" Suze looks pleased.

"You know, it really inspired me. I'm thinking of starting the frame business again."

"You should!" I say with enthusiasm. Suze used to make brilliant photo frames till she had the children. They were stocked in Liberty's and everything!

"I mean, the children are getting older now," Suze is saying. "And if Lulu can write cookery books, why can't I make frames? It won't kill the kids if I work a few hours a day, will it? I'll still be a good mother."

I can see the anxiety in her eyes. I totally blame that cow Lulu. Suze never worried about being a good mother till she met her.

OK. Payback time.

"Suze . . . I've got something for you," I say, reaching into the kitchen drawer. "But you can't show Lulu, *ever*. Or tell her. Or tell anybody."

"I won't!" Suze looks intrigued. "What is it?"

"Here."

I hand Suze the long-lens photograph—the only thing I saved from the original folder. It's of Lulu in the street with her children. She looks pretty frazzled—in fact, she seems to be yelling at one of them. In her hands are four Mars Bars, which she's doling out. She's holding a couple of cans of Coke too, and under her arm is a jumbo packet of chips.

"No." Suze appears almost too staggered to speak. "*No*. Are those—"

"Mars Bars." I nod. "And Cheesy Wotsits."

"And Coke!" Suze gives a gurgle of laughter and claps a hand over her mouth. "Bex, that has made my day. How on earth . . ."

"Don't ask." I can't help giggling too.

"What a hypocritical . . . cow!" Suze is still peering at

the picture in disbelief. "You know, she really got to me. I used to feel so *inferior*."

"I think you should go on her TV show after all," I say. "You could take that photo with you. Show the producer."

"Bex!" Suze giggles. "You're evil! I'm just going to keep it in a drawer and look at it when I need cheering up."

The phone suddenly shrills through the kitchen and my smile tightens. What if this is the press again? What if it's Luke with more news?

"Hey, Suze," I say casually. "Why don't you go and make sure everyone's OK? I'll be out in a minute."

"Sure." Suze nods, and picks up her juice, her eyes still fixed on the photo. "I'll just put this somewhere safe...."

I wait until she's gone and the door is firmly closed, then steel myself and pick up the phone. "Hello?"

"Hi, Becky." The familiar drifty voice comes down the line. "It's Fabia."

"Fabia!" I subside in relief. "How are you? Thanks *so* much for letting us use the house the other day. The *Vogue* people thought it was amazing! Did you get my flowers?"

"Oh, wonderful," Fabia says vaguely. "Yeah, we got the flowers. Listen, Becky, we've just heard you can't pay cash for the house."

Luke must have called the agent and told him. News travels fast.

"That's right." I nod, trying to stay upbeat. "There's been a slight change in our circumstances, but it should only delay us by a couple of weeks...."

"Yeah..." Fabia sounds distracted. "The thing is, we've decided to exchange with the other buyers."

For a moment I think I've hallucinated. "Other buyers?"

"Did we not mention the other buyers? The Americans. They made the same offer as you. *Before* you, in fact, so strictly speaking..." She trails off.

"But...but you took our offer! You said the house was ours."

"Yeah, well. The other buyers can move faster, so..."

I'm light-headed with shock. We've been screwed.

"Were you just stringing us along the whole *time*?" I'm trying to keep control of myself.

"It wasn't my idea." Fabia sounds regretful. "It was my husband. He likes to have a fallback position. Anyway, good luck with the house hunt...."

No. She can't really be doing this. She can't be leaving us in the lurch.

"Fabia, listen." I wipe my clammy face. "Please. We're having a baby any day. We don't have anywhere to go. Our flat is sold—"

"Mmm...yeah. I hope it all goes well. Bye, Becky...."

"But what about the Archie Swann boots?" I'm almost crying in anger. "We did a deal! You owe me a boot!" I realize I'm talking into silence. She's rung off. She doesn't care.

I switch the phone off. Slowly I walk over to the fridge and lean my head against the cool steel, feeling dizzy. We don't have our dream house anymore. We don't have *any* house anymore.

I lift the phone to call Luke, then stop. He's got enough on his plate as it is right now.

In a few weeks we have to move out of our flat. Where are we going to go?

"Becky?" Kelly bursts into the kitchen, giggling. "We've put candles on your cake. I know it's not your birthday, but you should blow them out anyway."

"Yes!" I jolt into life. "I'm coming!"

Somehow I manage to hold myself together as I follow Kelly back to the sitting room. Inside, Danny and Janice are playing guess the baby food and writing down their answers on sheets. Mum and Jess are perusing pictures of celebrity babies.

"It's Lourdes!" Mum is saying. "Jess, love, you should be more *aware* of the world."

"Pureed beet," says Danny knowledgeably as he tastes a spoonful of purple goo. "All it needs is a shot of vodka."

"Becky!" Mum looks up. "Everything all right, love? You keep running off to answer the phone!"

"Yes, Bex, what's up?" Suze's brow wrinkles.

"It's..."

I wipe my damp upper lip, trying to keep steady. I don't even know where I'd start.

Luke's fighting to save his company. He's hemorrhaging money. We've lost the house.

I can't tell them. I can't spoil the party—everyone's having such a good time.

I'll tell them later. Tomorrow.

"Everything's fine!" I force my brightest, best, happiest smile. "Couldn't be better!" And I blow out my candles.

At last the tea and champagne are all drunk and all the guests gradually leave. It was *such* a great baby shower. And everyone got on so well! Janice and Jess made up in the end, and Jess promised she'd look after Tom in Chile and not let any guerrilla bandits get him. Suze and Kelly had a long conversation while they played guess the baby food, ending up with Suze offering Kelly a job as au pair during her year off. But the *really* amazing thing is, Jess and Danny have hit it off! Danny started talking to her about some new collection he wants to do using shards of rocks—and she's going to take him to a museum to see some specimens.

The bike arrived while everyone was eating cake, and the package went off OK. I haven't heard back from Luke, though. I guess he's in talks with his lawyers or whoever it is. So he doesn't know about the house yet, either.

"Are you all right, Becky?" says Mum, giving me a hug at the front door. "Would you like me to stay with you till Luke arrives home?"

"No, it's OK. Don't worry."

"Well, have a nice afternoon rest. Save your energy, love."

"I will." I nod. "Bye, Mum."

The place feels silent and flat with everyone gone. It's just me and all the stuff. I wander into the nursery, gently touching the handcrafted crib and the little white rocking cradle. And the Moses basket with its gorgeous linen canopy. (I wanted to give the baby a choice of sleeping accommodations.)

It's like a stage set. We're just waiting for the lead character to appear.

I prod my tummy, wondering if it's awake. Maybe I'll play it a tune and it can be a musical genius when it's born! I wind up the mobile I ordered from the Intelligent Baby catalog and press it against my tummy.

Baby, listen to that! That's Mozart.

I think. . . . Or Beethoven or someone.

God, now I've confused it. I'm just looking on the box to see if the tune is by Mozart, when there's a small crash from the hall.

Christmas cards. That'll make me feel better. Abandoning the Intelligent Baby mobile, I head to the front door, pick up the huge pile of post lying on the doormat, and waddle back to the sofa, leafing through the envelopes.

And then I stop. There's a small package, labeled in distinctive, flowing writing.

Venetia's.

It's addressed to Luke, but I don't care. With trembling hands I rip it open, to find a tiny leather Duchamp box. I wrench it open, and there's a pair of silver and enamel cuff links. What is she doing sending him cuff links?

A small cream card falls out, with a message written in the same script.

L
Long time no see. "Nunc est bibendum?"
V

I stare at the note, the blood rushing through my head. All the stresses of the day seem to be focusing in a laser of fury. I've had it. I've just *had* it. I'm going to send this package straight back, return of post—

No. I'm going to give it back to her myself.

In a daze, I find myself getting to my feet and reaching for my coat. I'm going to find Venetia and I'm going to finish this. Once and for all.

TWENTY

I'VE NEVER BEEN more itching for a showdown in my life.

It didn't take long to track down Venetia. I phoned the Holistic Birth Center, pretending to be really desperate to talk to her and asking where she was. After saying she was "unavailable," the receptionist let slip that she was at the Cavendish Hospital, in a meeting. They offered to page her, as I'm still on the system as a patient, but I hastily said don't bother, actually I was feeling better all of a sudden. Which they totally swallowed. They're obviously used to flaky pregnant women phoning up and dithering.

So now I'm standing outside the Cavendish Hospital's private maternity wing, my heart racing, clutching a carrier bag from The Look. It contains not only the cuff links but also the support stockings, the fanny pack, every single little note she ever sent Luke, the brochures and medical notes from her stupid holistic center... even the freebies from the goodie bag. (It was a bit of a wrench putting in the Crème de la Mer. In fact I scooped out most of it and put it in an old Lancôme pot. But Venetia needn't know that.)

It's like a breakup box. I'm going to hand it to her and say, very calmly, "Leave us alone, Venetia. Luke and I and the baby don't want anything to do with you ever again." She *has* to realize she's lost, after that.

Plus I phoned up my lovely professor on the way here, and he gave me a brilliant Latin insult, which I've learned by heart. It goes *Utinam barbari provinciam tuam invadant!* and it means "May barbarians invade your province."

Ha. *That'll* teach her.

"Hello?" A tinny voice comes through the intercom system.

"Hi!" I say into the grille. "It's Becky Brandon, a patient." I won't say any more. I'll just get into the place and take it from there.

The door buzzes and I push it open. Normally this place is pretty tranquil, but today it's full of activity. The seats are filled with women in various stages of pregnancy, chatting with their partners and holding leaflets entitled "Why Choose the Cavendish?" Two midwives are walking quickly down the corridor, saying words like *operating* and *stuck,* which I *really* don't like the sound of, and I can hear a woman's screams emanating from a distant room. My stomach curdles at the sound, and I fight the urge to put my hands over my ears.

Anyway. It wasn't necessarily a scream of agony. She was probably just shouting because she couldn't see the telly or something.

I approach the reception desk, breathing hard.

"Hi," I say. "My name's Rebecca Brandon, and I need to see Venetia Carter straightaway, please."

"Do you have an appointment?" the receptionist demands. I haven't seen her on duty before. She has graying curly hair, and glasses on silver chains, and a pretty abrupt manner for someone who's dealing with pregnant women all day long.

"Well . . . no. But it's really important."

"I'm afraid Venetia is busy."

"I don't mind waiting. If you could just tell her I'm here . . ."

"You'll have to phone for an appointment." The receptionist taps at her keyboard as though I'm not even there.

This woman is *really* winding me up the wrong way. Venetia's only in some stupid meeting. And here I am, practically nine months pregnant. . . .

"Can't you page her?" I try to stay calm.

"I can only page her if you're in labor." The woman shrugs, like it really isn't her problem.

I stare at her through a fine mist of anger. I've come here to have it out with Venetia, and I'm not letting some woman in a mauve cardigan stop me.

"Well . . . I *am* in labor!" I hear myself saying.

"You're in labor?" She eyes me skeptically.

She doesn't believe me, does she? What a nerve. Why would I lie about a thing like that?

"Yes." I plant my hands on my hips. "I am."

"Are you having regular contractions?" she says, challenging me.

"Since yesterday, every three minutes," I shoot back. "And I've got back pain, and I've been vacuuming non-stop . . . and . . . and my water broke yesterday."

So there. *Now* tell me I'm not in labor.

"I see." The woman looks a little taken aback. "Well . . ."

"And I want to see only Venetia, no one else," I add,

pressing home my advantage. "So, can you page her immediately, please?"

The woman is regarding me with a narrowed gaze.

"Your contractions are coming every three minutes?"

"Uh-huh." Suddenly I realize I must have been standing in this reception area for at least three minutes.

"I'm coping with them silently," I inform her with dignity. "I'm a Scientologist."

"A *Scientologist*?" she echoes, putting her pen down and staring at me.

"Yes." I meet her gaze, unflinching. "And I need to see Venetia urgently. But if you won't let in a woman whose water broke yesterday and is silently suffering in great pain . . ." I raise my voice a little so that it carries to all the waiting pregnant women.

"All right!" The receptionist clearly realizes she's defeated. "You can wait. . . ." She surveys the packed seating area. "Wait in that room," she says at last, and gestures to a room called Labor Room 3.

"Thank you!" I turn on my heel and head into Labor Room 3. It's a big room, with a scary-looking metal bed and a shower room and even a DVD player. No minibar, though.

I sit on the bed and swiftly get out my makeup case. Everyone knows the first rule of business is "Look good during confrontations." Or if it isn't, it should be. I put on some blusher and apply some fresh lipstick—and am practicing my steeliest expression in the mirror, when there's a knock at the door.

That's her. With the most enormous lurch of nerves I grab the breakup bag and stand up.

"Come in," I say as calmly as possible, and a moment later, the door swings open.

"Hello, love!" A jolly-looking Afro-Caribbean midwife comes bustling in. "I'm Esther. How are you getting on? Contractions still coming thick and strong?"

"What?" I stare at her. "Er...no. I mean, yes...." I break off in confusion. "Listen, I really need to see Venetia Carter."

"She's on her way," says the midwife soothingly. "I'll get you sorted out in the meantime."

I feel a tweak of suspicion. They haven't paged Venetia at all, have they? They're trying to palm me off.

"I don't need sorting out," I say politely. "Thanks all the same."

"Darlin', you're having a baby!" The midwife peals with laughter. "You need to get into a gown. Or did you bring a T-shirt? And I'll need to examine you, see how you're progressing."

I need to get rid of this woman, quick. She presses a hand on my abdomen and I shrink away.

"Actually, I've already been examined!" I say brightly. "By another midwife. So I'm all set...."

"Another midwife? Who? Sarah?"

"Er...maybe. I don't remember. She suddenly rushed off, said she had to go to theater or something?" I blink innocently.

"I'll start you a new chart." Esther shakes her head, sighing. "I'll have to examine you again...."

"No!" I squeak before I can stop myself. "I mean... I have a phobia about being examined. They said I could have minimal examination. Venetia understands. I really need to see Venetia, no one else. In fact, could you leave me alone till she comes? I want to focus on my . . . my inner womanhood."

Esther rolls her eyes, then heads to the door and leans her head out.

"Pam. We've got another one of Venetia's wacky patients here. Can you page her? All right." She draws her head back in. "We're paging Venetia for you. I'll just fill this in. So, your water broke at home?"

"Uh-huh." I nod.

"Did the other midwife say how far you'd got?"

"Um . . . four centimeters," I say at random.

"And you're coping with the pain?"

"Fine, so far," I say bravely.

"Well, now." The midwife finishes writing. "I really must examine you, so if you pop up on the bed for me. . . ."

"No!" I back away. "Don't touch me! I only want Venetia!"

There's a knock at the door and a woman pops her head round it. "Esther? Can you come?"

"We're busy today." Esther sighs and hangs the chart on the end of the bed. "I'll be back. And Venetia should be here soon. Sorry about this."

"That's all right," I say, trying to hide my relief. "Thanks!"

The door closes behind her and I sink back on the bed. For a few minutes nothing happens, and I start to flick through the TV channels. I'm just wondering whether they have any DVDs for hire, when there's another knock at the door.

It has to be Venetia this time. I grab the breakup bag, struggle to my feet, and take a deep breath to prepare myself.

"Come in!"

The door opens and a girl of about twenty, in a mid-wife uniform, looks in. She's got blond wispy hair tied back and looks very apprehensive.

"Um, hi," she says. "My name's Paula and I'm a student midwife. Would you mind if I come and observe you in the early stages of labor for a while? I'd be really, really grateful."

Oh, for God's sake. I'm about to say "No, go away." But she looks so shy and nervous, I can't bring myself to. After all, I can always get rid of her when Venetia arrives.

"Sure." I wave an arm. "Come on in. My name's Becky."

"Hi there." She smiles shyly as she tiptoes in and sits down on a chair in the corner.

For a minute or two neither of us says anything. I've flopped back on the pillows and am staring at the ceiling, trying to hide my frustration. Here I am, all ready for a confrontation, and there's no one to confront. If Venetia doesn't show in the next five minutes, I'll just go.

"You seem very...serene." Paula looks up from scribbling on her notepad. "Do you have any particular coping mechanisms for the pain?"

Oh, right. I'm supposed to be in labor. I'd better put on a show or she'll have nothing to write down.

"Absolutely." I nod. "I'll just move around a bit, actually. I find that really helps." I get up and walk around the bed, swinging my arms back and forth in a businesslike way. Then I rock my hips around a few times, and do a stretch I once learned in Yoga-lates.

"Wow," says Paula, impressed. "You're very mobile."

"I've done yoga," I say with a modest little glow. "I think I'll have a Kit Kat now. Just to keep my energy levels up."

"Good idea." Paula nods. As I reach for my bag I can see her writing down "Eats Kit Kat," on her notes, and underneath, "Using yoga for pain relief." She riffles back in her file, then looks up sympathetically. "During contractions, where's most of the pain focused?"

"Er...just...around," I say vaguely, munching on my Kit Kat. "Kind of here...and here..." I gesture at my body. "It's hard to explain."

"You seem amazingly calm, Becky." Paula is gazing at me as I check my teeth in my hand mirror for Kit Kat crumbs. "I've never seen a laboring woman with such self-control!"

"Well, I'm a Scientologist," I can't resist saying. "So I'm trying to keep as quiet as possible, obviously."

"A Scientologist!" Her eyes open wide. "That's amazing." Then she frowns in alarm. "Aren't you supposed to be in total silence?"

"I'm the sort that's allowed to talk," I explain. "But not scream or anything."

"Wow. You know, I'm not sure we've ever had a Scientologist in here before!" She looks quite animated. "Do you mind if I just tell a couple of my colleagues?"

"Go ahead!" I nod absently.

As she hurries out, I crumple up my Kit Kat wrapper and throw it in the bin, frustrated. This is stupid. Venetia's not coming, is she? They're never going to page her. And I'm not even in the mood for seeing her anymore. I think I'll go home.

"She's in here!" The door is flung open and a whole crowd of young midwives floods into the room, led by

Paula. "This is Rebecca Brandon," she addresses the group in an undertone. "She's four centimeters dilated and is using yoga to help deal with the pain. Because she's a Scientologist she's keeping very quiet and calm. You'd barely know she was having contractions!"

They're all gawping at me as though I'm an extinct animal. I'm almost sorry to let them down.

"Actually, I think it might be a false alarm." I pick up my bag and shrug on my coat. "I'm going home now. Thanks very much for all your help—"

"You can't go home!" says Paula with a little laugh. She consults my chart and nods. "I thought so. Rebecca, your water has broken. You'll run the risk of infection!" She pulls off my coat and takes my bag. "You're staying here till that baby's out!"

"Oh," I say, stymied.

What do I do now? Should I tell them I made up that my water has broken?

No. They'll think I'm a total loony. What I'll do is wait till they leave me alone and then sneak out. Yes. Good plan.

"She could be in transition," one of the student midwives is saying knowledgeably to another. "They often want to go home at that stage. They get quite irrational."

"Rebecca, you really need to put on a hospital gown." Paula is surveying me with anxiety. "The baby could be well on the way. How are the contractions feeling? Are they coming quicker? Can I examine you?"

"She's requested minimal monitoring and examination," chips in another student midwife, looking at my chart. "She wants everything natural. I think we should get a senior midwife in here, Paula."

"No, don't!" I say hurriedly. "I mean . . . I'd like to be left alone for a while. If that's OK."

"You're very stoic, Rebecca," says Paula, resting a sympathetic hand on my shoulder. "But we can't leave you alone! You don't even have a birth partner!"

"I'll be fine, honestly." I try to sound casual. "Just for a few minutes. It's . . . it's part of my beliefs. The woman in labor needs to be on her own every hour to say a special chant."

Go on. I'm willing them silently. *Just leave me alone. . . .*

"Well, I guess we should respect your beliefs," Paula says uncertainly. "OK. We'll pop out for a while, but if you feel *anything* moving on, just press the buzzer."

"I will! Thanks!"

The door closes and I subside in relief. Thank God. I'm out of this place as soon as the coast is clear. I grab my bag and coat and open the door a chink—but two midwives are still standing right by the door. Hastily I close it again, trying not to make any noise. I'll have to wait a few moments more. They're bound to move away soon, and I'll make a dash for it.

I can't believe I'm in this situation. I should never have said I was in labor, I should never have pretended my water had broken. God, it's a lesson. I am never doing that again, *ever.*

After a little more time I check my watch. Three minutes have gone by. Maybe I'll check the corridor again. I pick up my coat, but before I can creep forward, the door bursts open.

"Oh my God, Bex!" Suze bursts in in a flurry of blond hair and Miu Miu embroidered coat. "Are you OK? I came as soon as I heard. . . ."

"*Suze?*" I stare at her, poleaxed. "What—"

"Your mum's just coming," she says breathlessly, throwing off her coat to reveal Danny's "Yummy Mummy" T-shirt. "We were all together in a taxi when we got the news. Janice is getting some magazines and drinks and Kelly says she's going to wait down in reception...."

"But how..."

I don't understand. Is Suze *psychic* or something?

"I rang your mobile and the woman who answered told me it was the Cavendish ward." Suze is babbling in excitement. "She said you'd left your phone in reception and you were in labor! We all freaked! So we told the taxi driver to turn round straightaway and I've canceled this dinner party we were throwing—" She stops abruptly as she notices my appearance. "Hey, Bex, why are you holding your coat? Is everything OK?"

"Rebecca's doing great!" says Paula. She comes into the room and gently takes my coat out of my hands. "Four centimeters dilated already and she's had no pain relief!"

"No pain relief?" Suze looks staggered. "Bex, I thought you were having an epidural!"

"Um..." I swallow hard.

"But she won't put on a hospital gown for us," adds Paula in reproof.

"Of course she won't!" says Suze indignantly. "They're revolting. Bex, didn't you bring your bag? Don't worry, I'll go and buy you a T-shirt. And we need some music in here, and some candles maybe...." She looks around critically.

"Um...Suze..." My stomach is bunched with nerves. "Actually..."

"Knock, knock!" There's a fresh voice at the door. "It's Louisa here! Can we come in?"

Louisa? This can't be happening. She's the aromatherapist I hired for the birth. How the hell did she . . .

"Your mum's been busy calling all the people on your list, just to make sure they knew!" Suze beams. "She's so efficient! They're all on their way."

I can't cope. Everything's moving too quickly. Louisa has already got out some little vials of oils and is rubbing something orangey on the back of my neck. "There!" she says. "Does that feel good?"

"Lovely!" I manage.

"Becky!" Mum's shrill voice is sounding from outside the room. "My darling!" She comes rushing in, clutching a bunch of flowers and a paper bag full of croissants. "Sit down! Take it easy! Where's your epidural?"

"She's managing without one!" says Suze. "Isn't she amazing?"

"*Without* one?" Mum looks appalled.

"Becky's using yoga and breathing techniques to cope with the pain," says Paula proudly. "Aren't you, Becky? She's already four centimeters!"

"Love, don't put yourself through it." Mum grabs my arm, looking close to tears. "Accept the pain relief! Take the drugs."

I feel like my tongue's glued to the bottom of my mouth.

"Now, this is jasmine oil," comes Louisa's gentle voice in my ear. "I'll rub it into your temples. . . ."

"Becky?" Mum says anxiously. "Can you hear me?"

"Maybe she's having a contraction!" exclaims Suze, grabbing my hand. "Bex, breathe...."

"You can do it, love!" Mum's face is screwing up tighter and tighter, as though she's in labor herself.

"Focus on the baby." Paula's eyes are gazing intently into mine. "Focus on that lovely baby of yours coming out into the world...."

"Look." I finally find my voice. "I...the thing is, I'm not in labor...."

"Becky, you *are*." Paula rests her hands on my shoulders.

"Bex, conserve your energy!" Suze shoves a straw into my mouth. "Have some Lucozade. Then you'll feel better!" Helplessly I suck at the sickly drink, and then stop dead as I hear hurried footsteps approaching. I know those footsteps. The door swings open and this time it's Luke, his face pale, his eyes dark and tense as he surveys the room.

"Thank God. Thank *God* I'm not too late...." He seems almost speechless as he comes toward me on the bed. "Becky, I love you so much....I'm so proud of you...."

"Hi, Luke," I say feebly.

Now what the fuck do I do?

The thing is, in a lot of ways this is the perfect birth.

It's twenty minutes later and the room is full of people. Felicity the reflexologist has arrived and is manipulating my toes. Maria the homeopath is measuring out some pills for me to take. Louisa is arranging essential oil burners around the place.

I have Mum and Suze sitting on one side of me, with

Luke on the other. I've got a flannel on my forehead and a water spray in my hand and I'm wearing a long baggy T-shirt which Suze and Mum basically manhandled me into. I'm relaxed, music is playing, I'm managing without an epidural. . . .

There's only one tiny hitch. And I still haven't plucked up the courage to tell anyone.

"Becky, would you like some gas and air?" Paula is approaching me with a face mask attached to a tube. "Just to take the edge off the pain."

"Er . . ." I hesitate. "Well, OK. Thanks!"

"Breathe it in just as you feel the contraction beginning," Paula instructs, handing me the mouthpiece. "Don't leave it too late!"

"OK!" I put the face mask over my nose and mouth and breathe in deeply. Wow. This is *fantastic*! I feel like I just downed a bottle of champagne!

"Hey." I take the mask away and give Luke a beatific smile. "That's really nice. You should try it."

"Becky, you're doing amazingly." He's clasping my hand tight, not taking his eyes off me. "Is everything OK? Is everything going according to your birth plan?"

"Er . . . most things!" I say, avoiding his eyes, and quickly suck in some more gas and air. Oh God. I have to tell him. I *have* to.

"Luke . . ." I lean forward, feeling a bit tipsy from the gas and air. "Listen," I whisper in his ear. "I'm not having the baby."

"Darling, don't worry." Luke strokes my forehead. "No one's in any hurry. It takes as long as it takes."

Actually . . . there's a thought. I mean, the baby's going to come out *sometime*, isn't it? I could just stay here and not say anything and drink Lucozade and watch the telly. And eventually something will happen and they'll just say, "Becky was in labor for two weeks, poor thing!"

"I spoke to Dr. Braine, by the way," Luke adds. "He's on his way over from the Portland."

"Oh." I try to hide my dismay. "Great!"

In desperation I breathe in the gas and air again, trying to come up with a plan. Maybe the bathroom has a window I could climb out of. Or I could say I want to walk down the corridor, and then find a newborn baby and just quickly borrow it for a moment. . . .

"I thought you were with Venetia Carter?" Paula stops writing on my notes. "Isn't she on her way?" She glances at her watch. "If not, one of the senior midwives will need to examine you soon. Are you feeling any pressure, Becky?"

"Um . . . a bit, yes!"

She has *no* idea.

"Here." Louisa gives me a pot of oil to sniff. "Clary sage for stress."

"So, Paula, does labor ever go . . . backward?" I ask the question casually, trying to hide my sudden spark of hope.

"No." Paula laughs. "Though it feels like it sometimes!"

"Ha-ha!" I join in her laughter and flop back on my pillows, inhaling the clary sage for stress. What I need is an essential oil for telling people you're not in labor and they've all got to go home.

There's a knock at the door and Suze looks up. "Ooh. That might be Jess. She said she was on her way. . . ."

"Come in!" calls Paula. The door opens. And I freeze.

It's Venetia. She's wearing operating scrubs with her hair all bundled into a green cap, and she looks totally glamorous and important, like she's been saving lives all day.

Bitch.

For an instant Venetia looks pretty shocked too, but then almost at once she comes over to the bed, a professional smile at her lips.

"Becky! I had no idea the patient they paged me about was you. Let's have a look and see how you're getting on...." She takes off her green cap and her hair tumbles radiantly down her back. "Luke, how long has she been in? Fill me in on what's been happening."

She's doing it again. She's cutting me out. She's trying to bewitch Luke.

"Leave me alone!" I exclaim in fury. "I'm not your patient anymore and you're not having a look at anything, thank you very much."

Suddenly I don't care about being in labor. Or pretend-labor. Or whatever I'm in. It's not too late; I can still have my big confrontation. As everyone gapes, I cast away the gas and air mask and heave myself off the bed.

"Suze, can you give me that bag please?" I say in a trembling voice. "The carrier under the bed."

"Yes! Here." Suze hands me the carrier bag. "Is that *her*?" she adds in my ear.

"Uh-huh." I nod.

"Cow."

"That's a good idea, Becky!" Paula's saying in bright,

uncertain tones. "Keeping upright will help the baby descend...."

"Venetia, I have something to return to you." My voice is very slightly slurred, which is the fault of that stupid gas and air. And I keep breaking into a smile, which is a bit annoying. But anyway, she'll get the message.

"Luke doesn't want these." I reach into the bag and throw the support stockings at her. They land on the floor and everyone looks at them.

Oh. I've got a bit confused.

"I mean...these." I chuck the cuff link box, hard, and it hits Venetia on the forehead.

"Ow! Shit!" She clasps her head.

"Becky!" Luke remonstrates.

"She's still after you, Luke! She sent you a Christmas present!" Suddenly I remember my Latin. *"Uti...barberi..."* My tongue keeps tripping up. *"Nam...I mean...tui..."*

Fuck.

Latin's a stupid language.

"Love, are you delirious?" Mum looks anxious.

"Becky, I have no idea what you're talking about." Venetia looks as though she wants to laugh.

"Just leave us alone." I'm quivering with anger. "Leave me and Luke *alone*."

"You paged me," Venetia reminds me, and takes the chart from a nervous Paula. "Now, where are we at with this baby?"

"Don't change the subject!" I yell. "You told me that you and Luke were having an affair. You tried to freak me out."

"An *affair*?" Venetia opens her eyes wide. "Becky,

Luke and I are just old friends!" She gives her silvery laugh. "I'm sorry, Luke. I realize Becky has a problem with me. But I had no idea she was *quite* so possessive...."

She looks totally reasonable, standing there in her green medical-authority uniform. And I'm the deranged, drugged pregnant woman in a baggy T-shirt.

"Ven, it's fine," says Luke, looking uncomfortable. "Listen, we've got Charles Braine coming to supervise. Maybe you should...leave."

"Maybe I should." Venetia nods conspiratorially at Luke, and I feel a stab of white-hot rage.

"Luke, don't just let her get away with it! She said you were lovers! She said you were leaving me for her!"

"Becky..."

"It's *true*." Angry tears are running down my face. "No one believes me, but it's true! She said the minute you saw each other again it was just a question of when and where. She said you were intoxicated with each other, and it was like Penelope and...someone. Othello."

"Penelope and Odysseus?" Luke stares at me.

"Yes! That's it. And you were meant to be together. And that I didn't have a marriage anymore...." I wipe my runny nose with my T-shirt sleeve. "And now she's pretending I'm a completely deluded psycho...."

Something has changed in Luke's eyes. "Penelope and Odysseus?" he says, an edge to his voice. "Ven?"

There's a prickling silence.

"I don't know what she's talking about," Venetia says smoothly.

"Who are Penelope and Odysseus?" Suze whispers in my ear, and I shrug helplessly.

"Venetia…" Luke looks at her directly. "We were never Penelope and Odysseus."

For the first time ever, I see Venetia falter. She doesn't say anything, but just stares at Luke with a kind of defiance. Like she wants to say, Yes, we were.

OK, I *have* to know. "Luke, who are Penelope and Odysseus?" I ask.

I'm really hoping they're not a PR guy and an obstetrician who get together after the wife is pushed out of the picture.

"Odysseus left Penelope to go on a long journey," says Luke, his eyes still pinioning Venetia's. "The *Odyssey*. And Penelope waited faithfully for him. For twenty years."

"Well, she hasn't waited faithfully for you!" Suze says, pointing an indignant finger at Venetia. "She's had affairs all over the place!"

"Venetia, did you tell Becky we were having an affair?" Luke's stentorian voice makes us all jump. "Did you say I was leaving her for you? Did you try to break her confidence?"

"Of course I didn't," says Venetia coldly. Her eyes are hard but her jaw is trembling slightly, I notice.

"Good." Luke's tone is still scathing. "Well, let's make it crystal clear once and for all. I would never have an affair with you, Venetia. I would never have an affair with anyone." He turns to me and takes both my hands. "Becky, there is nothing whatsoever between me and Venetia, whatever she might have said. We dated for a year. As teenagers. That's *it*. OK?"

"OK," I whisper.

"How did you break up?" Suze says with interest, then flushes as everyone turns to look at her. "It's relevant!" she says defensively. "You should be open about past relationships! Tarkie and I know *everything* about each other's old flings. If you'd *told* Bex, instead of..." She trails off.

"Maybe you're right." Luke nods. "Becky...maybe I should have explained what happened between us. How it ended." His face twists fleetingly. "Venetia had a pregnancy scare."

"She was *pregnant*?" I feel sick at the thought.

"No. No!" Luke shakes his head vigorously. "She thought she might be, briefly. But anyway, it...clarified things. And we ended it."

"You panicked." Venetia's voice is suddenly throbbing, as though she can't control a long-buried anger. "You panicked, Luke, and we lost the best relationship I've ever had. Everyone was jealous of us at Cambridge, everyone. We were perfect together."

"We weren't perfect!" He looks at her incredulously. "And I didn't *panic*—"

"You did! You couldn't cope with commitment! It frightened you!"

"It did not frighten me!" Luke shouts, exasperated. "It made me realize you weren't the person I wanted to have children with. Or spend the rest of my life with. Ever. And that's why I ended it!"

Venetia looks as though he hit her. For a few seconds she appears speechless—then her eyes focus on me with such aggression that I shrink away.

"And she *is*?" she demands with a savage gesture. "This mindless consumer little...*girlie* is who you're going to spend the rest of your days with? Luke, she has no depth! She has no brain! All she cares about is her shopping, and her clothes . . . and her girlfriends. . . ."

The blood has drained from my face and I feel a bit shaky. I've never heard such vitriol.

I glance over at Luke. His nostrils are flared and a vein is beating in his head.

"Don't you dare talk about Becky like that." His voice is so steely, even I'm a bit scared. "Don't you dare."

"Come on, Luke." Venetia gives a mocking little laugh. "I grant you she's pretty. . . ."

"Venetia, you don't know what you're talking about," Luke says evenly.

"She's beyond frivolous!" cries Venetia. "She's nothing! Why the *hell* did you marry her?"

There's a tiny intake of breath around the room. No one moves for about thirty seconds. Luke looks a bit stunned to have been asked such a blatant question.

God, I wonder what he's going to say. Maybe he'll say for my brilliant cooking and repartee.

No. Unlikely.

Maybe he'll say . . .

I'm a bit stumped, to be honest. And if *I'm* stumped, Luke must be too.

"Why did I marry Becky?" he echoes at last, in such a strange voice that I think maybe he's suddenly wondering himself, and realizing he made a terrible mistake.

All of a sudden I feel a bit cold and a bit scared.

And still Luke hasn't said anything.

He walks over to the sink and pours himself a cup of water as everyone watches nervously. At last he turns. "Have you spent time with Becky?"

"I have!" says Suze, as though she's going to win the

Jackpot prize. Everyone turns to look at her, and she colors. "Sorry," she mutters.

"The first time I ever saw Becky Bloomwood..." He pauses, a tiny smile at his lips. "She was asking a bank marketing department why they didn't produce checkbook covers in different colors."

"You see?" Venetia tosses a hand impatiently, but Luke doesn't even flicker.

"The next year they *did* produce checkbook covers in different colors. Becky's instincts match no one else's. Becky has ideas no one else has. Her mind goes to places no one else's does. And sometimes I'm lucky enough to go along with her." Luke's eyes meet mine, soft and warm. "Yes, she shops. Yes, she does crazy things. But she makes me laugh. She makes me *enjoy* life. And I love her more than anything else in the world."

"I love you too," I mumble, a lump in my throat.

"Fine," says Venetia, her face pale. "Fine, Luke! If you want a shallow little airhead—"

"You have no idea, so shut the fuck up." Luke's voice is suddenly like a machine gun.

Mum opens her mouth to protest Luke's language— but he looks so livid, she closes it again, looking nervous.

"Becky's a lot more principled than you *ever* were." He's regarding Venetia with contempt. "She's brave. She puts other people before herself. I couldn't have got through the last few days without her. You guys probably know what trouble my company is in at the moment...." He glances at Suze and Mum.

"Trouble?" Mum looks alarmed. "What kind of trouble? Becky never told us!"

Luke turns to me, incredulous. "Becky, haven't you *said* anything?"

"I knew something was up," Suze gasps. "I knew it. All those phone calls. But she wouldn't say what it was...."

"I didn't want to spoil the party." I flush as everyone turns toward me. "Everyone was having such a lovely time...." I break off, realizing I still haven't told him. "Luke...there's something else. We've lost the house."

As I say the words I feel a wave of crushing disappointment again. Our beautiful family house, gone.

"You're kidding." Luke's face darkens in shock.

"They're selling it to someone else. But...it'll be fine!" Somehow I force a bright smile. "We can rent a flat somewhere.... I've been looking on the Net— we'll easily find somewhere...."

"Becky..." I can see it in his eyes too. Our dreams, destroyed.

"I know." I blink back the tears. "It'll be fine, Luke."

"Oh, Becky." I look over, and Suze is practically in tears too. "Have our castle in Scotland. We never use it!"

"Suze." I can't help a half-giggle. "Don't be silly."

"You'll come and live with us, love!" Mum chimes in. "You won't rent any nasty flat! And as for *you,* young lady..." She turns on Venetia, her face pink with outrage. "How dare you upset my daughter when she's in labor!"

Shit.

I'd forgotten about being in labor.

"God, of course!" Suze claps a hand over her mouth. "Bex, you haven't made a peep! You're amazing!"

"My darling, you are such a star." Luke looks absolutely awestruck. "All this, and you're in labor. . . ."

"Oh . . . er . . . it's nothing!" I try to sound modest. "You know. . . ."

"It's not nothing—it's incredible. Isn't it?" Luke appeals to the student midwives.

"She is pretty special," agrees Paula, who has been following the exchange with Venetia with a wide-open mouth. "That's why we're all observing her."

"Special, huh?" Venetia suddenly says. She comes over and looks me up and down, her eyes narrowed. "Becky, when exactly was your last contraction?"

"Er . . ." I clear my throat. "It was . . . er . . . just now."

"She's a Scientologist," puts in Paula eagerly. "She's managing the pain silently. It's wonderful to watch."

"A *Scientologist*?" echoes Luke.

"It's my new hobby!" I say brightly. "Didn't I tell you?"

"I never knew you were a Scientologist, Bex!" says Suze in surprise.

"Is that the Moonies?" Mum demands of Luke in alarm. "Has Becky joined the Moonies?"

"Well, now." Venetia's eyes gleam. "Let's have a look at you, Becky. Maybe this baby's ready to be delivered!"

I edge away. If she gets to examine me, I'm basically dead.

"Don't be shy!" Venetia is advancing on me, and in panic I hurry round to the other side of the bed.

"Look at that mobility!" one of the student midwives is saying admiringly.

"Come on, Becky. . . ."

"Go away! Leave me alone!" I grab the gas and air

mask and start gulping it in. That's better. God, we should have a tank of this stuff at home.

"We're here!" The door is thrust open and everyone looks up to see Danny bursting in, followed by Jess. "We're here! Did we miss it?"

Jess is wearing her *She's a Yummy Mummy and We Love Her* T-shirt, to match Suze's. Danny is wearing a blue cashmere tank with *She's a Red-Haired Bitch and I Hate Her* printed in khaki on the front.

"Where's the baby?" Danny looks around the room with bright eyes, taking in the tense scene. His eyes alight on Venetia. "Hey, who invited Cruella de Venetia?"

Luke is staring at the slogan on Danny's tank top. He gives a sudden snort of comprehending laughter.

"You're so *juvenile*," spits Venetia, who has also clocked the tank top. "All of you. And if Little Miss Becky is really in labor, then I'm—"

"Oh," I shriek. "Oh! I'm leaking!"

God, that's the weirdest feeling. Something somewhere has just burst, and a pool of water is gathering at my feet. I can't stop it.

"Jesus!" says Danny, shielding his eyes. "OK...*way* too much info." He takes Jess's elbow. "C'mon, Jess, let's go get a drink."

"Your water has gone," says Paula, looking puzzled. "I thought that happened yesterday."

"That could have been her forewater," another student pipes up, looking all girly-swotty and pleased with herself. "This could be her hindwater."

I'm in a state of shock. My water has broken.

That means...I'm in labor.

I really, genuinely, truly am in labor.

Aaaargh. Oh my God. We're going to have a baby!

"Luke." I grab him in total panic. "It's happening!"

"I know, my darling." Luke smooths my brow. "And you're doing amazingly. . . ."

"No!" I wail. "You don't understand—" I stop, suddenly breathless. What was that?

It felt like someone squeezed my abdomen and then squeezed it some more and then squeezed it even tighter, even though I was begging them to stop.

Is *that* what a contraction's like?

"Luke . . ." My breath is suddenly rather snatched. "I'm not sure I can do this. . . ."

It's even tighter now, and I'm almost panting, my hands gripping Luke's forearm.

"You'll be fine. You'll be wonderful." He's stroking my back rhythmically. "Dr. Braine's on his way. The red-haired bitch is just leaving. Aren't you, Venetia?" He doesn't take his eyes off mine.

The contraction seems to have finished. The clenching sensation has died away. But I know it'll be back, like that scary guy on Elm Street.

"I think I'd like an epidural after all," I gulp. "Quite soon."

"Of course!" says Paula, hurrying over. "I'll page the anesthetist. You've done so well to last this long, Becky. . . ."

"*. . . ridiculous.*" I hear the last word of some muttered epithet of Venetia's before she bangs the door closed.

"What a cow!" says Suze. "I'm telling *all* my pregnant friends what a cow she is."

"She's gone." Luke kisses me on the forehead. "It's over. I'm sorry, Becky. I'm so sorry."

"It doesn't matter," I say automatically.

And actually . . . I mean it.

Already I feel like Venetia's irrelevant, drifting away from us like smoke. It's Luke and me that matters. And the baby.

Oh God, another contraction's starting already. This whole labor malarkey is a complete pain. I grab the gas and air mask and all the student midwives gather round, encouraging me as I start to inhale.

"You can do it, Becky . . . stay relaxed . . . breathe. . . ."

Come on, baby. I want to meet you.

"You're doing great . . . keep breathing, Becky. . . ."

Of course you can do it. Come on. We both can.

TWENTY-ONE

IT'S A GIRL.

It's a little girl, with scrunched-up petal lips and a tuft of dark hair and hands in tiny fists, up by her ears. All that time, that's who was in there. And it's weird, but the minute I saw her I just thought: It's *you*. Of course it is.

Now she's lying in a plastic crib beside my bed in a gorgeous little white Baby Dior babygro. (I wanted to try a few different outfits on just to see what suited her, but the midwife got a bit stern with me and said we both needed our sleep.) And I'm just staring at her, feeling fuzzy from the broken night, watching every rise and fall of her breath, every squirm of her fingers.

The birth was ...

Well, it was what they call "straightforward and easy." Which *really* makes me wonder. It seemed pretty complicated and bloody hard work to me. But anyway. Some things are best left a blur. Births and Visa bills.

"Hi. You're awake." Luke looks up from where he's been dozing in a chair and rubs his eyes. He's unshaven and his hair is askew and his shirt is all rumpled.

"Uh-huh."

"How is she?"

"Fine." I can't help a smile licking across my face as I look at her again. "Perfect."

"She *is* perfect. You're perfect." His face has a kind of distant euphoria even as he's looking at me, and I know he's reliving last night.

In the end, just Luke stayed in the room, and everyone else went out to wait. And then they went home, because Dr. Braine said it would be a long while before anything happened. But it wasn't! It was one thirty in the morning when she was born, and she looked all bright-eyed and alert, straightaway. She's going to be a party girl, I know it.

She doesn't have a name yet. The list I made is discarded on the floor beside the bed. I got it out last night when the midwife asked what we were going to call her—but all the names I'd thought about are wrong. They're just...wrong. Even Dolce. Even Tallulah-Phoebe.

There's a gentle tapping at the door. It opens very slowly and Suze puts her head round. She's holding a giant bunch of lilies and a pink helium balloon.

"Hi," she breathes, and as her eyes fall on the crib she claps a hand over her mouth. "Oh my God, Bex, look at that. She's beautiful."

"I know." With no warning, tears spring to my eyes. "I know she is."

"Bex?" Looking anxious, Suze hurries over to the bed with a rustle of flowers. "Are you OK?"

"I'm fine. I just..." I gulp, wiping my nose. "I had no idea."

"What?" Suze sits down on the edge of the bed, her face full of dread. "Bex...was it really awful?"

"No, it's not that." I shake my head, struggling for the words. "I had no idea I'd feel so ... happy."

"Oh yeah, that." Suze's face lights up as if in memory. "You do. It doesn't last forever, mind you." She seems to think again and gives me a tight hug. "It *is* amazing. Congratulations. Congratulations, Luke!"

"Thanks." He smiles. Even though he looks knackered, he's glowing. He meets my eye and I feel a catch in my heart. It's like we have a secret together, which no one else can quite understand.

"Look at her little *fingers*. . . ." Suze is bending over the crib. "Hello, darling!" She looks up. "Does she have a name?"

"Not yet." I adjust myself on the pillows, wincing a little. I feel pretty mashed up after last night. Although the good thing is, the epidural hasn't completely worn off yet, and they've already given me a stash of painkillers.

The door opens again, and Mum appears. She's already met the baby, at eight this morning, when she arrived with brioches and hot coffee in a flask. Now she's laden with gift bags and Dad is following in her wake.

"Dad ... meet your granddaughter!" I say.

"Oh, Becky, darling. Congratulations." Dad gives me the hugest, tightest hug. Then he peers into the crib, blinking slightly harder than normal. "Well, then. Hello, old girl."

"Here are some clothes for you, Becky, love." Mum heaves an enormous weekend bag stuffed full of garments onto a nearby chair. "I wasn't sure what you'd want, so I just rooted around. . . ."

"Thanks, Mum." I undo the zip and pull out a chunky cable cardigan which I haven't worn for about five years. Then I glimpse something else. A familiar pale blue glimmering, beaded, velvety softness.

My scarf. My precious Denny and George scarf. I still remember the first instant I clapped eyes on it.

"Hey look!" I pull it out, careful not to snag any of the beads. I haven't worn this for ages, either. "Remember this, Luke?"

"Of course I remember!" Luke's face softens as he sees it. Then he adds, totally deadpan, "You bought it for your Aunt Ermintrude, as I recall."

"That's right." I nod.

"Tragic that she died before she could ever wear it. Her arm fell off, wasn't it?"

"Her leg," I correct him.

Mum has been listening to this exchange, perplexed.

"Aunt who?" she says, and I can't help breaking into a giggle.

"An old friend," says Luke, tying the scarf around my neck. He looks at it for a moment in a kind of wonderment, then down at the baby. "Who would have thought..."

"I know." I finger the corner of the scarf. "Who would have thought?"

Dad is still totally fixated by the baby. He's put a finger into the crib, and the baby has wrapped her tiny hand around it.

"So, old girl," he's saying. "What are we calling you, then?"

"We haven't decided yet," I say. "It's so hard!"

"I've brought you a book!" says Mum, rootling in her holdall. "What about Grisabella?"

"Grisabella?" echoes Dad.

"It's a lovely name!" says Mum defensively, pulling

out *1,000 Girls' Names* and putting it on the bed. "Unusual."

"She'd get called Grizzle in the playground!" Dad retorts.

"Not necessarily! She could be Bella . . . or Grizzy. . . ."

"*Grizzy?* Jane, are you *mad*?"

"Well, what do you like?" says Mum, affronted.

"I was thinking . . . possibly . . ." Dad clears his throat. "Rhapsody."

I glance at Luke, who mouths *Rhapsody*? with such an expression of horror, I want to laugh.

"Hey, I have an idea," chimes in Suze. "Fruit's been done to death, but not herbs. You could call her Tarragon!"

"Tarragon?" Mum looks appalled. "You might as well call her Chili Powder! Now, I've got some champagne to wet her little head. . . . It's not too early, is it?" She pulls out a bottle, along with a piece of paper. "Oh yes, and I took a message from your real estate agent. He phoned while I was at your flat, and I gave him a piece of my mind, I can tell you! I said, 'A newborn baby is homeless at Christmas because of you, young man.' That stopped him in his tracks! He said he wanted to apologize. Then he started talking some nonsense about villas in Barbados! I ask you." She shakes her head. "Now, who wants champagne? Where are the champagne glasses?" She puts the bottle down and starts searching in the cupboards under the telly.

"I'm not sure they've got any champagne glasses," I say.

"Well, for goodness' sake!" Mum clicks her tongue and stands up again. "I'll speak to the concierge."

"Mum, there *isn't* a concierge."

Just because they have posh menus and tellies, Mum seems to think this place is some kind of Ritz-Carlton.

"I'll find something," Mum says firmly, and heads to the door.

"D'you want some help?" Suze gets to her feet. "I've got to phone Tarkie anyway."

"Thank you!" Mum beams at her. "And Graham, you fetch the camera from the car. I forgot to bring it up."

The door closes behind Dad, and Luke and I are alone in the room again. With our daughter.

God, that's a weird thought. I still can't quite believe we have a daughter.

Meet our daughter, Tarragon Parsley Sage and Onion.

No.

"So." Luke pushes a hand back through his rumpled hair. "In two weeks' time we're homeless."

"Out on the streets!" I say lightly. "Never mind."

"I guess you expected to marry someone who could put a roof over your head, didn't you?"

He's joking, but there's a wryness in his voice.

"Oh well." I shrug, watching the baby's hand unfurl like a little starfish. "Better luck next time . . ."

There's silence and I glance up. Luke seems genuinely stricken.

"Luke, I'm joking!" I say hastily. "It doesn't *matter*!"

"You've just had a baby. You should have a home. We shouldn't be in this position. I shouldn't have—"

"It's not your fault!" I grab his hand. "Luke, we'll be fine. We'll make a home wherever we are."

"I'll get us a home," he says, almost fiercely. "Becky, we'll have a wonderful house, I promise you."

"I know we will." I squeeze his hand tight. "But honestly . . . it doesn't matter."

I'm not just saying that to be supportive. (Even though I *am* a very supportive wife.) It really, truly doesn't seem to matter. Right now, I feel like I'm in a kind of bubble. Real life is on the other side, miles away. All that matters is the baby.

"Look!" I say, as she suddenly yawns. "She's only eight hours old and she can yawn! That's so clever!"

For a while we both gaze into the crib, awestruck, hoping she might do something else.

"Hey, maybe she'll be prime minister one day!" I say softly. "Wouldn't that be cool? We could get her to do all the things we wanted!"

"She won't, though." Luke shakes his head. "If we tell her to do them, she'll do exactly the opposite."

"She's such a rebel!" I run a finger down her teeny forehead.

"She has her own mind," Luke corrects me. "Look at the way she's ignoring us now." He sits back on the bed. "So what *are* we going to call her? Not Grisabella."

"Not Rhapsody."

"Not Parsley." He picks up *1,000 Girls' Names* and starts flicking through it.

Meanwhile I'm just gazing at her sleeping face. This one name keeps popping into my head every time I look at her. It's almost as if she's telling it to me.

"Minnie," I say aloud.

"Minnie," Luke echoes, experimentally. "Minnie Brandon. You know, I like that." He looks up with a smile. "I really like it."

"Minnie Brandon." I can't help beaming back. "It sounds good, doesn't it? Miss Minnie Brandon."

"Named after... your aunt Ermintrude, obviously?" Luke raises his eyebrows.

Oh my God! That hadn't even occurred to me.

"Of course!" I can't help giggling. "Except no one will know that except us."

The Right Honourable Minnie Brandon QC OBE.

Miss Minnie Brandon looked radiant as she danced with the Prince in a floor-length ball gown by Valentino....

Minnie Brandon has taken the world by storm....

"Yes." I nod. "That's her name." I lean over the cot and watch her chest rising and falling with each breath. Then I smooth back her tuft of hair and kiss her tiny cheek. "Welcome to the world, Minnie Brandon."

TWENTY-TWO

SO IT'S HAPPENED. The Karlssons have moved in to our flat. All our furniture has been packed up and moved out. We're officially homeless.

Except not really, because Mum and Dad are having us stay for a while. Like Mum said, they've got heaps of room, and Luke can commute from Oxshott station, and Mum can help out with Minnie, and we can play bridge every night after supper. Which is all true, except the playing bridge bit. No way. Uh-uh. Never. Not even with the Tiffany bridge cards Mum bought me as a bribe. She keeps saying it's "such fun," and "All the young people are playing bridge these days." Yeah, right.

Anyway, I'm too busy looking after Minnie to sit around playing bridge. I'm too busy being a *mother*.

Minnie's four weeks old already, and is a total party girl. I knew she would be. Her favorite time is one in the morning, when she starts saying "ra ra ra" and you struggle out of bed, feeling like you only fell asleep three seconds ago.

Plus she quite likes three in the morning. And five.

And quite a few times in between. To be honest, I feel totally hungover and knackered every morning.

But on the plus side, cable telly is on all night. And Luke often gets up to keep me company. He does his e-mails and I watch *Friends* with the sound turned low, and Minnie breast-feeds like she's some starving, deprived baby who wasn't fed just an hour ago.

The thing about babies is, they really know what they want. Which I do quite respect. Like, it turns out Minnie doesn't like the hand-crafted crib after all. It makes her all cross and squirmy, which is a bit crap considering it cost five hundred quid. Nor is she impressed by the rocking cradle, nor the Moses basket, even with Hollis Franklin four-hundred-thread-count linen sheets. What she likes best is to be cuddled in someone's arms all day and all night. And second best is my old carry-cot, which Mum got down from the attic. It's all soft and worn-looking but pretty comfy. So I returned all the others and got a refund.

I returned the Circus Tent Changing Station too. And the Bugaboo and the Warrior—in fact, loads of stuff. We don't need them. We don't even have a house to put them in. And I gave all the money to Luke, because . . . well, I wanted to help. Even a little bit.

The good news is, things are looking up a tad for Luke. And the best bit of all is that Iain Wheeler lost his job! Luke didn't hang around—the day after we had Minnie, he paid a visit to Iain's bosses, along with his lawyer, and they had a "short conversation," as Luke put it. The next thing we heard was that Iain Wheeler was announcing his decision to move from Arcodas. It's nearly a month later and Gary, who knows these things, says he hasn't had any job offers yet. Which is apparently because everyone has heard the rumor of some incriminating dossier on him. *Ha.*

Luke won't work with Arcodas, though, even with Iain gone. He says their attitude is just as obnoxious as ever. And he still hasn't got any money out of them. He's just closed down another three European offices and things are still pretty tense. But he's OK. He's thinking positive, already planning new pitches, new strategies. We sometimes talk about them at night, and I tell him everything I think. And then somehow the conversation always drifts to Minnie and how amazing and beautiful and gorgeous she is.

And now I'm standing in Mum's driveway, joggling her in my arms, watching the delivery men unload all our things. Most of our stuff has gone into storage, but obviously there were a few essentials we had to bring with us.

"Becky..." Mum approaches me from across the drive, holding a teetering pile of old magazines. "Where shall I put these, love? In the rubbish?"

"They're not rubbish!" I protest. "I might want to read them! Can't they go in our bedroom?"

"It's getting a little full...." Mum looks at the magazines and seems to make a snap decision. "I think we'll have to give you the blue bedroom as well."

"OK." I nod. "Thanks, Mum."

We didn't give up the house without a fight. Luke phoned Fabia to plead with her, and so did I and so did the real estate agent. But they exchanged contracts with the other couple two days after Minnie was born. The only tiny silver lining was that I got my Archie Swann boot back, after I sent Fabia about five threatening e-mails. Otherwise there really *would* have been trouble.

"More shoes." A delivery guy comes by, carrying a cardboard packing box. "That fitted wardrobe's full, you know."

"It's all right!" says Mum briskly. "Start filling up the blue bedroom. I'll show you...."

"How are you doing?" Luke comes by in his shirt-sleeves, carrying my Pilates ball and two hatboxes.

"Fine." I nod, watching a delivery guy carry in my vanity case. "This is weird, isn't it?"

"It's pretty weird." He puts his arm round me and I nestle into his shoulder. Last night was even weirder, with all the furniture packed up in the van and just a big empty flat filled with boxes. At about four A.M., Minnie just wouldn't sleep, so I wound up her mobile with the Brahms Lullaby and put her in the baby sling. Luke wrapped his arms round us both and we kind of danced around the room in the moonlight.

I never realized that song was a waltz before.

"Luke!" Dad approaches us, holding a pile of post. "You've got a letter."

"Someone's very efficient," says Luke in surprise. "I haven't given this address to many people...." He glances at the logo on the back. "Ah. It's from Kenneth."

"Great!" I feign enthusiasm and make a face at Minnie.

Luke rips open the envelope and scans the text. After a second he peers harder. "I don't believe it," he says slowly. At last he raises his head and stares at me in disbelief. "It's about you."

"Me?"

"There's a duplicate letter in the post for you too. As Kenneth says, it's quite a big matter, so he wanted to contact both of us."

Oh, this is all I need. Letters of complaint from Kenneth.

"He hates me!" I say defensively. "It's not my fault. All I said was that he was narrow-minded—"

"It's not that." Luke's mouth twitches into a smile. "Becky...it looks like you beat me."

"What?" I say in astonishment.

"One of your investments has done exceedingly well. I'm not sure Kenneth can quite cope with the news, to be honest."

I knew it. I *knew* I'd win.

"What is it?" I demand in excitement. "What did well? It's the Barbies, isn't it? No, the Dior coat."

"The Web site fabbesthandbags.com is going to be floated. You'll make a stack."

I seize the letter and run my eyes down it, taking in words here and there. *Three thousand percent profit... extraordinary... unforeseen...*

Ha-di-ha! I beat Luke!

"So, am I the most financially astute and clever person in this family?" I look up in triumph.

"Your Antiques of the Future are still a worthless pile of crap," Luke says, but he's grinning.

"So what? I still beat you! You've got lots of lovely money, darling!" I kiss Minnie on the forehead.

"When she's twenty-one," Luke puts in.

Honestly. Luke's so boring. Who wants to wait till they're twenty-one?

"We'll see about that," I murmur into her ear, pulling the blanket over her head so Luke doesn't hear.

"Right!" Mum appears in the front door, holding a cup of tea. "That's your bedroom pretty much full. But it'll take an awful lot of sorting out and tidying, I'm afraid. It's quite a mess."

"No problem," calls Luke. "Thanks, Jane!" Mum disappears inside again and he picks up the Pilates ball. "So, shall we make a start?"

I loathe sorting out. And tidying. How can I get out of this?

"Actually, you know, I thought I might take Minnie for a walk," I say casually. "I think she needs some fresh air. She's been stuck inside all day. . . ."

"Good idea." Luke nods. "I'll see you later then."

"See you later! Bye-bye, Daddy!" I wave Minnie's tiny hand as Luke vanishes into the house.

I never realized it before, but having a baby is just the *best* excuse. For anything!

I put Minnie in her pram, all wrapped up cozily, and tuck Knotty next to her for company. I think Minnie's quite fond of Knotty, actually. And Double-Knotty, which Jess gave her.

We're using the old-fashioned gray pram I got at the baby fair, first of all because I got a bit carried away sending back all the other prams, and secondly because Mum reckons it's the best one for supporting Minnie's back, "not like these newfangled buggies." I'm planning to get it sprayed hot pink as soon as I can—only it's not that easy to find a custom pram paint-sprayer over the festive season.

I tuck her up in the gorgeous pink-and-white blanket that Luke's parents gave her when they visited over Christmas. They were so sweet—they brought me a basket of muffins and invited us to stay (only, Devon's a bit far) and said Minnie was the most beautiful baby they'd ever seen. Which shows what good taste they have. Unlike Elinor, who hasn't even visited and just sent Minnie this hideous antique china doll with ringlets and spooky eyes, like something out of a horror film. I'm going to auction it on eBay and put the money in Minnie's account.

I put on my new Marc Jacobs coat which Luke got me for Christmas and tie my Denny and George scarf round my neck. I've been wearing it all the time since I got out of hospital. Somehow I don't feel like wearing any other scarf at the moment.

I always *knew* it would be a good investment.

There's a little parade of shops quite near to Mum and Dad, and without quite meaning to, I head that way. Not because I'm planning to go shopping or anything. Just because it's a nice walk.

As I reach the newsagents it's all warm and bright and welcoming, and I find myself pushing the pram in. Minnie is fast asleep and I head toward the magazine rack. I could get a magazine for Mum—she'd like that. I'm just reaching for *Good Housekeeping* when my hand freezes. There's *Vogue*.

A brand-new issue of *Vogue*. With a bright blue cover line shouting, *London's Yummiest Mummies-to-Be*.

My hands fumbling in excitement, I pull it down, tear off the free travel supplement, and flick through the pages. . . .

Oh my God! It's a huge picture of me! I'm standing on the sweeping staircase in the Missoni dress, and the caption reads: "Rebecca Brandon, shopping guru and wife of the PR entrepreneur Luke Brandon, is expecting her first baby."

Based in Maida Vale, the text below reads, *former TV presenter Becky Brandon's elegant style is obvious throughout her palatial six-bedroom house. She designed the stunning "his" and "hers" nurseries herself, with no expense spared. "Only the best will do for my baby," she says. "We hand-sourced the furniture from a tribe of artisans living in Mongolia."*

I turn the page—and there's another picture of me, beaming as I stand in the fairy-princess nursery, my hands resting on my bump. A big pull-out quote reads: "I have five prams. I don't think that's too many."

Becky is planning a natural water birth with lotus flowers, and is under the care of It-obstetrician Venetia Carter. "Venetia and I are good friends," enthuses Becky. "We have such a great bond. I might ask her to be a godmother."

It all feels like an age away. Like a different world.

As I gaze down at the beautiful designer nursery, I can't help feeling a pang. Minnie would have loved it. I know she would.

Anyway, she'll have a lovely nursery one day. Even *better* than that one.

I take the *Vogue* to the counter and put it down, and the assistant looks up from her magazine.

"Hi!" I say. "I'd like to get this, please."

There's a new display in the corner with a sign reading GIFTS—and while the assistant is unlocking the till, I wander over to have a look. It's mostly photo frames and small vases and a rack of thirties-style brooches.

"You've been here before, haven't you?" says the assistant as she scans my magazine. "Over Christmas you were in all the time."

All the time. Honestly. People do exaggerate.

"I've just moved back into the area." I give her a friendly smile. "My name's Becky."

"We noticed you." She puts the *Vogue* into a plastic bag. "We call you the Girl—" She breaks off and I stiffen. What was she going to say?

"Shh!" says the other assistant, going pink and nudging the first one.

"Don't worry, I don't mind!" Nonchalantly I flick my hair back. "Do you call me . . . the Girl in the Denny and George Scarf?"

"No." The assistant looks blank. "We call you the Girl with the Crappy Pram."

Oh.

Huh. It's not *that* crappy. And just wait till it's sprayed pink. It'll be totally fab.

"That'll be three pounds, please," she says, and holds out her hand. And I'm just about to get out my purse, when I spot a display of rose quartz necklaces nestled among the other gifts.

Ooh. I love rose quartz.

"They're on sale," says the assistant, following my gaze. "Really nice."

"Right. Yes." I nod thoughtfully.

The thing is, we're supposed to be tightening our belts at the moment. We had a big talk when I came home from hospital, all about cash flow and bank debt and stuff. And we agreed that just until Luke's business is more stable, we wouldn't buy anything unnecessary.

But I've been wanting a rose quartz necklace for *ages.* And this one's only fifteen quid, which is a real bargain.

And I deserve a little reward for winning the investment competition, don't I?

Plus I can use my new online Indonesian overdraft,
which Luke doesn't know about.

"I'll have one," I say on impulse, and reach for a
string of the iridescent pink beads.

If Luke finds it, I'll tell him it's an educational toy.
Which the mother has to wear round her neck.

I hand over my Visa card, tap in my pin number, and
slide the bag containing *Vogue* onto the pram tray. Then
I tuck my lovely necklace right under Minnie's blankets
where no one can see it.

"Don't tell Daddy," I murmur in her ear.

She won't say a word.

I mean, obviously she can't speak. But even if she
could, I know she'd keep quiet. We've got a special
bond already, Minnie and me.

I wheel the pram out of the shop and look at my
watch. There's no hurry to get back, especially if
they're still tidying. Anyway, Minnie will want feeding
soon. I'll go to that Italian café where they don't mind.

"Shall we go and have a nice cup of coffee?" I turn
my steps toward the café. "Just you and me, Min."

As we walk past the antique shop I catch a glimpse of
my reflection and can't help feeling a tiny jolt at the
sight. I'm a mother pushing a pram. Me, Becky Brandon
(née Bloomwood), an actual mother.

I turn into the café, sit down at the table, and order
a decaf cappuccino. Then, gently, I lift Minnie out of
the pram, cradling her soft downy head. I unwrap her
pink-and-white blanket and feel a swell of pride as two
elderly ladies look over from the next table and start
saying to each other, "What a dear little thing!" and

"What a smart outfit!" and "Is that a real cashmere cardigan, do you think?"

Minnie starts making her snuffling "Where's the food?" noises and I give her tiny cheek a kiss. I'm the Mother with the Fabbest Baby in the World. And we're going to have a blast. I know it.

Bambino

975 Kings Road
London SW3
...for children of all ages...

Miss Minnie Brandon   5 January 2004
The Pines
43 Elton Road
Oxshott
Surrey

Dear Miss Brandon,

Congratulations on being born!

We at Bambino are delighted to celebrate your arrival into the world—and would like to mark it with a very special offer. We hereby invite you to become an Infant Gold Card Member of the Bambino Club!

As an Infant Gold Card Member you will be entitled to:
- exclusive preview afternoons to try out new toys (with a carer!)
- a complimentary juice at every visit
- 25 percent off your first shopping spree with your Gold Card
- annual Christmas party for all Gold Card holders
- ...and much more!

Joining could not be simpler. All Mummy or Daddy has to do is fill in the enclosed form—and their little princess Minnie will have her first-ever Gold Card!

We look forward to hearing from you soon.

Yours sincerely,

Ally Edwards
Marketing Manager

Acknowledgments

My heartfelt thanks to the endlessly wise and supportive Susan Kamil. Huge thanks also to Irwyn Applebaum, Nita Taublib, Barb Burg, Sharon Propson, Carolyn Schwartz, Betsy Hulsebosch, Cynthia Lasky, Cathy Paine, and Noah Eaker. To my fabulous agents, Araminta Whitley and Kim Witherspoon; to David Forrer and Lizzie Jones. As ever, a big wave to the Board and to my expanding family: Henry, Freddy, Hugo, and Oscar.

And finally thanks to the real "must-have" obstetrician, Nick Wales, who aided the delivery of latest baby *and* book—and the "must-have" maternity nurse, Michelle Vaughan.